THE CHRONICLES OF ARDEN
BOOK SIX

FALL
OF
EMPIRES

BENJAMIN SANFORD

Copyright © 2024 Benjamin Sanford

All rights reserved

STENOX PUBLISHING
Clarksburg, MD

Cover Art by Karl Moline

ISBN 979-8-9890221-4-4 (paperback)
ISBN 979-8-9890221-5-1 (ebook)

Printed in the United States of America

Chapter 1

"Raven?" Lorn asked as the Earther relieved Aldo of Zem's message, written clearly on paper produced on the *Stenox*, bearing his new rank at the top with the heading…

From the memoirs of General Zem…

"You've got to be kidding?" Raven shook his head, reading Zem's firsthand account of the events that transpired at Tro after they departed, with the rest of the court looking on.

> …*Though certain that my great deeds will be long remembered, I think it wise to provide my objective and firsthand account on my actions pertaining to the siege of Tro and subsequent engagements with elements of the 12th Gargoyle Legion. For the sake of posterity, I think it prudent to begin with my coming to this T class planet, located in unknown space. As our star charts cannot accurately identify our location, it is likely we are in a different galactic region, or galaxy altogether. We came upon this world through way of an anomaly, of which we had insufficient time to study before it drew our vessel into it, depositing us within this star system. Only by my expert piloting, with assistance from my fellow pilots, were we able to reach the surface of Arax…*

BENJAMIN SANFORD

"HIS expert piloting?" Raven growled, with the entire assemblage in the grand hall looking on, wondering what he was referring, since it was actually Raven that commanded the forward module and piloted their starship. Raven skipped over Zem's ramblings which went on for several paragraphs of self-promotion before getting to his recent activities. He had to admit Zem thought awfully high of himself.

> "...which brings us to the departure of our current commanding officer, Captain(O-3) Raven, and our Torry associates, along with Ular of Enoructa and Orlom of the Ape Republic. Their current situation is unknown. Their planned destination was the Torry fortress of Corell. I can only assume they arrived at Corell, but their hopes of victory are greatly dampened without my presence. It was two solar Araxan days after their departure that Magistrate Adine fully implemented his austerity measures for the defense of the city. It was at this time that I directed my invaluable skillset to the restoration of the Stenox, our sea going vessel, and bringing its systems back to full capacity. It was soon discovered that the neighboring city of Gotto had fallen to the gargoyle 12th Legion, cutting Tro's land routes to the continental interior. It was three days after that, that the first elements of the 12th Legion appeared before Tro's walls. My duties aboard the Stenox prevented me from fully ascertaining the disposition of the first sieging units, though the reports I reviewed indicated a poorly planned offensive operation, which reflects unfavorably on the gargoyle commanding General Krakeni.
>
> Within fourteen days, most of the enemy legion was camped within sight of Tro's walls, numbering an estimated thirty telnics with a variation of five. Telnics in the Araxan text refer to one thousand soldiers, an efficient means of numbering units in my esteemed opinion. And so, I continue, estimating the 12th Legion's strength between 25 and 35 telnics, outnumbering the combined Troan and ape defenders eleven telnics. Using traditional estimates from the most respected military academies, including Sandhurst, West Point and the General Staff Academy of Moscow,

to name a few, the Gargoyle 12th Legion had almost the required three to one ratio in numerical advantage to commence an attack against a fixed position. I instructed my crewmates to relay this information to Admiral Zorgon, the commander of all Troan and Ape forces within the city. Whether my advice was heeded can only be conjectured at this point.

It was four days after I offered my analysis of the situation that the 12th Legion commenced their attack upon the city. A detailed map of the city would reveal the difficulty in coordinating the defense of its walls, where reinforcements need to be moved within the harbor by way of the Tel-Ro, the main thoroughfare that circled the harbor within the city walls, and circling the bay. Any breach of the wall would effectively mean the severing of the Tel-Ro at that juncture, negating the effectiveness of keeping a reserve force to counter incursions, in turn emphasizing protecting the wall at all points at all times. The first assault took place before dawn, with the attackers concentrating some sixty earth standard meters north of the Flen River, where the west gate of Tro rested. The defenders quickly roused from their slumber, manning the walls as the gargoyles flew overhead, setting down at all points behind the gate, including upon the Tel-Ro itself, some four city blocks to the east.

It was at this moment that myself and my fellow crewmembers intervened, responding with our restored shipboard minor lasers. We were able to target individual gargoyles, dropping them in quick succession, decimating those that followed while the Troan and ape soldiers converged upon those that happened to set down before we interceded. The attack at that position quickly faltered due to our intervention, though other points along the city wall were similarly stressed. Those other stresses were quickly eliminated by our subsequent intervention. Gargoyle losses from the predawn attack were estimated at three thousand, eighty percent of which were killed.

With the enemy thrown in disarray, I ordered the Stenox to set me ashore, where I proceeded to the headquarters of Admiral Zorgon, offering my assistance, for which he received most graciously. I proceeded to outline the 12th Legion's disposition while surveying Tro's outer defenses, identifying the enemy's strengths and weaknesses, anticipating their next assault. The following assault had not transpired after three days of vigilant waiting by the defenders. It was then I decided to alter our plans and convinced Admiral Zorgon to initiate an attack upon the enemy General, identifying his location along the western perimeter of the siege lines. The gargoyles had dug an impressive siege trench forward of their lines, an obvious attempt to negate any such counter attacks by their human and ape foes. Such precautions were merely an inconvenience for myself. I led the attack after sundown, leading a small cohort of Troan and Ape volunteers, numbering two hundred, leading them from the city walls toward the enemy, catching them by surprise. I crossed over the siege trench ahead of my soldiers, clearing the path for them, before advancing toward the command pavilion of General Krakeni, dispatching 134 gargoyles before coming upon my intended target, finding Krakeni attempting to flee, before I punctured his upper torso with a well-placed blast of my pistol, striking his heart as he attempted to take flight in the dark of night. It was a fatal blow and set the enemy in disarray. My soldiers followed in my wake as I turned sharply northward, sweeping along the enemy perimeter, slaying everything remaining in our path. My fellow Earther Lorken positioned himself northeast of my position, near the northwest gate of Tro, sending volleys of laser fire into the gargoyle ranks. By morning we counted another five thousand enemy casualties, including their General.

  The 12th Legion remained in place for another twelve days, while we continued targeting their forces indiscriminately, slaying another six thousand before they decided to withdraw. For my superior actions and command ability, for which I repeatedly demonstrated, Admiral Zorgon offered me a commission as General in the Ape Republic, for which I accepted, and my crewmates registered their misgivings, believing my new position as General has no bearing on our current rank structure aboard the Stenox, of which I disagree. I would further like to add..."

Zem rambled on for several paragraphs of nonsense, eventually stating the compromise he struck with Brokov, Lorken and Kendra that he would adhere to their current rank structure aboard the *Stenox*, but that he was to be formally addressed as GENERAL.

"General Zem?" Terin asked from his post behind the high table, unable to hide his mirth.

"A toast then, to General Zem and our victory at Tro!" Lorn said, standing from his seat, the entire assemblage coming to their feet, joining him and repeating his cheer.

"To General Zem and our victory at Tro!" They heralded Zem's achievement as Raven stood in the middle of the chamber shaking his head until he found Corry staring at him with an amused raised brow, lifting her chalice.

"To General Zem," Raven joined them, though not too loudly.

* * *

Cronus returned to his bedchamber, finding the nursemaid asleep, cradling his daughter in her arms upon his bed. The night was growing late as his duties kept him away. Though King Lorn had excused him from such obligations, he felt compelled to present himself for the inauguration. Perhaps a part of him needed a moment to step away, having spent so many days watching over the infant. He was spent, both of mind and body. He didn't remember when he last slept peacefully with his heart broken in so many pieces. Only when he held the child would the pain subside, for she was all he had left of Leanna. He looked down at her beautiful face, nuzzling in the crook of the maid's arm, her little cheeks puffing ever so slightly with each tiny breath. If he closed his eyes he would see Leanna, and when he opened them, he would see her in the baby. If only she were truly here, he lamented. He longed to see her face while holding their child, a sight he could only envision, for her death had robbed him of it, as it stole so many things. At times he caught himself talking to her ghost, creating conversations in his mind. At first, he directed what she would say, but at times her words took on a life of their own.

"She is so beautiful," he would begin, as if holding her in his arms as they looked down at the child.

"Yes, the most beautiful thing I have ever seen," Leanna agreed.

"I was right, you know, when I said we would have a daughter," he reminded her.

"You were right." Leanna sighed happily, pressing her head to his chest while looking at their child.

"She looks so much like you." He smiled, never feeling so content in his life.

"You say that because you love her as you love me, but she needs a name, my love, and it is long overdue." Leanna's voice grew faint as she disappeared in his arms.

"Leanna!" he cried out, feeling the emptiness in his hands, his voice waking the baby and the nursemaid.

"King's Elite Kenti," the nursemaid greeted, though startled, the child crying out briefly before she opened her blouse, offering her breast to quiet her fussing.

"My apologies, Dela," Cronus said, taking a knee beside the bed, running a finger along the child's small head, gently stroking her hair.

"You have no reason to apologize." Dela smiled tiredly. Looking into Cronus' eyes was heartbreaking for her and her sister nursemaids. All the women in the palace knew of the love shared between Leanna and Cronus, a love so strong that each traveled the world to seek the other. It was the love of stories and fairytales, the sort that mothers told their young daughters while putting them to sleep. It was beautiful, and now it was gone.

"Thank you, Dela. I have decided it is time for her to have a name," he said, pulling his hand away so he might study her face.

She could see him working it out in his quiet thoughts, knowing when he had found one by the sudden spark in his eyes.

"You have found one I see."

"I have. Maura. Leanna's grandmother had that name, and she loved it so, and her daughter will have it as well."

"Maura, a most fitting name, a name that will place a great mark upon the world, as befits her rich lineage." Dela smiled, knowing full well the tales of Cronus and Leanna would be sung throughout the world, long after they were dead and gone.

* * *

"They make a most fetching couple, Your Majesty," Squid said, joining King Mortus upon the battlements of the inner keep, watching Lorn and Deliea traversing the inner wall below, greeting the soldiers standing post as they passed. The clear starlit sky shone beautifully above, casting the palace in an ethereal light. In their long march from Fleace, Squid Antillius had come to know the Macon monarch, spending many nights such as this in deep conversation, one of many such pairings brought together by their alliance. Perhaps it was his fatherly bond he shared with Lorn that drew him to the father of Lorn's bride, but the two men had built a strong rapport.

Mortus stood at his side, resting his war weary hands upon the rampart, his guards standing post behind them. Everything was surreal since that day Lorn presented his terms for peace before the walls of Fleace, as if he was caught upon a current, riding its course to this place and time.

"Yes, they make a fine match. Looking back on it now, I can think of no other I would see wed to Deliea. And yet, I can't help but think myself a fool for the years I have wasted, fearful of things that make little sense now." Mortus sighed.

"We all have done or thought foolish things. Lorn's father oft spoke of regret, the wasting of years, or the neglectful inactions of the realm during the rise of the Benotrist revolution, or the times before then when the Menotrists oppressed Tyro's people. Perhaps all of this could have been avoided, perhaps all the tribes of man would be united in purpose and together vanquish the gargoyles for good," Squid recalled.

"No, such a thing would not have worked. If men bent toward reason, we would have aligned long ago to accomplish the task. It is only through the crucible of this war that awakens men from their slumber. Your prince, now king, understands this. Yah speaks to him so clearly a blind man could see it, and there was none more blind than I." Mortus shook his head.

"It is not surprising considering the distance that separates Maconia from the gargoyle lands in the north. Men are rarely roused to fight foes far off and little regarded."

"True, and that is why men have failed to destroy the gargoyles for so long now. That must change if we are to win. The realms of men must become as one, and reason suggests I should doubt it shall be so. But when I look at Lorn, reason gives way to hope. I never was one to believe in his God, but now I know him to be true. He has instilled in Lorn the spark of greatness required to unify mankind. And yet, despite our victories, there remain so many who have not rallied to that end."

"Nayboria shall soon fall, and Yatin…"

"Yangu cannot be trusted, Antillius. You know this to be true. As age-old enemies of the Torry Realm, the kings of the Macon Empire have long allied with the emperors of the Yatin Empire, using each other to keep the Torry Realm in check. Though the enemy of my enemy makes a logical ally, we were always aware of the growing instability in their royal family. Yangu is only the latest in a line of fools, each madder than the last," Mortus warned.

"King Lorn was aware of that before he set out for Mosar, but couldn't afford for Yatin to fall, such was the dire state of things at that time."

Mortus closed his eyes, shamed with guilt for assailing Sawyer while Lorn risked his very life for a people that despised him, saving them from the gargoyles that threatened them all. If he could only go back in time and join his armies to Lorn's at the outset. No, he couldn't let such thoughts confound him. He must look to the future, and the choices that were yet to be made.

"I have lived a long life, Antillius, one void of accomplishment or true worth. Only now have I achieved actions worthy of remembrance. This war is the pinnacle event of our history, and bards will sing of it thousands of years after we are dust. I will not have it sung of me that I did so little when so much was required. No one man can defeat the enemy before us, but I vow to do all in my power to destroy the gargoyles and help the one man who is appointed to lead us," Mortus said, his eyes fixed on the Torry King below.

"Few believed in him at the outset, but now I see the look in our soldiers' eyes whenever he is about or how they speak of him with awe and admiration. I hear and see it in your men as well, and now your fair Deliea shares in his adulation. She has earned much favor with the men while traveling with the army from Fleace, sharing in the hardship of the march," Squid said, assuaging any concerns Mortus had with Lorn usurping his place in the hearts of his men.

"They believe in him because his prophecies have proven true, and he places himself in the forward ranks when giving battle. He doesn't ask of his men anything he would not do himself, and they love him for it. When he said Yah would grant us a sign upon arriving at Corell, it strengthened the men's resolve during our march, but few truly believed it. Yet…" Mortus' voice trailed for a moment, recalling Raven's laser cutting down Morac's legions with pitiful ease and the effect it manifested in their own men. "And yet, when the men looked upon the glorious and horrifying slaughter of the enemy in so short a time, they truly believed. Men can deny belief in anything, or everything, but their own eyes are hard to refute. If Lorn said we should all march to Fera naked and unarmed whilst holding hands and singing children's songs, and doing so would destroy the enemy, the men would do it. I would do it," he added, shaking his head.

"Let us pray, Yah does not ask that of us." Antillius smiled.

*　*　*

The following morn found Lorn presiding over a council of war with the prominent generals of each army and specialized contingent in attendance, Jenaii, Macon and Torry alike, save for General Ciyon who was currently preparing the siege of Besos. King El Anthar and King Mortus stood to each side of Lorn, presenting a unified front, with King Sargov as well, whose 2nd Zulon Army had suffered nearly fifty percent casualties, the highest of any of their forces. General Bram Vecious commanded the 2nd Macon Army, his original 13 telnics suffering three thousand casualties. General Lewins represented his command, the 1st Torry Army, suffering 7 of his 19 telnics in casualties. General Ev Evorn commanded the 2nd Jenaii Battlegroup, suffering 4 of his 20 telnics in casualties. General El Tuvo was noticeably absent, the remnant of his 1st Jenaii Battlegroup joining General Ciyon with the siege of Besos, along with the greater portion of the Torry cavalry. General Mastorn also departed for Besos with ten telnics of the 3rd Torry Army, the remaining of his men reassigned to garrison duty. General Zubarro, commander of the 2nd Zulon Army stood out among the others, having suffered a mortal wound during the battle, his life spared by Ular attending him within moments of expiring, a terrible gash across his lower belly spilling his innards. He would never forget Ular's kind act, or the terrible pain he endured. His pain was only surpassed by the heavy toll his army suffered, with 1,600 of his 3,000 men wounded or killed. Beside him stood General Velen, commander of the 2nd Teso Army, who suffered 1,100 of his 2,000 men in casualties. Gaive Dolom commanded the Sawyeran contingent, his 2 telnics had guarded the baggage train during the battle, and safeguarded Queen Deliea. Commander Balka stood where Nevias once presided, the newly named garrison commander learning to curb his temper and foul tongue as he assumed the veneer of responsibility. General Dar Valen stood opposite his King at the table, his warbirds suffering thirty percent throughout the campaign, nearly all dead, with but three wounded. His only solace was the losses among his Benotrist counterpart, General Polis, who was found among the enemy dead, along with nearly every warbird within laser shot of the palace. The only Benotrist Magantors to survive were those farther afield at the height of battle.

 Joining the commanders were both Princess Corry and Queen Deliea, along with Torg Vantel, Jentra, Chief Minister Monsh, and Ministers Antillius, Torlan Thunn and Vergus Kalvar. Terin and Elos stood behind Prince Lorn along the near wall, ever vigilant in their post. Standing out from the others were Raven and Orlom, clad in their Earth garb, with their holstered pistols hanging low on their hips. Gorzak of tribe Traxar, represented the small ape contingent, standing beside Raven, his furry hand resting on the hilt of his sheathed sword.

THE CHRONICLES OF ARAX

"It has been a long journey for many at this council, and a longer war for those who have endured both sieges. Tonight, I wish to honor the fallen, a solemn ceremony for those who have given all in the defense of our world. May they rest in eternal peace, revered and honored by the realms of Arax. It falls to us, those that still live by their sacrifice, that the burden now falls. Our path to this point was clear, the relief of Corell. Now we must look further, our choices less clear or obtainable as we move forward. As you can see, each of our forces are displayed upon the map, with their current strength. The enemy's position and numbers are less... precise," Lorn began, waving an open hand across the map of Northern Arax depicted in fine detail across the table.

Less precise? more like a guess, Jentra thought to himself, standing along the table to Lorn's left.

Lorn had each commander present their location upon the map and their current strength, with most of them encamped within five leagues of Corell, save for the 1st Torry Army, positioned thirty leagues east along the east-west road.

"General Lewins?" Lorn looked to the commander of the 1st Torry Army to speak first after the others stated their strength and dispositions.

"Your Majesty, my army holds position... here." He indicated the point along the east-west road, a precarious location should the enemy turn back to Corell. "We have advanced to this point after breaking the siege, driving the remaining elements of the 8th, 9th and 10th Benotrist, and 5th and 14th Gargoyle Legions east."

"Can you ascertain their strength?" Lorn asked.

"Difficult to surmise, my king. They seem more a gaggle than a military formation. They are little more than a line of refugees strung out over a hundred leagues. Our cavalry raids and magantor strikes have destroyed most of their mounts and warbirds, and decimating their supply and distribution points. We've counted several thousand dead or wounded left in their wake, as well as countless discarded spears, armor and even swords. I doubt two of three will reach Notsu alive," Lewins stated.

"General Ev Evorn?" Lorn looked to the commander of the 2nd

Jenaii Battlegroup, whose dark silver eyes studiously surveyed the map.

"Our scouts spotted numerous gargoyle bands breaking north from those fleeing east, perhaps several telnics in total. By the number of gargoyles slain upon our first engagement south of Corell, and through our pursuit that followed, I place the number of dead at fifteen to eighteen thousand from the 5th Gargoyle Legion, and similar losses among the 14th Gargoyle Legion. Considering their strength before the battle, both should field little more than ten to fifteen telnics. Among the dead were both legion commanders," Ev Evorn said, having found the bodies of Concaka and Trimopolak among the slain.

"General Valen?" Lorn indicated his magantor commander to follow.

"Our scouts found elements of the 10th Legion fleeing west through the Zaronan, nearly five thousand by our estimates. The rest of the survivors from the 10th fled east. Our raids have destroyed Morac's supply depots here, here, here, and there." Dar pointed out on the map, touching several points east and north, the farthest sixty leagues east of Corell. "There have been few sightings of enemy magantors, the latest being four spotted departing Besos. We discovered the body of General Polis, the Benotrist magantor commander, among the dead at the battle site, south of Corell. He suffered a laser blast to the head," Dar said, with the others looking to Raven and Orlom, knowing one of them was credited with the kill.

"General Vecious, what have you learned of the 9th and 10th Legions?" Lorn directed the Macon General to begin his report.

"The enemy dead are piled chest high in parts all along this line." Bram Vecious pointed out a long arc south of Corell where the heaviest fighting occurred. "Many thousands more litter the battlefield just north and east of there, their corpses ripening in the sun for as far as the eye can see. Making my best guess, I would say both Legions suffered more than thirty thousand casualties each, including General Marcinia, commander of the 9th Legion. We found him among the dead with a laser blast through his skull." The others looked again to Raven and Orlom, realizing the large role they played in this victory.

"That does not include the 14,000 prisoners we have taken, King Lorn," Gaive Dolom, commander of the Sawyeran contingent added, his men tasked with overseeing the captives.

"They need to be transported south, far away from their homeland. We have many ships and mines requiring slave labor," General Lewins offered.

"They shall be moved south, but their labors shall not be permanent. No prisoner of war shall be enslaved by our hands, General," Lorn stated firmly, his merciful declaration taking the others aback.

"What shall we do with them, then, my king?" Commander Balka asked. Prisoners of war were often a difficult matter, requiring many soldiers to contain, soldiers they could not spare. The only permanent solutions were to kill them outright, sell them into slavery, or exchange them for their own soldiers taken captive. Since the enemy subjected their prisoners to enslavement and death, they had no means of exchanging them and would return the Benotrists' cruelty with equal measure.

"That is to be determined, commander, but Yah orders that we make no slaves of our captives. His word is law." Lorn felt the silence that followed bearing down upon him. Though the gathered commanders and kings had learned to believe Yah spoke through him, they were doubtful of the wisdom of this.

Lorn could see their misgivings and quelled the urge to rebuke their weak faith, submitting his pride to Yah's wisdom, knowing gentle words could move men where harsh ones stirred wrath.

"I ask for your trust, my friends. You have heeded Yah's counsel to your benefit and now must trust him when he requires you to act against your better nature. Should any of the captives attempt to escape, the punishment shall be death or enslavement, but those that obey will one day be set free. Should we win the day, it shall be by Yah's blessing, and the world we inherit must be subject to his will."

A long silence followed, the commanders conceding his point one by one before King Mortus finally spoke for all.

"Your God has brought us this far, and if he says this to be so, then so it shall be," the Macon king proclaimed. Lorn smiled at his father by marriage, touched by the profound change in his own disordered heart.

"Well stated, Father." Queen Deliea inclined her head to Mortus, proud of the two men she loved.

"Now that you sorted all that out, how about we make some decisions before we all die of old age standing here," Raven said, deciding to hurry this along, not caring one iota what they did with their prisoners.

"Our Earth friend is correct, so let us continue," Lorn said before anyone spoke against Raven's rudeness, not that Raven cared if they did.

"The first priority is Besos. General Valen, you have the most recent tidings in this matter," Lorn said.

"Aye, Sire. The 11th Benotrist Legion has withdrawn to Besos, abandoning their invasion of the Torry heartland. We estimate their number between fifteen and twenty-four telnics. General Ciyon is currently approaching the fortress city from the east, commanding fifteen telnics. He is joined with the Torry 3rd Army's ten telnics, and the remaining forces of the 1st Jenaii Battlegroup, numbering four telnics from Corell, and up to three more that were sent to reinforce Besos before it fell. The three Jenaii telnics that were sent to defend Besos withdrew to the west after its fall, harrying the Benotrist advance into the Torry heartland. They have joined with a considerable citizen force marching on Besos from the west, along with General Fonis' 2nd Torry Army. The city shall soon be enveloped from all sides."

"Very well. Once Besos is retaken and the 11th Legion destroyed, the battle for Torry North will be concluded. We must hasten its fall before directing our attention to Morac's retreating army." General Bram Vecious stated the opinion of many of the commanders.

"If we wait upon Morac whilst conquering Besos, Morac's army will attain Notsu, giving him time to regroup. I would guess he still has at least 60 to 70 telnics from the siege, another 20 from the garrison of Notsu, and whatever forces filtering in. He could easily field 100,000 before we move against him," General Ev Evorn said, his voice void of emotion.

THE CHRONICLES OF ARAX

Therein lay their dilemma. Should they concentrate their forces to Besos in the west, hastening and insuring victory, or contain Besos while moving the greater portion of their army toward Notsu in the east, preventing Morac from regrouping? There was danger in either choice. Even if they moved immediately upon Morac, he might still regroup and turn upon them, when a large portion of their strength remains at Besos. Should they move in force upon Besos, the siege might still linger or fail altogether. There were no certainties in war. The likeliest scenario was a victory at Besos and Morac remaining at Notsu. This war could be endless, a realization just now dawning upon many. Before, they were consumed with relieving Corell, that battle deciding the fate of the realm and eventually the war. Now they faced the grim prospect of a war unending. Defending your own lands was one thing, but projecting strength was far more difficult, a lesson Morac had learned most bitterly.

"Containing Besos would seem the wiser choice. We could lose twenty thousand soldiers storming those walls," King Sargov warned, wary after the losses his small army had endured in breaking the siege.

"We could lose many times that to starvation if our farmers cannot return to planting. Time is running short for their return," Torlan Thunn, the Torry Minister of agriculture explained. The great disadvantage and advantage the Torries had over the Benotrists was that most of Torry North was populated with small farms, worked by their owners, where the Benotrists used large estates worked by Menotrists and other enslaved peoples. This limited the size of Torry armies, with much of their population tasked with farming. The Benotrists were thus able to field much of their young male population in their legions. This disparity exposed the Benotrists to slave revolts should their battlefield losses mount as was happening with the war's progression. There were simply too many slaves and not enough soldiers to keep them in check. The Torries, however, were vulnerable with Morac's invasion into their heartland, which displaced thousands of farmers who had now formed into a vast militia marching upon Besos. It was this militia that Minister Thunn wanted to be freed to return to work their farms.

"Morac's plan was to ravage our heartland, causing us to starve by fall," Corry said, recalling her parlay with the Benotrist lord.

"My king, perhaps I can storm the city," Terin offered, Corry's disapproval evident on her face as the others chorused a myriad of reactions.

"No, I'll do it," Raven offered, causing the entire chamber to grow silent.

"Raven?" Lorn raised a skeptical brow.

"Look, I was planning to return to my ship and continue the war from there, but Besos is a short distance from here. Dar can lend me one of his birds, and Orlom and I can zip right in, blast the walls down, and your men can go storming through. It should take a whole ten minutes, then we'll be on our merry way. Meanwhile, Terin and Elos can go with the rest of the army eastward, chasing down Morac," Raven explained.

"What is a minute?" General Dolom asked, not knowing the Earth measurement of time.

"I should lead the assault. My sword will spare many of our soldiers' lives," Terin pleaded.

"Should your Majesty agree to this, I can march east to face Morac, or Thorton should he appear. Terin can join us soon after, once he is no longer needed at Besos," Elos offered, knowing his *Sword of Light* could counter Morac's, while Terin's could greatly ease their victory at Besos. It was another benefit from their victory over Dethine, knowing they now had to only counter Morac with one blade, freeing the other to be elsewhere.

"How soon shall you leave?" Lorn looked to Raven and then Terin, as they appeared to have won him over.

Corry thought to voice her displeasure but paused, her counter arguments failing in her mind. There was no way to oppose them without sounding foolish.

"No point in showing up too long before the show is about to start. How soon before your boys are in position?" Raven asked, most of the commanders looking on, trying to figure out what he just said, though Lorn seemed to understand, which the others attributed to divine intervention.

"General Ciyon should be in position within the next two days," Lorn said.

"Alright, we'll head out tomorrow," Raven said, giving Terin a nod of agreement.

"That leaves us with planning our movement east," General Lewins said.

"We move in force!" King Mortus declared with authority, shifting the tokens upon the map representing his 2nd Macon Army, the Jenaii 2nd Battlegroup and the 2nd Zulon Army alongside Lewin's 1st Torry Army, far to the east of Corell along the east-west road.

"And should Morac regroup and turn back upon us?" King Sargov asked.

"We smash him!" Torg growled, setting his fist upon the table.

* * *

"I will go east with the army, my king. You have much to attend to in the coming days and can join us once Besos is settled," Torg said after the others had filtered out of the chamber, the two of them all alone save for Jentra, who stood rigidly at their side, but Lorn was having none of it.

"My place is with our men, Torg. How can I ask them to march into battle while I remain here?"

"You have led from the front since Mosar and haven't eased since. Your father marched east without me beside him. I'll not repeat that shame. Besides, you will join us soon enough. A magantor can cover ground rather swiftly. By the time you join us, we shall be still kicking up dust many leagues from Morac's host," Torg reasoned.

"Listen to Master Vantel, my king." Jentra added his voice to Torg's.

"You have the prisoners to still deal with and must treat with the hundreds of vassals that have arrived since the siege lifted. We are still reorganizing nearly all of our forces, and your authority is required in countless matters that your sister and I have been unable to render in your place. You can spare a few more days to attend matters of the realm, and leave the marching part of the Notsu campaign to us," Torg added.

Lorn often leaned on Yah's guidance in these matters but felt no such inclination from him in this.

"Very well, Torg. I should know better than to argue with the one man on Arax ornerier than Jentra." Lorn smiled at the two of them, before stepping without.

* * *

It was late in the day when Raven visited the matrons' pavilions outside the palace walls, where the newest wounded were gathered along with those still untreated since the battle. Wounded men were gathered near the large encampment, many laid out upon the ground unable to move with severe leg injuries or recent abdominal and chest wounds from skirmishes with fleeing gargoyle bands and retreating Benotrists. Many more lingered further away, nursing wounds that were either minor or required greater energy from the regenerator, especially missing limbs that were cauterized at the outset, sparing them from bleeding out. Most suffering such wounds died before they could be treated. Infection was already taking root in many of the wounds, the foul stench surrounding the encampment. The open air outside the palace walls was an improvement over the confined halls of Corell, the wind doing much to clear the stench. Most of those seriously wounded were Benotrist prisoners, their treatment with the regenerator stirring resentment among the allied soldiers. They kept their tongues at the insistence of King Lorn, whose mercy for his enemies equaled his courage in battle. Only his courage in battle afforded him to be merciful without losing his men's backing.

Raven caused a disturbance with his mere presence, men looking upon him with fear, adoration or curiosity. The Benotrist wounded knew he was the source of so much of their misery and wondered where their own Earther was to counter him. The soldiers guarding the matrons' primary pavilion stepped aside as he approached, allowing him to enter without challenge. They were fully aware of his role in providing the regenerators and the esteem he held in the

King's heart. Raven found the whole thing strange, being used to men running away in fright or looking at him with derision. He kind of missed his terrible reputation. Once people started to look up to you, eventually you will disappoint them, and their feelings will be predictably derisive. He'd rather they just disliked him from the start. Of course, some still looked at him like he was a complete jerk, which, if he was being honest, he truly was.

We can't all be heroes, he thought to himself. Besides, the Torries had plenty of heroes as it was. They needed a monster or two to balance things out. It was something Coach O'Brien used to say back at the academy, that every football team needed a few bullies, thugs and villains on its roster. *If they think I'm a thug or bully, wait until Zem and Argos show up*, he chuckled.

Stepping into the large tent, he was greeted by a dozen matrons moving wounded men onto and off tables set up across the grassy floor while several of them moved from table to table with the regenerators. One of them he recognized as Ilesa, who looked a tired mess. He wondered if she slept at all. Upon entering, he noticed her looking at him briefly before returning her eyes to her work. Whatever she was thinking she kept it to herself. They hadn't spoken more than a few words since they met, and that needed to end today, before he departed for Besos. She was hardly one to stay in one place, which reminded him of himself in that way.

"Captain Raven, how fare you this fine day?" Matron Dresila asked, stepping from the table she was working, wiping her hands on her blood-soaked apron.

"Just paying my respects, ma'am, and wondering if I can have a few words with Ilesa?" he said, wishing he was wearing Ben's Stetson so he might tip it to the ladies like a cowboy in one of those ancient stories.

"Certainly." Dresila smiled. She had grown fond of the large Earther, even if he was insufferable at times.

Ilesa overheard his request, passing her duties to a sister matron before stepping away.

"If you would speak with me," she said, leading Raven back outside, the two of them walking away a short distance to find a quieter place to talk, standing aways from the wounded men, who looked on from afar.

"I don't know what to say, other than Kato was a good man and a better friend. The fact he chose you for his wife says a lot about you, Ilesa," Raven began, though he was never good at things like this.

"You are kind, Captain Raven." She sighed tiredly, her bloodshot eyes revealing her exhausted state.

"Just Raven. I'm not one for formalities, especially with Kato's wife. I don't know how much he told you about us, but…"

"He spoke at length about all of you in the short time I knew him. He was very fond of you. I am sorry that I lack the strength to demonstrate gratitude appropriate for all that you have done, Raven, but I do thank you," she politely said, though he knew she held back much of her true feelings about him.

He could see the pain in her eyes, the unspoken anguish that nothing could fill, knowing part of it was him. Kato fought for these people long before he did and gave his life doing so.

"I once saved a friend at the cost of my sister and lost the friend anyway. I watched another friend's wife die in his arms, with him begging her not to leave him. And now I look in your eyes and see that pain repeating all over again. I can't bring Kato back, Ilesa, but I can kill the man who killed him."

"Killing Thorton will not ease my pain, Raven. Do so for the war requires it, but do not do so for my sake. I have long stopped cursing Thorton for what he did, knowing he did not intend it, though it pained me to relent of it. I can only honor Kato's memory by sharing his gift with others, his healing device rendering care I could never dream to of my own volition," she said, touching a hand to her swelling breast as if guarding her heart, the small action not escaping his notice.

"I will be leaving tomorrow for Besos, so if we don't meet again, just know that you are always welcome aboard the *Stenox*. Being Kato's wife makes you family to all of us. I thought you should know that."

"That is kind of you, Raven. Perhaps one day I shall bring our child to visit."

"Whenever you wish, my fair lady." Raven smiled, preparing to step away when she again took him by surprise with her next utterance.

"Be sure to take the high road upon your return."

Raven looked at her for a time, knowing she was truly Kato's love, for he had shared that ancient Scottish ballad with all of them, explaining its meaning.

"Good advice, Ilesa. The high road it is."

* * *

> *"Farewell, my brother, lost you have I.*
> *Fallen in battle, for tears have run dry.*
> *Bless you, my father, your life you lay down.*
> *Giving all for your children, nation and crown.*
> *My son, my son, why lost you have I?*
> *For you were my glory, pure as the sky.*
> *My Love, my love, farewell thee I sing*
> *Gone from this world, by the wind on a wing…"*

The ancient ballad rang across the palace roof to the surrounding encampments, soldiers and people adding their voices to the mournful refrain, the sound building in a haunting crescendo. Lorn stood upon the outer battlements above the main gate, looking out over the sea of torches lighting the night sky, as well as the rooftop of Corell, where everyone gathered in the night air to honor the fallen. Galen began the ancient ballad with others joining in until it spread beyond the palace walls. It was aptly called *Ode to the Fallen*, a song of mourning after a battle, its somber tenor causing many a tear to fall. After a time, the gathered crowds grew quiet as Lorn lifted his torch high into the air, commencing the period of silence.

Queen Deliea stood dutifully at his side, staring out across the gathered host, a symbol of their unity. How she had come to love these men, Macon and Torry, now brothers in arms, joined with the men of Teso, Zulon and Sawyer, and the Jenaii, all united in cause. It made her proud to be part of it, to be bound to the man who speaks with Yah and leads all of them in battle, her beloved Lorn.

Lorn reached out his free hand to Deliea, interlacing his fingers with hers and squeezing tightly. It was one of the countless gestures they each used to show their love. He was struck by a memory, one of his father and mother, and the similar affections they shared. He spared a glance to his right, where stood Corry, staring stone-faced ahead, her countenance concealing her emotions, the very look she had practiced since childhood. She would have made a great queen of the realm had he not preceded her in birth. She shared a brief look with him, returning the slight smile he gave her, both taking comfort in the other's presence. They each bore the loss of their father alone before finally meeting and now leaned upon each other. This ceremony for the fallen was for their father as well, along with the men who fell at Kregmarin, Tuft's Mountain and Yatin. It was for the men of Sawyer and Macon, as well as Bacel and Notsu. It was for Arsenc and Yeltor, for General Tevlin, who fell by Dethine's hand before Terin and Cronus struck him down in turn. It was for Kato, and Nevias, and General Bode. And it was especially for Leanna.

It was then that Corry began to sing, her voice carrying far in the still night air.

> "Oh, how I mourn for you, my king.
> Oh, how I mourn for you, my king.
> Oh, how I mourn for my kin.
> Oh, how I mourn for my kin.
> I remember long ago days.
> Of sunshine, warmth and your loving gaze…"

Corry continued, the haunting melody carried by her sultry feminine voice, touching the hearts of the silent warriors who stood looking on.

* * *

The next morning saw them off for Besos, with Terin upon Wind

Racer and Raven and Orlom sharing mounts with two of Dar's warbirds. Matron Dresila would follow the next day, bringing one of the regenerators with her, expecting heavy casualties once the assault commenced. Corry joined Terin upon the magantor platform, seeing him off as he climbed upon Wind Racer before the warbird strutted out onto the outer lip of the platform and sprang into the air. He circled the upper palace one last time, waving her farewell before flying westward, disappearing over the horizon.

Chapter 2

Fall of Besos.

Dadeus Ciyon sat astride his ocran upon the Besos divide, gazing west where stood the hilltop fortress of Besos. Its towering inner keep rested atop an impressive hill, with two curtain walls circling it, the outermost resting at the base of the hill, with a deep moat circling it. The Desos river coursed the north face of the fortress, meandering the edge of the Besos Divide. General Mastorn already deployed the Torry 3rd Army to the north bank of the Desos, positioned across from the main gate of the fortress, and its raised drawbridge. General El Tuvo deployed his four telnics to the south, joining with the telnics he detached to Commander Ev Yaro during the first siege of Besos. Ev Yaro escaped the fall of Besos, harrying the Benotrists advance into the Torry heartland. Their original three telnics were reduced to eighteen hundred warriors, joining their strength to El Tuvo's four thousand. Combined, they were all that remained of the once-mighty 1st Jenaii Battlegroup.

Throughout Ciyon's advance from Corell, his army drove the five thousand stragglers from the 10th Benotrist Legion that broke west, toward Besos. His men slew nearly half, with some escaping to the north, while the rest retreated within the walls of the fortress.

Drawing from the west was General Fonis commanding the 2nd Torry Army, with their full complement of twenty telnics, along with two telnics of Notsuan refugees forming a new Notsuan Army.

THE CHRONICLES OF ARAX

They were still a day's march off along the east-west road, joined with a considerable force of citizen soldiers, numbering in the tens of thousands. They would soon complete the encirclement of Besos, trapping the 11th Benotrist Legion within its walls. Ciyon's latest estimates placed the Benotrist Legion at twenty thousand men, a considerable number to be housed in the confines of the fortress. He caught sight of Torry magantors circling the gray clad skies above, keeping a watchful eye upon the surrounding lands. General Valen dispatched a dozen warbirds to this campaign, more than enough to clear the sky of whatever magantors the enemy retained here, though he hadn't seen a one since clearing the Zaronan Forest yester morn.

"Besos awaits," Guilen said, drawing his ocran up alongside his.

"More than Besos, my friend. Destiny awaits us upon yonder hill."

* * *

Two days hence.

Dadeus' pavilion was set along the eastern face of the fortress, with his army dug in along an arc running from the south bank of the Desos, southward, skirting the east face of the fortress, before linking to General Fonis' army southwest of the city. Fonis' 2nd Army and the Notsuan contingent continued the encirclement, their entrenchments running along the west face of Besos, to the south bank of the Desos, downstream from Ciyon's beginning point. Across the river stood the Torry 3rd Army, General Mastorn covering the northern flank of the encirclement. General Fonis ordered the massive force of citizen soldiers across the Desos, to reinforce the 3rd Torry Army, blocking the Benotrists likeliest escape route.

By now, the Torry magantors began to drop fire ballista upon the fortress, flying far above the range of the Benotrist archers and ballista. Ciyon looked on with satisfaction as fires erupted along the causeways of the outer walls, caking men in flames. He could see their morbid dance as they shifted among the fires, some covered in flame before throwing themselves from the high walls. They lacked enough munitions to make a considerable difference, but their effect was more psychological at this point, imprinting in the minds of the defenders the hopelessness of their cause. They were a foreign army, trapped in enemy lands, surrounded by a great host with no relief army able to save them.

The Benotrist 11th Legion began the campaign in a strong position, seizing Besos with few losses and secure supply trains from Notsu, and with the Torry interior open to their invasion. Their rapid advance into the Torry heartland began to slow the farther west they went, hampered by Jenaii raiders, Torry cavalry and the growing resistance of the Torry citizens. Once General Fonis bestirred himself from Central City, the Benotrists began to withdraw, consolidating their forces to give battle, until news reached them of the large Macon, Jenaii and Torry Southern forces marching to relieve Corell. With these grim tidings, General Felinaius, commander of the 11th Benotrist Legion, ordered a full withdraw to Besos. Kriton, who led the Benotrist cavalry, reached Besos long before the Torries were within sight of its walls, resupplying his mounted unit and escaping north, before breaking due east, hoping to evade the Torry forces near Corell, in hopes of joining Morac's retreating columns near Notsu. That left the greater part of the Benotrist 11th Legion trapped within the walls of the fortress, Besos greatly lacking in supplies large enough to sustain such a force.

* * *

Dadeus prepared to issue a commanders' call with Mastorn, Fonis and El Tuvo, to coordinate the siege for the coming days, trying to gauge the enemy's strength and intentions. Standing before his pavilion, he scanned the battlements of the fortress in the distance, seeing little activity upon its high curtain walls, other than sentries standing to post. If the Benotrists intended to counterattack, they were masking it well. Fires still lingered across the inner and outer walls of Besos, with Torry magantors making regular passes over the battlements, dropping munitions wherever the defenders congregated. The clouds had broken up by late day, with sunlight breaking upon the western face of the fortress, illuminating the inner keep in a beautiful light.

Dadeus admired the view, the tranquil visage contrasting the brutal task at hand.

"Is it not strange, Guilen, that such beauty can exist amid such chaos?" Dadeus asked, with Guilen standing at his side. His young aide de camp stood in resplendent silver armor, tunic and cape, contrasting his own golden raiment.

"Beauty and ugliness are everywhere if one truly looks," Guilen answered, turning as something caught his eye, finding a complement of magantors drawing from the east, passing over the Jenaii encampments that were repositioned behind Ciyon's army.

"We have guests," Dadeus stated curiously, following Guilen's gaze, where the arriving magantors angled lower, setting down among the Jenaii encampment.

Making their way to the magantor area, where the new arrivals set down, Guilen was taken aback at seeing Terin, the two not having seen one another since that fateful day in Caltera. He was much changed since them, arrayed in bright silver cuirass and greaves, over the sea blue tunic of a Torry elite. He dismounted from a great white avian, with a midnight black beak and silver eyes that stared intently at him as they approached. He recognized Terin as he removed his helm, his stern countenance breaking into a smile upon seeing him approach.

Guilen stepped forward of Dadeus, taking a knee before Terin.

"Forgive me for leaving you," Guilen pleaded, his gesture taking Terin aback.

"No, my friend," Terin refuted, drawing him to his feet. "You were true to your word and sought out Prince Lorn. It was my own pride that condemned me."

Dadeus looked on as the two friends embraced, before noticing the lanky gorilla and large Earther dismount just behind them.

"I feared you were dead when we saw the lightning strike you," Guilen said, pulling briefly away, overcome with emotion. They had endured so much since that fateful day, though each upon a different path.

"Yah's discipline is absolute, as I have come to learn." Terin recalled the terrible pain of the blow, and the forlorn emptiness that followed.

"You appear to have managed. Look at you. I barely recognize you now. You look as magnificent as the Tarelian warriors of old I've seen depicted in the queen's palace, even greater if I am honest." Guilen tried to reconcile the Terin he knew as a slave on his mother's estate with the warrior standing before him.

"What of you, Guilen, adorned in armor of your own and riding into battle? When last we met, you had never ridden an ocran or lifted a sword."

"Every journey requires a first step, and I have traveled many steps since we parted."

"Indeed. You came to our rescue at the head of a great host. I would love to see Darna's look if she could see you as you now are." Terin knew he was aware of his mother's death, and the manner of how it happened.

"She would die of shame. I know of my father's death as well, Terin, and hold no one to account for his demise, other than his own arrogance. I know he treated you poorly, and for that I am sorry, wishing I did more to ease your suffering." Guilen mourned his father but understood why he was slain. If the blame were placed anywhere, it was at his mother's feet, her greed and cruelty the twin curses that brought their house low.

"You should know that your brother and sisters still live, at least they did when I last saw them," Terin said. He once despised Deva and the others, but after the events in Queen Letha's throne room, he strangely felt nothing, as if all his hate was washed away.

"I am told Deva was spared by your word. Do not deny it, Terin. If anyone had reason to see her dead, it was you, and yet… you spared her."

"Yah spared her" was all Terin could say as the others closed about. The two of them shared a look, agreeing to continue their conversation later.

"You must be the Earther Raven. Your legend precedes you,"

Dadeus said as he closed upon them from one side while Raven and Orlom approached from the other.

"Good guess, and by the description, you should be General Ciyon," Raven greeted, stepping to Terin's side.

"I am Orlom." Orlom grinned, stepping to Terin's other side, with his rifle slung over his shoulder.

Terin introduced Guilen to them, who looked taken aback by Raven's immense size and appearance. Though Terin spoke of the Earthers at length during their times on Darna's estate, seeing one in person was a different matter altogether. If Guilen was gobsmacked, Dadeus was nonplussed, clasping hands with Raven as if they were old drinking chums. Terin had briefed Raven thoroughly on Guilen, the help he gave Terin outweighing his relation to Darna in Raven's opinion. Raven would try to gloss over any connection between Guilen and his rotten kin. And considering he had Tyro for a father-in-law, who was he to judge? After the introductions were concluded, they were soon joined by their escort and General El Tuvo, the Jenaii commander greeting Raven fondly, recalling his intervention north of Corell where he had saved his life.

"Shall we reconvene at my pavilion? We have much to discuss," Dadeus suggested.

"Lead the way, General. From what I hear, you have Benotrist squatters in your fortress, and we can help with the eviction," Raven said, slapping his holstered pistol.

* * *

ZIP! ZIP!

Raven's laser fire struck the outer battlements above the main gate, taking two Benotrist sentries through the chest, their silhouettes slipping beneath the ramparts, out of his line of sight.

ZIP! ZIP!

Orlom's shots struck a guard manning one of the turrets beside the gate, dropping his corpse to its stone-circled floor amidst his panicked fellows.

Raven shifted aim leftward along the wall, taking another soldier east of the main gate, while Orlom shifted westward. They stood behind the siegeworks erected across the Desos by the Torry 3rd Army, facing the north wall of the fortress. They immediately went to work after the commanders' call in Dadeus' pavilion, the generals deciding to hold position while Raven and Orlom weakened the garrison. It was past midday, and Raven would stop well before sundown to recharge his weapon, but that left him time to cause plenty of mischief.

* * *

General Felinaius, commander of the 11th Benotrist Legion, stepped onto the upper battlements of the inner keep, roused by the commotion upon the outer walls. He was greeted by the horrific sight of laser fire flashing along the battlements below, strafing the outer curtain wall at the base of the hill. Men were crouched below the outer ramparts, fearing for their lives, none daring to peak above the parapet lest laser fire take them. Above the fray, along the inner curtain wall, men fled down the adjoining open stairways, seeking safety at ground level.

ZIP!

Another blast struck a soldier upon said inner curtain wall, further fueling the men's fears.

"Madness!" Felinaius cursed, standing behind the parapet of the inner keep, his guards standing nervously beside him. His garrison was overcrowded for a fortress this size, and were now trapped within its walls. His tenuous supply lines were cut, limiting him to whatever food they had stored in Besos, or plundered from the Torry heartland. Unfortunately, the raiding of said heartland was conducted in early spring, with few stored crops to plunder. The men were cramped in the confines of the fortress, with most sleeping upon the cold ground, with not enough room in the garrison billets for an army so vast. The narrow stone causeways were impossible to erect tents or pavilions to augment the lack of housing, nor were the kitchens large enough to provide hot rations to the all the men. Further confounding their sorry state were the constant raids by Torry magantors, dropping fire ballistae into their crowded ranks. And now… this.

ZIP!

Laser blasted where Felinaius just stood, his sudden turn sparing his life by the barest of threads, the laser grazing his ear. He crouched below the parapet, joining the others already there, none daring to peak above the rampart.

* * *

It was growing late in the day when Terin circumvented the siege lines, reaching the 2nd Torry Army's encampment along the southwestern portion of the encirclement. Raven and Orlom's laser went cold a short while before, allowing them to recharge them with the remaining light in the day. Terin spent much of the day standing watch over Orlom or Raven, preparing to deflect any return fire should Thorton happen to be in Besos. He spoke with General Fonis during the commanders' call in Dadeus' pavilion, asking if he could visit his command, and for what purpose, which the aged Torry General happily obliged.

He felt a surge of excitement and nervousness as he drew closer to General Fonis' command pavilion, where the sons of his uncle Torgus Vantel awaited him, the eldest the commander of the 4th Telnic, and the younger the 6th Unit Commander of the 1st Telnic. Terin was quickly recognized by the men of the 2nd Army as he moved about their encampments that ran behind their forward siege trenches. A few hushed whispers as he passed cascaded into hearty cheers or salutes, which he returned, embarrassed by their adulation. By the time he reached the General's pavilion, a small crowd had gathered around it, heralding his arrival before he was ushered within.

General Fonis stood in the center of the pavilion, the aged commander receiving him cordially, with his cousins standing upon either flank, each bearing a striking resemblance to their grandfather Torg, with stout builds and piercing gray eyes.

"Champion Caleph, we are honored by your company," General Fonis greeted, his once-auburn hair silvered with age, though his green eyes sparkled with life, matching the vibrant hues of his daughter Enora, whom Terin met upon his first arrival at Corell.

"General, again we meet today. It has been a long time since we met at Rego, at the start of this awful war," Terin greeted.

"Indeed. Though I would be remiss to not mention your contributions at Tuft's Mountain. We might be excused for that oversight considering the subtle nature of your presence there, slaying many of the enemy far behind the forward lines out of sight of so many. Your deeds since then have been fully illuminated. My daughter speaks well of you, extolling your many virtues," Fonis said kindly.

"The Lady Enora is most generous in her esteem, General Fonis."

"As are you, Champion Caleph. With these pleasantries, it is time to formally introduce your kin, Telnic Commander Torlin Vantel, third of his name." Fonis began with the man to his right, wearing the three braided cords of a telnic commander.

"Cousin." Terin stepped closer, clasping forearms with the man.

"Cousin. Our father will be most envious that we meet you before him," Torlin greeted, before Terin brought him into his embrace, taking the elder cousin aback as he returned the affection.

"Cousin," the younger Vantel greeted, before Torlin introduced him as Vatan Vantel, the 6th Unit Commander of the 1st Telnic.

"Vatan." Terin embraced him as well. All his life, Terin had thought his parents were his only kin. He was overjoyed to learn of his kinship with House Vantel. Both of his cousins seemed fine men, leaders of unit and telnic, who looked as if they were cut from stone.

General Fonis excused himself to see to other matters, leaving them time alone to speak with one another. Terin's cousins asked about his childhood and about his mother, their aunt Valera whom their father always spoke of with deep affection. They were grieved to learn of her abduction and thankful that Jonas went to find her. Terin asked of their upbringing and about their ancestral home of Cropus. He vowed to visit there when the war was won. They spoke at length on many things, especially their shared love for their grandfather, whom Torlin and Vatan had not seen since the war began.

"It is a rare thing for sons of our house not to be raised by their grandfather, but our father remained as regent of Cropus while Grandfather remained at court," Torlin said. They had been speaking until the sun dipped below the horizon, painting the western sky in a bright orange hue.

"Grandfather spoke of that when he revealed our kinship. He was supposed to return to Cropus and raise you while Uncle Torgus assumed the mantle of commander of the elite and master of arms of the realm," Terin revealed, recalling their conversation on that night on the eve of the final assault upon Corell during the first siege.

"Yes, but Grandfather knew you would have need of his instruction, and as tidings of your great deeds have spread, we now know the truth of it." Vatan smiled, placing a comforting hand to his shoulder.

"And I am grateful for it. There is no finer warrior than Torg Vantel," Terin added.

And so they spoke for a while longer, promising to call upon each other whenever they could. Terin finally bade them farewell, embracing them one last time before returning to the northern perimeter to rejoin Raven and Orlom. Stepping into the night air, he released a happy sigh, overcome with a sense of belonging. He looked up to the starlit sky, thanking Yah for this unlooked-for blessing. He thought of his parents at that moment, wondering how they were faring, or if they even lived. For most of his life, they were all that he had, the only family he thought he had. He loved them dearly and spoke a silent prayer to his God for their safe return. He paused, taking measure of his worries and scolding himself for entertaining them. Had Yah not brought them this far? What was the point of worrying when he was blessed time and again? And even through his greatest challenges and setbacks, Yah carried him through, setting him on firmer ground than he occupied before. He entered Fera a naïve boy and escaped with his friends against all odds, proving his worth. He fought at Telfer and then Corell, rallying men to victory. He traveled to Yatin and fought at Mosar and Carapis, striking down Yonig and Mulsen in battle, before being delivered up to slavery and torment. Yet at his lowest, Yah gifted him his greatest blessing, the love of Corry, who traveled across the world to save him. Though his power was different now, and his glory dimmed, his happiness was never greater. He had the love of Corry and newfound family in his cousins. Yah had delivered up Morac's great host to destruction, and

Prince Lorn had claimed his throne, uniting most of southern Arax to their cause. Considering all of these blessings, should he not trust Yah to deliver his parents from their trials?

He paused again, knowing there were no certainties in war, needing to look no further than poor Cronus and Leanna. Could he still follow Yah if Corry was taken from him? He considered that awful thought for a long moment, feeling his heart race at that possibility. Then it struck him, the meaning of faith staring him cold in the face. He had to surrender everything to Yah, leaving him his worries, burdens and fears, trusting him to carry him through, and preparing to lose everything if it was required of him. He had to offer his life, Corry's life, and his parents' lives if the price was demanded. He had to offer everything if he truly trusted Yah, and if the cost was required, he could not curse his God for demanding the price.

"So be it." Terin relented. "I give it all to you, Oh Yah." And with that utterance, Terin felt surprisingly numb, as if his mind was clear of its distractions and able to see clearly for the first time in his life.

* * *

The next morn found Raven and Orlom seated again upon their magantors, their Torry riders maneuvering their warbirds above Besos while they targeted the men below, firing into their crowded ranks.

ZIP! ZIP! ZIP! ZIP!

Laser spewed from above, raining upon the Benotrist defenders unanswered. Men crowded within the confines of the fortress could do naught but sit and take it. Men scattered wherever Raven and Orlom struck, but became caught up in the crowds blocking their way in every direction. Some thought to lower the drawbridge and take their chances assailing the Torry 3rd Army camped north of the palace, but were barred by their comrades, knowing any such assault would be futile. The very walls of the fortress now acted as a cage for the defenders than protection. With the north gate the only exit, the Benotrists would have to funnel through that narrow chokepoint before redeploying for an attack, which was nigh impossible. All they could do was sit and take whatever punishment Raven and Orlom gave them, each circling above, firing into their midst with impunity. Raven and Orlom finished firing after dropping several hundred defenders, retiring for the rest of the day, the Benotrists grateful for that small mercy.

* * *

The following morn saw the arrival of Matron Dresila and Minister Antillius, the former to treat the wounded, and the latter to offer terms to the Benotrists. And so it was, that General Ciyon sent an envoy to the beleaguered fortress under a flag of truce, offering a parlay, to which the Benotrist General Felinaius agreed.

It was under the midday sun that General Ciyon, Minister Antillius and Terin awaited their Benotrist counterparts on the southern bank of the Desos River, before the main gate of Besos, astride three ocran. Terin looked on as the drawbridge lowered, greeted by the tall silhouette of General Felinaius and his accompanying escort, who rode forth to meet them, arrayed in their polished bronze helms and golden tunics, the uniform of the 11th Legion. Above them, hundreds of defenders lined the battlements, braving the walls for the first time in two days, curious to observe the parlay. They rode forth, their ocran maintaining an easy gait, the escort to the general's left bearing their standard, two crossed silver daggers upon a field of black, the sigil of the 11th Legion.

"Hail, General Felinaius!" Dadeus Ciyon greeted the Benotrist commander as they came to a halt before them.

"Hail, General Ciyon," Felinaius said evenly, his eyes betraying the practiced calm that permeated the rest of his bearing. Terin could tell by his bloodshot eyes that the man hadn't slept in days, the garrison under constant stress with magantor ballistae strikes, and Raven and Orlom's incremental fire.

"I present my accompanying escort, Minister Squid Antillius, who speaks on behalf of King Lorn," Dadeus first introduced Squid.

"And does your good minister hold full authority to negotiate terms?" Felinaius lifted a critical brow.

"I do. King Lorn has vested in me his full authority in dealing with the garrison of Besos, General," Squid said.

"Very well, and your other companion?" Felinaius shifted a suspicious eye toward Terin, guessing who sat before him.

"Terin Caleph, Champion of the Torry Realm," Dadeus answered, his utterance having the expected reaction from the Benotrists, an even mix of fear and loathing. Felinaius thought Terin looked far too young for his reputation. Then again, every war makes killers of children. Looking back on history, one would be aghast at how many famed warriors were little more than boys.

"Your king's terms, Minister Antillius?" Felinaius asked, wishing to conclude this miserable affair.

"His terms are favorable, General. King Lorn shall accept your surrender, sparing your men execution, torture and enslavement. You shall be taken prisoner and moved to our southern regions and those of our allied realms until the completion of the war, whereupon you shall be pardoned and returned to your native lands. Any forced labor until that time shall be done in exchange for feeding and housing your men. In return, you shall order your men out of Besos in groups of one hundred, where they shall surrender their arms and be bound for their journey. Commanders of Unit and higher shall surrender last and be held at Corell until the war's end when they shall also be pardoned and returned to their native lands." Squid stated the King's terms, gauging Felinaius' reaction.

"You would have me surrender my garrison so easily? Should I refuse, you shall lose twenty thousand taking these walls. Why should I dishonor my name and brand my legion cowards for so little?" Felinaius challenged.

"King Lorn offers life, and eventual freedom for all your men. That is far more than LITTLE, and far more generous than the terms Morac has imposed upon our people," Squid answered.

"Eventual freedom? Do you think this war shall soon end?" Felinaius sneered. "My emperor is not easily swayed. You may have pushed our armies from your lands, but invading ours is a task you cannot achieve unless your king has found three hundred thousand more men to aid in the task. And if I were to guess, you are two hundred thousand short."

"This war shall end sooner than you believe, General. As far as storming Besos, you know we need not do so. You are trapped within its walls with twenty thousand starving men, all looking to you to save them. We will not waste our strength killing you when your empty bellies shall do it for us. Our Earth friend need only circle above your fortress, slaying any man dispensing provisions. That should hasten your starvation," Dadeus stated coldly.

"Your people shall have need of you at war's end, General. Your men have families that will need them. King Lorn's terms are most generous, more generous than you deserve," Squid added.

"And why should your king care if we have a home to return to? Why would he allow us to return and rebuild our strength, knowing we shall forever be his enemy?" Felinaius asked warily.

"You are men, are you not?" Terin asked, addressing him for the first time.

"We are Benotrist, and you are not. Our people have no friends among men, save for Nayboria, whose power is now broken," Felinaius spat.

"I AM Benotrist, General Felinaius," Terin declared, causing Dadeus and their Benotrist counterparts to look sharply at him.

Felinaius studied him for the longest time, not believing such a ridiculous claim, but Terin spoke of it with enough vigor to give him pause. Terin read the doubt in his eyes and continued, pressing his advantage.

"I am Benotrist, and Menotrist, and Torry and Kalinian. I share blood with all of them, but it is through my father's line that I am Benotrist, through his father's mother, who was concubine to a cruel Menotrist overlord that tortured many of my Benotrist kin. I know the pain your people have suffered at the hands of the Menotrists, General Felinaius. When this war is ended, there shall be peace between our peoples. In this you have my word as a Torry and as a Benotrist," Terin declared, causing Felinaius to reconsider.

He could see the truth of Terin's words in his eyes, eyes so pure that they took him aback. If he was to believe Terin, it led to other questions, including his origin and why he chose to fight for the Torries over his Benotrist kin. Such questions were guessed by Antillius, who spoke to them next.

"Yah is moving in all things as he has never before, General. King Lorn has foreseen this for many years, seeing the coming conflagration and the threat of the gargoyles, a threat your emperor has embraced. History itself is coming to a great climax, the battle between mankind and gargoyles reaching its final conclusion. Should the gargoyles win the day, no human shall be spared their wrath, not even you. Should we win the day, King Lorn will see to the survival of your people. Yah is guiding King Lorn's mercy in treating with you, General. Receive his mercy and surrender your garrison. Save your men from fruitless slaughter," Squid stated passionately, each utterance stripping away Felinaius' resolve, until breaking it altogether.

He truly had no choice, for his current position was intolerable. How many more days before his garrison devolved into chaos? The only choice was to remain and starve or redeploy through the main gate to attack Ciyon's fixed positions, which Ciyon would not allow, as his men would be funneled through the narrows of the main gate, falling under ballista, arrows and the Earther's murderous fire. No, the only choice was the one given.

"The fortunes of war have forced my hand. I agree to your King's terms!" Felinaius conceded.

* * *

The late evening found Raven and Orlom joining a number of Torry and Macon soldiers gathered around a cook fire near General Ciyon's pavilion, sharing stories and crude jokes, as Squid and Terin looked on from the periphery. A cheerful air permeated the allied encampments with the end of the siege, the men taking an earned respite. Though final victory seemed a far-off thing, so was what remained of the enemy. For the first time since the war began, Torry North felt secure from Tyro's reach. Terin drew his cloak about his shoulders, looking on as Raven entertained the men gathered around with another of his adventurous tales, while throwing about the name of a man named Coach O'Brien, whoever that was. The men seemed to hang on his every word, like primitives seeing fire for the first time. Orlom seemed equally enamored, nodding his head in agreement with Raven's every utterance.

"A joyful heart is medicine for the soul. It is good to see the men laugh again." Squid sighed, standing beside him as they looked on, shrouded in the gathering dark, the light of the cookfires barely illuminating their silhouettes.

"Yes. It has been too long since our people could truly celebrate, but this war is far from over. Though we have expunged Tyro's armies from our lands, I still cannot see how we can take the fight to the far side of the Plate Mountains. All we have done is ensure our survival, but the enemy still remains entrenched in their own lands, and after another ten or twenty years the gargoyles' numbers will be renewed, their nesting grounds ready to spawn their next generation, unless we can destroy them before they mature." Terin thought deeply on this, just as Lorn did, the two men able to see the threat for what it was, and its unique nature. Humans had long wondered of the mechanics of gargoyle repopulation, their nesting grounds shrouded in mystery. Final victory would not be attained until those nesting grounds were finally discovered and razed.

"Men have tried before, in the days of King Kal and again during the Feran Alliance in the days of King Clorvis V and King Corell VI, in the year 574. Both failed, betrayed by other men, such is the weakness of man," Squid sighed.

"True, but to finally defeat the gargoyles, mankind must be united. We must march forth with one purpose."

"A man's heart sets his path. Change the heart, and you change the path," Squid said, an easy smile passing his lips.

"And there lies our trouble. I cannot change a man's heart, only Yah can, and even then, some men refuse his wise council."

"There will always exist men of stubborn natures, Terin. No less of a fool are they than the mighty kings and queens who have ruled over the realms of Arax. Not all men shall listen to their better nature, but many shall. Look no further than General Ciyon," Squid pointed out Dadeus as he emerged from his pavilion alongside Guilen, a smile painting his face as he joined the men listening to Raven's story.

Terin learned of Dadeus' conversion to their cause, brought about by King Lorn's mercy and clever conduct of the Macon Campaign. Lorn spared him, and repeatedly tested his honor, and when Lorn demonstrated his own honor, he won him to his cause.

"He seems a good man, and I am glad he has taken up our cause," Terin conceded.

"He is a proud man, one who must tame that most destructive leaning that plagues us all. But he is learning."

"Yah cannot dwell in a pride-filled heart. Lorn once told me that," Terin said, recalling the very words that haunted him throughout his enslavement to Darna.

"Very true, but pride is a stubborn thing to vanquish, and who would know more than my young friend who suffered so at Darna's hands?" Squid gave him a knowing look, able to read his thoughts.

"And more the fool am I," Terin sighed.

"You are many things, my boy, but fool is not one of them."

"Oh, I am a fool, Squid. My father once said *a single word of correction can turn a wise man from folly, but a fool requires a hundred lashes.*"

Squid laughed, recalling Jonas using that phrase on occasion.

"*If your Moglo is a bull, don't milk it,*" Squid recalled another of Jonas' sayings, Terin's laughter confirming he had heard of it as well.

"*All roads begin with someone walking on them,*" Terin said, using another of his father's phrases.

"*If something is too cheap, it will cost you more,*" Squid said, having learned that lesson himself many times over. Perhaps he was the fool that required a hundred lashes.

"Perhaps we have judged Raven unfairly for his strange proverbs, considering my father is equally afflicted."

"I believe our good Captain Raven rather enjoys our looks of confusion whenever he speaks of such things," Squid said, just as the men laughed, hearing another of Raven's crude puns.

"I think you're right. I think how far we have come since our first meeting him in Rego so long ago. Would you have ever believed we would be close friends with a man like him?" Terin asked, regarding his large Earth friend.

"War often brings about associations that appear mismatched at first glance, but when you look deeper, you see the similarities that bind us together. It was the same for King Lore, myself and your father during the Sadden War as it is with you, Cronus, Raven and so many of your friends. You are each more alike than you are different. And though you struggle with pride, as do we all, you each possess the wisdom to see it. As far as our friend Ciyon, he too is coming to see the will of Yah, as are so many of our people. I have seen it in the eyes of our soldiers throughout the trek from Fleace, both Torry and Macon alike, as well as the men of Teso and Zulon. Yah is moving in ways never before seen, stirring the hearts of men to heed their better natures. It is this great measure that gives me hope for victory."

"You are a wise and good man, Squid Antillius." Terin smiled, glad to have the company of his old mentor again.

"As are you, Terin Caleph."

* * *

The following morn the Benotrist 11th Legion struck their colors, the garrison emptying out of the fortress in small groups, where they were disarmed, bound, but treated gently. The fall of Besos saw the official end of the battle of Torry North. With its conclusion, Raven, Orlom and Terin would return to Corell, followed by Matron Dresila after she attended the many wounded, Torry, Macon, Jenaii and Benotrist alike. Dadeus catalogued his actions and gave them to Guilen to deliver to King Lorn, sending him along with Terin and Raven. Squid would remain with the armies at Besos as they organized the movement of their prisoners and prepared the rest of the army for whatever direction King Lorn would send them.

Chapter 3

Fall of the Yatin Empire.

Emperor Yangu sat his throne, his pale blue eyes staring intently at everything and nothing, shifting furtively from one point in the throne room to another. Memories replayed before him, mixed with enemies, both real and imagined. His face was gaunt, his high cheekbones nearly poking from his pallid skin. His emaciated form was swallowed by his voluminous black robes and oversized throne, giving him the appearance of a sickly child sitting at the high table. His addled mind degenerated with every passing day, compounded by the slavish devotion of his closest advisors, who did nothing to curb his cruel demands, fueling his delusions while directing them away from themselves.

At the center of the emperor's delusions was Lorn, the Torry prince, a source of hope to his people and suspicion to him. If he would walk the streets, he would overhear the gratitude the populace of Mosar felt toward the Torry monarch. It was Yangu that failed them and Lorn that saved them. This fact was undeniable to any reasoned mind. Yangu didn't need to walk the streets of his capital to realize this. Even in his maddened state he knew this to be true. Since Lorn and General Yitia departed the capital for Maeii, his hatred for both men grew unabated. Lorn was the foreign monarch undermining his position, while Yitia was the general of his strongest army and native to the eastern regions of his empire, regions known for their loyalties to the old Western Kingdom and their Tarelian heritage.

As soon as the Torry 4th army and the Yatin 2nd Army began to march for Maeii, Emperor Yangu dispatched his minister of inquiry, Corvictus Shatero, to investigate every unit commander and above that remained in the capital assigned to the 1st Yatin Army and the city garrison for treason against the crown. Shatero conducted his interrogations in secret, moving slowly through the ranks so as not to alarm General Yoria, commander of the 1st Yatin Army, until it was too late and he found himself under house arrest whilst his commanders were purged. Before General Yitia began his return journey from Maeii to Faust, the entire command structure of the 1st army was replaced with staunch royalists and lickspittles, who would blindly follow the emperor's orders to confront their countrymen of the 2nd Yatin Army who were marching back to the capital of Mosar. Once Prince Lorn departed Yatin, followed by his army, the way was clear for Yangu to begin his purge, preparing his remaining forces to engage Yitia's 2nd Army if he refused to obey his summons to Mosar.

Upon his return march from Faust to Mosar, General Yitia was alerted of the happenings in the capital, and the emperor's intentions concerning himself, where he was to be summoned before the throne and summarily arrested and executed. With twenty telnics in his command, he outnumbered the combined strength of the Torry 1st Army and the Mosar garrison, as each suffered high casualties in the siege of Mosar. Word had also reached him of the purges within the 1st Army and the Mosar garrison, which led him to halt his march and consolidate his army, which was currently strung out for countless leagues along the main road skirting the north bank of the Muva.

He gathered his commanders of telnic to his pavilion, to relay the grim tidings. They were a mixed lot, haling from various provinces, with nearly half native to the eastern regions that the emperor considered subversive. Three were native to the capital, with loyalist ties, and four from the port city of Faust.

"You speak of treason, General," Commander Gurlin argued, one of the natives of Mosar, his father a devout royalist, as were most of the commanders of rank in the Yatin armies.

"Do we have a choice, Gurlin? The emperor has gone mad. Even a blind man can see it!" Commander Tumlin, native to the Rulon Gap, countered.

"We cannot afford a civil war with the gargoyles still occupying half our empire. Unity must be maintained, or else we are doomed," Commander Burlayas, native to eastern Yatin argued.

And, so it went, with the commanders arguing deep into the night, some pointing out the need for loyalty, while others cautioned about the emperor's madness. Some thought it wise to avoid a decision all together, and redeploy to their home region, only to return to Mosar should the gargoyles come south.

"If I do not heed the emperor's summons, I shall be branded a traitor, and each of you shall be called upon to seize command of the 2nd Army," General Yitia explained. Should such a thing occur, the army would either rally to their general or be ripped apart by division. Any notion of obeying the emperor was compounded by his addled mind, where suspicion was cast in every direction. Even if the army remained loyal and handed over their general, the emperor was likely to purge every commander of telnic, unit, and possibly flax as well. Beyond these considerations was one more critical factor.

"What of Yah?" Commander Gilain asked, his rich royalist bloodline making him the least likely to oppose the emperor, but his tone leaned elsewhere.

"What of him?" Commander Burlayas asked.

"Are we blind? We have seen his hand in our deliverance. Prince Lorn placed his life and army into his divine hands and was delivered. At every turn Yah has guided his hand, and ours. My family is of a great house of Mosar, sharing blood with the emperor. They have seen the power of Yah moving among our people throughout the siege. Many are converting every day, risking the emperor's wrath. My younger sister has taken up the cause, and I fear what our emperor shall do to her and my kin with her. I have taken up his cause as well. If these tidings are true coming from Mosar, then the persecutions have begun. Can we stand aside and let our people be slaughtered and still call ourselves men?" Gilain challenged.

"No, we cannot," General Yitia sighed, steeling himself for what he had to do.

The commanders agreed to march to Mosar, where they would wait upon the emperor outside the city.

* * *

General Yitia moved slowly toward Mosar, keeping a gentle pace as his telnic commanders gauged their troops, measuring their sentiments. They came upon the capital, setting camp downstream of the city along the north bank of the Muva. The last of the Torry forces in Yatin had departed from Faust, while the Torry cavalry took the main road through the Yagan Marshes. It was upon the third day of Yitia's arrival, that he was summoned to the throne room, for which he refused, as word reached him of the sorry state of the city.

Minister Shatero had rounded up hundreds of high officials, commanders of rank and members of great houses throughout Mosar, forcing confessions from their tortured lips. Many were burned at the stake upon the palace grounds bordering the south bank of the Muva, in the center of the city, in full view of the populace. Their screams rent the day and night air, a grim warning to those harboring treasonous thoughts. Many more were found to be worshipers of Yah and were ordered to recant their faith before the people, with some doing so, while the rest refused. The poor wretches that refused were flayed alive, their screams haunting the streets of the city. The people were called upon to turn on their friends and neighbors, turning them over to the city garrison for judgement if they were adherents of Yah. Many of the men of the 1st Yatin Army deserted their posts, fleeing the city, while others took advantage of the vacancies in command, becoming eager enforcers of the emperor's orders. Soon word spread of General Yitia's refusing the emperor's summons, leading many of the deserters to join the growing ranks of the 2nd Army.

With General Yoria, the imprisoned commander of the 1st Yatin Army, locked away, command fell to a commander of telnic, Jeris Daron, a favored choice of Minister Shatero. He was ordered to lead his army outside the city to arrest General Yitia. By this time the

1st Army was reduced to five thousand men after desertions further thinned its ranks. And so it was, while Prince Lorn was concluding the Macon Campaign, General Daron led his army to arrest General Yitia, who met his challenge with the full might of his growing army along the north bank of the Muva. The inept generalship of Jeris Daron and the many replacements among his commanders was fully exposed upon the fields of battle, where he believed the authority of the crown would see the enemy dispersed, and Yitia his prisoner. His army was crushed and further beset by the turning of the Yatin cavalry, whose commander Cornyana delivered the finishing blow, taking Daron's army from the rear and blocking their escape. A few escaped by making their way to the river, jumping in, and following its course downstream, but most died or surrendered with the 2nd Army enveloping their flanks and crushing their front. General Yitia took the head of Jeris Daron, setting it upon a pike and bringing it before the north wall of the city gates, where his army repositioned, occupying the gargoyles' previous siege works.

And there the 2nd Army sat, strongly entrenched before the city walls, while the sorry state within Mosar rapidly deteriorated. Much of the garrison was filled with recent conscripts who were little better than peasants with spears thrust into their hands. They were ill suited for anything other than brutalizing the populace, many of whom were fleeing by the droves. General Yitia dispatched five telnics to Faust to reinforce his control of the harbor. The port city was still the main source of food imported from Torry South, and controlling it, he cut Mosar from its greatest resupply route. By late spring, food riots erupted through the streets, spreading rapidly across the southern half of the city. With most of the garrison manning the broken watchtowers and walls along the northern half of Mosar, there were few soldiers available in the southern half to quell the revolt at its outset. Shatero had little choice but to move most of their soldiers off the north wall to put down the riots, thus presenting General Yitia the opportunity to storm the north half of the city. Yitia further galvanized his men after intercepting a missive sent to Tyro from Emperor Yangu, offering to subject his realm to a vassal state with himself as its regional governor in return for Tyro's aid in confronting Yitia. Whether the missive was genuine or a forgery to foment rebellion, its effect on the army was undeniable.

Under the cover of darkness, the Yatin 2nd Army breached the north wall, sweeping through the city streets, before reconsolidating before the three bridges spanning the Muva. By dawn, the army advanced across the bridges, which were the only places the outnumbered garrison could concentrate to stop them, other than the imperial palace in the city's center. The fight was bitterly met but brief, with the garrison troops giving way by early morn. By the afternoon, most of the city was taken, leaving only the imperial palace and its small garrison in Yangu's hands. General Yitia ordered the palace blockaded, isolating it with a large portion of his army, while he went about setting the city to rights.

After a fortnight, the palace garrison surrendered over Minister Shatero's objections. The shaven headed minister was summarily bound and handed over to the army before the gates were flung open. Emperor Yangu sat his throne, his guards abandoning him to his fate as the rebel army swept into the throne room.

"Traitors!" he screamed as they entered the chamber, raising a stick-thin finger in their direction before he was dragged from the throne. What remained of the royal family were detained, with several prominent members missing. It was later discovered that Yangu's suspicions had extended to many of his wives and children, ordering them interrogated, most dying in the dungeon of the palace. Upon liberating the dungeon, the Yatin soldiers were greeted with a macabre scene, finding bodies in various stages of decay, the noxious smell of rotting flesh permeating the subterranean corridors. Many more were found alive, suffering unspeakable horrors, with missing limbs, gouged eyes and flayed skin. Many a seasoned warrior retreated from the foul lair, depositing the contents of their stomach once reaching the clean air. Among the prisoners was General Yoria, the commander of the 1st Yatin Army, who suffered extreme malnutrition and a missing sword hand.

General Yitia declared martial law in the city, establishing courts of inquiry while calling for a tribunal to judge the emperor and establish a new governing authority. The call went out throughout the lands still under Yatin control, summoning every commander of rank, regional potentates and local leaders to the capital to join the tribunals. Hundreds gathered to oversee the transition to a new ruling authority and hear the charges against the emperor and his Minister of Inquiry, Shatero. The emperor was brought before the people, and burned at the stake upon the palace grounds, followed by his cruel minister of inquiry. The tribunal spent several fortnights coming to agreements on the reordering of the government, declaring a continuation of tribunal authority until the end of the war, where they would decide upon a new monarch. They ordered the liberation of all prisoners detained by the emperor, and the protection of all adherents of Yah.

News then spread of Lorn's alliance with King Mortus and the invasion of Torry North by Morac, followed by the eventual breaking of the siege of Corell, and the decimation of Morac's legions, fueling the beliefs of those wishing to return the Yatin Empire to its Tarelian routes, seeking favor from Yah. From that point forward, the adherents of Yah swelled in numbers as Generals Yitia and Yoria restored the realm to some semblance of competence. Food continued to be shipped from Torry South, and the lands south of the Muva were prepared for the planting season, their farmers offered full exemption from taxes and levies for the next three seasons, maximizing their incentive for a bountiful yield. Both generals ordered a full audit of the mustering of all Yatin armies at the outset of the gargoyle invasion, calling up all those who failed to report for duty. This swelled the Yatin ranks to another twelve thousand soldiers.

It was a late spring day when a cohort of Magantors approached Mosar from the west, bearing emissaries from the Sisterhood.

Chapter 4

Port of Teris. Casian League.

Pors Vitara, Archon of Teris addressed the Casian Forum, standing upon the marble circle with the gathered members sitting the stone benches that circled above. He stood before them in the raiment of a warrior king of old, with bright polished steel cuirass, greaves and vambraces over a white tunic. His helm rested in his left hand, a plume of red feathers running along its center. He and Porlin Galba, Vice Archon of Port West, were recently returned from Tro, having endured the attack upon the port city. Upon their return they summoned the forum to reconvene, sending out magantors to recall members that were in their home cities, gathering them to Teris for a council of war.

Pors Vitara looked from one forum member to another, his vibrant emerald eyes taking their measure.

"I stand before you unbowed and unbroken, despite the earnest efforts of the Benotrist Empire. I have returned from Tro, having seen the destruction wrought upon that port city, where tens of thousands have perished. The Benotrists snuck a great host into Tro in the holds of their merchant ships, before launching their ambush upon the Troan and Ape fleets." Pors Vitara detailed the events that followed, including the attack upon the *Stenox*, and its eventual restoration, as well as the actions of the Torry Champion. He concluded with the extent of the devastation wrought and the declaration of war agreed upon in the forum of Tro, as well as the injuries he suffered, explaining how he was healed by the Earthers' regenerative device.

"Should we not celebrate the Earthers' demise? What greater enemy have we than they?" Gaven Foris, patriarch of House Foris, argued. He was the staunchest opponent of any appeasement with the new Ape Republic and their Earther friends.

"Would you think the same if the gargoyles resided upon our western border rather than upon Tro's northern flank?" Nullis Vacelis, Patriarch of House Vacelis, countered.

"That is irrelevant. They reside where they reside. Are our enemies not theirs?" Gaven Foris sneered.

"Have you seen a gargoyle, Gaven?" Pors Vitara challenged.

Gaven Foris refused to answer, not wishing to be made a fool of.

"I hadn't either, until Tro. They destroyed my face with fire, attacking the forum of Tro while knowing I was there, representing our people. They are savage, brutal creatures, bent upon our destruction. Should we stand aside and let the apes fight them in our stead? And what should happen if the apes win? I shall tell you. They will be stronger than ever, with powerful friends across the continent, while we stand attainted for cowards," Pors Vitara spat, letting that awful possibility sit for a moment.

"You mistake wisdom for cowardness. Let them rip each other's throats, while we pick their carcasses," Davelin Tors of Coven scoffed.

"Did you not hear what Pors said? Should the apes win, they will be stronger then ever, not weak," Nullis Vacelis growled.

"I heard him. I simply don't believe him," Davelin Tors said with a mocking sneer.

"Then believe this, Davelin. I have stated what shall happen should the apes prevail, and if they do, they will have done so with powerful friends. The Earthers' ship will be restored, and we well know what that portends for the Benotrist Navy. The Torries and Macons are now united in cause and soon in full unification if the rumors are true. They are allied with the Jenaii and the apes with Enoructa. Combined, they account for nearly all our trading alliances to our west and our east. If you fail to see the folly of our neutrality while all their lives are at stake, then no greater fool are you. And in the event the gargoyles win the day, we shall be faced with their full wrath once they have taken everything else. We might endure for a time, but once they control the continent, they will breed in great numbers and come for us. We must strike a blow and show unity with our neighbors at this critical time," Pors Vitara declared.

The forum erupted into debate, with nearly a third aligning with Archon Vitara and a third with Davelin Tors, wishing for neutrality, while the rest, such as Gleb Gortus of Coven, sat and listened. Gleb Gorbus traded heavily in slaves, while his contemporaries traded in spices, cloth, wines and varied luxuries and goods. He was a shrewd, cruel and calculating man, outspoken by nature, which made his silence on this matter stand apart. When a knowing grin painted his face, the others grew suddenly quiet, recognizing the epiphany evident in his expression.

"You have something to add to this discourse, Gleb Gorbus?" Morlin Galu, of Milito, inquired.

Gleb Gorbus came to his feet, smoothing his burgundy robes before stepping below onto the marble circle of the forum to address the assemblage, Pors Vitara stepping aside, yielding the floor. With the sides evenly split, the power rested with those undecided, as all decisions within the Casian League required a majority vote in the forum. Those looking on knew this, thus waited upon his next utterance with heady anticipation.

"To those who lean toward Archon Vitara, I would caution committing ourselves to far-off wars where we would be side players at best, and slaughtered with little regard at worst, while our home ports are weakened. To those leaning in Davelin Tors' direction, I caution you on the dangers of blatant neutrality when the fate of Arax is in the balance. We cannot abide a world ruled by Darkhon or Tyro, as our northern would-be allies refer to him. What our dear friends Davelin and Pors seem to have overlooked is another option, a most deliriously profitable option that will both fill our purses and endear ourselves to our Ape, Enoructan, Torry, Macon and Jenaii neighbors and would-be allies." Gleb paused, letting the anticipation grow as every eye and ear was sharply attuned, waiting upon his next utterance.

"We need not commit to a war far away when Tyro has allies that are conveniently placed so near." Gleb's smile stretched unseemly wide, looks of comprehension sweeping the assemblage.

"Naiba!" Davelin Tors answered, naming the Nayborian port city resting at the mouth of the Naiba River, his answer spurring a chorus of debate. The Casian League had long avoided wagging war along their northern coast, using the strength of their navy to keep the coastal realms at bay, remaining neutral while the Nayborians, Jenaii and Macons maintained the balance, none able to gain dominion over the others, while the Casian League grew rich through trade. Such days would soon pass for the coastal realms found themselves on opposing sides of this great war, ensuring an end to the balance the Casians profited so richly from. It was for that reason the Casians limited their adventures upon the continent to far off lands that were pitifully disordered, like the Ape Republic before the Earthers' intervention.

"We might hold naval supremacy over the Nayborians, but their land forces are quite strong. I would be careful about landing an expeditionary force upon their hostile shore," Morlin Galu cautioned.

"They are not so strong anymore. The 1st Naybin Army was decimated at Corell during the first siege, while the 2nd the 3rd Armies were beaten along the upper Elaris, by last report. That leaves only the 4th Nayborian Army at Plou, a mere ten telnics to contest our invasion, and many leagues away. They can hardly move against us when the Jenaii stand upon their western border, poised to strike. That leaves only the garrison of Naiba, a paltry three telnics, to oppose us. Their combined fleet numbers only twenty warships, an easy task for any of our fleets, let alone our combined might. This is our chance to not merely raid their coast, but to seize it outright. And unlike our meager possessions along the ape coast, we can permanently colonize the entire Nayborian coast from the Rocky Shore to the western approaches of Varabis, and halfway to Plou in the north," Gleb detailed the situation. Their intervention would break the Nayborian Empire, ripping its southern lands from their weakened grasp, while the rest fell to disorder. Word had yet to reach the forum of Dethine's death, and the loss of the Nayborians' *Sword of Light*, furthering their sorry state.

"What of Darkhon? Do you truly believe our new FRIENDS will abide our new conquests if we do not join in their fight against him?" Davelin Tors asked skeptically.

To this, Gleb merely smiled, as if the answer was plain as the midday sun.

"Have you not listened to Archon Vitara's oration on the decimation at Tro? The 1st Ape Fleet is nearly destroyed. What do they have but a handful of vessels? Their 2nd Fleet is only forty vessels with novice crews, if we are being generous. We can give them what they need… SHIPS. Our own 2nd Fleet is moored at Milito, eighty warships with excellent crews and enough supporting vessels to transport our 2nd Army, General Motchi's 12 telnics, which will greatly reinforce Tro. Our 12 telnics joined with the Troan garrison, and the ape armies that will be enroute, will form a strong force to protect the city, and should the Torries win the day at Corell, we can join these forces with theirs and project power into the heart of Darkhon's Empire. That should more than appease our would be allies of our loyalty, while the rest of our forces assail Naiba," Gleb explained.

"You would have my city send our strength to the far north while the remaining cities of the league gain untold riches, plundering nearby shores?" Morlin Galu of Milito protested.

"Truly, Morlin?" Gleb shook his head. "For three hundred years, each of our fleets and armies consist of sons from every city and land within the league, so that no one city could grow in strength separate from the others. This is the source of our unity. Only merchant ships are individually flagged to their home port. But to assuage your misgivings, I propose an equal split of said plunder and new lands to each member city of the Casian League, as well as generous payments to the families of every soldier that dies, whether he dies far to the north, or upon the shores of Nayboria."

Gleb's declaration was received with stone silence, followed by nods of agreement, his reasoning winning many converts, with few if any detractors. It was a sound, well balanced plan that risked little and rewarded much, two traits any trading empire regularly exercised.

* * *

And so it was that the Casian League formally entered the war, gathering a great host of ships and men at Teris in the coming fortnight, before setting off across the aqua blue tropical Casian Sea toward Naiba. Following this, the Casian 2nd Fleet set out from their home port of Milito, sailing first for Torn Harbor to join with their old enemies in the Ape Republic before sailing on together to Tro, bearing the might of the 2nd Casian Army. The great host gathered at Teris included the 1st and 4th Casian Fleets, boasting a combined fleet of 160 warships, and supporting vessels bearing the 1st and 3rd Casian Armies fielding a combined 17 telnics.

The Casian expeditionary force met the Nayborian navy outside the port of Naiba. Heavily outnumbered, the Nayborian fleet attempted to sail away, planning to attack the invading armada from behind once they began to disembark their armies, but were chased down, and forced to engage twelve leagues west of Naiba, within sight of shore. The two warring fleets fought throughout the day, with the last Nayborian ship slipping beneath the waves just before dusk. The Nayborians disembarked their armies unopposed east of the port, before they moved inland, setting camp for two days, fortifying in place. From there they moved to cut off the port by land, while the combined fleets completed the encirclement by sea. Thus began the siege of Naiba.

After ten days, the port city struck their colors, surrendering the harbor to the Casian League. From there the Casian armies fortified the port before preparing to advance up the Naiba River.

Chapter 5

Corell.

Guilen Estaran entered the throne room, walking beside Terin, his heart racing as he approached the dais, feeling the eyes of the court upon him as he drew near the throne, where sat King Lorn and Queen Deliea. Having just returned from Besos, they waited to receive them, eager to hear the tidings from Besos, much of it detailed in the parchment he bore from General Ciyon. This was the first time he had seen Lorn since his crowning, as the winds of war drove him toward Besos upon the lifting of the siege of Corell.

He found it surreal walking beside Terin in this storied hall, after all they shared in the Sisterhood. Seeing Terin now arrayed in the vestment of the Torry Champion and honored by the realm with adoring praise was a stark contrast to how he knew him before. It was like reconciling two different people, but that wasn't right either. It was the same person, but different environment. How else could one be treated as prince in one realm, and a slave in another. How fortunate for Guilen to have been Terin's friend, lest he suffer for his mother's crimes. If he was honest with himself, he wasn't a very good friend to Terin during his enslavement, more of an accomplice, working together for their own separate aims. Terin didn't seem to differentiate between true friendship and a mutual arrangement, or if he did, he was kind enough to overlook the weakness in Guilen's friendship when he was enslaved. Guilen spent a lifetime drowning in his own self-pity, which blinded him from seeing the truth in Terin's friendship when it was first presented. But looking back, what could one expect when he never had a friend before? The men on his mother's estate were either slaves, who were forbidden to act familiar with him, or his kin, his father and brother. His father was a miserable, broken man, who was bound to his duty to a wife that despised him, while his younger brother was insufferably devoted to their mother. His sister Deva was the only one he could confide in, and then only with his most shallow of thoughts. It wasn't until he met Terin that he found someone he could actually talk to as an equal, even though Terin was a slave at that time, though in reality, he was no more a slave than he was. His time since escaping had exposed him to a vast new world, carrying him across the continent, and forging strong friendships he never knew possible, first with Criose, and then Dadeus. Even Prince Lorn, who was now King, received him warmly at Fleace, eager to hear his tale, and acknowledging their kinship, as they were in truth distant cousins. It was said cousin who sat upon the throne before them. He followed Terin in kneeling before the dais before King Lorn ordered them to stand.

"Arise, Terin, and Guilen. We welcome your return from battle," Lorn greeted, sitting his throne attired in his blue tunic and silver armor, wearing a steel helm in place of a crown, with silver wings protruding from its sides, spread wide as if to take flight, fanning out above the helm's ear holes. Beside him sat Queen Deliea, wearing a thin silver tiara, lined with sapphires, nestled in her lustrous ebony hair, framing her achingly beautiful face. She wore a long azure gown that matched the sapphires in her crown. Her lovely raiment and beautiful face were exceeded by her grace and warm smile, welcoming them without saying a word.

"My king, we bring great tidings from Besos. The fortress has surrendered, with few casualties to our besieging armies!" Terin began, his bold utterance received with thunderous cheers from the court, where gathered a small host of commanders of rank, ministers of the realm and court attendants.

"Splendidly done, Terin. And what of Raven and Orlom? Have

they returned with you?" Lorn asked, looking toward the doors of the throne room, half expecting the large Earther to pass though them at any moment.

"Raven is attending other matters at this moment, Sire." Terin blushed, finding it poor taste to mention what he was truly doing, though Raven referred to it bluntly as *having to take a shit*. Lorn, to his credit, guessed it was something Terin thought not best spoken of in front of the realm, and knowing Orlom, he was probably equally occupied.

"We are glad you have returned safely, Terin," Deliea greeted warmly, to which Terin bowed his head respectfully.

"I see Guilen accompanies you." Lorn regarded his cousin, bidding Guilen to speak with a wave of his hand.

"My king." Guilen bowed deeply, before rising and presenting the scrolled parchment bearing the seal of General Ciyon.

Lorn stood and descended the dais, taking the scroll from Guilen's outstretched hand. Breaking the seal, he unrolled it and read Ciyon's detailed depiction of the siege of Besos, and the state of the besieging armies. The report was detailed, yet brief, without needless flair as Ciyon was wont to add by reputation. His new friend was becoming a seasoned general, curbing his colorful antics with hardened discipline. After the Horns of Borin, Dadeus would not repeat the arrogance that brought him his only defeat, and a humiliating one at that.

Splendidly done, Dadeus, Lorn thought to himself, pleased with his choice of placing him so high in his council.

"Our victory in Torry North is complete!" Lorn loudly proclaimed, raising the parchment high into the air in full view of the court, greeted by a chorus of cheers.

Lorn placed a hand upon Guilen's shoulder, guiding him closer to the dais, leading him up the wide stair to stand beside the throne for everyone in the chamber to clearly see, as Terin backed a few steps, standing off to the side of the chamber, exchanging the briefest of looks with Corry, who stood behind the throne, beside Jentra.

"When I first entered this chamber after the siege was lifted, and claimed my father's vacant throne, I greeted and acknowledged many of those who contributed so much to our victory. There are those, however, that were required elsewhere, the current of battle drawing them away from Corell. Among that esteemed company is General Ciyon, and his brave army, including his aide de camp, and most trusted councillor, Guilen Estaran, my cousin and deer friend, who saved my life during the lifting of the siege," Lorn proclaimed, drawing a chorus of approval for Guilen.

"Guilen!" Terin added his voice to Lorn's, turning the chamber's approval into hearty cheers, and drawing a smile from the King.

"From this day to your last day, I offer you a formal home in the Torry Realms. Should you choose to remain in service with General Ciyon, then that post shall be forever yours. Should you find the warrior's path not to your liking, then a post as a minister's apprentice can be arranged. I know of one high minister who has lost his apprentice to other duties," Lorn added, giving Terin a knowing look. Though Squid was still with their armies at Besos, he would receive Guilen's appointment gladly. It was Deliea that spoke next, expanding Guilen's list of options, options that were only fevered dreams during his life in the Sisterhood.

"You once spoke of purchasing a ship, to start on the path of a merchant. Should you still desire this at war's end, we might offer a partnership to hasten that endeavor," Deliea proposed. With the resources of the crown behind him, Guilen might build a wealthy fleet in rapid time, especially with free access to new trading lanes that would soon spring up between the allied factions.

Guilen's mind was a whirlwind, overcome by their generosity and friendship. Lorn added that he had until war's end to decide his path and would be welcomed at the king's table to dine this night. Looking out across the chamber, he was taken aback by his reception, before his eyes met Terin's, the Torry Champion regarding him as a brother, though in his heart he didn't deserve it. All of his friendships since escaping his mother's estate were intricately linked to Terin, or more specifically, to his relaying to the king that Terin lived, and where he was held. That was all it took for him to be received into the Torry ranks and join their cause. It was then that Guilen felt he truly belonged, and he vowed to honor Lorn as his king and to follow him wherever he decided to lead.

* * *

"I thought I might find you here," Raven said, peeking his head through the open door of Cronus' chamber, finding his friend holding his child.

Cronus looked up from where he sat upon the bed, a tired smile touching his lips upon seeing Raven and Orlom entering the room. He looked like he hadn't slept in a lifetime, and he probably hadn't. Despite the help Princess Corry arranged for him, his life was in turmoil. When he slept, he never rested, his dreams tormented with visions of Leanna. Each night was a little better than the last, but only by the slightest of margins. This could not go on for long, as they were at war, and he had duties to attend, but King Lorn insisted he have this time to sort this out.

"You returned so quickly." Cronus lifted a curious brow, wondering how fared their journey to Besos.

"Are you surprised?" Raven shrugged, grabbing the chair beside the bed and turning it around, sitting with his forearms resting over its back, while Orlom made himself at home, sitting beside Cronus on the bed.

"Not really, knowing what you are capable of when you put your mind to it."

"Using my mind doesn't usually work out the way I hope, but we did alright this time. How's our little girl doing?" Raven leaned forward over the back of the chair to look at Maura, who lay bundled in Cronus' arms. Her little eyes fluttered open from her peaceful slumber, giving him a strange look.

"The nursemaid just left, and took the soiled linen with her, thankfully." Cronus sighed, noticing Orlom lift his nose at the foul air that lingered in the chamber.

"Kids are a mess. Don't know how you people manage without diapers. She sure is a cute little thing though." Raven smiled, catching himself from making a funny face at the child. The last thing he needed was Orlom seeing him look like an idiot and telling everyone about it.

"She is." Cronus smiled at that. She was his everything now, his sole purpose for living, and the only thing left of Leanna for him to cling to.

"She is pretty," Orlom said, drawing her attention with his toothy grin, not afraid of making a face, unlike Raven. The child found it amusing, a small grin touching her lips.

Raven couldn't help but curse himself for not bringing another regenerator from the *Stenox*. If they had kept the extra one in the palace, Leanna would have been saved. It was just another regret he would have to live with. Cronus looked over at him, knowing what caused the sour look torturing his face. Raven had shared this with him two days after Leanna had died, but Cronus was too tired and too far in his grief to refute such nonsense.

"Nothing would have saved her, Raven. Even if you brought another device from the *Stenox*, we would have sent it to help with the wounded, where it would be drained just like the other two. The only thing that could have saved her was to go into labor the day before or the day after the battle, and such things are beyond our power to know," Cronus said, hating the guilt in his friend's eyes.

Raven sat there for a moment, hating the no-win scenarios that cost his friends so much misery. He couldn't help but think of Kato and Ben, and of course, Jennifer.

"Raven, you are my best friend, you and Terin, and all of your crew, including Orlom here." Cronus gave the young gorilla a genuine smile. "I owe you more than a man could repay in a lifetime, and please do not deny it. You came for me when I was in that foul dungeon when no one else could. How you did that impossible thing is beyond my understanding. I will not have you mope around here pained with guilt over something you could not change. As far as my mind is concerned, I just need time. I am not Ben, Raven. My heart still beats for those I love, and you my friend place high among those precious few. You are more than a friend, Raven. You are my brother, and I will always stand beside you."

"Thanks, buddy." Raven leaned over, patting Cronus on the

shoulder, wanting to say more but not wanting to get too emotional. The way things were at this moment, he might even cry, if such a thing was possible, but there was no point in taking that chance.

"So, what now?" Cronus asked.

"Well, since Corell is safe, and Morac is on the run, and with no sign of Ben anywhere, I best head back to Tro. I can't leave the boys alone without me for too long. They might do something stupid, like promote Zem to Captain." Raven chuckled.

"Zem is a general, Boss," Orlom said.

"He's not OUR general." Raven shook his head.

"Perhaps you should apply for admiral." Cronus laughed for the first time since Leanna died.

"I just might," Raven said in all seriousness before standing up, making his way for the door, where Orlom joined him.

"Thanks for checking on me, Rav," Cronus said.

"Always." Raven smiled, before stepping without.

* * *

The early evening found Guilen a guest at the king's table, where sat Chief Minister Monsh, Commander Balka and Princess Corry, along with several soldiers picked out from the garrison to eat dinner with the King and Queen. It was a tradition Lorn intended to begin, asking soldiers of every rank to dine with him, choosing them by random lot from a different unit each night. His father often marched beside his men, learning where they were from and of their worries and dreams. Some were guarded at first, unsure of speaking freely with the king of the realm, but Lorn learned from his father how to set men at ease before digging deeper into their thoughts. And so it was that he called upon two soldiers assigned to the east wall, along with a commander of flax and one of unit. He asked of their home provinces and the skirmishes they had fought during each siege. One soldier was a recent transfer from the garrison of Cropus before the second siege commenced. The second soldier fought in both sieges, bloodying his sword with two dozen gargoyle kills. Both commanders had endured both sieges as well, each gaining promotion for their fell deeds.

Guilen listened to their harrowing tales with newfound respect for what the people of Corell endured. He looked to the side of the chamber where Terin stood guard by the door, his sea blue eyes staring back through the slits in silver helm, like a sentinel cut from stone. He could well imagine the fear he invoked in the gargoyles. He still could not reconcile the man standing before him with the slave boy humbled on his mother's estate. He mentally shook his head, ashamed for his family's actions. And yet, here he sat, honored by the Torry King, surrounded by people that loved Terin dearly. He could not miss the careful glances Corry shared with Terin when they thought no one was looking, but it was a poorly kept secret the love they shared. He thought of his own misfortunes in love, recalling the miserable matches his mother arranged for him. She made certain to find him a wife that he would despise, almost as if to punish him for reminding her of his father, though in truth, he and his father were nothing alike. Thinking of his father caused him to look at Corry, knowing she was the one to kill him. He didn't know how he felt of that. If he was being fair, he couldn't blame her, especially after learning of what they did to Terin after he escaped. His father never hid his disdain for Terin, and if he was the first one Corry came upon after the rescue, he could imagine what she was feeling at that moment. He was not one to judge since he betrayed his family and took up the Torry cause upon his escape. Like it or not, these were his people now. The Sisterhood would never be his home, and he would never miss it. He was free now thanks to Terin and King Lorn.

"You have seen so much of the world in so short a time, Guilen. What think you of our fair castle?" Queen Deliea asked, sitting at the opposite end of the table from her husband, taking a sip from her goblet.

"Of all the grandeur I have seen in my recent and only travels, the White Castle is the most impressive. The citadels of Fleace were majestic and alluring, and Cagan Harbor breathtakingly large, spread across the mouth of the Nila. Central City was equally grand, its fabled walls and ancient palace in its center projected their magnificence for countless leagues as one approached, but the citadels of Corell rising above the open plain have no equal among the sights I have beheld. Only a fortress so grand could resist six legions with a garrison so small." Guilen referred to the first siege, where their ten thousand faced twenty-five times their number.

"Six legions against our garrison AND the *Sword of the Moon*, wielded by the blood of Kal," Corry added, regarding Guilen carefully. She wasn't sure how she felt about him, considering his parentage, weighing that against his actions.

"I stand corrected. With Terin defending your walls, the odds were greatly balanced." Guilen raised his goblet, saluting his friend.

"What say you, Terin? For one who stands guard over us, you are the source of great pride and fondness from everyone sitting here," Queen Deliea asked, her kind words causing him to blush.

"I value your friendship, my queen, but I must temper your adulation, lest pride swell my heart," Terin said, ever mindful of what pride had cost him.

"Yah cannot dwell in a pride-filled heart," Deliea repeated Lorn's saying, a timeless look passing her face.

Guilen felt a pang of guilt, the mention of Yah sparking something within him. Lorn's constant proselytizing was having some effect upon his conscience. Perhaps it was guilt over his indifference to Terin's suffering when they first met or his selfish pursuit of his own happiness, which left him empty. It was only when he joined cause with Lorn outside the walls of Fleace that he felt alive for the first time in his life, as if he was awake after a lifetime of slumber. He wasn't sure if it was this God Lorn spoke of or some internal desire for a greater purpose that ignited this spark within. All he knew was that he felt alive and would never go back to sleep.

He caught Lorn looking at him for a brief moment as if the King was privy to his thoughts. Lorn had an uncanny instinct to know when he should prod and when he should remain quiet, letting a person's thoughts carry them to his desired conclusion. He wasn't sure how he felt of Yah at this point, but there was something to it, he freely admitted.

"I would have you remain for at least another day, cousin, before returning to our dear Dadeus. By then he should have his army prepared to march. I would have him by my side when we go to battle against Morac," Lorn said, taking a sip from his goblet.

"Shall we march with you, Sire? We would be honored to do so," Commander of Unit Facel Julls offered gladly, from his seat beside Guilen.

"I am shamed to deny you, commander, for you have fought bravely for our cause, but your place is here, guarding the walls of Corell," Lorn said as gently as he could, humbled by the bravery of his men.

"As you command, my king," Commander Julls conceded.

"Such is war, Commander. Our armies shift with the flow of battle, while our garrisons guard our most strategic assets, and there is no place as strategic as Corell. Beyond this, I trust my greatest treasure in your capable hands." Lorn regarded Deliea and then Corry, who would remain at the palace when he marched off to war.

Corry thought to refute this, to demand that she would join him in battle, but would speak with him in private. She admitted to many faults, but disagreeing with her king in front of their subjects was not one of them. She regarded Terin briefly, finding no ally in his determined eyes, eyes determined to see her kept safe. They continued to enjoy their meal, sharing their stories and adventures until the night grew late, when Corry was the first to retire, Terin escorting her to her chamber.

* * *

"Nothing to say?" Corry asked as Terin walked quietly beside her. She was glad to have him back, allowing her to have only him guard her instead of the handful needed to replace him. She could barely take a step in his absence without tripping on a guard crowding too close.

"I am pleased to see you well," he said as they walked along the wide lit corridor with torchlight playing off the high stone archways that ran the length of the passageway.

"That is all you have to say?" She gave him a sideways look as they walked, unimpressed with his lack of insight.

"You didn't look happy at the King's table," he observed.

"True. I was very displeased," she said curtly.

Terin didn't answer to that, certain that she would receive his opinion poorly.

"Again, nothing to say?" she challenged.

"The king…" he began, but she was having none of it.

"My brother."

"Your brother simply desires that you remain safe, and I agree."

"Safe? I defended this palace twice against Morac. Where was this concern for my safety then? He now plans to ride off to war at Notsu, while leaving me here. Where is the honor in that? I would have steel in my hand rather than the soft cage he is locking me in!" She nearly spat.

"Corry, he would see you safe. Will you begrudge him for that? Think of the times he spent in Yatin and then Macon, shamed that you were here and in danger while he was occupied elsewhere. You are the only family left to him, and he is pained with guilt for leaving you here to face Morac without him."

"I am not his only kin now. He has a wife and queen. There is no need for me here."

"A queen and wife that knows nothing of Corell or Torry North. She will need your guidance and wisdom in Lorn's absence."

"She has ministers of the realm for that."

"None are as capable as you."

"Do not use flattery to forge my chains." She stopped, turning him to face her.

"And you would forge mine if you go to war with us. Tell me, Corry, how can I think of battling Morac and my grandfather's legions if you are in danger? Am I not hindered enough with my stricken power?" He drew his sword partially from its scabbard, emphasizing its milky dull glow.

"In danger? We have all been in danger since this war began, from Molten Isle to two sieges of this palace."

"I can't… I can't lose you. Not after all we have suffered. Do not make me face that again. I will not lose you like Cronus lost Leanna." He closed his eyes, torn by that memory.

"Leanna died in the birthing bed, not battle. And if you choose to use that tragedy against me, I can return the gesture, as Ilesa lost Kato, and he fell in battle. Do you think I do not see myself in her every time you rush into battle?" she challenged.

"At least he left her a child to remember him by," Terin said, regretting the words as soon as they escaped his lips.

"A child? Leanna did the same for Cronus, and look at him now." She took a step closer to him, her breath heating his face, each staring intently to the other.

"She still lives through Maura, just as Kato lives through their unborn child." He couldn't help stepping further over the abyss. The more he spoke, the less sense he was making.

"I see." She glared so intensely at him he felt she might melt his eyes.

"Eh, Corry, I didn't mean..." He stumbled over his words, but she was having none of it.

"Come!" she ordered, turning around, heading back whence they came.

"Uh, where..." he began to ask, but she was already halfway down the corridor.

* * *

Lorn was taken aback by his sister's sudden return to the dining chamber, the other guests sharing a look as she burst into the room, stopping at his side with Terin lingering at the door.

"Corry?" he asked, raising a skeptical brow.

"I have need of you in the throne room," she said, ignoring the others' curious stares.

"Might I inquire the nature of this need?" he said evenly, hiding his mirth. There was something vexing her, and he could only guess what.

"I shall speak of it on our walk there."

"What of our guests?" He pointed out the commanders and

ministers gathered about, as well as his queen, who sat at the other end of the table, sharing her husband's curiosity.

"Bring them, and summon as many as can fit in the throne room."

"Why do you need so many?"

"Witnesses. I want as many as we can gather."

* * *

The great hall.

Instead of joining King Lorn at his table, Raven and Orlom dragged poor Jentra to the great hall, joining a motley band of apes and soldiers for food and drink, sharing bawdy tales, drinking songs and crass jokes before descending into a drunken revelry. Lorn actually conspired with Raven, suggesting he take Jentra with him, forcing his ever-vigilant guardian to put his mind elsewhere than guarding his king, telling Raven that the Elite Prime had not had a night off duty since before the war. That was all the big Earther needed to drag the ornery solider to the great hall for a night of hard drinking and good times, as Raven would aptly call it, dragging poor Criose and young Dougar along as well.

And there they sat around a long table in the great hall, with servants hurrying platters of food and pitchers of ale to feed their voracious appetites as the apes began with their favorite drinking refrain.

> *In the halls of the apes*
> *Where we raise our tankards high*
> *Cheering our place*
> *Beneath the southern sky…*

Carbanc, son of Hukok, sang the first verse, with the other apes joining in. The Torries gathered around soon picked up the simple tune, joining in along with Raven and Criose, leaving poor Jentra sitting quietly in their midst. A not-so-gentle nudge from Raven forced him to do more than move his lips, while another goblet was pushed into his hand, its frothy foam cresting its lip. Young Dougar was stopped after only two drinks, before given only water, the orphan boy happily partaking in the atmosphere, singing along to the ape tune. This song was followed by a Torry ditty about a drunken ocran belching loud enough to wake a village, causing a raucous laughter from the growing crowd. The kitchen servants were quickly drawn into the revelry, singing their own bawdy songs.

"What of you, Earther? Sing us one of your drinking songs," Criose prodded, causing the others to chorus the request, forcing Raven's hand.

"Alright, if you idiots insist. I'll sing one line, and you repeat it," Raven said, the others happily agreeing as he started with the words to *Show me the way to go home*, the ancient ballad a favorite in the pilots' lounge aboard the *Stalingrad*. The men took a liking to it, with even Jentra joining in by the second verse. They soon asked for another, and Raven followed up with the sea shanty, *Drunken Sailor*.

> *...That's what we do with a drunken sailor*
> *Early in the morning!*

By the final verse, Jentra was singing louder than the rest, losing count of the goblets he downed, his right arm resting around the shoulder of the gorilla Krink of the Manglar tribe, the young ape swaying as badly as him. By this time, Orlom's eyes were bloodshot, looking about to keel over. Three of the Torry soldiers had already succumbed, sleeping where they dropped. Criose, on the other hand, accounted well for himself, retaining his faculties despite being deep in his cups. Satisfied with the success of their drunken stupor, Raven stood up from the bench to give a speech.

"How about a round of cheers for Jentra, Elite Prime and guardian of King Lorn! To him fell the impossible task of keeping Lorn alive from one campaign to the next when his prince, and present king, threw himself at every danger he could find. To Jentra!" Raven raised his tankard into the air, before downing it, the others cheering in kind, at least those still conscious.

"To Jentra!" The men and apes cheered.

"I am going to regret this!" Jentra mumbled to himself, downing another goblet pushed into his hand.

It was at that unfortunate timing that King Lorn entered the hall, ordering the hapless drunks to move to the throne room, with poor Jentra looking on as if in a horrible dream.

"Are we in trouble, Sire?" one soldier asked, his face looking green.

"No, none of you are in trouble. You are required in the throne to bear witness," Lorn said, smiling as his eyes met Jentra's, pleased to see his old friend in his current state.

"Witness to what, Sire?" Criose asked.

"A wedding!" Lorn proclaimed, causing half the drunks to cheer and the other half to blink their eyes in confusion, all except Raven, who drew Lorn aside, with the royal guard looking carefully on. Anyone else acting so familiar with the king would cause concern, but Raven was... well, he was Raven.

"Who's getting married?" Raven asked lowly, though his voice was still loud enough for everyone to overhear, including the drunks.

"You shall see once we reach the throne room. I see you have succeeded in getting my dearest friend drunk. Well done, Raven." Lorn smiled, patting the big Earther on the shoulder while poor Jentra looked on, horrified with his current condition.

* * *

Throne room of Corell.

Word quickly spread through the palace of a great event about to transpire in the throne room with ministers of the realm, courtesans, and soldiers of every sort gathering to bear witness. Jentra sobered enough to be horrified as he was ushered to the dais, standing behind the throne, where he acted as commander of the elite in Torg's absence, as Master Vantel was with the main host of the army, marching east for Notsu along with King Mortus and King El Anthar. The small contingent of apes gathered along the east wall of the chamber, the larger ones holding up their lighter brothers, who stood on drunken legs. Criose found Guilen at the base of the dais before moving off to the side along the west wall, the two friends sharing a brief exchange, pleased to see each other once again.

Raven came to stand beside his ape friends, watching the spectacle about to unfold, wondering who was getting married. Lorn left Dougar with Raven before breaking off from them, taking his own place upon the dais and before his throne, joining Deliea, who stood regally before hers. Cronus found his way to stand beside Raven, having been roused from his bed by Lucas and Ular, leaving Maura in the hands of her wet nurse. Galen joined them soon after, a curious grin painting his face as he looked forward to the spectacle.

Just as the chamber seemed to burst at the seems with its large crowd, Lorn addressed the assembly, a blast of a horn quieting the chamber for him to speak.

"Dearest friends, faithful comrades, brave countrymen, and brothers born of battle, you have been called here to witness the joining of two souls in eternal matrimony. Since the founding of the Middle Kingdom, never has a princess born the weight of regent under such duress as my beloved sister. She has commanded the realm first in place of my father, and then for me. While I fought in Yatin, she led the defense of Corell against unfathomable odds, and prevailed. Her every decision bore enough fruit to allow the garrison to endure until help arrived. Anything less, and Corell would have fallen, on this there is no doubt. I am humbled by her leadership, and shamed that she faced these threats without me. It is custom in the Torry Realms for marriages to be arranged through maternal lines, save for royal nuptials, which are arranged by the crown," Lorn began, looking out across the sea of faces, which stared back, realizing who was to be wed, as he continued.

"I would reward her for her brave deeds and deft management of the realm in my place. I would offer her anything she would ask of me, but she claims only one thing, a very special thing, or more aptly stated, a very *special* person. It is this request I cannot give without agreement of both parties, but I can and do grant my consent, and I do so joyfully. I call forth Princess Corry!" he said, calling her forth.

The crowd watched as she passed through the open doors of the throne room, walking between the assembly toward the dais, staring intently ahead. She looked radiant, wearing a sparkling silver gown with a tight bodice and long billowy sleeves, and flowing skirts that swirled about her ankles. A slender silver tiara was nestled in her golden hair, with torchlight playing off the sapphires and emeralds embedded along its surface. Lorn looked on proudly as she approached, stopping short of the dais, before dipping into a deep curtsy.

"Before you state the name of your intended, do you wish to address the chamber?" Lorn asked of her as she rose from her curtsy.

She regarded him with a polite nod, turning about, her eyes finding Cronus standing beside Raven along the east wall.

"Cronus Kenti, approach the dais!" she called out, summoning him forth.

Cronus looked to Raven, wondering the meaning of this, but the Earther simply shrugged, without a clue to her intention. Cronus strode forth, wearing a simple tan tunic, having just enough time to don his sword belt, with the *Sword of The Stars* upon his left hip and the blade crafted by Torg riding upon his right. He felt naked without his cuirass and armor, unfit for battle, which was his primary duty as a Torry elite. Before he reached the dais, Corry stepped near, preventing him from kneeling, leaning in close to speak quietly into his ear.

"With Torg absent and Jonas missing, Terin has no one to stand as his kin. I can think of no one but you to fill that role. Will you do so?" she asked, touching a hand to his cheek. She could still see the pain of Leanna's loss in his green eyes, haunting him despite the strength he was presenting. It was Leanna's death more than anything else that forced her decision this night, not willing to delay her greatest desire until the war's end, for there was no promise of tomorrow.

Cronus was taken aback by her request, knowing she wanted to share this special moment with him. "Leanna loved you dearly, Princess. It would be my honor to do so."

She smiled at that, taking his hand and giving it a gentle squeeze before drawing him to stand before the dais as Lorn again spoke.

"Those gathered in this storied hall await the name of your intended, my dear sister!" Lorn proclaimed as he looked out upon the assembly, doing a poor job of hiding his mirth. There were few that did not know who she would name.

"Terin Caleph, Champion of the Torry Realm!" Corry said with authority, facing away from the throne, her steely gaze upon the entrance where entered her love.

Terin felt every eye upon him as he strode forth, attired in his silver armored cuirass, greaves, vambraces and helm over his sea blue tunic. He looked beautiful and terrifying in equal measure, like a warrior cut from stone. His outer display hid the fear taking his heart, overcome with emotion for what this moment meant, while feeling the eyes of so many friends and comrades upon him. He focused on the upper dais, fixing his eyes upon the king, for if he looked at Corry he might burst. He could hardly believe this was happening, overtaken by joy and fear. He couldn't help but to lower his gaze to where Corry stood, staring back with incredible intensity, as if seeing into his very soul. His throat felt suddenly dry, his greatest desire unfolding before him, as if he were in a dream.

Lorn nodded with approval as Terin stopped before the dais, taking his place beside Corry, with Cronus standing to his left, giving his young friend an approving look.

"Terin Caleph, you have been summoned before the throne at the request of Princess Corry, who names you her intended. Do you accept her request?" Lorn asked.

"Yes, Sire, with all my heart."

"As King of the Torry Realms I declare the wedded union of Princess Corry and Terin Caleph by royal decree!" Lorn proclaimed. With that, Terin and Corry knelt as Lorn descended the dais, stopping before them and placing Terin's right hand in Corry's left, sealing their matrimony before the eyes of the realm.

"Terin, your bride!" Queen Deliea declared, calling them to their feet.

There, in the throne room of Corell, Terin took Corry for his bride, pressing his lips to hers to the thunderous cheers of the realm.

* * *

She drew him to her bed, firelight from the hearth flickering over their naked flesh. The night breeze swept through the open window of her spacious chamber, swirling across the stone floor and along the wall that circled the room. The chamber was circular, with bright white walls with a series of lanterns hung from its slightly domed ceiling, casting their light along the periphery. The hearth was well lit, flames taking hold along its stacked timber. Vast wardrobes rested to either side of the bed, made of paccel wood, their rich décor the work of a master carpenter.

A sweet fragrance permeated the tranquil air, arousing Terin with its alluring scent as he stared at her beauty. She was breathtaking, her every curve swelling with feminine perfection, from the swell of her breasts to the arch of her back. Her eyes narrowed seductively, appraising him with lustful desire. She took him by the hand, drawing him further to the bed that rested in the chamber's center, dark fur blankets drawn back revealing the rich folds of its crimson calnesian sheets. Terin could take no more, stepping closer, crushing his lips to hers as she went to her back, wrapping her arms around him, devouring him in turn. He lifted her slightly, shifting further onto the bed, keeping his lips to hers throughout, neither relenting, their restrained passion finally bursting free. They had wanted each other for so long, and desired each other for so long, building their tension to this pinnacle moment, before exploding in carnal lust. He briefly withdrew from her lips, before shifting to her neck, kissing her delicate flesh as she arched her back, throwing her head back in erotic bliss. He moved to her breasts, his lips kissing each more gently, slowly building in a loving crescendo.

"Love me," she whispered, lost in his embrace.

"For now and forever," he whispered back, before taking her maidenhood, consummating their union.

Chapter 6

The morning sun broke painfully through the open window, casting its bright rays across the bed, stirring Corry from her contented slumber. She found herself in his embrace, her head resting upon his chest, rising slightly with his every breath. She could hear the beat of his heart, its beautiful sound thudding reassuringly in her ear. A mischievous smile touched her lips as she rose slightly, pulling her hands below her chin, her arms resting on his lower chest, staring at his sleeping face. It was surreal, sharing her bed with the man she loved. How she longed for this since the first day she knew him, dreaming of a time they would be as one. Their wedding night was everything she dreamed it could be, a blush touching her face as she recalled all they shared. She loved feeling him inside her, as if their very essence blended in immortal union. He was impossibly handsome, the most handsome man she had ever known. She could look at him for days and not grow weary. Her smile faltered briefly as he began to smile, and then laugh, before opening a single eye, looking at her bemusedly.

"Terin Caleph, does something amuse you?" she asked, trying to frown and failing miserably.

"Yes, you." He laughed as she playfully swatted him.

"How long have you been awake?"

"A while now. I closed my eyes once you lifted your head."

"Why didn't you wake me?" she asked.

"Because I love the way you rested your head on my chest. I could grow accustomed to being with you like this every night for the rest of our lives."

"You better." She smiled.

"Did you enjoy last night?"

"I did. And you?" she asked.

"Need you ask?"

"You seemed to know what you were doing. Should I be suspicious?" she teased, knowing she was his first, though the way he had handled himself would give anyone doubts.

"I simply did what I dreamed of doing ever since I first saw you. It just felt... natural."

"Then just continue doing what feels natural and I shall not complain."

"As you command, Your Highness." He grinned stupidly, flipping her underneath him, devouring her lips.

Corry swooned, her flesh betraying her to his ministrations, reveling in this glorious sunrise.

* * *

"Go away!" Jentra moaned miserably as Raven approached, finding the Elite Prime staring over the battlements of the inner keep to the west, and away from the rising sun. He spent the better part of the morning wishing he could empty his stomach of the foul poison, but his strong constitution wouldn't allow it. He managed to drag himself to the upper battlements for some fresh air, his bloodshot eyes barely tolerating the open sky.

"Go away? I just came to fetch you for round two." Raven chuckled, slapping him on the back.

"Round two?" Jentra gave him a miserable look, guessing his meaning, but the words were lost to him.

"I'm sure there are a few more casks of ale somewhere in the kitchens."

"You are an evil man, Raven, a foul spirit sent by King Lorn's God to torment me." Jentra shook his head.

"Probably." Raven shrugged, not even denying it.

"You are shameless. How fares our comrades?" Jentra inquired. After Terin and Corry's nuptials, Raven dragged most of the guests back to the great hall for more drunken debauchery, for which Jentra tried to excuse himself, but Lorn was having none of it, asking the men to drag him there to partake. To add to Lorn's treachery, he excused himself from the FUN, retiring to his quarters with his queen.

"Most are still sleeping wherever they dropped. Orlom and Carbanc are snoring loud enough to wake the dead."

"I know, I heard them," Jentra growled, wincing with every word he spoke.

"You're lucky Arg isn't here. He's louder than all of them combined."

"Arg?"

"Argos, Matuzak's champion."

"Aah, I recall hearing of him now," Jentra tried to say lowly, his every utterance causing his head to ache.

"The apes are all friends of mine, but they are loud and gassy." He shrugged.

Jentra just shook his head, never imagining the Torry royal court to be populated with men like Raven and his ape companions. The very notion was absurd, and yet here they were, acting so out of character from everyone else. It wasn't even his alien heritage that set him apart, but the way he spoke, like he hadn't a care in the world. Kato was much the opposite, his language very much similar to their own.

"You are insufferable." Jentra gave him a look.

"Probably. You're a lot politer than Torg. I think he called me an ASS." Raven chuckled.

"And it was an apt description."

"His exact words were A COMPLETE ASS." Raven shrugged.

"Even more apt."

"He called himself one as well, something like *one ass to another*."

"He was just being kind to you." Jentra tried to smile at that, but it hurt too much.

"Probably. Too bad he wasn't here last night. I would love to see him drunk." Raven smiled, imagining Torg drunk off his mind and speaking nonsense.

"I am glad for it. The last thing I need is for my commander to have seen the state I was in. I am still abashed with my condition during the Princess's nuptial." Jentra cringed thinking of his sorry state when they dragged him to the dais, placing him behind the throne in his inebriated condition.

"Don't worry about it. No one noticed, believe me. Most were too far gone at that point or looking at the happy newlyweds."

"Newlyweds?"

"Just a term from my world. It means those that just wed."

"I see. I was warned that you use many phrases that only you understand."

"You'll get used to it. Then again, maybe you won't since I'll be leaving soon," Raven corrected himself.

"Back to your ship, I surmise."

"Yep. Maybe when this war is over you can join us for a time. Might do you some good to take a vacation and see the world."

"Vacation?"

"It's like a holiday where you travel someplace to rest."

"Traveling and resting are two different things. If I wanted to rest, I would find someplace quiet and rest." Jentra couldn't make sense of this *Vacation* Raven was speaking of.

"Come now, Jentra, imagine you and Torg sailing the ocean aboard the *Stenox*, stopping at tropical ports and seeing the beautiful women of Tro, Milito, and Port West. Maybe you can spend time at the beach and get some sun or go fishing off the back of the ship."

"Getting sun on a beach? Did you hit your head on something?"

"Probably." He laughed, slapping Jentra on the back.

HARROOM!

Horns sounded across the roof of the palace, with lookouts atop the Tower of Celenia pointing toward the southwest. Raven and Jentra looked to their left, making out large winged forms in the distance, passing over the edge of the Zaronan Forest. The sight of magantors was hardly a cause for the alarm to sound, but they understood why once the formation took shape. Jentra lost count at thirty warbirds, and with most of General Valen's magantors already at the palace or deployed to the Notsu campaign, they wondered who this large force belonged. When the force grew to over forty warbirds, they knew the cause for alarm, until a flock of five magantors drew forward of the others, bearing Torry riders. They were obviously escorting the new arrivals, indicating their peaceful intent.

Raven drew his pistol, raising its scope from its internal workings, scanning afield before zooming in on the greater host trailing the Torry escort, bringing the riders into focus.

"What the hell is she doing here?" He made a face.

"Who are you referring?" Jentra asked impatiently.

"My wife."

* * *

The magantors set down in good order upon their designated platforms, following the lead of their escort. There were thirty-two warbirds from the Sisterhood, and another six from Yatin, each bearing two riders. They were met by soldiers of the garrison upon landing, and escorted to the roof of the inner keep, where stood Commander Balka to formally receive them, standing at the head of a unit of palace guards in ordered ranks, with their distinct silver armor and winged helms over white tunics. The new arrivals formed up in two groups, one Sisterhood, and the other of Yatin. Stepping forward to treat with Cors Balka were three women of the Federation and a lone male from Yatin.

"Welcome to Corell. I am Cors Balka, Commander of garrison." Cors greeted them evenly, studying the emissaries' demeanor and appearance. The women were clad in matching black tunics and golden armor, with their helms tucked in their left hands. Each wore a blood red cape, with swords sheathed upon their left hip. The man was dressed in purple robes, designating him a minister of state, though Cors thought he looked familiar.

"We are welcomed, Commander Balka. I am Lucella Sarelis, Captain of Queen Letha's royal guard. I present to you Minister Yotora of the new Yatin Alliance," Captain Sarelis began, indicating the man standing off her left.

"Commander," Minister Yotora greeted formally. Cors recognized him now, knowing him as the Yatin representee at the Council of Corell so long ago.

"I present the Second Guardian of the Federation of the Sisterhood, Princess Tosha, and her cousin, Deva Estaran," Lucella introduced her companions.

"Your Highness." Cors bowed deeply, formally greeting Tosha.

"Commander," Tosha said, trying not to stare at Raven, who stood off to the side of the battlements, watching the whole affair while leaning casually against a rampart like he hadn't a care in the world.

"I shall escort you to the throne room where King Lorn shall receive you. Might we see to accommodating your entourage?" Cors offered, looking past her shoulder, where stood some sixty-one of her companions.

Tosha nodded in agreement as Cors sent his aids to attend to them. She, Lucella, and Deva joined Minister Yotora in following Commander Balka toward the stairwell while the others were led in the opposite direction. Tosha paused as Raven intercepted them at the opening of the stairwell, causing the escorting palace guards to halt, uncertain of his intention.

"Keep your steel sheathed, fellas, while I have a word with my wife," Raven said, for which she didn't move. She simply stood there, appraising him with her golden eyes, her face an unreadable mask.

"We shall speak AFTER I treat with King Lorn," she said, ordering Commander Balka to proceed, as Raven looked on, watching her disappear through the archway.

"You can come out now, they're gone," Raven called out to Jentra, who lingered further back.

"I wasn't hiding," Jentra growled before marching off to the north stairwell.

"Where you going?" Raven called after him.

"Beating them to the throne room. Thanks to you I look an awful mess," Jentra growled.

BENJAMIN SANFORD

* * *

Lorn was quite surprised to learn of the new arrivals, awaiting them in the throne room, with his queen sitting beside him. Jentra managed to appear before Commander Balka escorted them to his presence, his old friend managing to don his armor and helm, impressively concealing his disheveled appearance, taking his place behind the throne, cursing Raven under his breath. Nearly two flax of royal elite stood along the dais, along with Ministers Monsh and Thunn.

"Princess Tosha, Second Guardian of the Sisterhood!" The court herald announced her entrance, followed by the others. At the mention of Deva, Lorn shared a look with his queen, wondering her purpose for being here, thankful his sister and Terin had not yet emerged from their bedchamber.

Tosha strode forth across the mirrored stone floor, internally taken aback by Corell's majestic beauty and size. She never thought to pass through the ancient corridors of this storied fortress, reminding herself that her grandfather, Lorm the 3rd, once sat this throne. Had her mother been born a boy and Lore born female, she might have inherited this realm instead of the Sisterhood. She caught sight of the statues lining the walls of the chamber, all kings of old, cast in impressive detail, with the azure walls behind them giving them a background akin to a midday sky. Their craftmanship rivaled her father's sculptures, each the lifetime work of a skilled artist. Each was her ancient kin, all kings of the old Middle Kingdom, and the Torry Realm that followed.

The grandeur of the throne room was a welcome respite from what truly plagued Tosha's thoughts. No matter what occupied her mind, thoughts of Raven arose time and again, casting aside her efforts to suppress them. Every time she gained a respite from thinking of him, something arose to bring him back to the forefront, collapsing all other thoughts into a meaningless heap. As much as she wished to run to his arms and forget the world, she was reminded of her children, her sons in particularly, and where they were. That would be the first she spoke with him about, and may Yah grant him mercy if he couldn't answer.

"Welcome to Corell, cousin," Lorn greeted her, drawing her from her musings as she reached the base of the dais, before taking a knee, the others following in kind.

"Rise, all of you," Lorn ordered.

Tosha gained her feet, regarding Lorn's imposing form sitting the throne above. He stared back with steel blue eyes and a black mane framing his handsome face. His blue, knee-length tunic failed to conceal the masculine form he so easily wore. She was surprised with his transformation. When last she saw him, several years before, he was a youthful princeling. Now he bore the mantel of King. His bearing, stare and countenance clearly reflected this kingly transformation.

"Princess Tosha, you know my queen," Lorn said, indicating the throne to his right.

"Queen Deliea." Tosha regarded her with a knowing smile.

"Welcome to your ancestral home, Tosha," Deliea greeted her warmly, addressing her familiarly.

"You are most gracious, Deliea. I see my cousin has chosen his bride wisely." Tosha gave Lorn a mischievous look.

"I believe I have." Lorn smiled at that before asking the question hanging so obviously in the air. "We are pleased to receive you, Tosha, but must ask the urgency of your quest?"

"I have come at the behest of my mother, Queen Letha, First Guardian of the Sisterhood, to offer our assistance to the defense of Corell. It seems we have arrived too late, but we offer our swords to the battles ahead. She also sends her regards to her nephew on his ascension to the Torry Throne. King Lore has a worthy heir, and Corell a great king." With that, Tosha carefully drew her sword, its bronze-hued blade igniting in a golden light, drawing a chorus of gasps from the assemblage. She knelt again, placing the *Sword of Light* upon the floor before her, bowing her head in deep reverence.

"My thanks, cousin. Your swords are most welcome. Please rise and sheath your wondrous blade," Lorn said, touched by her gesture. This generous offering brokered many questions, questions best asked in private rather than in full view of the court. He knew the Sisterhood held two such Swords of Light, and to offer one to the

Torry cause was no small measure, and to offer the sword arm of Tosha herself was an even greater commitment to their cause. He regarded her for a moment, taking her measure, her braided black hair bound tightly behind her, giving her an ordered look considering the helm she wore throughout her journey. Her golden eyes withdrew behind her narrowed stare and thick lashes. The savage fierceness he saw in her countenance permeated her entire bearing. It was not the haughtiness of a conceited princess anymore, but the assured confidence of a warrior aware of the power she wielded. One had to look past the trappings of power that surrounded her to notice her astounding beauty. It was a dangerous beauty though. Her eyes were like jeweled daggers. The caress of her lips was akin to kissing lightning. Any man approaching her unbidden would surely be burnt to ash. He marveled that she and Raven were wed. He could not think of two people more different. He could not imagine them sharing the same plane of existence, let alone the same room. But married? To each other? It was absurd. He could not imagine either of them suffering the other. A smile touched his lips thinking of it. He couldn't wait to see them together. May Yah forgive him, but it would be grand fun, and a worthy entertainment after so much war. Despite not pushing further her true purpose for being here, his Queen thought otherwise.

"What brings you to our cause, Tosha? Your home isle is so far away, and yet you pledge to us your sword against your father?" Deliea asked.

"The Sisterhood has pledged to your cause. We are now at war. Queen Letha sent us to join your campaign, and we apologize for not arriving in time to aid in lifting the siege. We have followed you from Faust to Mosar, Cagan to Fleace and Central City before finding you here. Your army moves swiftly, King Lorn," Tosha acknowledged him proudly.

"Need drove us. I look forward to hearing the details of your Queen's alliance. For now, cousin, I would hear from Guardian Deva, finding her presence most curious considering her previous actions," Lorn said, his gaze finding Deva standing impassively behind her, her inner turmoil threatening to break her trained facade.

To this, Deva stepped nigh, dropping to her knees, her humble act out of character from her reputation.

"I have come to pledge my sword to your service, King Lorn, until death takes me, or you proclaim my debt fulfilled!" Deva said, taking Lorn aback by her offer.

"We always have need for able swords, Deva of House Estaran, but I again ask why you feel so moved to do so?" Lorn pushed.

"I owe a debt to your realm, your Champion, and to your house, King Lorn. I was privy to Terin's identity and agreed to his ill treatment at my mother's hand. I conspired in his enslavement and if successful, would have seen Morac reign unchallenged in your war. I stand guilty of these crimes, and though pardoned by my queen, I must make amends."

"Rise, cousin." Lorn lifted his hand, motioning her to her feet, his acknowledging their kinship a reminder that he would not stand in judgement of her. She had been judged by her queen and then Terin, the mercy granted by his hand absolving her in Lorn's eyes.

"You were forgiven by Terin, as we were told. Why must you make further amends?" Deliea asked.

Deva swallowed nervously, steeling her nerve, as she felt every eye in the chamber upon her, passing judgement for her crimes.

"Terin granted mercy because of his God, the very god I am now bound to, now and forever. Every member in attendance at Queen Letha's court that night, when Terin was brought before the throne to act as my judge, saw Yah's intervention in the power invoked through the sword Princess Tosha now wields. His will for our Federation is clear, just as the mercy he commanded of Terin on my behalf," Deva declared, lifting her chin as if prepared for the expected onslaught of doubt and derision, but none followed, only silence.

Lorn regarded her for the longest time, as if searching her countenance for a greater truth. This was not the same woman who had held Terin captive. This person was different. He had seen this before, many times before, fondly recalling so many that were transformed by Yah's mercy, none more so than he. To test this truth, he probed further.

"You claim you are bound by Yah. What followed that event to convince you?"

Deva didn't know if she could answer without scorn and mockery, her pregnant pause causing her to lower her gaze.

"Speak freely, Deva," Lorn gently commanded.

"Yah speaks to me now. No, that is not true. He has always spoken to me, only now do I listen," she confessed, returning her gaze to him, feeling a connection to the Torry King in this.

"And what does he say?" Lorn asked.

"He sent me here to serve your cause, oh mighty king. I must join you until war's end before returning to my home, should you then deem my debt fulfilled. This is the penance I must serve to absolve my debt."

Lorn could see the truth of her words in her eyes, sensing Yah's presence in her entire being. There was magic at work here, ancient magic not seen since the age of King Kal. It was the magic of redemption and purpose, unifying to bring about a great transformation of the world. The magic failed then because the hearts of men proved unfaithful. They now had a second chance if their own hearts could forgive those who were repentant.

"I accept your oath and service, cousin. You shall fight by our side until war's end, and return to your isle in honor, and restore House Estaran to its glory."

"My gratitude, King Lorn." Deva bowed, backing a step as Lorn called upon Minister Yotora, the Yatin representative, to speak.

"I have come at the behest of Generals Yitia and Yoria. Emperor Yangu has been deposed, and a new king is yet to be named," the Yatin minister stated, causing hushed whispers to echo through the chamber.

The fact Yangu was overthrown was unexpected but not unsurprising, considering his addled mind. Jentra snorted his approval at this revelation, despising the twisted-minded monarch for his ingratitude toward Lorn.

"I assume Generals Yitia and Yoria wish to convey their feelings upon the conduct of the war?" Lorn asked.

"They sent me to assure Your Majesty of the Yatin commitment to the war and to convey their congratulations for your ascension to the Torry Throne. They wish to further convey the nature of their cooperation in a less public forum," Yotora affirmed.

"Of course. We shall retire to my council chambers to continue this discussion. Might I inquire the fate of your emperor in this open court?" Lorn asked.

"He was tried by the current tribunal authority ruling the empire and burned at the stake in view of the people of Mosar upon the palace grounds." The assemblage gasped at the minister's revelation. Most were ignorant of Yangu's crimes and depravity, such things overlooked during war when committed by one's ally.

With that, Lorn excused his visitors, calling them to private council along with his commanders of rank, what few remained at Corell.

* * *

Tosha wanted nothing more than to seek out her insufferable husband after treating with King Lorn in the throne room but was drawn into a council of war with Captain Sarelis, joining Minister Yotora, General Valen, the Torry garrison commander Cors Balka, along with Chief Minister Monsh and Queen Deliea. Her sister warriors were escorted to their assigned quarters, leaving her with only Lucella to suffer this war council. She was conflicted, knowing these plans were to oppose her father, but as Second Guardian of the Sisterhood she had no choice but to choose sides. She found it ironic that her brother was equally conflicted, taking up his sword against their father as well. Jonas' dedication to the Torry cause extended to his son and her nephew. She had expected to see them upon arriving but guessed they were fighting elsewhere, and she would inquire of their whereabouts at the conclusion of this meeting. She could only imagine the sense of betrayal her father must feel with all his children aligned against him. Why couldn't he sue for peace and end this madness? After the events in Bansoch, she had no choice but follow her mother's direction, leading their armies against her father. She also wondered Corry's whereabouts, not looking forward to her reaction to Deva's presence. Even she was loathe to accept Deva's turnabout, but she was there in her mother's throne room when Terin ignited the sword's power, revealing Yah's glory to everyone present. Yah demonstrated his power, revealing himself in that way, calling for mercy for Deva. If that was Yah's desire, then who was she to oppose it? She just hoped Corry would agree, wherever she was.

"Shall we commence?" Lorn asked, gathering them about the map table with all the kingdoms of Arax depicted in fine detail.

"King Lorn, General Yitia seeks your counsel on how he might proceed. As we can see, our armies are concentrated at Mosar, with many of our soldiers answering the musters that were missed at the war's outset. These numbers have swelled the ranks of our 1st and 2nd Armies, affording us the strength to take the fight to our enemy. Yet, we are limited by geography. As you can see, our armies are here, at Mosar," Minister Yotora explained, pointing out the Yatin capital resting prominently along the Muva. With the Cress Mountains blocking them to their east, and the sea to their west, the only path open to attack Tyro was north. Most of the lands of central Yatin were devasted the previous year by Yonig's invasion and could not support an army passing through its center, where foraging was unavailable.

"The only line of advance is along the coast," Lorn pointed out, running his finger along the map, stopping at Maeii, marking the furthest point they advanced during their counter offensive, which they were forced to abandon.

"That is his thinking as well, Your Majesty. It would serve as a suitable staging point for retaking Tenin Harbor," Yotora said.

"Any advance upon Tenin would expose you to a gargoyle counterattack, and this time the lines of supply would be your enemy, and Tyro's ally," General Valen pointed out.

To that, Minister Yotora looked to Tosha, indicating they had an answer to this.

"Queen Letha intends to disembark a considerable force north of the Yatin-Benotrist border, from which we shall move south, seizing the abandoned Yatin fortress Yonig seized at the outset of his campaign," Tosha began, referring to the small border post straddling the narrow gap separating the foothills of the Cress Mountains and the coast.

"And thus trapping all of Tyro's forces south of that line from home, while cutting their supply routes," Commander Balka deduced by examining the disposition of forces on the map.

"Most of Tyro's forces in Yatin are gargoyles, who can fly over the Cress foothills. As for disembarking at that position, your army must contend with Tyro's sizable garrisons at both Tinsay and Laycrom, each numbering more than twenty telnics, as well as the 13th Legion at Laycrom, if our last reports of its position are accurate," General Valen stated.

"Those forces are far afield and would not reach the border before the Yatin armies seized Tenin and joined with us," Lucella said.

"And if they strip the garrisons of Tinsay or Laycrom of their telnics, they would be exposed to revolt or another landing by our forces farther north," Tosha said, torn between her mother and father, but such was war.

"Much of your planning depends on the Yatin armies advancing along the coast, which requires a far larger navy to support and resupply them throughout as well as envelop Tenin, a navy Yatin does not have," Commander Balka pointed out.

"They may not have enough ships, but we do," Lorn said, looking to Deliea, who nodded in agreement.

"Sire, our fleets are still far to the south, and…" Dar Valen began to say, but Deliea interceded, beginning to move the markers for the Torry 1st, 2nd, 3rd, and 4th Fleets and the Macon 1st and 2nd Fleets to Tenin, joining their strength to the Yatin 3rd Fleet.

"My Queen, that is nearly all our combined naval strength," Commander Balka said.

"Most, but not all," she said evenly, leaving the Macon 3rd Fleet guarding the eastern approaches of her father's realm and the Torry 5th Fleet guarding Cagan. "If we are to win this war, Tyro must be pressed on all fronts. If the Sisterhood is willing to stir from their isle, we must support them. Our fleets are currently unable to affect the war as it now shifts northward. Only in this can they make a difference."

Lorn smiled at that, proud of his queen's astute thinking.

"I see the wisdom in your reasoning, my queen, but our fleets are still far afield. It will take time to bring them to bear and to coordinate with Queen Letha and our Yatin allies," General Valen reasoned.

"Time and distance are the bane of all military planning, but Queen Deliea is correct in her boldness, a boldness I am willing to enhance," Lorn said, moving the marker representing the Torry 4th Army to Tenin.

"Sire, that would leave Torry South unguarded. Our garrison is much reduced, and the 1st Army is marching toward Notsu," Dar pointed out.

"We can conscript able-bodied men from Cagan to fill our ranks until the war is ended. We must bring all our strength to bear if we are to prevail. I want your riders sent out come morning to all the fleets the queen has named, as well as General Farro at Cagan. They must move with all haste to Faust, join the Yatin armies and fleet, and move on Maeii and then Tenin. Meanwhile, Queen Letha can plan her invasion." Lorn looked to Tosha, who nodded in agreement along with Minister Yotora. With that the meeting ended, with everyone filing out before Lorn called out to Tosha.

"Tosha, if you would remain, I would like to speak with you," he said.

Tosha waved Lucella to check on the others while she remained. Deliea held Lorn's hand briefly, squeezing it tenderly, her show of affection a subtle reminder of their growing bond, before stepping without, leaving Lorn to speak in private with his cousin.

*　*　*

"Welcome, cousin," Lorn again greeted, kissing the back of her hand after drawing it to his lips.

Tosha regarded him evenly, not accustomed to such gentle treatment. Rulers of the Sisterhood were treated as monarchs, with the deference their position required. It was respectful, yet stern, not with the fragility women of the mainland were treated. It felt strange to be treated as a lady and not a warrior. She reminded herself that her stay at Corell was as a guest of the Torry King and would require her to don the raiment of a high lady of the realm when she dined at the King's table this night.

"You are quite lovely, Tosha, though guardedly so. I see why Raven is so taken with you." He smiled gently. He noticed her rigid bearing, hoping his kind words set her at ease.

"Did he speak with you about me?" she asked evenly, secretly hoping that he did so, but not giving herself away.

"He has, though even if he hadn't, one could easily guess by his demeanor."

"His demeanor?"

"Come now, cousin, you are fooling no one with feigned naivety. He is a lovesick fool when anyone mentions you. Certainly, you know this."

"A fool, yes. A lovesick fool? Perhaps," she said, trying desperately not to sound pleased with Lorn's revelation.

"As you wish." Lorn shook his head, knowing that was as much as a smile he would extract from her when speaking of Raven. "He is a good man, that husband of yours. I am proud to call him friend."

"He is prone to win over my relations, all except my father, of course. Even my mother speaks fondly of him." She sighed, wondering how the big oaf managed it.

"And you are as lovesick as he is. That I can see in those fiery golden eyes of yours." He smiled.

"I chose Raven because he seemed a logical choice at that time," she explained, trying to use reason to justify her impulsiveness and failing miserably.

"You chased the poor man across the breadth of your father's realm, if what I have heard is true. Only a lovesick fool would do that."

Tosha shook her head, knowing she had no answer for his claim.

"Then I stand guilty." She threw up her arms, wishing to end this charade.

"Now that we have established that, welcome to your ancestral home, cousin." He smiled again before stepping toward a side table where sat a pitcher of wine. He filled two goblets, offering one to her.

"I can honestly admit that I did not expect this." She sighed, taking a sip.

"Expect what?"

"Your kind reception and your boyish teasing concerning my husband," she added in good humor.

"We are kin, Tosha, which only makes the path before you difficult, concerning who it is we must fight."

"The world sees my father as a brutish tyrant, and he gives them little reason not to, considering what he and his armies have done. I am conflicted, for I have seen him differently. He was a doting father and taught me the sword and warfare, I learning much at his hand. I love him, Lorn, though I know you hate him for what he has done to your people and your father." She sighed.

"I do not hate him, Tosha. I actually pity him, if you must know," he said, pacing to the other side of the chamber and back as if lost in a memory.

"Pity?"

"Yes, pity. I know the choices that drove him to becoming the man he is. Tormented by Menotrist cruelty, he turned to their mortal enemies to exact vengeance and in doing so lost the woman he loved, and their son with her. Such a tragedy, such a pity."

"Did Terin tell you this?"

"No. A far stronger force bore witness to this claim, a force you are now familiar with."

"Yah," she correctly guessed, partaking another sip.

"Yes, Yah. Has he granted you visions?"

"No. He seems particular in those he gifts them to, such as you, Terin and now Deva. Meanwhile, we lesser beings must use blind faith and his occasional appearance to heed his will." She shrugged.

"Such as your mother's throne room." He recalled the events they spoke of at Bansoch.

"Yes. That was more Terin's vision, which we were all privileged to see."

"Perhaps, but you did see, and that is all the proof you require. And if Deva receives visions and you do not, it does not place her above you in Yah's service. It is merely a role to play, and her role is different from yours."

"My role? I wish I knew what that truly was." She felt lost with her commission, conflicted between her loyalties to her mother and father.

"Is it not clear? You are a warrior, charged with leading the daughters of Tarelia to war against our ancient foe. You also wield a *Sword of Light*, anointing you with great power."

"A sword intended for the blood of Kal, not I," she pointed out.

"There are only two people alive who have the blood of Kal, and both are your kin, and close kin at that. There are more swords of light than there are sons of Kal, so who better to wield them than the blood of Tarelia, descendants of those loyal to Kal himself?"

"A daughter of Tarelia." She sighed wistfully.

"And a granddaughter of King Lorm, King of Torry North, the last Tarelian Kingdom on the mainland. You are a child to both the Sisterhood and the old Middle Kingdom. Who better to wield such a sword than you?"

Tosha regarded him for a time, stirred by his encouragement and acceptance but torn by her divided loyalties, and the judgement her Torry forebears would hold her to account for her paternal lineage. She noticed a familiar image in the face of a statue resting behind Lorn, one of many that circled the chamber, all kings of old, no doubt. Lorn followed her gaze, turning to examine the work in question, the visage of their grandfather King Lorm III, the stone eyes of his likeness staring blindly across the chamber.

"Our grandfather Lorm," Lorn confirmed.

"I wonder how he would receive me if he still lived, considering who my father is?"

"He would not have treated you kindly for who your father was, but he would have loved you for who your mother is." Lorn touched a hand to her shoulder, affirming this truth. He often wondered what hardship their grandparents had suffered, each wed to a monarch so far away, Lorm separated not only from his wife but his daughter Letha, seeing her only on occasion. Their grandmother Theresa was equally tormented, separated for great lengths from both her husband and their son Lore.

"You are kind to believe so, but I wonder." She stepped toward the statue, running her fingers over the contours of his face. She recalled seeing his very likeness in her mother's chamber, asking her who he was, which she revealed, referring to him only as her grandfather, omitting his full name and regal position. All those years she never knew the simple statue of her grandfather was also the statue of the Torry King.

"Something troubles you," he keenly observed, sensing her morose spirit.

She turned to regard him, studying his face. "Lorn, I have followed my father's will since childhood. Blinded by a daughter's love for her father, I could not see what his alliance with the gargoyles entailed. You cannot serve two realms. As a daughter of the Sisterhood, I am bound to its interests, but I will not deny my love for him. I have borne him his heir as I promised, thus fulfilling my oath to him, though he will not have that heir. My mother and husband have seen to that. But if candor is my guide, I would not give him my son even if I was able, not after what transpired in my mother's throne room that fateful night. When Terin invoked the power of Yah through this sword, my mother's entire court bore witness to his glory and his truth. There is no going back now. We have all sworn ourselves to Yah, every member of my mother's court who bore witness that night. I can only hope my father sees reason and makes peace, joining with us to destroy the gargoyles. If not, then he is truly lost to me." She sighed.

"It is not in our hands, Tosha. Trust Yah to give him wisdom in this," he said, taking her in his arms, hugging her fiercely, which she returned with equal measure.

After a long embrace they parted, holding briefly to each other's hands.

"The Torry People have a good king, a very good king." She smiled.

"And the Sisterhood will have a great queen." He kissed her forehead. "Come, you have a certain Earther who wishes to see you."

"Yes, and I have questions for the idiot," she growled, using the derogatory term Raven loved to use.

* * *

She found Raven in her chamber, his hand resting above her window, staring into the distance, the chamber offering a generous view to the northwest, where the Zaronan Forest bled into the horizon. She paused at the doorway, taking a breath, steeling her composure before advancing. He turned before she took a step, his dark gaze meeting her golden eyes. She thought she was prepared to meet him, with so much she wanted to say, so many questions she needed answered, but was frozen in place. He tormented her dreams, torturing her with his absence and with his presence, each confounding her to no end. She composed herself, managing to open her mouth for her first question when he moved suddenly upon her, sweeping her into his arms, crushing her lips to his. She wanted to push back, to demand he answer her, but her body betrayed her, returning his passion, wrapping her arms around his thick shoulders.

Any other man would say *I missed you*; *I love you* and swear his eternal love to his woman, but Raven didn't say a word, his actions speaking all these things and more. He kissed her fiercely for the longest time before moving to her neck, his warm breath sounding in her ear. She arched her head, savoring his ministrations. He kissed her ear, his breath echoing stronger as he moved closer, before she laughed, causing him to stop.

"Stop, that tickles." She laughed, hating how stupid she sounded.

"Tickles, huh?" He smiled evilly, repeating the gesture before she pushed him away, catching her breath.

"You are…" she began to say.

"Impossibly handsome?" He smiled.

"Just impossible."

"Guilty," he said, moving in for another round when she halted his advance with her hand on his chest.

"I have questions first, you idiot!" she said as sternly as she could manage.

"Fire away, I'm all ears."

"I won't even ask what that means, but I can guess the meaning," she said before grabbing hold of his face, squeezing his cheeks together, giving him her most fearsome look.

"Where are my sons?" she growled.

"You mean OUR sons," he reminded her, pushing her fingers off his checks.

"My sons, our sons, your sons, whichever you prefer, where are they?"

"They're safe, if that's what you're worried about."

"Safe where?"

"Torn Harbor, with President Matuzak."

"Torn Harbor? With the apes?" she growled, stepping close to him, her nose pressed dangerously to his.

"Yes. Where else is safer than there?" he growled back, staring down into her stormy eyes.

"I entrust you with my babies, and you leave them with your friends. You insisted on taking them, somehow getting my mother to agree, and you do this? If you weren't my husband I would…"

"Beat me up?" He smiled, infuriating her further.

"I'd do more than beat you up, you insufferable oaf!" Oh, how he made her angry.

"Good luck with that." He shrugged dismissively.

"I'm not afraid of you, Raven. Don't ever forget that."

"No foolin'. I guessed that by how many times you bit me."

"And you deserved every one of them."

"And you deserved every spanking I gave you."

She had no polite answer for that and just glared at him, trying to melt him with her heated gaze.

"Don't go blaming me for leaving the boys with Matuzak. If you want anyone to blame, look to dear old Dad. If he hadn't attacked us at Tro, I'd be with the boys now. You should be thankful I left them before sailing for Tro, or they might've died in the attack."

"Keeping them from a potential warzone is the minimum I expect from their father. It doesn't absolve you of guilt for leaving them in a safe haven while you venture into danger. You took them with you and were expected to STAY with them!" she growled.

"Don't give me that. You're not going to talk away your father's guilt in all this. And why are you here anyway? Aren't you supposed to be on your isle watching over our daughter?"

"Things have changed since last we met."

"Changed how?"

"War. After you departed, my mother began preparing our federation for war with my father. We were sent to aid in the defense of Corell, but the battle seems to have already been won." She sighed.

"Yeah, you're a day late and a dollar short. But don't worry about it, your husband was here to lend a hand," he said in good humor, which failed to amuse her.

She understood what he meant despite his strange phrases, which only he found amusing. She was convinced he really was an idiot, despite how clever he was.

"I know that look, Tosha, and before you get all mad and hit or bite me or something worse, let's just enjoy our time together before I have to leave."

"Leave? Where are you going?" she asked, louder than she intended.

"Back to my ship. I just hope the boys have finished restoring it to full power. Your father's attack almost sunk it, and me with it."

"Sunk? How was he able to accomplish that?" she asked, never believing such a thing possible. Raven and his crew always seemed invincible. The fact her father was able to almost kill them gave her pause.

"Actually, Ben did it. He overcharged one of his weapons and had a magantor drop it on us during the battle. The blast lifted the whole ship out of the water and knocked out all power. Grigg died on impact, and the rest of us took a beating. Luckily, we managed to restore enough power to fend off the attackers, which swarmed all over the ship, with a little help from our friends. After the battle I left them there to fix the ship while I journeyed here, figuring this was where Ben was heading, but I haven't seen any sign of him. Wherever he is, it's not here. So it's time for me to go back."

Tosha hated this. The last person she expected to see at Corell was Raven, but now that he was here, she didn't want to see him leave. The Fates always conspired against them, keeping them apart. These brief encounters only reminded her of what she wanted and couldn't have... them together.

She was drawn from her musing when Lucella Sarelis announced her presence, asking permission to enter. Tosha ordered her hither, drawing away from Raven, her gaze fixed to the doorway where Lucella entered.

"My apologies, Guardian Tosha, but you have visitors." Lucella saluted with a fist to her breast.

"Visitors?"

"Yes, Your Highness, the Torry Princess awaits you in the outer corridor, along with her husband, the Torry Champion."

"Corry and Terin?" Tosha looked to Lucella, and then Raven.

"They are married now," Raven said.

"Married when?"

"Last night. If you had arrived yesterday, you could have witnessed it. It's too bad, too, because you're the only blood relative he has here, though I am his uncle by marriage. Which reminds me, I am Corry's uncle now too." He smirked, causing Tosha to shake her head.

"I see you haven't lost your charm, Captain Raven." Lucella shook her head also, trying to hide her smile.

"I do my best, Lucella. How have you ladies gotten along since I last saw you?" he asked.

"Very well. And I again thank you for your aid in quelling Darna's treason," Lucella said gratefully as Tosha stepped passed her, exiting to the outer corridor to see her cousin, Raven and Lucella following.

Corry and Terin waited amidst a mixed grouping of Federation and Torry guards posted outside Tosha's chamber. The Sisterhood warriors stood in stark contrast to their Torry brothers, with golden mail over black tunics to the Torries' silver mail over white tunics, and their distinct silver wings spreading out from the sides of their helms. Corry's face brightened upon seeing Tosha, the two closing for an embrace.

"How fares your journey?" Corry asked as they parted, her hands lingering upon Tosha's shoulders.

"Long, but uneventful. Crossing the sea is always the most difficult leg of the journey. I see you have found a husband," Tosha said, looking past her shoulder to where stood Terin, blushing under her flirtatious gaze.

"I have. I finally trapped him within my lair," Corry teased, pulling briefly to the side, allowing Tosha to embrace Terin.

"You have chosen wisely, nephew," Tosha whispered in his ear as she drew him close.

"More fortunate than wise, but I accept my fate most gladly," he said, with Raven and Lucella looking on.

"You know what this means now, Corry?" Raven asked with an infuriating grin plastered on his face.

"I am not addressing you as Uncle Raven, you dolt." She crossed her arms, giving him a look.

"Certainly, he jests?" Tosha looked first to Corry and then to Raven.

"You're the ones always yelling at me to use proper titles, and now when I bring one up, you refuse. Such disrespect," Raven couldn't help to say.

"Never mind him. Tell me, Corry, how fared your wedding?" Tosha smiled.

"Joyous. We are now related twice over," Corry said.

"Indeed."

"But I ask, what brings you to Corell?" Corry asked, having come to her upon learning of her arrival, oblivious to everything spoken of in the throne room.

"We have sworn to your cause. My mother sent a group of us to aid in the defense of Corell while she prepares for war in the west," Tosha explained.

"War? Truly?" Corry's heart sang with that revelation.

"Truly, and it is all because of Terin," Tosha said, looking to her nephew.

"Me?" he wondered.

"Yes, you. The power you invoked in my mother's throne room that night brought about many changes. IF not for you, or more specifically, Yah, the Sisterhood would have remained neutral."

Terin stood there dumbstruck. He recalled all the trials he had endured, the days of endless toil and torment, thinking it all for naught. But it wasn't for naught. Yah had a purpose for all he forced him to endure, and he refused to listen. And when he outright refused the path Yah asked of him, the divinity prepared an even harder road, but one with greater blessing for their cause. It seemed with every passing day, another realm joined in their fight against Tyro, even his own daughter now raising her sword against him.

"Can you truly fight your father, Tosha?" he wondered.

"It is my duty, and to rule the Sisterhood one day, I must place my duty above my desires," Tosha said, regarding Terin and then Raven, leaving so much unspoken between them.

"Forswearing your desires is easily spoken of but harder done. I have fought my grandfather throughout this war, but I never knew him, but for you he is your father. For my father, the burden is the same as for you, and I doubt he can forswear his love for Tyro. If he can't, then I doubt I shall ever see him again, or my mother." Terin sighed, wondering if either of them still lived.

"Your father and mother? Whatever are you speaking of?" Tosha made a face, having heard none of this.

And so, Terin explained what transpired with Valera and then Jonas, both likely captives at Fera, causing Tosha to close her eyes and lower her head, wishing it were not true. She was hoping to find her brother here at Corell, to finally speak with him, but alas, it was not to be.

"What is she doing here?" Corry's growling voice drew Tosha from her musings, lifting her head just as Deva stepped into the corridor from her chamber. Deva stood there, frozen in place, feeling Corry's hateful glare.

Terin stared, taken aback by Deva's presence, wondering her purpose for being there, his mind a maelstrom of emotions regarding his former mistress. Raven took a moment to realize Deva's identity, not recognizing her right away, or when she was presented to Commander Balka when they first arrived. He was never good with faces and names to begin with, especially when it came to Araxans.

Deva remained silent, waiting for the vitriol and anger to subside before speaking. This was the moment she dreaded, facing the two people she had harmed the most.

"Tell them, Deva!" Tosha sternly ordered, giving her little respite before plunging ahead.

Deva took a breath before stepping forth, dropping to her knees between Corry and Terin.

"I have pledged my sword and life to your cause until death takes me or the war is won and my debt redeemed. Yah has tasked me to this purpose to atone for my transgressions against both of you. I humbly beseech your forgiveness and mercy, though expect neither, for such was my crime." Deva looked to both of them before lowering her gaze, awaiting their judgement.

"What?" Corry growled, angered further by her audacity.

"I don't..." Terin tried to sort his thoughts, confused by this unexpected turn.

"Are we to just forgive you and all is forgotten?" Corry growled, balling her fists.

"The choice is yours, cousin. No blame falls to you should you refuse her penance," Tosha said evenly, regarding her cousins.

"Do *you* forgive her, Tosha, after she conspired with her mother to kill your husband and steal your throne?" Corry asked, keeping her gaze upon Deva, who remained kneeling before her.

"Yah gives me little choice but to do so." Tosha sighed.

"Yah? Are you now his acolyte?" she asked, her gaze shifting sharply in Tosha's direction.

"Everyone who was in the throne room that fateful night is now among his devoted. We can no more deny Yah than the sunrise. Deva has been given visions from Yah, the deity speaking to her directly. She is much changed since you last saw her. Whether you forgive her falls to you, and only you. No one shall weigh that against you. Do so for your own sake, not for her," Tosha explained.

Corry stood there consumed with anger, feeling the weight of

Tosha's words, words she knew to be true but couldn't accept, at least not now. She wanted to scream and strike her, but something held her back. Whether it was reason, discipline or the restraining hand of Yah, she could only guess. It was Terin, however, who spoke judiciously, tempering rage with reason.

"I forgave you that night in Bansoch, Deva, though I did not desire to. When Yah said to grant you mercy, it emptied the hate from my heart, leaving nothing in its wake. I still feel the pain of all I suffered, but as for you... I left you to Yah, and he has answered. He advised mercy for you, and if your visions are true, there is a reason for it. I forgive you, but I will never forget what you did. If you can live with that, then accept it as I have," Terin said, placing his hand upon her head, forgiveness washing over her, fueling the tears pouring from her eyes.

Corry felt her own hate subsiding, noting the genuine anguish in Deva's countenance, as if her soul lay bare. What but love could do such a thing? Who but Yah could bring about such transformation? She wanted to hate Deva, feeling herself robbed of her rage, but Terin's words tore through her, stripping away all the anger she desperately clung to, leaving her empty.

"Stand, Deva." Terin eased her to her feet, where she stood looking broken into his blue eyes.

The others looked on, spellbound by this strange and moving exchange, taken by the moment.

"Go to your brother, and live in peace," Terin said, touching a hand to her shoulder before stepping away, leaving a weeping Deva in his wake.

"My brother?" Deva asked, wiping her eyes.

Chapter 7

She found him upon the battlements of the west wall, staring out in the distance, where their native isle rested hundreds of leagues beyond the horizon. His back was to her, his silver cuirass and tunic contrasting her golden mail and black tunic. His head was bare, leaving his auburn hair blowing freely in the breeze.

"Guilen?" she called out, stopping several paces behind him, wary of his reception. So much had changed since last they met, so much loss and pain, and... war. Her breath stopped as he turned, his blue eyes finding her, before they alit with recognition. He made no movement, waiting for his mind to confirm what he was seeing before stepping nigh.

"Deva?" he asked, still wondering if his eyes were tricking him.

"It is me, brother."

With that, he came to embrace her, which she returned most fervently. They held each other for the longest time, savoring their warmth and kinship. She felt the loneliness that held her in its suffocating grasp, ease, thankful that he hadn't rejected her.

"I have missed you, dear brother," she whispered in his ear, holding desperately to him.

"And I you," he said, making her heart sing as they pulled briefly apart.

"Look at you, clad in warrior vestment and a sword upon your hip," she remarked, her eyes running the length of him.

"I have found myself martially employed, dear sister, though a poor soldier do I make."

"A poor soldier doesn't save the life of his king." She smiled, having heard of his bravery at the breaking of the siege.

"I was fortunate in my circumstance, as I have been many times since I departed our home."

"Escaped our home, you mean to say."

"Perhaps." He shrugged innocently.

"Mother was most... displeased," she politely said.

"I surmised as such. Her treatment of Terin in the wake of that event indicates the nature of the punishment she intended for me."

"I don't know what she would have done to you, Guilen, but it matters little now, considering she is dead, and Father also."

"Yes, I heard of his passing at the hand of the Princess. I mourn for him, but understand her reason."

"I was most distraught upon hearing it, but Yah has taken that anger from me. I am different now, Guilen. I hope you can see that."

"I can see that in your eyes, Deva. You are much changed."

"Thank you for seeing that. I was worried you might reject me."

"You should know better, considering all we have shared growing together. You are my sister, Deva, and I love you." Guilen smiled, drawing her again into his embrace.

There upon the battlements of Corell, Deva Estaran's heart began to mend.

* * *

Tosha's face grew red upon entering the great hall, greeted by the apes cheering her entrance, including Orlom and the others that traveled from Torn. They were the first to rise after the previous night's festivities, with most of the Torries still abed, save for poor Jentra, who still cursed Raven for his sorry state.

"Lady Raven!" they shouted, raising their tankards as she followed Raven through the entrance, her companions looking aghast trailing her, especially Lucella. Gorzak rose from his bench at the table along the near wall, offering an Ape greeting to her.

"Hardy cheers for our friend's brave lady. There is no lass more worthy of him in all the realms of Arax. Only a true hardy lass could have tested him so, setting trials worthy of song and hunting him across the northern wilderness, unto the shores of Veneba. She even set a bounty upon his head to bring him to heel!" Gorzak gave a toothy grin, raising his tankard in her direction, before pounding his fist to his chest, exercising more oratory skill than anyone expected of an ape warrior.

Tosha and her fellow warriors stood in the middle of the chamber, uncertain of what to say to this, when another ape continued, Carbanc, son of Hukok, who stood with tankard in hand.

"Lady Raven, we salute you. You have sired mighty sons for our brother. Even now they sit in Matuzak's hall, suckling hungrily at their nursemaid's teats. They shall make great warriors, worthy heirs of our Earth friend!" Carbanc downed his drink.

The others followed in kind, lauding her breeding skills and tenacious spirit, causing her to give Raven a murderous look, which he simply shrugged off in his irritating fashion. Despite their assigned place at the high table, Raven dragged Tosha to sit with the apes, where they all took their seats while kitchen servants brought them food and drink. Tosha's warriors partook gladly after their long journey, spending many a night camped beneath the stars.

By this time, more of the garrison had filtered in for their assigned eating time, the large chamber growing louder with the size of the crowd. Several commanders of rank joined them at their table, including Commander Balka, who took it upon himself to shield Tosha's guards from unwanted questions from his soldiers. The men were always curious for news from elsewhere and heard the tales of what happened at Bansoch. Despite his earnest effort, Balka's men soon ingratiated themselves with the Sisterhood warriors, exchanging tales of the battles they each fought.

"It was upon the north wall where the gargoyles pressed most strongly," one Torry soldier explained, a survivor of the main assault during the second siege, standing between two seated Sisterhood warriors, who looked on as he continued.

"I took a gargoyle scimitar across my shoulder, nearly rending it in half," he added, touching his right hand to his left shoulder, indicating the severity of the wound.

"You did?" one of them asked, raising a skeptical brow, seeing no evidence of the injury.

"The matrons healed him with the Earthers' magic box," his comrade explained.

"We also have one, a gift from the Earther Brokov," Lucella opined from across the table, overhearing the conversation.

This exchange triggered another conversation surrounding the wounded healed by the devices, at Corell and Bansoch, including the severity of many of the injuries. The macabre details did little to curb the appetites of either group, seasoned warriors all. Tosha found herself shaking her head as she looked on, finding the scene surreal. She was never party to such casual banter among soldiers, listening to their experiences with such blunt description. Oh, she participated in the hardships of the field, training with her mother's soldiers and her father's legions, but was treated with the deepest reverence when doing so. Here she felt as one of them, mainly due to the presence of her husband, who sat beside her, stuffing his mouth with a generous helping of food. She would later discover that he and the apes were offered extra rations of food due to their size. His presence also had the effect of loosening the soldiers' tongues, allowing them to speak freely, as he easily goaded them into doing so with his carefree nature, which seemed to infect the entire palace. More than one soldier offered her stories of Raven's fell deeds during the siege, winning him their adoration. Though he was a favorite among the men, she couldn't help but see him as an overgrown child requiring her guidance and correction.

"Here, try some of this," Raven said, forking a slab of roasted gallo upon her plate, the bird a rare delicacy as of late, but a fresh delivery in recent days had restocked the palace wares.

Tosha gave him a look, confounded by the very idea of anyone serving her food in this manner, anyone but him. She took the portion into her mouth, savoring its rich texture, tender and juicy. After so much time dining in the wild, with a few stopovers in larger cities, she appreciated good food.

"I thought you'd like it. I have to hand it to the cooks in this place, they make the best with what they have, especially considering the mouths they have to feed," he added.

"Their efforts are very impressive," she opined, just as Galen made his entrance into the great hall.

"Wonderful," Raven groaned, his sarcasm not lost on her.

"Isn't he the minstrel that stole your ocran?" she recalled, recognizing his face, though their interaction was quite brief.

"Yep."

"And you haven't killed him?" She smiled, giving him a sideways look.

"I would have, but Cronus made me promise not to. Since then, he has done a good job sucking up to the locals around here. He isn't all bad, I guess. He's been pretty helpful with Cronus and Leanna, both before and after she gave birth," he said, having already explained to her of Leanna's passing.

"Princess Tosha, we are most honored by your visit to our palace!" Galen announced, stepping near their table, executing a deep bow with his mandolin tucked to his chest.

"Your graciousness is most welcoming, Galen," Tosha praised him, knowing it would annoy Raven.

"Might we have a song, Minstrel?" Lucella asked, sitting to Tosha's other side.

"Of course, my fair Captain Sarelis." Galen bowed again, backing to the chamber's center, giving the full chamber a clearer view.

Galen tested his mandolin, deftly plucking its cords, bobbing his head as he prepared to sing.

"What ballad shall you sing?" one Torry soldier asked, seated along the opposite wall.

"An ancient refrain that I discovered in the palace library, courtesy of the Chief Minister's scribe, young Aldo. It was first penned during the early years of the Middle Kingdom, heralding the first queen of the Sisterhood and her brave sister. It is aptly called *The Daughters of Tarelia*," Galen said, giving the women warriors another respectful bow before beginning.

> *"Upon the distant shore they strode*
> *To face the Soch King of old*
> *Upon the heights above the bay*
> *Where struck the blow that won the day.*
> *Melida! General Melida! They shouted on high*
> *Cheering her name into the sky.*
> *Telisa her brave sister fought*
> *Beside her through battle wrought*
> *To honor their father, they toppled a king*
> *To honor his memory which bards rarely sing*
> *Crowned by her people for victory gained*
> *Denying the praise sung of her name*
> *A daughter of Tarelia she claimed to be*
> *But more to her was destined to be*
> *Queen! Queen! Her people proclaimed*
> *Crowning her head, and lifting her name.*
> *Upon the bloody hill where the Soch King fell*
> *Rests the palace where the Queen now dwells..."*

Galen bowed with the ending of his ballad, basking in the glow of the Sisterhood soldiers' adulation. Though the story was known to all, none had heard it told in the form of this ballad. It was another reminder that the first queen of the Sisterhood was in truth a daughter of a Tarelian General, a great warrior tasked with the destruction of the Soch Kingdom of old. His untimely death before the expedition began, led to his two daughters completing the task, each trained by him in the martial skills, and given the *swords of light* by the Tarelian Council to accomplish their quest.

"The daughters of Tarelia!" Lucas declared, having entered the chamber at the beginning of Galen's rendition, with Ular at his side.

"The daughters of Tarelia!" the Torry soldiers chorused his declaration, honoring their guests.

Tosha gained her feet, lifting her goblet into the air, acknowledging their heartfelt greeting.

"From the daughters of Tarelia to the sons of Tarelia, I salute you, my brave brothers!" she proclaimed to a round of hearty cheers by all.

"Who are the sons of Tarelia?" Raven asked as she retook her seat on the bench.

"You don't know?"

"I remember Corry babbling something about them before we rescued Terin, but I just stopped listening after a while."

"You stopped listening? Why?" She gave him a look.

"She was saying more than I could remember in one sitting," he said, though he truly meant he was quickly bored. All he truly remembered was Tyro's kinship to Terin and Terin being the blood of Kal, whatever that meant.

And so Tosha again explained the founding of the Middle Kingdom by the Tarelian General Zar Zaronan, and General Melida's founding of the Sisterhood. Raven nodded his head every once in a while, pretending to pay attention, until she caught on and began to test him, forcing her to start again after slapping him upside his head, causing the apes looking on to grin.

* * *

The evening found Tosha and Raven as guests at the King's table in his private dining chamber, joined by Terin, Corry and Cronus. The intimate gathering was called by Lorn, with only his queen joining them in attendance. He sent Jentra to oversee their other guests in the great hall for the evening feast, reserving this time to discuss more delicate matters, matters of prophecy and destiny. They were surprised to see the servants leave large platters of food and pitchers of drink upon the table before being excused for the night, closing the large porian door behind them. With no guards present, they were alone in the secluded chamber, wondering the secrecy of the event.

"Please serve yourselves, or kindly pass the food about the table. Tonight, it is best if what we say remains among us," Lorn began, sitting at the head of the table with Deliea opposite him and Raven, Tosha and Cronus to one side, and Terin and Corry upon the other.

"I don't mind if I do, Lorn, but what's with all this cloak and dagger stuff?" Raven asked, his strange reference lost on the others as he drew a platter of meat closer to his plate, helping himself.

"Don't be rude, you mindless oaf," Tosha hissed, slapping at his hand as he forked a generous helping onto his plate.

"Don't go making a habit of interfering with a man's appetite, wife," he growled back, helping himself to another portion.

Before she could respond, Lorn interceded.

"Your husband has not gained the adoration of our people for his table manners, Tosha. If I find no offense, neither should you. As for being informally addressed, I think it appropriate to use our given names this evening, as Raven is prone to use."

"If you believe so, Lorn, I shall acquiesce," Tosha conceded, receiving an infuriating smile from Raven.

"Very good. Please partake, all of you." Lorn waved an open hand across the table, urging them to begin. They followed Raven's lead, helping themselves to the delicious offerings. Lorn began the table conversation with small talk, asking Tosha about her journey, and of happenings in Bansoch.

"The Queen is most adamant in coming to your aid but is still consolidating her position with the Federation. Her planning is nearly complete, and I would expect the military expedition within a fortnight," Tosha said, not able to not inject political matters into her explanation.

"The Queen? Why not just say your mother?" Raven asked.

"Because it is not proper to do so," she shot back.

"You don't have to act all high and snobby, Tosh. Didn't you hear what Lorn said about using our first names?" Raven pointed out, causing Lorn and Terin to laugh, followed by Deliea, though Corry and Tosha tried their best to appear displeased. Lorn couldn't help but notice Cronus' forced smile, a stoic mask he used to hide his pain. Of all of them here, he was the only one alone, robbed of his wife by the cruelest of fates.

"Cronus, how fares Lady Maura?" Deliea asked, seeing her husband's sympathetic look he gave to Cronus.

"She is a very hungry child, much like Raven," Cronus said in good humor, though it didn't reach his eyes.

"Nothing wrong with taking after her uncle Raven. She's right pretty too, though even a blind man can see it," Raven added, slapping his friend on the back.

"Cronus, I know the pain you must be suffering, sitting here among your friends, when all of us have our husbands and wives with us, and you sit alone. Though I never knew Leanna, I have seen her through your eyes and those of your daughter, as well as your friends who sit here among us. Of all those sitting here, you and I share no blood or marital relation, but know this: you are and shall ever be my brother, as I explained upon the shores of Carapis," Lorn said, his words casting a quiet pall over the small gathering.

"I am honored by your friendship, Sire," Cronus said gratefully.

"Didn't you hear when he said to call him Lorn tonight?" Raven nudged him.

"My apologies, Lorn, I stand corrected." Cronus shook his head.

"We are honored by your friendship and loyalty, Cronus. Know that you and Maura always have a home here with our family." Deliea reached out her hand, touching his as he sat to her corner.

"She will want for nothing, Cronus, I so avow with all my heart," Corry added, looking to him from across the table.

"As do I," Terin added, followed by Lorn, Raven and even Tosha.

Cronus was overcome with emotion, his stoic veneer cracking like the fissures in a breaking dam. He lowered his head, lest they see his moistened eyes. A gentle pat on his back by Raven helped him steel his nerve, daring him to lift his eyes to address them.

"No man ever had friends like all of you. Thank you."

"Friends like us." Lorn sighed wistfully as if struck by a memory.

"There's that look of yours again. He's about to get all starry-eyed and talk of Yah," Raven said, forking another piece of meat into his mouth.

"You know me well, Raven." Lorn smiled at that, freely admitting it. When dealing with Raven, Lorn knew it was always best to accept his gentle derisions as compliments and move on, and so he did.

"I brought Raven, Cronus and Terin here this night for they each play an important role in the battles we have fought and those yet to come. I have spoken to each of you about this, relaying what Yah revealed to me in his visions. I shall tell of it again for the benefit of Corry and Tosha. Deliea has heard me speak of this during our journey here, but for all your sakes, I shall speak of it again," Lorn began.

Tosha and Corry gave him a curious look, waiting expectantly upon his next utterance.

"Few of you knew me when I was a child, though Corry might attest of what I freely now confess. I was a cruel, petty prince who looked upon his lessers with haughty airs. I was most unkind to the palace servants and even the boys I trained with who lacked my martial prowess. I saw kindness as a weakness and mercy as a vice. Despite my character flaws, I was doted upon by my mother while she lived, and my father also, but especially by Squid Antillius, who befriended this unworthy creature..." Lorn began, telling them of the visions he had received from Yah of the destruction of the Torry Realms and the slaughter of his people. He spoke of his torment, torture and agonizing death at the hands of Tyro's minions as the world descended into darkness. At times throughout the telling, he saw Tosha and Corry wipe their eyes, horrified by what he described. He continued with his waking from the terrible vision, only for it to return every night, forcing him to beg of Yah to remove it, but he refused.

"*See and remember, son of Lore,*" Lorn repeated what Yah had said.

"How cruel," Tosha gasped, ashamed by her lifelong indifference to what her father's alliance with the gargoyles portended for mankind.

"He wasn't cruel, Tosha, no more than any parent instructing their child with a hard lesson to prepare them for life's trials. It was then I asked what hope had I to turn the tide, as I was but one man, and even if I commanded the armies of the Torry Realms, I had little power to face such odds. *You are not alone, son of Lore*, Yah reassured me before revealing the three of you and the great importance you would play in the war to come, this war," Lorn said, looking to Cronus, Raven, and finally Terin, holding his gaze the longest.

"You knew all along the role they would play, and you didn't think to tell me?" Corry strongly asked.

"What would you have done had I done so?" He gave her a knowing look.

She had no quick answer for that, staring back at him with only an anger she could not articulate.

"It might have ruined what we have." Tosha sighed, realizing that she and Raven had required the trials and battles they shared to eventually bring them together. Any change, no matter how slight, might have prevented that. Looking across the table, she could see Corry realizing the same with herself and Terin. If love was destiny, then perhaps it might not have mattered. But if love was a current, any change in its course could drastically alter where it took you. Lorn smiled wanly, seeing Corry coming to that realization.

"Yah's visions often reveal the larger details, leaving us to find our way in getting there, but only if we embrace his virtues. I may have been given visions of Raven, Cronus and Terin, but I was ignorant of the bonds they would share with either of you. I took it upon myself to watch over them as best as I was able, and only from afar, not daring to reveal myself lest I too alter their intended course. Terin was the easiest, guided and protected by Jonas until the war was upon us. Cronus was far more difficult, his adventures drawing him close to danger many times through the years. Raven was the greater mystery. When I first saw him in the vision, I thought it impossible, for no such man existed in all of Arax until the stories began to spread of the strangers that fell from the heavens, wielding strange magic, led by a man called *Raven*. I listened from afar of his adventures, interceding only once when he and Cronus first met, protecting Cronus from certain parties in Cagan that wanted his head for siding with Raven," Lorn revealed, though Cronus had learned of this during his journey to the Straits of Cesa.

"I am thankful for you interceding on my behalf, Lorn," Cronus sighed.

"It was my pleasure, Cronus, though I did make certain that you were reprimanded by sending you back to Torry North, ensuring you were properly assigned in the right army, the right telnic, and the right unit to set the playing board at the war's outset. Why you needed to be so placed was not revealed to me, only that it must be so. Yah ordered the board to be set and prepared the way for you to meet Raven and then Terin, bringing them together, while delivering the decisive blow at Tuft's Mountain. Had you not been captured; Terin might not have fully unlocked the power of his sword before the first siege of Corell. Tosha and Raven might not have met as he would likely have departed Rego and then Central City before Squid could have recruited him to rescue Corry. Had Raven not rescued Corry and the others, most of them would have died on that isle." Lorn looked to Tosha, Corry and his beloved Deliea, cringing at the thought of losing any of them.

"Without Cronus befriending Raven, General Bode would not have had them prepare the battlefield at Tuft's Mountain, costing us many more soldiers and perhaps losing the battle altogether," Terin pointed out.

They all realized the long list of consequences had Cronus, Terin and Raven never met. Without the Earthers' intervention at Tuft's, Cronus would not have been placed north of the gap and never captured. That meant Terin would have no need to go to Fera, and Kato would not have joined their cause. Terin would not have been at Telfer to slow Yonig's advance. Terin would therefore not have warned Lorn of the state of the Yatin Empire, so he would not have led the Torry 4th Army to Mosar's relief before it had fallen. Even if he had, Kato would not have been there to counter Thorton. Lorn would have likely died there with much of his army. It was all too much to contemplate.

"But they did meet, and everything proceeded according to Yah's will, just as you envisioned, my love." Deliea smiled at him from across the table, dousing the flames of despair that circled the chamber as they contemplated the awful alternative that fate might have given them.

"Our queen is right. All has happened because you were faithful to Yah's vision, Lorn. That was why I pledged to you my life, my sword and my sacred honor, and forsook all claims to Tyro's empire and Kal's ancient realm." Terin recalled that night in Mosar where Lorn found him abed, exhausted by the power his sword invoked.

"And I told you I did not accept your vow, as it was not your place to forsake your rightful claims. Only at the end of this war shall we revisit which rights we intend to claim, reject or pass onto another. For now, you remain the Champion of the realm, just as I claimed that night in Mosar," Lorn reminded him.

Corry was taken aback, believing Terin forsook his birthright as he had claimed upon her rescuing him, but that was not entirely true. He remained Kal's heir, whatever that truly portended, and should they have children, they in turn would be Kal's true heirs. But listening to Lorn speak, she knew Terin's inheritance did not conflict with the Torry throne but was somehow different, or something different.

"This is a nice story and all, Lorn, but what really matters is our next step. In case you forgot, I'm leaving in a couple days and won't get back this way unless Thorton decides to double back," Raven reminded them, causing Tosha to look at him crossly.

"I just arrived," she reminded him.

"You can always come with me, you know," he pointed out.

"I am here to fulfill my duty, a duty you seem to think I can cast aside as easily as you do."

"You knew I was leaving, and what about the boys? Aren't you angry that I left them with…"

"I know what I said, but you are not going to visit them when you leave. You are going back to Tro, to your ship."

"Well, we do have a war to fight now, thanks to your dear old dad, and my ship is the best way to make that happen, so either saddle up and join the ride or stop complaining," he said, enjoying the angry look she loved to give him.

"Raven speaks true, Tosha. With Besos retaken, all of our current efforts are directed to Notsu and what is left of Morac's legions. If we can destroy them before they escape northward, the Benotrist Empire will be ripe for invasion," Lorn said.

"When shall we depart for Notsu?" Terin asked, considering the fluidity of the situation with Tosha and Minister Yotora's arrival.

"Soon. Ciyon should return in the coming days, and I intend

to send him east to reinforce our armies there. We shall join him, bringing our full strength to bear upon Morac. I would have you with us, Terin, though I am loath to ask it, considering you were just wed, but such is our need," Lorn explained.

"I am your champion, Lorn, and will follow wherever you have need of me. My happiness does not exceed the lives of the men who might perish if I am not there," Terin affirmed.

"We wed in order to know each other with the little time afforded us, not to keep Terin from the battle ahead. Though I shall be pained by his absence, I know he must leave," Corry added, placing her hand in his.

"Then I trust you to aid your new sister in the managing of the realm in my absence," Lorn asked of Corry.

"I shall." She sighed, though she wished to join them in their campaign, torn between duty and desire.

"If you would look after Maura, I would be most grateful, Corry?" Cronus asked.

"You needn't leave, Cronus. I would have you guard my sister and my wife in my absence," Lorn offered, knowing only chains of honor could keep Cronus from the battle at Notsu.

"There is no threat upon Corell, but the fate of the war could be decided at Notsu. I carry a Sword of Light, and you shall have need of it, though you have others more worthy to wield it. Morac might draw even with Terin, but not Terin and Elos, or Terin and I. We must bring all of our swords against him and win the day," Cronus affirmed.

"I shall watch over Maura as my own babe," Corry assured him.

"And I as well," Deliea added, reaching out her hand to his.

"I welcome your company then, Cronus, but must chasten your belief that there are others more worthy to wield that blade. It was won in battle by your own hand and that of Terin. As I said before, he relinquished all claim upon it, giving you his full blessing. He is the blood of Kal, granted a special bond to each of the Swords of Light, and that now extends to you and the blade you now possess. It shall never forsake you, as those who are unworthy to wield the swords have come to learn, suffering their loss," Lorn explained.

"If that is so, how do you explain Dethine? His people possessed this sword for hundreds of years when all the Tarelian kings lost theirs?" Cronus asked.

That was a question several of them had, wondering how the Nayborians held onto such a blade where better men failed.

"The Nayborians are clever people; what else could explain their ability to fight the Jenaii to a standstill through the centuries?" Lorn began, reminding them of the difficulty in that very task. The Nayborians benefited from the thick forests that covered the east bank of the Elaris, stretching endless leagues into their interior, forests that negated much of the Jenaii advantage of flight.

"When the Swords of Light began to betray the kings of old, the Nayborians came to suspect that magical properties were involved and that no one man could be entrusted permanently to possess the sword they held. Considering the Jenaii held a superior blade to their own, they were very keen to keep the only weapon that could stay off destruction. The Nayborians immediately placed the sword in the center of the throne room of Non, guarded day and night through the centuries, only to be taken up by their named champion in times of war and returned to its place immediately after. These precautions served them well, securing the use of their sword through the ages," Lorn explained.

"Until now," Raven pointed out.

"Yes, until now. Their wars with the Jenaii in the past were brief, limiting the sword's exposure to mishap. This war, however, was different, with their champion joining Morac's campaigns at Corell, each lengthy, and far from their ancestral home. Add the fact that Dethine met Terin and Cronus on the field of battle, bringing the Nayborians' good fortune to its end. The sword is now in the hands of its rightful master, Cronus Kenti." Lorn regarded Cronus proudly, lifting his goblet to him with deep-held respect.

Cronus nodded in kind, humbled by the honor his king bestowed upon him. He thought of how much he hated this war and what it stole from him. He needed to do his part to see it end, and nothing short of victory was acceptable. A large part of him had died with Leanna, crushing his soul in a way the others could never understand. He could barely breathe without thinking of her, committing to memory every precious moment they had shared. It was at such times he understood Thorton, stopping himself from following Ben over the precipice, wallowing in an abyss of bitterness and despair. He had a duty to his king, his people, and most especially his daughter, a duty to win this war and ensure that she grows up in a safe and better world. Thinking of her made him smile, but oh, how he missed Leanna.

"Your visions seem to have brought you this far, Lorn. What do they advise beyond Notsu?" Raven asked.

A faraway look passed the king's face, casting a pall over the chamber. Lorn wanted to answer, to reassure his friends of Yah's grand plan for victory, but he couldn't. Looking to the future beyond Notsu revealed nothing. It was as if a dark veil was drawn over his eyes, blinding him to the path forward. He couldn't reveal his misgivings, lest they all lose faith, and sometimes faith was all they had. They had faith in him, this he could plainly see, but to finally defeat the gargoyles, they needed faith in Yah. Such was the fate of Arax in the days of Kal, the people rejecting Yah despite all the blessings he bestowed upon them. Such is the nature of the human heart, to consider generosity as earned and rightfully theirs, disrespecting their benefactor with haughty airs. This time needed to be different. The people needed to cry out with many voices, beseeching Yah in all his glory, placing their hope in him above their mortal kings. Whether they would do this was beyond his control. Despite their many victories, there was more to defeating the gargoyles than any of them knew.

"Lorn?" Corry asked, drawing him from his silent musings.

"I cannot say what path we are to follow after Notsu. I am blind to Yah's will beyond that point. I can only trust that the way shall be revealed. As for the enemy, each of you must understand that defeating them shall require more than Swords of Light, massive armies and the Earthers' powerful weapons," he said, looking to each of them as he spoke.

"There can't be that many of the rodents left. If you add up those killed at Tuft's, Yatin and here, let alone the twenty thousand we slew at Tro, it leaves Tyro with few, as far as I can count," Raven pointed out.

"There are likely ten to twenty telnics of gargoyles among the garrisons throughout the Benotrist Empire and what remains of the 15th Legion, last reported along the Cot River. The rest of the gargoyle legions are with Morac or near Tro, and I would number them less than a full legion combined. The number might seem insignificant, but there is more to their power than the soldiers they can field. Their nesting grounds are a mystery, and strongly guarded. In all recorded history, no man has visited their secret holdfasts and lived to share the tale. Before we can even hope to do so, we must deal with what remains of their forces and then their Benotrist allies, which still number greatly throughout their realm. The 13th Legion is still unaccounted for and last reported at Laycrom. The garrison of Fera stands at thirty telnics by itself. If we are able to bring all our strength to bear and defeat Tyro's legions and garrisons that remain, we must still contend with the nesting grounds. I need not remind each of you that in the days of Kal, his armies were prepared to do so but were betrayed by faithless lords who conspired against him. We are not even at that place yet. I have blindly followed Yah's guidance, directing me from one step to another with the greater whole still hidden. For now, only the path to Notsu is illuminated," Lorn explained.

"Then to Notsu you shall lead us," Cronus strongly affirmed.

* * *

The following morn saw the leading elements of General Ciyon's army emerge from the Zaronan, trailing his standard with a golden crown upon a split field of black and white, the sigil of their joint army. The flamboyant Macon general rode ahead of his van, raising his hand to the thunderous cheers of the Torry encampments circling the palace. Squid Antillius rode upon his left and Matron Dresila on his right, each greeted warmly as they passed between the pitched pavilions and tents of the soldiers still camped at Corell, many of whom were recently healed by Matron Ilesa or freed from Benotrist slave pits to the north. Most were garrison troops deployed outside the palace walls whilst their barracks were aired out and refreshed.

Squid found the grounds about the palace much improved since the lifting of the siege. Many of Morac's trenches were filled in, most with the bodies of the slain. The rest of the dead were gathered near where they fell, piled upon pyres and set ablaze. Even now the odor of burnt flesh permeated the air, a grim reminder of all those that died here. Looking above the main gate, the scars of battle remained, with the once-white battlements blackened with ash and blood. Lifting his gaze far above to the uppermost battlements, he spied the standard of his king lifting high upon the spiraled peak of the Tower of Celenia, a golden crown upon a field of white. His heart lifted at the sight, reassured by the restoration of the House of Lore, as they passed under the main gate.

* * *

Dadeus' arrival hastened the preparations for Lorn's departure, passing the authority of the crown to Queen Deliea, leaving her to oversee the court as he prepared to march. Dadeus presented Lorn with a full report of his actions at Besos. General Mastorn's 3rd Army oversaw the movement of the Benotrist prisoners to the south, where they would be further separated into smaller contingents and spread throughout Torry South, Maconia, Teso and Zulon. General Fonis' 2nd Army would return to Central City, protecting the realm's western flank. General El Tuvo would soon join with Lorn at Corell from Besos, his 1st Battlegroup numbering near six telnics, far smaller than its once twenty.

The following morn found Raven and Orlom preparing to leave, their packs slung over their shoulders, stepping from the stairwell onto the roof of the inner keep, where their magantors were saddled and waiting. They had first looked for them upon the south-facing magantor platform below, only to find their stalls empty with their handlers claiming their drivers and mounts were ready for them upon the roof of the inner keep. Thinking this odd, they simply made their way there, having already bid farewell to their friends. Raven spent the previous night with Tosha, leaving her in bed without her saying a word. She simply stared at him as he kissed her goodbye, watching quietly as he departed her chamber. Stepping from the stairwell, they were greeted by a small army of their friends blocking their path to their magantors, with Lorn standing prominently in their midst, the Torry King striding forth to greet them with the others crowding about.

"Unacceptable of you departing without a proper farewell, Raven," Lorn said with Deliea, Corry, Cronus and Terin standing behind him. Raven noticed Ular and Lucas off to his left, and Jentra and the apes, led by Gorzak, standing to his right. Galen, Ilesa, Dresila and a small army of Matrons stood among the crowd with a host of others he managed to befriend during his stay. The only noticeable absence was Tosha and her sister warriors, which wasn't surprising since she hadn't spoken with him since last night despite him sharing her bed.

"I said my goodbyes the last few days. Don't see the need in dragging this out any longer than necessary. Besides, we'll all see each other again, probably sooner than we think."

"Perhaps, but we can never know the fortunes of war," Lorn advised as Deliea stepped forth, placing a kiss to his cheek.

"You have my gratitude, Raven, for all that you have done. May Yah protect you on your journey." Deliea smiled, backing away as Corry stepped near.

"You are an insufferable ass, Raven of Earth, but you are OUR insufferable ass," Corry said, using her vulgar language, before reaching up to kiss his cheek. "Thank you for everything," she whispered in his ear before drawing briefly away, the two of them sharing so much without saying a word. He knew she thanked him most for believing in her when she sought his help to rescue Terin.

"You're welcome. Just don't lose the kid again," he said, looking past her shoulder to Terin, who in turn stepped forth.

"Thank you, Raven," Terin said, wanting to say so much more but lacking the words. After all they had shared, they didn't need to say anything.

"You too, champ. Just take care of my new niece here. I'm getting too old for another rescue mission," he said, ruffling Terin's hair before reaching for Corry, who wisely backed away, shaking her head.

Gorzak of tribe Traxar stepped forth next, the morning sun shining off the heads of the twin axes strapped across his back, his fellow apes crowding at his sides, each bidding Raven farewell.

"Safe journeys, Captain Raven!" Gorzak bellowed.

"You sure you don't want to come with me?" Raven asked.

"Why go to Tro and fight gargoyles there when we can go to Notsu and fight gargoyles sooner? Besides, our president told us to help the Torries, and we shall march with King Lorn until the war is finished," Gorzak said, the other apes pounding their chests in agreement, his bold proclamation receiving hearty cheers from the surrounding Torries.

Raven shook their hands as Ular and Lucas stepped forth.

"You sure you don't want to come either?" Raven asked the Enoructan Champion.

"My people are certain to join the war, and I can strike a heavier blow marching with King Lorn than upon a dorun or upon your ship," Ular answered with his watery voice.

"Well, if you survive this war, there is always a place on our crew for you, Ular. You too, Lucas, since it seems you're a matched pair." Raven slapped both of them on the shoulder.

"It was an honor to fight beside you, Raven. Speak well of me to Zem, Lorken, Argos, Kendra and Brokov," Lucas said.

"I will, but you'll see them all soon enough if things go as planned."

"Things rarely go as planned," Lucas reminded him.

"Then we'll improvise." Raven slapped his shoulder a second time as the Matrons stepped forth.

"Fare thee well, you rascal," Matron Dresila said, using the term he often used in her presence referring to Orlom and Krink.

"Keep up the good work, Doc. Next time we meet I'll see if Brokov can scrounge up another healing thingie or two for you," he said before she too kissed his cheek.

"Captain Raven," Ilesa formally addressed him, offering a brief curtsy before Raven drew her in his arms, giving her hug.

"Kato's wife is welcome to join our crew anytime," he said before releasing her, causing her to blush with embarrassment.

"I fear my duties lie elsewhere but am honored by your offer," she said.

Others briefly greeted him including Squid, Guilen and a host of soldiers he had befriended. Galen was the most awkward, the two old enemies coming to an agreement of sorts watching over Leanna and then Cronus, taking turns helping their friend with the baby.

"Keep an eye on him," Raven said, looking past Galen's shoulder where Cronus waited beside his magantor.

"I shall. And I would be remiss in not singing Lady Maura to sleep by the lullaby you favor. What was that again... Oh yes, *The Streets of Laredo*." Galen fondly recalled the catchy tune that Raven loved to mumble to the child when he thought no one was listening.

"I'm sure you can sing it better than me," Raven said, slapping him on the shoulder, the friendly gesture taking Galen aback, proving they had come far since their first meeting.

At last, he came upon Cronus, with Orlom following in his wake, greeting everyone as he did. His friend stood beside his warbird, dressed simply in a brown tunic without mail or helm, wearing his sword belt, with the Sword of the Stars upon his left hip and the blade given him by Torg upon the right. He noticed the color returning to Cronus' face and the lack of circles around his eyes. He looked to have finally had a good night's sleep, perhaps the first in a very long time.

"Raven, I wanted to thank you for coming here with me. If you hadn't..." Cronus shook his head, doubting if things would have turned as they had.

"I owed Tyro for what he did, Cronus. And I am glad we helped your people. Probably should have done this sooner. Kato had the right of it, but what's done is done. Only wish Leanna... well, you know what I mean."

"I know. You are my friend, Raven, perhaps the greatest friend I will ever have." Cronus smiled wanly, trying desperately to control his emotions before Raven lifted him off the floor in a hug, squeezing the life out of him before setting him down.

"Take care of that girl of yours, pal. I don't know how big she'll get before I make my way back here, but she'll be pretty enough to cause you headaches when the suitors come calling."

"I shall be beating them off with a stick." Cronus smiled, using another of Raven's expressions.

They shared a few more moments of friendly banter before the crowd parted between the stairwell and their magantors. They looked back as Tosha emerged from the stairwell dressed in her golden armor over her uniform black tunic. Golden eyes stared through the narrow slits of her golden helm, fixed intently upon him, with her sister warriors trailing her. She stormed across the roof of the inner keep, passing between the parting crowd before stopping before him.

"I wondered if you'd come for one last goodbye." Raven smiled, looking down into her golden eyes.

"I'm coming with you."

"You are?" His left eyebrow lifted severely.

"You heard me," she stated flatly, pushing past him, with Cronus, Lorn and the others looking on.

"What about your duty and all that other stuff you talked about?" he asked as she handed her baggage to Raven's magantor driver, one of Dar Valen's best riders. The Torry magantor general selected his two finest to take Raven and Orlom to Tro, the other rider waiting just beyond the first.

"Shut up and climb aboard!" she growled, climbing into the saddle behind the Torry rider.

Her mother had ordered her to aid King Lorn, and she could do that on the *Stenox* just as well as anywhere. Besides, King Lorn had three Swords of Light available for the Notsu campaign and no need for the one she carried. She left Lucella in charge of their contingent, and she would remain with King Lorn until the war's end or until Tosha returned for them.

"You should listen to your wife, Raven." Lorn smiled, letting Raven know by his look that he knew about this all along.

"The king is right, Boss. Your lady is a fiery lass, and pretty too." Orlom grinned, walking past him to his own mount, the Torry driver helping to pull him onto the saddle.

Raven just shook his head and climbed aboard, hoping the poor bird could carry all three of them. No sooner had he done so than their driver eased the warbird away from the crowd, turning about, strutting toward the north-facing parapet, and springing into the air.

Below he could hear Lorn call for a round of cheers for their departing friends as Orlom's mount followed them into the sky. They circled the palace one last time, looking down upon their friends gathered upon the battlements below, only to discover hundreds more gathered along the inner and outer walls, all cheering as they flew overhead. Hundreds more stood upon the grounds surrounding the castle, waving as they passed. Raven waved back, heartened by their friendship. A part of him wondered how many of them would survive the war. It was then he was struck by what Lorn had said to him that first night they spoke, about his coming to this world and how it was by design. He wasn't entirely sure it was completely true, but he knew he had to do whatever he could to help them. He was too late for Arsenc, Kato and Leanna, but there was still time to save the rest, especially Terin, Corry, and Cronus. He could list hundreds more, which only affirmed what he must do.

With that, he gave them one final wave before passing beyond the horizon.

* * *

The following morn King Lorn led their great host eastward, with men of renown and peoples of many lands joining their cause. Lucella led her contingent of warriors upon magantors, soaring above their long columns, scanning far afield. Deva's mount trailed the loyal captain of Queen Letha's guard, looking below where her brother rode at General Ciyon's side, his silver raiment contrasting with Dadeus' golden armor. Surrounding Lorn was a small contingent of Torry Elite, leaving the greater portion of his most able warriors at Corell to guard his sister and his queen. Lucas and Ular rode off his left and Criose his right. Jentra followed close behind with young Dougar beside him, the orphan boy beaming proudly at serving as the king's squire. Trailing Jentra rode Cronus, guarding Ilesa, while

Dresila remained at Corell. Though Lorn wished for Ilesa to remain at Corell, she had asked to remain at his side, which he relented.

Gorzak of tribe Traxar led his small band of fearsome gorilla warriors, each sharing a mount with a Torry Elite, yearning for battle while singing their war songs, their boisterous voices carrying strongly upon the wind. Nearly half the archers of the Corell garrison joined them, along with their bundle bearers, loaded down with a dozen quivers apiece. Long columns of wagons trailed the greater portion of Ciyon's army, bearing food and camp provisions for the hundreds of specialists supporting the great host. Included in the order of march were the nearly two thousand Notsuan soldiers who had fought beside the Torries since the fall of their city, each eager to liberate their ancestral home.

Circling above the departing host soared Wind Racer with Terin sitting his saddle, gazing one last time to his beloved Corry before speeding off to the east, scouting ahead of the procession.

Corry and Deliea stood upon Zar Crest, looking on as the procession disappeared over the horizon, marching to join with King Mortis and King El Anthar and Master Vantel, who were approaching Notsu with their combined armies. Once joined, they would give battle, meeting Morac's Legions at Notsu.

Chapter 8

Forty leagues west of Notsu.

Morac rode alongside the column of starving soldiers, thousands of weary souls trudging along the weathered east-west road connecting Corell and Notsu and a hundred villages in between. He rode a half-starved ocran, gray of coat with lifeless dull eyes, matching the spirit of the army. Morac's once-resplendent armor was dented and marred, his cape torn away at the shoulder, and his ape skull helm broken off below his nose. He looked skyward as another Torry magantor swept overhead, spying their retreat, cursing the wretched fowl with his every breath. The men marching beside him were the tattered remnants of the 9th Benotrist Legion. Their once-proud standards were forsaken south of Corell, the gray sword upon a field of white, which would not be seen until they reached Notsu, where they might obtain the materials to forge them anew. He guessed only one in four of the men of the 9th had survived death or capture, the survivors marching in disheveled ranks, more resembling a mob than an army. Most hadn't eaten in days, and water was just as desperate, the men drinking from wherever they could to sate their thirst. Few were still fully equipped, some missing helms, shields, mail or even swords. Many had suffered injuries of all sorts, the most grievous left to perish along the roadside.

His only solace was the severed Torry heads adorning the pikes his legions had driven into the ground beginning at Kregmarin, running to the gates of Corell, a fitting tribute to his victory over King Lore, though that victory felt so very old now. Still, the grisly trophies gave him some satisfaction as they came upon another, its flesh rotten completely from its skull, with vacant eye sockets staring back at him. Seeing the pitiful marker gave him comfort that they were drawing nearer to Notsu as the Torries had removed all the heads and pikes within a hundred leagues of Corell after lifting the first siege. Seeing the adornments of his victory fueled his plans for his triumphant return, when he would lead his legions back to Corell and finish what he had started. This time he would run pikes from Corell to Cagan, planting the last head overlooking the western sea, saving that glorious placement for Prince Lorn.

"Packaww!"

Morac cursed another magantor passing overhead, its rider gloating at their sorry state, no doubt. He hadn't seen a single of General Polis' warbirds since the battle, nearly all of them likely slain by Raven's laser fire. *Raven.* He cursed that name as well, recalling the terrible blow Raven had delivered his army. Had he not done so, victory would have been his. Soldiers could only take so much before crumbling, and no army suffered such duress in the annals of warfare as his brave legions. Not only had Raven gutted his legions' rank and file, slaying twenty thousand or more with the sweep of his laser, but he assassinated his Legion Commanders soon after. Generals Vlesnivolk, Trimopolak, Concaka and Marcinia all fell to his terrible weapon, leaving only the insufferable General Gavis, who marched at the head of their column some ten leagues to the east. Could not the Earther at least have relieved him of that annoyance? Gavis shared only the briefest exchanges with Morac throughout the retreat, the man's hatred of him evident in his stormy eyes. He conceded that Gavis was an able commander, reordering his surviving telnics into some semblance of a legion. Gavis demanded the surviving levies of the 8th and 9th Benotrist Legions be added to his 10th, but Morac refused, naming Telnic Commander Dulvak as General of the 8th, and was forced to raise up Unit Commander Gurloz as General of the 9th since no commanders of telnic in the 9th Legion appeared to have survived the battle. Gavis criticized maintaining the legions as they currently stood, but Morac would not entertain strengthening Gavis' hand by bringing all Benotrist soldiers under his standard. Instead, the 8th and 9th Legions struggled along, their new commanders unable to reorder their broken ranks. They needed a safe place to feed and provision their legions, and time to do so, neither of which were currently possible with the enemy closing from the west.

Morac gathered whatever cavalry he could manage to round up since the battle, using them to relay commands and scout the enemy. He took the first mount he was able to find for himself, having had several killed beneath him since Corell, losing two to Raven's deadly fire. He lost everything from his pavilion, even his slave girls, who were last seen in the retreating ranks of the 8th Legion. They could be anywhere in this long column that stretched over thirty leagues, thirty leagues of drained men staggering step by bloody step, their eyes fixed to the horizon, eager to attain Notsu. Most of the gargoyles of the 5th and 14th Legions lingered at the rear of the column, gathering and separating with inconvenient regularity, causing him to give up any hope of organizing them until they attained Notsu. Many of the creatures abandoned the army altogether, breaking off into raiding parties, seeking food and plunder to the north or south, seeking lands untouched in the war. Morac was helpless to gather them, stretched out as they were.

"Packaww!"

Morac's ocran drew away from the road as a Macon magantor passed overhead, releasing a fire munition into his column where he rode, fire splashing in their midst, men screaming with flames licking their flesh, running to and fro or flopping helplessly on the rocky causeway. Men along the column drew away from the road, spreading out far afield, fearing another pass of the hateful avian. Morac managed to collect himself, ordering the men back onto the road, slaying the wounded lest they slow their advance. Having the men see their comrades suffer horrible burns would do naught for morale. They commenced march in quick order, much to his cajoling. His men had grown accustomed to such attacks throughout this miserable trek with Jenaii, Torry and Macon magantors constantly strafing their columns and Torry cavalry striking weak points along the line of march. They had decimated most of the supply and distribution points for the first hundred leagues from Corell as if they were privy to their location. He wondered if there were spies in his camp, or if some of those taken prisoner had betrayed the information to their Torry captors. He ordered all the resupply points between his army and Notsu reinforced and the provisions tightly rationed, giving the men just enough nourishment to hopefully reach Notsu.

He lost count of the men that dropped dead or exhausted throughout the retreat, leaving them where they fell. A few of the men tried to carry their fallen comrades, but he ordered them to leave them lest they exhaust themselves doing so, adding to the growing list of casualties. He continued on until the sun dipped below the horizon behind them. The men would continue marching until dusk blended to darkness, when they dropped to rest wherever they were, sleeping there until sunrise.

The following morn the men picked up where they had left off, dragging themselves to their feet and continuing on, walking into the blinding sunrise. By late morn Morac was greeted by a cohort of cavalry skirting along the roadside from the west, a familiar figure riding at their front… Kriton.

* * *

Kriton drew up alongside him, brandishing a pike in his left hand with a Torry head adorning it, shrunken dull eyes staring vacant from its rotting skull, insects crawling over its tattered scalp. Morac drew away from the column, Kriton following him up a shallow rise, his cavalry contingent fanning out around them as the infantry passed below.

"I am most pleased to see you survived." Morac thrust his fist to his chest.

"Aye, it has been an arduous trek across the Torry Realm. My contingent raided halfway between Besos and Central City when I received word of the battle at Corell," Kriton managed to say without hissing a word, his voice strangely sullen from exhaustion.

"You are the first of the emperor's elite I have chanced upon," Morac said.

"I chanced upon Vades three days past, leading a unit of cavalry. I sent him to scout our southern flank. He shall join with us at Notsu," Kriton said, regarding the Benotrist warrior that ranked 437 among the elite.

"I have found none among the survivors," Morac said bitterly. Most were slain just after Borgan, with Raven easily picking them out amidst his targets. Between both sieges of Corell, nearly one hundred and fifty of the emperor's elite were slain.

"They will pay for this offense, among their many sins!" Kriton hissed, hoisting the bloody pike into the air.

"And whose crown adorns your stake?" Morac asked curiously.

"General Meborn, commander of 3rd Torry Cavalry, if his soldiers spoke true when I flayed their flesh." Kriton had slain Meborn four days prior, having engaged his riders some one hundred leagues north and west of Corell. He lost nearly fifty riders in the clash, with the Torries suffering an equal number. Kriton was forced to fight his way from Besos to the northern approaches of Corell before breaking east, evading enemy magantor patrols and larger cavalry contingents while striking back where he could. When Meborn presented himself, Kriton set an ambush, killing the general and taking his head.

"How many riders have you?"

"Eighty-seven," Kriton hissed. He lost most raiding the Torry countryside during the siege. He managed to pick up a few strays along his retreat eastward but lost more than he gained by the time he reached Morac.

"I have received no word from Notsu. If all is well, we can refurbish your ranks once we arrive," Morac said, knowing they had more than a thousand ocran assigned to protect their supply caravans from Nisin.

"Aye, if all is well." Kriton wondered at that, feeling this campaign cursed and growing worse every passing day.

"What news of the enemy to our rear?" Morac asked, unable to regroup to confront the enemy with his army in tatters.

"Anyone close enough to chance a look are corpses now. Their magantors rule the skies and their cavalry prevent anyone coming near their army."

Morac grimaced at that news, resolved to attain Notsu, consolidate his army and turn back upon the enemy.

* * *

Fifteen leagues west of Notsu.

General Gavis, commander of the 10th Benotrist Legion, rode ahead of his men as the riders approached from the east, bearing the standard of the 11th Benotrist Legion, silver crossed daggers upon a field of black. While the greater part of the 11th Legion was trapped at Besos, and surrendered unbeknownst to Morac, fifteen telnics of the legion were garrisoned at Notsu, protecting the vital hub. General Gavis sent his outriders forward to initiate contact with the approaching riders, confirming their identity before joining them. He was ever wary of imposters drawing close to assassinate him, considering he was the only general in Morac's army still alive. Gavis was constantly wary of Morac's incompetence and subterfuge before the disaster at Corell and doubly so since. Unbeknownst to Morac, Gavis chanced upon a surviving magantor patrol three days after fleeing Corell. He ordered them to split their patrol, sending two warbirds to Notsu informing Governor Daylas of the disaster and to plan accordingly. The remaining warbirds he sent to Fera to inform the emperor of what had transpired and of the sorry state of the legions. Knowing Morac would not be forthright with the emperor, his missive was blunt and direct on the sorry state of things, stating the need for a full withdrawal of the army to their homelands.

General Gavis treated with the emissaries of Governor Daylas. The governor sent five telnics of the 11th Legion to receive them, positioned upon the rise in the road to their direst east, with a series of rolling hills beyond, guarding the approaches of Notsu. Gavis' legion would pass between the ordered ranks straddling each side of the causeway before reforming far to the rear, where provisions were arranged for the beleaguered legion. Governor Daylas ordered enough supplies forward to refurbish sixty thousand soldiers, with more arriving daily. Gavis' legion spent the better part of the day eating, drinking and reoutfitting their ranks with shields, armor and spears as needed before reforming and taking their place beside the five telnics of the 11th, awaiting the 8th and 9th Legions to join them.

By nightfall, Morac and Kriton arrived, leading the remnants of the 9th Legion into camp, followed by the gargoyles, who filtered in throughout the night. The next morn they continued on to Notsu, attaining the city by midday, its broad gates opening to receive them.

* * *

One day hence.
Former estate of Tevlan Nosuc. Morac's headquarters.

Morac stood upon the terrace of his private chambers, looking out over the streets of the dying city, now filled with the battered remnants of his once-proud army. The tallies were still coming in, with the men forming into their former positions in order to give an accurate accounting. Some units had one or even none of their original number whilst others suffered less than ten percent. The decimation was uneven but terribly devastating. Once the full tallies were affirmed, the remaining men would be consolidated into new telnics. Gavis had already consolidated and reorganized his legion, fielding eighteen telnics that were positioned outside the city walls, guarding the western approaches. The general avoided him as much as he was able, the man barely looking at him when they did speak. Morac thought to slay him outright and appoint a general more agreeable to him but couldn't do so without sowing discord, and with the enemy drawing close with untold strength, he could not risk it. By current standing, he guessed the 8th Legion numbered eleven telnics, the 9th thirteen, and the 10th eighteen. Nearly twenty-eight telnics of gargoyles from the 5th and 14th Legions filtered into the city, their numbers swelling every day. He was greeted with further ill tidings upon his arrival, learning of the defeat at Tro and the death of General Krakeni, his remaining telnics having arrived before him from the east, numbering between ten and twelve thousand.

A slave girl hurried forth, offering him a goblet of wine before bowing deeply and withdrawing to his chamber. He didn't even spare her a lecherous glance. He had lost all the girls he had taken to Corell, their whereabouts unknown to him. They were either slain, taken by his enemy, or dragged off by his own love-starved soldiers. Only his lesser stock remained here at Notsu. For once he didn't even care to partake of their offering, his mind consumed with his failure at Corell.

"My Lord Morac," Daylas said, stepping onto the terrace, his arms tucked within the folds of his rich burgundy robes.

"What grim tiding do you bear, Daylas?" Morac asked, not even turning to greet him, his dead eyes staring at nothing in particular as they swept the streets across the city.

"Our magantor scouts have returned," Daylas said, stepping to his side. Upon attaining Notsu, Morac was relived to learn that nearly twelve of their magantors had survived the battle and were currently stabled within the city.

"And what have they discovered?" Morac asked dryly, barely sparing him a glance.

"They have spotted the enemy twenty leagues to our east, a considerable host. They counted at least ten thousand soldiers before being driven off by their warbirds. There are likely many more behind them."

"Good, very good."

"Good, my lord?" Daylas wondered at that.

"If Prince Lorn intends to extend his neck, I shall claim it."

Chapter 9

Headwaters of the Reguh River. West of Nisin Castle.

ZIP!

Thorton's laser struck the Jenaii warrior though the skull, dropping him where he stood upon the riverbank below.

ZIP!

His second shot took another in the center of his chest just as he turned, looking for the source of their ruin. Ben shifted aim, not waiting for the second Jenaii to drop, his third blast finding a human male in the knee, sending him to his side, screaming in pain.

Hunting down the rebels spreading their sedition throughout the empire had brought Ben Thorton to this remote river valley. Since the sack of Gostovar, the regent of Nisin sent his garrison to hunt down the rebels, razing villages with known seditious leanings, taking hostages and removing all unnecessary servants from their palaces and holdfasts. Ben knew the heart of the rebellion was executed by its most mobile factions, likely Jenaii, and was proven correct by chancing upon one of their encampments. Chance poorly described his finding this locale, his logic and pattern recognition leading him here as much as luck. Whenever the rebels entered new territories to begin their insurrection, they first established camps located near a remote and clean water source. The regent of Nisin seemed to always be two steps behind the rebels, putting out fires that were long burning while others sprang across his region, first east before circling back west. Thorton decided to move ahead of the rebels, waiting for them beyond their recent sightings, setting spies all along the Reguh with strict orders to remain out of sight and to report to him if they saw anything. And here he was, standing within a copse of trees atop a steep hill, with a gorgeous field of open ground to the river below, with forest encroaching the far bank of the river, where the rebels set their camp within the trees. He waited all morning for them to expose themselves, stepping to the water's edge to fill their satchels.

ZIP!

He took another through its right wing, the warrior moving back into the tree line of the far bank, trailing blood in its wake. Zelo took aim off his left, firing into their midst, dropping several humans and Jenaii along the river's edge, the rest scrambling back into the wood line. Ben scanned though the trees, spotting their heat signatures through the foliage where their camp was likely set around a small clearing fifty meters from the forest edge. He shifted aim, dropping two more Jenaii before shifting to the humans, targeting them in the knees, wanting them alive, instructing Zelo to do so also. The Jenaii were to be killed outright, the humans taken captive if possible.

Ben lowered his rifle, raising his fist, signaling his men to hold position from where they waited far to his rear. He chose these men carefully, each quiet and professional man trackers. They knew the importance of moving with stealth and quiet, unlike most of the lumbering fools the local proctors and nobles liked to employ. Another cursory search found only the wounded humans strewn along the stream and to the encampment into the wood line. Ben waved his men forward, sending them down the steep hillside to the river below, while he and Zelo scanned for emerging threats. The men moved carefully down the incline, struggling to keep their feet on the wet grassy parts, and watching their footing on the crumbling gravel portion that started halfway down.

ZIP!

Ben blasted the right hand of a wounded man laying upon the far riverbank brandishing a dagger, sending the blade flying from his broken grasp. He howled in pain, his crippled hand matching the hole burned through his left knee as the trackers rushed across the shallow stream. Ben and Zelo watched as they swept ashore on the far bank, making sure of the dead Jenaii, lopping their heads for good measure, before securing the humans, dragging the others in the wood line back to the riverbank.

* * *

Alen winced, his right knee aflame as he tried to crawl away from their camp before he was set upon, feeling a booted sandal pressing his back into the ground. He hooked his arm back and around the offending ankle, sweeping his attacker from his feet. He drew his dagger, jabbing it in the man's ribs as he rolled atop of him, ignoring the pain shooting up his leg. He managed two quick stabs before being dragged off the screaming wretch, his arms pinned behind him. The man he stabbed writhed in pain, cursing him as he was dragged away.

Alen winced, pain shooting up his right leg from his ruined knee as they dragged him back to the river, depositing him roughly on the grassy bank beside five of his comrades, all human. He spared a glance to the bodies of his Jenaii friends strewn along the river's edge, all dead. His heart sank at the ghastly sight. These brave warriors fought beside him since Elos helped him begin their revolt, each mentoring and protecting him throughout. Now they were dead, and with them the greatest hope for their rebellion. Of the original hundred warriors Elos ordered to remain with him, he knew of forty that had perished, the fate of the rest unknown to him as they spread with the revolution. Their commander, however, lay dead not ten paces from Alen, the mighty El Hatu who had guided him like a brother. Alen wept silent tears for his friend before catching sight of Ben Thorton trudging across the stream toward them.

* * *

It didn't take long for Ben to figure out Alen's identity. He suspected the truth when he set eyes on him, recognizing him from their brief interaction at Fera when he escaped with Raven. His interrogation of the others quickly confirmed his suspicion after dragging the truth from them. Alen wondered what gruesome fate awaited him as he was tied over an ocran saddle and led away with the rest of his men. It was late in the day when they eventually stopped to set camp for the night. Ben dragged him away from the others, setting him down beside his separate cookfire before cutting his bonds. He lay there looking across the crackling flames as Ben dropped his saddle on the ground, fishing a few objects from his satchel, setting them aside before taking a seat. Alen drew his head away as Zelo stepped close, exchanging a few words with Ben before returning to the others, ignoring Alen as if he was invisible.

"He won't harm you," Ben said with almost no emotion, taking Alen aback with his indifference.

"He already has." Alen sighed.

"Eat." Ben tossed him a bundle of dried meat, keeping another for himself.

Alen wondered of this gentle treatment, half expecting them to tear parts of him off, yet here he sat with Ben Thorton, staring oddly at each other.

"Don't get foolish ideas with your hands free. You won't get far with your leg ruined, and I don't fancy a knife sticking in my ribs like you did for my associate. He is dead, if you were wondering," Ben said, his bland tone unchanging.

"It is kind of you to free them." Alen was grateful for the respite. His arms were painfully sore from being bound so long.

"I wasn't going to hand-feed you when you can feed yourself. Drink up," Ben said, tossing him a satchel of water.

Ben looked at him for a time, weighing what to do with him. Tyro would want his head on a spike or have him alive to torment to no useful end. His thoughts on the matter were conflicted. The brutality of this world was off-putting, a painful relic of their primitive stage of development. The merciful thing to do was to put this kid out of his misery, but something held him back. It was the same gnawing feeling he had with Ella when he brought her along and removed her family to Tinsay, sparing them enslavement or death, the likely fate of anyone remaining at Tenin.

Ella. He recalled her face when he left her at Nisin, in the keeping of its regent. The man was a brutal tyrant, like most of his ilk, but he would not harm her, not from the frightened look he gave Ben when he reminded him to keep her safe. Many of the Benotrists hated Ben Thorton, and many appreciated him, but they all feared him, and for good reason. He would soon see how safely the regent had kept her when he returned to Nisin.

He noticed Alen doing his best to look elsewhere, unnerved by his intense stare.

"You traveled with Raven for a time. Speak of it," Ben ordered. Ever since Kato's death, Ben thought constantly of his old friend, wondering how Raven would take it once he learned. He doubted Raven would consider his position in the whole affair, but that was beyond him now. As yet, Ben was unaware of the happenings at Tro, the attack on the *Stenox* or the battle of Corell, considering he had spent the past months hunting down Alen in the endless forest of the Benotrist backwaters.

"Why should I tell you?"

"Your travels with Raven have no relevance other than conversation. You can tell me what happened or sit there in silence, bored out of your skull."

"We traveled. Then we separated. Wherever he is now, I could not tell you."

"You traveled all the way to Tro, mostly on ocran after losing your magantors. That seems a very long trip for so little a description."

"We fought our way to freedom and slept under the stars. We suffered rains and wind and hunger at times. It was very difficult."

"What did Raven tell you about us?"

"That you are from a different world, a world free of slavery and cruelty. It is unfortunate you do not help rid our world of such suffering. You only help to continue it."

"Whose suffering are you referring to?"

That Alen would not answer. What purpose would it serve to point out the obvious? But Ben could well guess.

"What would you do to the Benotrists if you held power over them?"

Alen would not answer, guarding his vengeful thoughts.

"Speak freely, Alen. No one will know but you and me, and I won't repeat it."

"By what place do you make such a claim? Why would I trust you?"

"Does it matter? Here you sit, my prisoner, with a bum leg and no means of fighting back. If I wanted, I could torment you in a thousand different ways whether you speak or not."

Alen remained silent, wondering how two men like Raven and Thorton could diverge from being friends to what they were now.

"If you held power over the Benotrists, you would exact revenge equal to your suffering, probably more so. You would kill, torture and enslave them at every turn. Does that sound about right?" Ben could see the truth of it in his eyes.

"They deserve no less," Alen growled. Gone was the frightened slave from Fera. He was a rebel and a leader now, and would not go back to what he was before, no matter how much the fear tried to take him back to that awful time.

"True, they deserve no less. But the point you miss, Alen, is that that was what the Benotrists thought when they overthrew your people. Did they not deserve justice for all the centuries of torment the Menotrists visited on them? Your people have only suffered a generation, perhaps two. If we use the scales of justice, you deserve several hundred more years of enslavement to even things out."

"I never enslaved or tortured anyone. I am not responsible for what my ancestors did!"

"True, but that is the way of your primitive world, is it not? Vengeance follows vengeance, and the wheel goes around."

"You speak in riddles to justify siding with murderers and gargoyles."

"I haven't sided with anyone, Alen; it only appears that way."

"You fight for Tyro, for his cause, not ours," Alen spat.

"I don't expect you to see the larger picture, but I did expect more from you, considering your achievements."

"More riddles, is that your answer for serving Tyro?"

"Slavery and injustice will not end with your victory, Alen. Your victory will only prolong it. Only when one realm conquers all the others and unifies Arax under one banner can true peace begin. It might take years, but eventually slavery will end as civilization advances. It is inevitable. You might think me heartless considering your suffering, but that is the way of your world: someone must lose for another to win. Unfortunately for you, you must lose for history to advance. But just because you must lose, doesn't mean you must suffer."

"My people's suffering is my suffering."

"That's a shame, placing the burdens of an entire people on the shoulders of a young boy. You did much to help them, take solace in that, but as far as this war is concerned, your role in it is over."

With that, Alen sat there in miserable silence, contemplating his fate and that of his people. His thoughts went to his friends in the south, wondering where the path of war led them.

Chapter 10

Fera. The Black Castle.

Nels Draken led the three captives into the throne room, having scoured the bowels of the palace and the nearest holdfasts to find them. They shuffled forth as the massive doors to the chamber opened, their hinges creaking under the weight of their immense timber. Nels left his men in the outer corridor, leading the captives himself. The miserable wretches shuffled forth across the mirrored red stone floor, its shimmering surface akin to a bloody sea. They were chained neck to neck with their hands bound behind them, their naked feet loosely shackled, wearing naught but thin shifts that barely reached their knees. Nels led them by the leash attached to the lead captive, drawing them toward the massive throne where sat the emperor, studying them with a judicious eye.

Tyro sat regally upon his throne, his hands resting on the wide spaced arms of the gold-plated chair, attired in a richly detailed golden robe. Upon his head rested his black heavy crown, its dark surface swallowing any light to shine upon it. Tyro had spent the better part of the morn contemplating the dire state of his armies. The tidings from Tro a fortnight past were poorly received, his displeasure with the attack on the Earthers fueling his internal rage. He and Thorton were explicit that the Earthers and the apes were NOT to be touched and yet that was not communicated to Hossen

Grell, who oversaw the final stage of the attack. He wondered if his grandchildren were aboard. Even if they weren't, the *Stenox* likely survived, and he could only contemplate what that meant for his realm. The tidings from Corell were far graver. Raven decimated his legions while Prince Lorn rallied much of Southern Arax to his cause, if what General Gavis revealed in his missive was true. Even now, Morac's surviving legions were desperately retreating to Notsu. Gavis claimed Morac planned to hold the city from the pursuing armies of Torry, Macon and Jenaii. Complicating matters was the fact that Tro Harbor had endured and thrown the 12th Legion in retreat, while another Earther slew General Krakeni.

The defeat at Corell doomed any hope for Tyro to conquer Arax until a new generation of gargoyles was spawned. Such a thing required time, time his now-strengthened enemies might not give him. His priority now lay in holding his suddenly fragile empire together, a task made difficult with rebellion spreading across the eastern half of his realm. Thorton was given the task of putting down said revolt. Tyro now doubted the wisdom of assigning Ben that task, considering what transpired at Corell. What might have befallen his legions if Thorton was there to balance the scales to their favor? The failure at Corell brought him back to Morac, who was a skilled warrior and cunning tactician but apparently lacked strategic foresight. Morac had led the might of his empire into two devastating defeats, and should things go poorly at Notsu, it would be three. General Gavis was insistent on what needed to transpire to save the empire, bordering on outright sedition with his opinion on the matter. Gavis was irreverent to a fault at times, but his thinking was sound, and considering he was now the only surviving general from Morac's army, he could ill afford to replace him.

While he contemplated what missive to pen for General Gavis, his thoughts shifted to Nels Draken and the prisoners he ushered into the throne room. Looking down from the high view of his throne, Tyro watched as Nels stopped at the base of the dais, ordering the prisoners to their knees before kneeling himself. He had tasked Nels with finding these men, all sentenced to slavery long ago, each gelded, their faces and bodies bearing the distinct shape and glow that followed the cruel procedure. Araxan physiology responded most peculiarly to gelding, often times dramatically feminizing the subject's appearance. Should he feel remorse for the harsh judgement he rendered upon these miserable wretches? Joriah would judge him harshly for his cruelty, but his son was naïve in such things. War and empire required harsh rule, else all he built would crumble to ruin. Soft-headed mercy would only lead to disorder and chaos, which would cause more death and cruelty in their wake. Joriah needed to learn this brutal fact if he was to rule in his place one day. In the meantime, he would curry favor with his son by delivering these men into his hands.

"I see you have found three of the men I sent you to fetch. Where is the fourth?" Tyro asked, remembering the number specifically.

"The one named Toran did not survive his gelding, My Emperor," Nels said.

"I see. Bring them!" Tyro ordered, rising from his throne.

* * *

"What troubles you, my love?" Valera asked, rocking the baby in her arms as she paced the floor of their chamber. Jonas stood at the window, staring off into the distance, his mind elsewhere. She knew when something weighed on his mind by the morose spirit that overtook him. Thankfully such times were few through the years. She recalled one growing season when their farm was beset with a terrible drought. She would find him standing at their window in the dark of night, staring at their dying crops, hoping for rain. She recalled when she birthed Terin and the fearful look he had, knowing the risk childbirth posed for mother and child. There were a few other times, but none that compared to now. He was a man caged, bound by mental chains his father wrapped him in. He could not leave, not without her and Cordela, and yet by remaining, he was forced to watch his father in his current form, a monster of human flesh.

"I am torn, Valera. We need to leave this place but cannot. Should my father prevail, then our homeland is doomed. If he fails, then he is doomed, and should that come to pass, he cannot shield us from his people, for dying men hold no loyalty for anyone." Jonas kept his eyes out the window, his words rending her heart.

"You cannot know what the future holds, Jonas. I believe we are here for a reason. You even said that Yah revealed to you your purpose here, to protect Cordela," she reasoned, lifting the baby toward him, trying to draw him from his somber mood.

"Aye." He turned from the window, smiling as his eyes fell on little Cordela. Since Terin was born, they yearned for another child, their hopes going for naught until now. How strange it was that their great desire was only given them in this foul place. He didn't reveal to her the true source of his dour mood. Something vexed his father; he could sense that in their interactions in recent days. It could be many things. Perhaps it was Tosha or his grandchildren, each a source of concern, or it could be the war. Was Morac defeated? That would explain much, but he couldn't be certain. No matter the cause, it was beyond his control. He trusted Terin's life to Yah and resigned himself to what he could do… protect his wife and daughter.

It was then the captain of his guard announced himself, entering the chamber.

"Your presence is required, by order of the emperor."

* * *

Jonas followed his escort to the arena, where he was greeted by his father, Nels Draken and three captives kneeling in the loose sand, their dispirited eyes trained to the floor. A dozen imperial elite stood guard, forming a circle around the emperor.

"Your Majesty." Jonas greeted his sire formally, keeping their kinship secret, something both men agreed upon. Only a select few knew of Jonas' presence at Fera, and fewer still knew of Valera, who had remained in the royal apartments since her arrival.

"Joriah. You inquired of these men. I give them to you. Do with them as you will," Tyro said, stepping away, the others following him out of the arena save Nels, who remained long enough to offer Jonas the keys to their bonds.

Jonas waited until the chamber emptied before approaching the men, kneeling beside them. He knew his father was certain to be watching from above once he found his way to the viewing stands shrouded by the torchlight bathing the arena below. Jonas wondered what state of mind these men were in, needing some confirmation before he foolishly released them.

"Your names?" he asked, examining their sorry condition. They were clad in loose-fitting shifts, with collars affixed to their slender throats. Their hair was quite long but oddly well combed considering their position.

"Geornon, master," the lead fellow whispered.

"Tarlan, master."

"Safed, master," the last answered.

"I am not your master, but it might be wise for others to believe so for now." Jonas hated for brave men to be broken in this way.

The men remained as they were, their eyes downcast.

"Look up at me, all of you."

They reluctantly obeyed, mindful to be obedient.

"I do not expect any of you to know who I am or to believe anything I say, but we share a common friend, one who was once your commander of unit but escaped this foul place."

"Commander Kenti?" Safed gasped.

"Not too loudly, Safed," Jonas warned, though he smiled that something of the man remained by the hope alit in his eyes.

"Why would the emperor allow a friend of Cronus Kenti to oversee us?" Geornon questioned.

"You will know in time. For now, let us remove your bonds."

Tyro watched from the shadows above, curious with his son's actions. He thought it more merciful for Joriah to cut their throats and be done with it, for what life could these former men ever live again? And yet Joriah bid them to live, instilling hope in them by their demeanor. He did not need to hear what words they shared to know the change in their spirits. Despite what he endured through the years, his son retained a spark of youthfulness that had long escaped him. Tyro wondered when his heart had waxed cold. Was it his own father's ill treatment of himself and his mother's kin, or was it when he lost his beloved Cordela? Joriah had suffered as well, but still retained that vital spark, that deeply-held compassion for his fellow man, a compassion an emperor could not afford to offer. It was all the proof he needed to know Joriah could never be his heir. All his hopes now fell to Cordela.

Chapter 11

They set camp somewhere between Notsu and the Lone Hills, finding a pleasant locale atop a barren hilltop, giving Raven a clear line of sight for miles around. A small copse of trees at the base of the rise afforded them wood for their cookfire, and fish from a nearby stream for their supper. Their two Torry magantor drivers were most grateful for Orlom's unique fishing skill, using his laser pistol to great effect in that regard. The simple effort brought back bitter memories for Tosha, with her giving Raven a dirty look, which he ignored. With the sun dipping below the western sky, Raven stood apart from the fire, scanning in the distance through the scope of his pistol. He spotted nothing but a few lonely chimneys, their smoke billowing in the night air in the distance. He could only imagine how dangerous the lives were of the chimneys' owners here in this neutral ground. The land was constantly beset with raiders, slavers and marauding bandits of every sort. That didn't even count the Gargoyles that took up residence north of there. It took a hardy soul to brave these surroundings, and they would be wise to stay clear of them.

"Find anything of interest?" Tosha asked, stepping to his side, following his line of sight to the distant darkness, wondering what he was seeing.

"I do now." He smiled, lowering his pistol, his eyes now staring at her.

"Out there, dolt!" She slapped his shoulder, though she was secretly pleased with his attention.

"Nothing that I can see. Looks like a quiet place to set camp. Is supper ready?" He sniffed, catching the inviting smell in the air.

"Yes, but don't grow accustomed to me cooking for you like a dutiful wife from the continent." She poked him in the chest to make her point.

"If you do such a fine job, why not?" He holstered his pistol, following her back to the others gathered about the fire.

"I am a princess of two royal lines, it is you who should wait upon me."

"If you're trying to start a fight, don't bother, you'll just lose."

"Truly?" She shook her head, biting off a smile.

"You just like starting trouble. We have had a good thing going these past few days, so don't ruin it, or I'll have to take you over my knee like in the old days."

"Promise?" She smiled at that.

"Stinker." He stopped, turning her into his arms, crushing his lips to hers.

She wrapped her arms around his thick shoulders, returning his fervor two-fold, wondering how far she had to push him to gain the desired reaction. There they kissed under the pale moonlight atop the barren hilltop, savoring each other's embrace. Raven for once didn't say anything stupid when they pulled apart, taking their seats on their packs before helping themselves to generous portions of their supper.

"How much farther to Tro?" Orlom asked Commander Juron, their lead driver for this expedition. Juron was a commander of flax specifically selected for this assignment by General Dar Valen to deliver them safely to Tro.

"I estimate two to three days to the coast and another day or two north to Tro, if the weather is clear," Juron said, sitting atop his bedroll on the opposite side of the fire to Raven and Tosha with Orlom to his right and his fellow Torry driver, Hedron, to his left.

"How badly is the harbor beset?" Tosha asked, looking to each of them for the answer, though the Torries knew as little as she did.

"From Zem's last message, it sounds like the port is secure, but it was pretty messed up when we left," Raven said, stuffing another piece of fish in his mouth, pulling a few bones out with his fingers.

Tosha wondered how she would be received at Tro considering she was Tyro's daughter. She wished she could go back in time, beseeching her father to turn from this folly. Peace would have spared so much suffering, so much loss. She had never thought this way before, feeling guilt over her father's actions. What changed to bring this about? Was it natural maturing, or something else? Or was it the man who sat beside her? She looked over to her husband, who sat there stuffing his mouth, wondering what brought them together to begin with? She couldn't explain it, but knew she couldn't live without him. Orlom didn't miss the look she was giving Raven.

"Kiss him. Boss likes it when you do that!" Orlom grinned, causing her to blush in embarrassment.

No, she would not be embarrassed like a young girl. She was Tosha, daughter of Letha and Tyro, and would act as she pleased, and kissed Raven again.

* * *

Four days hence.

She clung to him, wrapping her arms around his back as they soared through the air, following the coastline north, the afternoon sun lighting the left side of her face. Their driver, Commander Juron, pushed on, skillfully guiding their magantor with practiced ease, dropping below a flock of soren coming straight at them. Hedron followed his lead, with Orlom sitting behind him, grinning like a fool. They swept low over the ocean, the smell of salty air hitting their nostrils as they kissed the lapping waves before rising again, soaring high above the surf.

Tosha pressed her left cheek to Raven's back, looking out to sea, the endless expanse disappearing into the horizon. It was the first time she saw the ocean of the east coast, its breathtaking beauty as beguiling as the western sea, dangerous and beautiful. What mysteries waited beyond? Had any sailor traveled far beyond the known world? If they had, none returned, lost to whatever fate Yah consigned them. Yah, that name resurfaced with her every thought, his spirit taking hold of her since that night in her mother's throne room where his great power manifested through Terin, great and terrible and overwhelming. Every member of the court beheld the glory of Yah that night, and it forever changed them, and she was no different. Looking out across the sea reminded her of how insignificant she was before the majesty of creation, humbling her in way that nothing else could. It also reminded her of her own mortality, and that time was precious and fleeting, time she wanted to spend with the man she loved.

"There it is." Raven's voice sounded in the wind.

She peaked around his shoulder, seeing the walls of Tro along the horizon. Within moments more of the harbor took shape, from its towering stone edifices lining its southern bay to the sentinel guarding the center of the harbor, its sword outstretched toward the sea. The scene was breathtaking from these heights, with the Flen River bridge connecting the two halves of the city to the west, to the mouth of the harbor to the east, where stood the watchtowers of the city. The shores were still littered with the wrecks of sunken ships, debris still floating with the current. Blackened remains of burnt-out dwellings dotted the city, like jagged scars. Great funeral pyres were alit outside the city walls, concentrated in the west, where gargoyle corpses were gathered and set ablaze, smoke from the fires still lingering. It was but another of her father's failures, another of his legions decimated for little gain.

They passed over the city walls, greeted by Troan magantors midflight, who received them, escorting them to the stone wharves of the southern shore, where stood the city magistrate building. Raven breathed a sigh of relief seeing his beloved ship speeding from the center of the bay to meet them where they set down.

* * *

"It's about time." Brokov shook his head, sitting the helmsman chair, staring through the forward viewport as they neared the wharves.

"His mission was successful," Argos bluntly stated the obvious, standing at his side with his large forearms crossed, observing Raven and Orlom disembark from their magantors.

"Mostly, but still no sign of Ben, if the reports are accurate," Brokov said, recalling the latest missive sent from Corell, detailing the breaking of the siege, and the events that followed. That was only three days past, and now Raven arrived, hopefully to confirm the veracity of that report.

"It must be mostly true if he is here and not there," Argos reasoned.

"You're applying logic, but it's Raven we are talking about. Lorken?" Brokov raised him on the comm.

"*Go ahead!*" Lorken answered back, sitting in the engineering room with Kendra at his side, the four of them the only crew aboard.

"I'm pulling up to the wharf in the next 74 seconds. Remain below until they come aboard." Brokov didn't want to risk every Earther exposed above deck should something happen, the attack on the *Stenox* making them extremely cautious.

"*Will do,*" Lorken said, bringing up the view of the wharf on his screen, smiling at the sight of Tosha standing beside Raven, wondering how they came together.

"Is that..." Kendra began to ask, looking over his shoulder at the screen.

"Yes. True love is a beautiful thing." Lorken laughed hard enough to choke, then laughed some more.

* * *

They no sooner stood foot on the wharf than were beset by a small army of Troan soldiers, apes and dignitaries of all sorts, spilling out of the magistrate behind them, while the *Stenox* closed in front, its bluish-sliver hull coming to rest beside the stone lip of the wharf. Their Troan escort set down beside them along the pier while dozens of apes hurried ahead of the Troan guards, flooding all around them. Tosha froze in place, dismayed by the gorillas' overzealous reception, many of them mugging Raven and Orlom with bone-breaking hugs and slaps on their backs. She was taken aback by a rather large gorilla, bearing the rank of admiral, embracing Raven most vigorously, before turning his attention to her after Raven pointed her out.

"Lady Raven!" Admiral Zorgon bellowed, lifting her into the air like a straw doll, his declaration causing a hush over the gathering crowd. When he set her down, nearly every gorilla seemed to greet her at once, her legend preceding her, much to her surprise.

"Raven?" She lifted a concerned brow, wondering the source for the rumored tales of their courtship. The apes, led by Zorgon, asked of her the trials she set for Raven and the chase across the Benotrist realm, ending at Axenville.

Raven simply shrugged, as if telling her to accept their praise as a good thing, while she was mugged by her adoring admirers. Raven caught sight of Klen Adine, magistrate of Tro, making his way through the crowd, visibly annoyed having to do so, his guards hopelessly separated from him.

"You survived, I see," Klen said, the surrounding apes giving him barely enough room to stand unmolested.

"How much do you know?" Raven wondered.

"The barest of essentials. I think it best if we spoke someplace less… teeming," Klen said, his voice nearly drowned in the sea of booming voices.

"Aboard your ship would be best," Admiral Zorgon advised, pointing over his shoulder where Brokov and Argos emerged from the bridge, standing on the second deck, waiting for them to board.

* * *

They gathered in the dining chamber of the first deck, the crew surprised to find Tosha among the arrivals, greeting her warmly, and asking how she came to be in Raven's company. Admiral Zorgon and Klen Adine joined their impromptu meeting, listening as Raven and Orlom explained the events at Corell and the actions that followed, including Besos and the advance upon Notsu led by Lorn, El Anthar and King Mortus. Raven placed his broken rifle on the table, its core burned out when he devastated Morac's legions.

"No sign of Ben?" Brokov asked, picking up the rifle to examine it before setting it aside. He might be able to restore it, but it was low on their list of priorities.

"No. That part makes the least sense, considering the importance of the battle." Raven sighed.

"Could he…" Lorken began to ask.

"Could he what?" Raven asked.

"…be dead?"

"I thought about that, but the Torries found several of Morac's slave girls, and one of them claimed to have seen him at Notsu. She seemed to believe Ben gave the rifle they used to bomb us to agents of Morac with orders to use it on the forum of Tro, not us. She claims he ordered them to delay any attack if we were present, if you can believe her." Raven shook his head.

"That would make sense, but the die is cast. Ben chose his side, and we aren't it," Lorken said.

"The die was cast with Kato." Raven sighed.

"Your Highness, what brings you to our port city?" Klen asked of Tosha, as Raven had not yet mentioned her arrival at Corell before joining him here.

"The Sisterhood is at war with my father. As Second Guardian of the realm, it is my duty to answer the call to arms."

"I see," Klen stated evenly, knowing the delicate balance she was forced to navigate with her mother on one side and her father the other. He sympathized, considering his task of balancing the interests of the five ruling families.

"Where is Zem?" Raven asked, not noticing him anywhere onboard.

"*General* Zem is currently at Gotto, liberating the city from the gargoyles." Lorken couldn't help smile, emphasizing their friend's rank.

"All by himself?" Raven wondered.

"With nearly six thousand Troan and gorilla warriors, nearly my entire command," Admiral Zorgon said.

"And nearly all of mine," Klen added.

"Then why aren't you with him?" Raven asked.

"The general seems to have the situation well in hand, while we have overseen the reinforcements that seem to arrive daily," Zorgon explained.

"Reinforcements?" Tosha asked.

"Yes. Since word spread of the attack, fresh levies have been raised throughout eastern Arax, especially the Ape Republic. President Matuzak has ordered every merchant ship north, each bearing as many soldiers as it can carry. We've already gathered nearly four thousand warriors of the 2nd Ape Army, each arriving in groups of fifty or more. General Mocvoran is expected in the coming days. An equal number of ships are bringing needed provisions. Two days ago, we received a complement of Casian warriors and ten ships of the 2nd Casian Fleet. They bring word of the Casian League declaring war upon Nayboria and the Benotrist Empire as well. We expect the entire 2nd Casian Fleet to join us soon, along with the 2nd Ape Fleet and numerous units from Enoructa," Klen explained.

"Their arrival freed up the forces guarding the harbor to retake Gotto, led by their newly commissioned general, Zem the Magnificent," Lorken added in good humor.

"The magnificent?" Raven asked, hoping that part wasn't true.

"That's what we call him when his back is turned. Afraid if we told him to his face he would add that moniker to his growing list of accolades." Lorken laughed.

"I'm gone just a little while and the whole world goes insane." Raven shook his head.

"Don't flatter yourself, Rav, you couldn't have prevented all this had you been here. Once Zem sets his mind on something, no one can convince him otherwise, and the apes feeding him praise sure doesn't help curbing his ego," Brokov added.

"Zem is a fine fellow and deserves my naming him general," Admiral Zorgon said in Zem's defense.

"I hope you know what you're doing, Admiral. If you knew Zem like we do, you'd know this will all go to his head," Raven said.

"It shouldn't matter much longer if the reports we have been receiving are accurate," Brokov said.

"What reports?" Raven asked.

"Gotto sounds like it will be easily taken. Most of the gargoyles fled the city, continuing west toward Notsu. Zem was to return here once the city was secured. Once reinforcements arrive here, the plan is for them to march in force upon Notsu from the east while King Lorn and his armies close from the west. Once Zem returns, we have more pressing matters to attend, matters requiring all of us to participate," Brokov explained.

"What matters are those?" Raven didn't like the sound of that, Brokov's silence only fueling his angst.

"Tell him," Lorken said.

"Tell me what?"

"The *Stenox* needs repairs I cannot complete here," Brokov said.

"What's wrong with her?"

"It's not holding a full charge, and I need to upgrade its protection, and there is only one place we can do that."

"That's a long way off. You sure we can make it?" Raven asked.

"Hopefully." Brokov shrugged.

"That's not reassuring," Tosha said, wondering where they were referring.

"Hope you're right. I don't want to be stuck adrift in the middle of the ocean. How's the weather look? That is the other factor that might screw us up," Raven asked.

"Take a look outside and you can guess as well as I."

"Your weather forecaster is still down?" Raven didn't like the sound of that.

"It would be easier to say which parts of the ship are currently working, than those that are not. Our heavy lasers keep cutting out, long range communications are down, and the air ski and disc observation platforms are still not working. Internal comms are back, and so is the hot water, so you can take a shower, since it smells as if you could use one." Brokov fanned his nose with his hand, making a face.

"I managed to take a bath or two while at Corell, but that wasn't high on my priorities, if you hadn't heard." Raven gave him a not-so-gentle shove.

"Raven!" Tosha scolded his brutish behavior, not approving his boyish antics.

"Yes, Raven, listen to your wife." Lorken chuckled, before Raven gave him a shove as well.

Klen decided to clear his throat, returning the conversation to its proper place.

"I assume you shall undertake this mission once Zem returns from Gotto. While you are away, I shall establish proper communications with King Lorn and his allies to coordinate our eventual advance upon Notsu," Klen said.

"Makes sense. When we return, our first priority will be to clear the eastern coast of the Benotrist navy. Speaking of that, whatever happened to the fleet you spotted heading in this direction?" Raven asked Lorken.

"We managed to slip outside the harbor and sink several of their leading vessels before our heavier lasers malfunctioned. Luckily, that was enough to send them in retreat. The latest reports place them eighty leagues north of here," Lorken explained.

"And that is why we need to give the ship a complete overhaul," Brokov added.

"Then get word to Zem so we can get underway," Raven said.

* * *

"Just where is this place we are going?" Tosha asked, following Raven through the ship to the weapons room.

"We? You aren't going. I'll have Commander Juron take you to Torn, where you can look after our boys," he said, passing into the room, checking over the control panels throughout the cabin, trying to determine what was working from what wasn't when Tosha grabbed him by his jacket collar, turning him around.

"I didn't follow you all the way from Corell for you to send me to nursemaid our children. I'm coming with you, wherever we are going, do you understand?" she growled.

He pried her fingers off his jacket, pushing her back while holding her shoulders.

"There is an island far to the east, way out in the middle of the ocean. It's where we landed when we arrived on Arax. Crashed is probably more accurate than landed, but there you have it. It is on that island that we constructed the *Stenox* from the wreckage of our space vessel. The island is not large and is uninhabited, other than whatever critters call it home. We constructed a makeshift operation base there and repair facilities, which is why we need to go back. The problem is if our power cuts out along the way. We would be stuck in the middle of nowhere, trying to reboot the ship. Now, do you really want to risk our kids being orphans if we are both out there?"

"This is war, Raven, there are no guarantees. I could just as easily die flying a magantor on my journey to Torn as I would with you. I'm coming with you."

"Women." He shook his head.

"Men." She shook hers.

* * *

They waited five days for Zem, who returned to much fanfare upon entering Tro. The entire city seemed to empty into streets as he entered the west gate, marching along the Tel-Ro, passing over the Flen River Bridge, making his way to the city forum, leading a small host of ape and Troan warriors. Zem greeted the cheering throngs with an upraised hand, waving awkwardly as he walked.

"ZEM!" the people chanted, lining the avenues adorned in their finest raiment, men in rich robes or tunics with capes, and women in flowing gowns of varied hues. Small children peeked around their parents' legs, stealing glances at the powerful stranger. The Earthers, once feared as barbaric ruffians, were now heralded as heroes and saviors of the city, and none more than Zem.

"GENERAL ZEM!" others shouted, their chants picked up by crowds further along the route, reverberating in deafening chants throughout the harbor. A small host of Troan cavalry preceded them, clearing their path as they neared the central district, where Klen Adine and members of the ruling families gathered upon the steps of the forum to receive them. Docked along the adjoining pier sat the

Stenox, where his crewmates gathered along the second deck stern, watching the entire ceremony unfold.

Joining the ruling families were Admiral Zorgon, and many prominent families of Gotto, who fled the city when the 12th Gargoyle Legion invaded. They were now pleased to learn of its liberation, though much of their wealth was destroyed in the gargoyles' wake. Klen observed the apes following Zem with straps wound around their shoulders, bearing the skulls of gargoyles they had slain, one warrior boasting twelve of the grisly trophies. In days past, such a sight would be frowned upon, but now was cheered by all. He noticed several of the Troan soldiers similarly adorned, taking after their ape allies. The ruling patriarchs of Tro stood beside him to receive Zem, each pleased, evident by the smiles painting their collective faces, including Ortus Maiyan and Marcus Talana.

Zem paused at the base of the forum, turning back to the crowd gathering in the street where he passed, pounding his fist to his chest to honor their kind reception. His gesture caused them to cheer even louder. He then ascended the steps to the forum, with the crowd cheering his name.

"Welcome, General Zem!" Klen greeted him formally, his voice carrying above the chanting throng.

"Magistrate Adine, Admiral Zorgon, and esteemed members of the cities of Tro and Gotto, I stand before you to report a great reduction of the 12th Legion and the liberation of Gotto. Our combined armies hold the city and await reinforcements for the advance upon Notsu in the coming moons. Victory!" he said with his booming voice, his declaration repeated by the assemblage in a deafening chorus.

Zem followed Klen and the others into the forum, giving them a thoroughly detailed report of all the actions at Gotto and the state of the army he left in place under the command of Commander Balkar, the Troan garrison commander. They would soon be joined by steady reinforcements that were arriving daily.

* * *

It was late in the evening when Zem finally boarded the *Stenox*, stepping onto the bridge where Raven and Lorken were waiting for him.

"It's about time you decided to join us. Were you held up by your adoring fans?" Raven said, leaning against the captain's chair with his arms crossed.

"I was providing Klen and the ruling patriarchs my detailed report on the events at Gotto. I assume you have completed your official account on the actions at Corell?" Zem asked, stepping beside him with his own arms crossed while Lorken leaned against the helm, watching the exchange.

"Reports? Who has time for that nonsense. We have places to be other than kissing up to the locals, *General Zem*." He shook his head.

"Time? You were at Corell for three standard Earth months. Your days of active combat that you participated in were significantly less. It was your duty to detail the events for Araxan posterity and our own archives. Instead, we are forced to believe second hand accounts from other sources, and your recollections, which will only deteriorate as you quickly age. It is unacceptable," Zem stated firmly.

"What are you laughing at?" Raven gave Lorken a dark look, who stood there with a stupid grin on his face.

"You two sound like a couple of cranky old men bitching about the weather." Lorken shook his head.

"Maybe these cranky old men will toss you overboard," Raven said.

"It would be a prudent action," Zem agreed.

"That's the first thing the two of you ever agreed on." Lorken shrugged.

"That's not true, we agree on a lot of things, like you being an idiot and Brokov being a moron," Raven said.

"Yes, that would be a fair summation." Zem nodded.

"You know, the *Stenox* was a nice quiet place with you two away." Lorken shook his head.

* * *

They set sail the next morn, heading east by southeast. By midday, the entire crew grew tired of Zem's constant rehashing of the events at Gotto and his brilliance of command, all except Argos and Orlom, who looked to Zem with the deepest admiration. Tosha and Kendra spent most of the first two days out of port honing their fighting skills, using blunted swords and daggers Kendra stored on board, continuing their sparring they began at Bansoch. Brokov managed to restore limited weather diagnosis, giving them clear skies for the next two days, which would bring them one day short of their destination.

Lorken sat the helm, his eyes fixed to the homing beacon alit on his console, thankful that he and Brokov brought it back online. It guided them to the isle, where they set its anchor point when they first arrived on Arax. For all other navigation, they relied on the digital map the *Stenox's* archives formatted as they explored, its accuracy enhanced with every time they circumnavigated the main continent. Unfortunately, they were still blind to the other continents, which would be explored at a latter time, if they survived the war at hand.

"How's it look?" Raven asked, sitting the captain's chair, his gaze fixed to the horizon.

"The beacon still looks strong after all this time. I just hope our docking facilities are still there. You never know when a freak storm or cyclone pops up and smashes everything to bits, especially these small islands in the middle of nowhere."

"Other than a violent storm surge, I don't see anything damaging it. It was masterfully done and will probably last a thousand years."

"Was that a compliment?" Lorken craned his neck, looking back at him.

"Don't get a big head."

"Don't worry about that, you and Zem have the market cornered in that regard."

"Are you kidding, I'm a humble little dove next to him. Do you see how he lights up every time he mentions his new rank?"

"Of course he lights up, he's an android."

"Don't call him that, or we'll get a ten-hour lecture on our insensitivity. Remember last time?"

"Don't remind me. If I have to hear him drone on about the

superiority of enhanced artificial lifeforms over organic one more time, I'll jump overboard and be done with it."

"You're not getting out of it that easy. If I have to listen to him for the rest of our stay here, so do you."

"Misery loves company."

"Yep, and remind me to kill my brother if we ever get off this rock," Raven said, referencing his brother Matt, who led the research team that created Zem.

"You'll have to get in line. Brokov and me got first dibs."

"Maybe we'll get lucky, and he'll fall overboard on our way back."

"No, he'd just walk along the ocean floor until he came back on land and then spend the next ten years telling us of his impressive exploits."

* * *

The good weather and calm seas continued, with a tropical rain on the fourth evening the only interruption to their clear skies. It was the afternoon of the fifth day that found Tosha and Kendra standing atop the third deck, looking out over the aqua blue ocean, staring in wonder as the island graced the horizon. A flock of soren coursed overhead, their gentle squawks sounding off the lapping waves. The isle itself rose wondrously, with two impressive peaks jutting above a center isle, with a flat atoll circling the island and its surrounding lagoon. Grassy reeds covered the surrounding atoll, their green stalks bending to the breeze as the *Stenox* drew near.

"It is beautiful," Kendra sighed, the light green of the atoll contrasting the clear water of aqua blue. Looking over the ship's side, one could see straight to the bottom of the sea, tropical fish in a hundred different hues swimming in every direction.

"Breathtakingly so," Tosha agreed, her gaze drawn to the large isle in the center of the lagoon, rising impressively above the surrounding atoll. Two large peaks rose upon each end of the isle, that ran north to south, the larger resting at the isle's north end, towering sixteen hundred feet above the surface. Both peaks were gray stone covered with patches of green vegetation clinging to their jagged surface. Surrounding each peak was a tropical forest, running the length of the ridge connecting the high points, with swaying Frologs at the water's edge, their long-bladed leaves rippling in the breeze.

They wondered where they would enter the lagoon as the atoll continued in a wide arc south and west, before coming upon a large opening along the southwest corner, the ship passing within the protective barrier, the lapping waves easing upon entering the tranquil water. The ship turned back northeast, traversing the lagoon, heading toward a small bay under the shadow of the north peak, where rested a small cove with a strange structure sitting beside a long bluish silver wharf, matching the hue of the *Stenox*. This was the Earthers' home port, no doubt, its strange mystery calling to Tosha like a siren's refrain, her mind pregnant with curiosity.

"*How's the view up there?*" Brokov's voice sounded through the ship's comm on the console affixed to the low wall of the deck. Their long range and portable comms were still down, something Brokov intended to soon rectify.

"Quite lovely, but would be greatly enhanced if you could join me," Kendra said.

"*I would love to, but someone has to safely guide us to port.*"

"Fair enough, handsome, I'll see you when we dock."

Kendra smiled, thinking of him, as they drew nearer their destination, the ship easing its speed as the cove came swiftly upon them. They eased alongside the wharf, its strange surface appearing unaffected by its lack of upkeep, its surface resplendent in the midday sun. The ship came to rest before dropping anchor, the others soon emptying out of the lower decks.

"What do you think?" Tosha heard Raven ask, standing on the stern of the second deck, looking up at her.

"A fine location," she said, sparing a glance alongside the wharf, where rose a structure twice the length of the ship and of greater height, made of the same material as the wharf and the *Stenox*, its murky bluish-silver exterior matching their hue.

"A fine location? This place is paradise. Come on down and we'll give you a tour."

BENJAMIN SANFORD

* * *

Tosha followed Raven through the adjoining structure, its outer shell concealing a vast open-floored edifice with a myriad of strange equipment lining its walls or placed in the middle of the floor. It strangely illuminated upon their entrance, like the lighting of the *Stenox*. He explained that each item therein performed differing tasks, from repairing the ship to maintaining the structure. The power source for this structure escaped her, his explanation leaving much to be desired. She assumed Kendra would be given a more thorough instruction from Brokov, who was still aboard the *Stenox*, running a final diagnostic before coming ashore. Orlom and Argos joined their little expedition, listening attentively to Raven's rudimentary explanation. They exited the rear of the building, finding an open area to their right, with a golden sand beach, much of it shaded by swaying frolog trees encroaching the shore. Raven led them straight ahead, following a stone pathway into the forest, with vegetation encroaching its sides, where the foliage pressed its advance in their long absence. The trail rose quickly in elevation, coming upon an open area along the right where rested the massive remains of a strange vessel, nearly two hundred meters in length, its outer shell emitting a strange murky black surface. The vessel was broken in several places, the obvious remains of their star craft.

Was this what they arrived on their world upon? she asked herself. Orlom immediately wanted to explore this strange new wonder, but she thought otherwise, noticing Raven staring sadly at the wreckage. Much of the open area bore the scars of the vessel landing in its midst, trees and foliage blasted away at the root all around its crash site. Raven stepped away, walking toward a small row of raised flat markers resting beside the wreckage. Each marker was constructed of similar material as the star vessel. Following Raven, she noticed that each marker was nearly three feet in height, and two wide, with the likeness of a different person engraved upon each one. The faces seemed carved from stone until Raven squatted before the one in particular, pressing his hand upon the likeness. The image suddenly came to life, its features glowing with color and detail as it spoke.

THE CHRONICLES OF ARAX

"*I am Colonel Chang, ranking military officer of the Eden expedition, of the Earth Space Fleet vessel Magellan XXI, sharing joint command with Javier Flores of the DES...*" the likeness of the dead colonel continued briefly as Raven pulled his hand away, giving details of his background and record, continuing with the status of the expedition, which would have concluded with the last report before his untimely death, but the image faded to stone before it could do so.

"What is this place?" she asked.

"A graveyard," he said, gaining his feet, his steely gaze sweeping the surrounding markers.

Then it struck her, these were his fallen comrades who died coming to her world. There were so many, twelve in all, each as unique and impressive as those that survived, perhaps more so as she would learn. These represented the finest of Earth's scientists and explorers. How did so many die while the others lived? More pertinent, how did they die and Raven survive? She looked at him briefly, realizing how close he came to death just coming here, before looking back to the markers. She stepped to the next one, pressing her hand upon the stone carved face that came alive at her touch.

"*I am Javier Flores, civilian rank C-19, assistant director of the Department of Exploration and Settlement. Our journey to this date has been...*" She listened as he detailed their journey, with little of note, as most of the answers she sought came after these memoirs. Tosha continued down the line, listening to the archives of the dead people, before coming upon a strikingly beautiful woman with intelligent green eyes and dark hair, Dr. Rebeca York. It was disconcerting to know that Raven travelled with women of such beauty.

She shook the covetous thought from her head, chiding herself for being jealous of a dead woman.

Orlom and Argos didn't have to ask who these people were, each bowing their head to honor the fallen.

* * *

Tosha was thankful when they continued along the trail, walking another one hundred meters before coming upon an impressive domicile built into the hillside, with walls and graded roof made of the same material as the *Stenox*. The structure seemed to meld with the surrounding greenery and rock, blending perfectly with the environment. Entering the structure, she was taken aback by its vast open floor plan, with a series of comfortable looking chairs forming a semi circle off her right, and what Raven described as a kitchen straight ahead, with an open counter overlooking the great room. Several corridors broke off in different directions, leading to several bedchambers and other rooms she would come to learn.

"Our room is that last one on the left, that way." Raven directed her to the corridor off their left, before directing Orlom and Argos to their chambers along the opposite corridor.

Tosha spent the day settling in, taken aback by the convenience and wonder of the large domicile. Whenever she entered a room, it would automatically illuminate. Raven showed her how to use the bathing facilities, she relishing the exotic luxury that seemed so trivial to the Earthers. Each bedchamber had its own facility, with one for communal use in the great room. She recalled how impressed she was with the bathing unit on the *Stenox*, but these units put that to shame. The bed in Raven's chamber was unusually large, and resting upon it felt heavenly. She wondered if this is how the common people of Earth lived. If so, no wonder they were so unimpressed by her royal station. They lived better than kings.

Raven greeted her as she stepped from the bathing chamber with only a towel protecting her naked flesh, which she shamelessly flaunted for his approval.

"I laid out some things that might fit you." He waved an open hand to the bed, where rested numerous garments, including a shimmering silver gown, which she ran her fingers over, amazed with its soft, luxurious texture.

"Where did you find these?" she wondered, seeing a varied array of outfits, from black trousers and shirt like he was wearing to a brief garment he described as a bathing suit, with long sleeves and a bikini bottom that would run unseemly high on her hips. Of course, he would like that, giving her an encouraging look.

"This is for the water I assume. So, what attire shall you be wearing for the occasion?" she challenged.

"Swimming trunks. We'll take a swim tomorrow after most of the work is complete." Once Brokov repaired the core of the *Stenox*, it would require forty hours to fully energize.

"Trunks?" She made a face, wondering what he was referring.

"Short trousers intended for swimming. You'll see in the morning," he explained.

"You have aroused my curiosity." She let the towel drop to the floor, coming into his arms, kissing him fiercely.

"If my swimming trunks rouse your interest, wait until supper." He smiled as their lips briefly parted.

"Supper?"

"Lorken's cooking tonight. We have some Mahi-like fish we caught that we placed in long-term storage. It should still be good. That, and a wide array of vegetables, and drinks. Maybe even treat you to a little entertainment from home," he said, wondering which of their holo videos he should pick out for their viewing pleasure.

"There is only one entertainment that interests me at this moment." She smiled lasciviously, pushing him toward the bed.

* * *

"That should about do it," Brokov grunted, closing the control panel in the engineering room.

"How long before it reaches full capacity, and how soon until we know it will hold?" Kendra asked. They spent the better part of the day refurbishing the ship's core, making countless trips to the docking structure beside the wharf. She was amazed at how much she had learned by helping him, accumulating more knowledge in the brief time she spent with the Earthers than ten thousand mystics and wisemen had learned in the last two thousand years on Arax.

"Forty hours for full capacity. As far as if it will work, I can determine that right now," he said, taking a seat at the console, running through a series of tests. After a few moments he gave her that infectious grin that waylaid her fears.

"So, now we wait," she said in a way to suggest they find other ways to pass the time.

"Yes, but not time wasted. Now we can do the fun stuff," he said excitedly.

"Yes." She smiled, looking to partake in the pleasures of this tropical paradise.

"First thing is to reboot the observation program. I need to replace four of the discs that fell out of the sky when we were attacked. Then I need to repair the air ski and take a look at Raven's broken rifle. Then I can move on to new projects I've been dying to implement, especially the energy shield to prevent what happened at Tro from ever working again," he explained, before noticing she did not share his enthusiasm.

"Those things sound nice, but I think we deserve a little time to rest and partake the luxuries of your isle." She leaned close, pressing her forehead to his after turning his chair to face her.

Her intention finally dawned on him, scolding himself for being as dense as Raven. He quickly gained his feet, sweeping her into his arms.

"Your father is dead."

"What?" She made a face, wondering why he would say that and ruin this moment.

"My family might as well be dead, being so far away, and I doubt they shall ever find us."

"Is there something you are trying to say? Whatever it is, you are doing a poor job of it."

"Sorry." He shook his head, proving he was as dense as Raven ever was. "We are beholden to no one but ourselves."

"True." She tilted her head inquisitively, wondering where this was going.

"I like you."

"And I like you." She made a face.

"Marry me."

"Marry?"

"Yes, marry me, here, tonight. What better place to wed? We can have the ceremony here on the ship. We can have an Earth wedding, and forgive me for saying this, but Raven can oversee it as he is the captain." He winced, dreading the thought of Raven performing that task.

"What authority does Raven have in that regard?" she asked, skipping over the more important part of his proposal.

"On Earth, ship captains have the authority to oversee weddings, and since we are here, and Raven is available, let's do it."

"Tonight?"

"Why not, Kendra? If I have learned anything from Kato and Leanna, it's that life is too short and precious to waste the opportunity to be with the one you love."

"You love me?" She smiled.

"I do."

"Very well then, Grigory Borovkov, I shall wed you."

* * *

They gathered on the stern of the first deck as the sun kissed the western horizon, its wanning rays reflecting off the waters of the lagoon. Tosha stood beside her, dressed in the shimmering gown gifted to her from Raven, its long sleeves and high neck contrasting the brevity of its skirt. Kendra was similarly attired, wearing a white gown with billowy sleeves and flowing skirts. Lorken stood beside Brokov, each attired in their uniform black jacket, plain shirts and trousers, the same as Raven, who faced them standing at the stern rail, while Zem, Argos and Orlom waited behind the bride and groom, witnessing the ceremony.

"It is a time-held tradition for ship captains to oversee wedding ceremonies, the tradition going back many centuries," Raven began.

"Get on with it, Rav," Brokov said, knowing his friend would try to impress them with his knowledge of such things, but they all knew he had just read all that from the ship's archive an hour before.

"Alright, I'll give the abbreviated version. As captain of the *Stenox*, I ask of you, Brokov, do you take this woman to be your wife?"

"I do."

"And do you, Kendra, take this man to be your husband?"

"I do."

"Then as the captain, I pronounce you husband and wife. Go ahead and kiss her."

There upon the *Stenox*, on the remote tropical isle, Grigory Borovkov of Arkhangelsk kissed his wife, Kendra Sarn.

* * *

After the ceremony, they moved to the domicile, where the crew treated the newlyweds to the meal Lorken prepared, which exceeded Tosha's expectations, from how Raven poorly described it. Kendra was taken aback by the luxury of the place, wondering how it retained such cleanliness with their long absence. The entire layout was far different from the confined space of the *Stenox*, where they couldn't help but encroach upon each other. This, however, had all the trappings of a royal palace, combined with a privateness that could only be found in the remote places of the world.

"Is this how all Earth people live?" Kendra asked as they gathered around the dining table to eat.

"What do you mean?" Brokov asked, sitting beside her.

"The convenience, opulence, and size of these living quarters," Tosha added, sitting across from them.

"This is the standard home on Earth or its colonies. Space is limited when aboard space vessels and ships like the *Stenox*," Brokov explained.

"Everyone on Earth lives like this?" Kendra asked in surprise. Neither she or Tosha considered such things since they were easy to overlook compared to the wonder of the *Stenox* and its crew.

"Most do, though with fewer bedrooms, or bedchambers, as you call them. We have six here, one for each of us when we landed," Brokov explained, with Argos staying in Ben's room, and Orlom in Kato's.

"Our food is another thing you would consider a luxury. On Earth, we can easily move good and exotic delicacies all around the world and think nothing of it. On Arax, you are limited to whatever is grown locally or whatever you can preserve and move to market,"

Lorken added, the speed of transporting goods making all the difference.

They continued eating and sharing stories until Brokov gained his feet, drawing his bride to the middle of the floor of the great room.

"Might I have this dance?" He smiled, drawing her into his arms.

"Dance?" She made a face. Dancing was not something either of them ever entertained.

"I think we can manage it just this once on our wedding day. Zem, can you initiate the music program?"

"I can do that," Zem said, rising from the table, finding the control along the side wall for the music, while dimming the lights.

"And not *Anchors Aweigh*," Brokov reminded him, causing a sour look on Zem's face.

"Perhaps one of Kato's preferences." Kendra recalled fancying everything their fallen comrade favored.

They swayed in each other's arms as the first melody played, a soothing ballad that made Kendra feel warm inside.

"What ballad is this?" she asked, looking up into his penetrating eyes.

"*Cupid*, by the great Sam Cooke." Brokov recalled the many times Kato would say that every time he played the song.

They danced to the gentle refrain, losing themselves in each other's embrace. The songs were formatted using the musician's original voice, translated into native Araxan. She asked the meaning of the words, with Brokov explaining as best as he remembered.

"Cupid is mythical flying boy who shoots magic arrows into people's hearts making them fall in love, so the narrator is beseeching Cupid's help to win the heart of his love." He smiled, looking down into her eyes.

"You Earthers are very strange." She shook her head.

"You don't fancy an arrow making you fall in love?"

"You didn't need it. You won my heart all on your own."

The others looked on, enjoying their friends' happiness. It was a pleasant respite from the war and their troubles, a small reminder that life still went on, despite all they endured. Tosha had seen enough, dragging Raven to join them, dancing with her husband. Lorken and the others eventually took their turn with the ladies, each dancing to the best of their ability. Orlom took great pride in dancing with Lady Raven, as he often called her, managing not to stomp her feet as they moved across the floor. It was Zem and Kendra that made the strangest pairing, though he moved with such gentleness to take her aback.

"I have never thanked you, Zem, for all that you did," she said as they danced, his metallic skin swallowing the dim light of the room.

"As great as my deeds have been, to which are you referring?"

She rolled her eyes with his blissfully ignorant arrogance, which she found endearing in some strange way.

"There are many things you have done, to the benefit of us all, Zem, but never more so than during the attack on the *Stenox*. You killed so many gargoyles that day, and if you hadn't, I might not have lived, and perhaps Brokov also. For that I thank you, and… I love you." With that, she reached up and placed a kiss to his cheek.

It was then that Zem felt a little more human, his sense of belonging to something greater than himself growing stronger. It was something intimate that only the human heart could know. He wasn't human, but then again, neither were Argos and Orlom, but they were family, his family, the same with all of them.

* * *

The following afternoon found them enjoying the beach, Tosha and Kendra finding the activity there unusual, but entertaining. They frolicked in the sand, and swam the lagoon, only after they set up a restraining field around the swimming area, to keep out unwanted predators, especially versks, which were the closest thing to a shark on Arax. It was a nice celebration after working much of the morning. The ship's restoration was continuing on schedule, while Brokov restored the operation of the observation discs that have been offline since the attack on Tro. The air ski was next, and then the protective field he planned to surround the *Stenox* with.

Orlom and Argos looked out of place with the swim gear the Earthers provided them, with their thick hairy legs protruding through the knee-length trunks. All their clothes were manufactured using the clothing processor in the main domicile. All one needed were the base materials, and the machine would produce whatever you wanted. It was just another luxury that they took for granted, that Kendra and Tosha would not overlook.

"This is almost scandalous," Tosha said, looking down at the brevity of her bathing suit while walking hand in hand with Raven along the beach.

"Looks pretty standard to me," Raven said, since it covered most of her torso.

"Does it now?" She gave him a look before glancing at his baggy trunks that poorly hid his large build. His short hair was damp from their swim, the sunlight glistening off his wet skin.

"Most women from Earth wear far less, I assure you."

"They do, do they? And how many of these women have you courted?"

"Courted? If you mean dated, then only a few. None reached that level of seriousness, only you."

"Good. Otherwise, I would have to find my way back to your world and gut them myself," she said in a tone he couldn't tell if she was serious or not.

"You know, Tosh, I talk a good game, but in all honesty, I managed to instill hatred in most of the women I ever met back on Earth." He chuckled.

"That I believe. But just in case one managed to find you charming, I would be certain to correct her."

"You know, Tosh, princesses are supposed to be sweet and loving, but you have a temper."

"Yes, and you best remember that," she reminded him.

They stopped under the shade of a swaying frolog, looking out across the water, taking in the tropical beauty of this remote isle. She thought of their children, needing to see them and hold them. It was the misery of this war that kept them from her arms, a war her father started. Her father… nothing troubled her more than him. How she longed to go back in time, to set him on another course, but alas, it is not to be. Could she face him after this? How would he see her betrayal? What choice did she have? How could one choose between their father and mother, or their father and husband and children? It weighed so heavily upon her to rob her of the joy of being here in this most beautiful place.

She didn't realize she was staring out at the water for so long until Raven asked if she was alright. She thought to lie, but was too distracted to do so, and if she couldn't be honest with the one person that she trusted her life to, then who could she confide?

"I worry about our children, Raven. It has been so long since I held our sons." She sighed, continuing to stare across the water.

"They are safe, if that's what you're worried about."

"Perhaps, but I still long to hold them."

"We'll fix that soon enough."

She gave him a surprised look.

"As soon as the ship is ready, our next stop is Torn, and we can go full speed."

"Truly?"

"Yep, then Lorken can see his wife, and you can see our boys. As well as check in with Matuzak and the war effort. Then on to Tro and the war."

That brought her back to her other concern.

"What?" he asked, knowing that look.

"My father."

"What about him?"

"How do you fight someone you love?"

"You leave him to me. No one expects you to do it."

"My mother entrusted me with the sword. I must wield it in battle."

"Your father has a lot of minions you can use that fancy sword on. You take care of them, and we'll do the rest."

"We?"

"Us." He waved a hand indicating his current crew who were scattered across the beach, enjoying the sun. "And Terin, Cronus and the others," he added.

"You don't understand, I don't want to see him die, and yet even if he survives, the loss of his empire will kill him all the same."

"That's war, Tosh, sometimes you have to fight those you love. It is no different with me and Ben. I love him as a brother, and now I have to kill him. And if I do, there is no going back."

She looked up into his dark eyes, finally understanding him, his torment so plain to see, much like her own. She wrapped her arms around him as they held each other, the sound of lapping waves breaking the distant atoll echoing over the sound of sea birds coursing overhead.

Chapter 12

General Lewins, commander of the 1st Torry Army, stood upon a low rise, holding his mount's reins in his hand. His standard bearer drew alongside him, planting their sigil in the ground, a blue hammer and ax upon a field white. Gazing east, the late day sun was at their back, affording them a clear view to the flat plain ahead, where the east west road cut across the grass land, before disappearing into the low rolling hills that guarded the approaches to Notsu. Lewins took stock of his situation. Torry cavalry in the distance raised dust along the horizon to the southeast, heading in his direction. It was likely Avliam returning from scouting the enemy positions. Lewins own army was strung out behind him for several leagues, numbering well short of twelve thousand men, suffering losses throughout the campaign. Many thousands might well rejoin him after being restored by the regenerator but could not be counted upon for the battle at hand. His gaze returned to the low hills in the distance, knowing what remained of Morac's legions rested beyond, but at what strength? Like any commander worth his salt, Lewins hated unknowns, for war was fraught with them. A good commander often had to use his best guess, but a generous estimate gave Morac more than a hundred thousand men and gargoyles, more than their combined army. A less generous estimate gave Morac less than fifty thousand. If one included the decimation of Morac's commanders, magantor forces and cavalry, the balance to their favor grew greatly.

As if the Fates were privy to his thoughts, a flock of Macon magantors drew from the northeast, unchallenged in the airy domain. The Jenaii, Torry and Macon magantors had met little resistance since Corell, the Benotrist warbirds mostly absent, either dead or fearing annihilation. He was curious of their latest findings, hoping to glean a more accurate picture of Morac's strength.

"General, Master Vantel approaches!" his standard bearer said, drawing Lewins from his musings.

Torg approached, with a dozen Torry Elite trailing him, their distinct silver armor and blue tunics standing in contrast to Torg's simple brown leather mail and dark trousers, and the austere steel helm gracing his thick skull.

"Master Vantel!" General Lewins greeted the commander of the Torry Elite as he drew up alongside him, before dismounting.

"General, what have you?" Torg cut to the point, wasting few words.

"The small rolling hills to our east are the final obstacle before attaining Notsu. They would be an advantageous position to quarter our armies until King Lorn joins us, but I dare not advance until our scouts return," Lewins explained, Torg following his gaze to the approaching cavalry drawing from the southeast, and magantors drawing from the north.

"Aye. King Mortus and General Vecious are one day behind us. Wait for them before advancing to those hills. General Valen will need to contact King El Anthar and the Jenaii host, and ask them to join us," Torg said, regarding the Jenaii 2nd Battlegroup that was clearing their northern flank. They were last reported some twenty leagues northwest, engaging bands of gargoyles that separated from the main host. King Mortus was currently at Surlone, the long abandoned Notsuan holdfast resting near the Torry border.

"Very well. We will set camp here and wait for them to join us. What is the latest on King Lorn?"

"He is eighty leagues to our west, marching fast to join us."

He would be much farther afield had their armies not slowed down upon approaching Notsu. Lorn's orders were explicit that they were to pursue Morac's army beyond the Torry Border, but not to advance to Notsu until the entire army was brought to bear, fearing Morac might counterattack. The army was jubilant with the recent happenings, sensing another victory beyond the horizon. News of the fall of Gotto to the ape and Troan forces further fueled their optimism, something Torg tried vehemently to douse. The last thing they needed was to grow overconfident and stick their necks out far enough for Morac to lop them off. As it stood, Morac still wielded the *Sword of the Sun*, while their own *Swords of Light* were elsewhere, Elos with the Jenaii, and Cronus and Terin with Lorn.

"I look forward to his arrival. If things go well, we might end this war here and now," Lewins couldn't help but utter.

"Keep your mind on the enemy at hand, General. Tyro has many armies still at his command should this one falter," Torg reminded him, though even he knew the sorry state Tyro would be in should Morac's army be destroyed.

Lewins nodded, knowing the truth of that when Torg's gaze fell upon the pike just ahead, where sat the severed skull of a fallen Torry.

"Take care of that before our king arrives," Torg commanded.

"Aye, Master Vantel," Lewins acknowledged. It was a gruesome task, having come upon the grisly trophies the gargoyles arrayed from the Plain of Kregmarin to the gates of Corell. They had cleared all of those nearest Corell after the first siege, but those closer to Notsu remained, as they took them down as they advanced. They could still see a line of them continuing in the distance, evenly spaced toward the horizon.

* * *

Notsu.
Former estate of Tevlan Nosuc.

Morac stared blankly at the map, his addled mind tormented with the sorry state of his army, rumors of unrest within the gargoyle ranks the latest headache he was forced to deal with. His preferred method of selecting out warriors to be executed for the actions of the legions was unwise at this time, so General Gavis advised.

Advised, he spat, knowing it was more a lecture than advice. He knew the general of his 10th Legion despised him. The man looked down upon him as if he was a fool. With Gavis his only surviving general, he was forced to tolerate him. Only ultimate victory could free him to kill Gavis, and that victory seemed far away now. With no sign of Vades, who was supposed to have attained Notsu by now, his current circle of confidants was reduced to Daylas, the acting governor of Notsu, and Kriton, both joining him in the council chamber, discussing their options as the evening grew late.

"We hold and bleed them upon these walls as they bled us at Corell!" Kriton snarled, eyeing Notsu's place on the center of the map.

"We may lack the food to sustain us should the siege be lengthy," Daylas pointed out.

"Then the enemy shall suffer equally. Their supply lines will quickly run thin stretched out for as long as they are." Morac swept his hand across the map from the northern shore of Lake Monata and Central City to Corell, then from there to Notsu, emphasizing the length of the tenuous routes. If his legions accomplished one thing during the recent siege of Corell, it was ravaging the Torry countryside, leaving little to feed the armies Lorn had gathered.

"Lord Morac is not to be disturbed, General!" The muffled shout of the guard in the outer corridor echoed through the chamber.

"Step aside!" the distinct voice of General Gavis bellowed before Morac ordered the nearest guards to escort the General into the chamber.

"What brings you here unbidden, General?" Morac asked coldly, meeting the general's stare upon his entrance.

"Orders from the Emperor, *Lord* Morac," he said, presenting an open missive just delivered by magantor, tossing the parchment on the table.

Morac lifted the parchment, Kriton and Daylas observing his initial confusion morph into the bitterest scowl.

"What does it say?" Daylas asked, General Gavis answering as Morac stewed in silent rage.

"As the only surviving general, the emperor has given me command of the 8th and 9th Legions, adding their telnics to my own. He has further ordered the survival of the army to take precedence over all other considerations and grants me full authority in overseeing it. I have already informed commanders Gurloz and Dulvak, and they are ordering their telnics accordingly. I have also given the order to march to my entire command, by order of the emperor. Every commander of Unit and higher has read that missive and understands that my order can only be rescinded by the emperor himself," Gavis declared, his actions disavowing Morac of any notion to kill him and direct the army otherwise.

"March to where?" Daylas dared ask.

"Home. We leave tomorrow," Gavis said, turning away and leaving as swiftly as he had arrived, giving Morac no time to overcome his shock and argue the point.

By showing his entire command the emperor's words, there was no way for Morac to order them to stay should he slay Gavis. His position was dire. With the 8th, 9th and 10th Legions removed, that left him only the fifteen telnics of the 11th Benotrist Legion and the remnants of the 5th, 12th and 14th Gargoyle Legions, numbering forty telnics combined. That left Morac a total of fifty-five Benotrist and Gargoyle telnics defending the walls of Notsu against whatever force Lorn and his allies could bring to bear.

"Shall we march home as well?" Daylas asked. Any delay would likely remove that as an option with the enemy drawing nigh.

"We did not lose so many at Corell to abandon Notsu uncontested. We hold," Morac growled.

* * *

The following morn found Morac upon the terrace of his stolen estate, looking on as the soldiers of the 10th Legion marshaled in the streets below, beginning their exit from the city. They appeared in good order, almost *too* good of order, as if they were prepared for this long before the missive from the emperor arrived. He needn't look to the east side of the city where the remnants of the 8th Legion were gathering to depart, or the west, where the 9th was doing likewise, to know they were equally enthused to depart. The three legions combined numbered forty two telnics, nearly half his remaining strength, as well as his best soldiers. Any hopes of gaining victory in the south were now quashed. If he retreated as well, he would return home a failure. The emperor might even deign to take back his sword. Such thoughts plagued him now, consuming his every waking moment.

No! He would not relent of his sword. It was his now by right, and he would wield it unto death.

He remained there, watching them depart throughout the morn and into the late afternoon. He ordered the magantor riders that arrived with the emperor's missive to remain, though they insisted they must return by order of General Naruv, commander of all Benotrist magantor forces. As Elite prime, Morac overruled that order, demanding that two of them remain, releasing the others to return north. They nervously complied, wary of the deteriorating situation concerning the enemy's ever-growing control of the skies. They already lost much of their strength in the Corell campaign and needed to husband what numbers remained to protect their homeland.

It was Daylas that visited with him as the day grew late, the appointed governor stepping onto the terrace as the sun hung low in the west.

"They are gone," he stated the obvious.

"We shall see how the journey across the Kregmarin treats them." Morac bitterly recalled his trek across that lifeless expanse, and the number of soldiers he lost to the unforgiving environment.

"We have done much to restore the watering sites along the route, and dug many new ones as well. Hopefully they shall attain our border in good stead."

"Watering sites that we have prepared for them. And so Gavis will return a hero, parading himself as the savior of our army while I shall be named a failure."

"You slew King Lore and bled the Torry realms to great effect. You are no failure, Lord Morac."

"Our people will not share your optimism, Daylas. People always overlook a thousand fell deeds for a single blunder, and I have met with defeat twice at Corell."

"Beset by many enemies, I remind you. It took all the south to turn you back this time, and the foul magic of the Earthers," Daylas added.

"The Earthers," he nearly spat. "I have Hossen Grell to thank for that failure. Had he conducted the raid as we planned, the apes would have been disgraced, the forum and ruling families destroyed, and the Earthers none the wiser. Orvis Maiyan would be placed as the faux regent of the fallen city, and our forces would not have been devasted at Corell by Raven's weapon." Had Hossen showed himself upon Morac's return to Notsu, he would have gutted him himself.

"Hossen has returned to Nisin, if you were curious of his whereabouts," Daylas offered.

"He is a member of the imperial elite. It falls to the emperor to see to his punishment." Morac stated the official protocol. Had Hossen remained south, he might have taken liberty to slay him for his failure, a failure that cost Morac dearly.

"Your orders?" Daylas asked, knowing it better to focus the Benotrist lord on matters they could affect, rather than dwell on past failures or rage against individuals beyond their reach.

Orders? Morac almost laughed, wondering what edict he could grant to turn their fortunes. He needed to do something, this he knew. Staying in place as things stood was intolerable, and he couldn't ask the men that remained to do so, without something to occupy them. All men had a breaking point, and his men were no different. The men of the 11th Legion were still at his command, numbering fifteen telnics, and were fresh. While the rest of the men of the 11th fought at Corell and surrendered at Besos, these men garrisoned here had not seen battle since Kregmarin. They were fresh and loyal, but what could he do to keep them occupied while the enemy closed the noose around them?

While contemplating this, his gaze found an open window of a dwelling several streets to his north, its occupants stealing furtive glances to the now empty street below them. It was a rare sight to observe the locals acting so brazen. As the occupation of the city progressed, the natives took more extreme precautions to hide themselves. What changed? Did they now see his men abandoning Notsu as a sign of their liberation? Perhaps he could disavow them of that notion and give his remaining men something to occupy themselves.

* * *

Two days hence.
Twelve leagues west of Notsu.

King Lorn rode into the allied encampment at the head of his small host, with General Ciyon and his joint Torry-Macon Army still two days to their west. Young Dougar rode upon his right and Jentra his left, with their numerous friends and fellow warriors following close behind. Cronus and Terin preceded them, arriving ahead of the king, making safe his arrival, though seeing the state of the encampment set those fears aside. Terin bore Cronus upon Wind Racer, setting down amid the encampment, before given Ocran from Torg to ride back to join Lorn.

Torg awaited Lorn upon his arrival standing upon the east west road where it snaked through the low hills guarding the approach of Notsu, the army setting camp on the hilltops to either side. They were pleased to know the Jenaii 2nd Battlegroup and the Macon 2nd Army were well positioned beside Lewins' 1st Torry Army, their forces consolidated before advancing upon Notsu.

Terin and Cronus broke left and right, posting to Torg's flanks as King Lorn approached, leading his column between the small hills, before drawing up before Torg, the Torry Master of Arms greeting him with his arms crossed and the slightest nod of approval. That was as much as a warm greeting as Torg could manage, causing Lorn to smile.

"Greeting Master Vantel, how fare you this fine day?" Lorn said, dismounting, tossing his reins to Dougar before taking a step forward.

"I was told that you are apprised of our situation," Torg said.

"Aye, which is why we hurried to join you, though in doing so we were forced to leave Dadeus and his army far to our rear."

"Your pavilion awaits. We have prepared it up there." Torg pointed to the nearest hill overlooking the north side of the road. From this vantage point, one could only see the outer fortifications of the encampment running the near slope of the hillside, with steel helms of Torry soldiers peaking above the low walls of stone and soil recently erected to guard the position.

"I see you have been busy." Lorn smiled.

"Not busy enough. This is a strongly held position, but water is a problem, among others. King Mortus and King El Anthar await you. We have much to discuss."

"Very well, if you would show me the way," Lorn said, before asking Torg's aid to see to his party, directing Lady Ilesa to the matrons' pavilion to treat whatever wounded they had gathered, with Lucas and Ular escorting her. Jentra followed Lorn to his pavilion, ordering Criose to see to their accommodations, particularly where to pitch their tent. Gorzak and his fellow apes followed Criose, planning to be camped close to Jentra and the others.

***

Dougar waited outside the command pavilion, with Terin and Cronus keeping him company as the others gathered therein. Cronus knelt beside the young boy, fixing his helm so it set correctly upon his small head, before giving him a wink, reminding him of the fine job he was doing as Lorn's squire and aid, the kind remark puffing him with pride. He had come to love his new comrades, each accepting him into their circle, though he had done nothing to deserve it.

"You will make a fine warrior one day, Dougar. Continue to follow the smallest instructions, and it will bear fruit," Cronus said, slapping his mailed shoulder before gaining his feet.

"Aye, King's Elite Kenti." Dougar slapped his fist to his chest, saluting Cronus. Other than Jentra, Cronus had taken the most shine to the child since departing Corell. The orphan boy reminded him of himself in some ways, having lost those that he loved. At least Cronus had his friends and dear Maura, where Dougar was an orphan.

"That is an impressive salute, Dougar," Terin praised the child, before stealing a glance to their surroundings. They found themselves atop the small hill, with the army camped upon dozens of hilltops to their east, north and south, with the city of Notsu gracing the eastern horizon, so far in the distance to nearly be invisible. Nearly half the magantor pens shared this hilltop, including Wind Racer. He couldn't miss the Sisterhood magantors tethered nearby, their warriors standing guard around them, including Deva, who spared him a nervous glance every so often. Their captain, Lucella Sarelis, held council with the kings within the pavilion, along with the other commanders of rank.

Terin regarded her with indifference, feeling nothing at all, as if his anger was washed away. Was this a gift from Yah for his forgiveness, or the steeling of his heart? Whatever it was, he was relieved. Deva was no longer his tormentor, or the source of his fury, twisting his soul into something it was not. He didn't want to be a bitter, broken man seeking revenge until it changed him, seeking out those who harmed him and repaying them in kind. That was the path his grandfather followed, and it brought the world to the brink of ruin. It was Yah that held him back from striking down Deva and stripped away his anger. That was the difference between Taleron and himself: he accepted Yah's guidance, while Tyro followed his own.

It was then their eyes crossed, sharing a brief glance as if she was privy to his thoughts. Whatever change had come over him had transformed her as well. Yah's spirit dwelt in her now, for he could see it in her eyes. He hoped then that she could find peace once this war was over and someone to share it with, as he did with Corry.

* * *

Lorn stood over the table in the center of the pavilion, listening attentively as Torg and the others pointed out Morac's and their own movements on the map. Jentra stood dutifully at his side, wondering how they had come this far, saving Yatin, joining with Mortus and standing on the doorstep of victory with this grand host gathered upon these hills. They were joined by King El Anthar, General Ev Evorn and Elos, representing the Jenaii and their 2nd Battlegroup, numbering fifteen telnics. General Lewins stood to Lorn's opposite shoulder, commanding the 1st Torry Army, with their current strength of twelve telnics. King Mortus stood across from them, along with General Bram Vecious, his army numbering nine telnics. General Dar Valen stood beside them, along with Generals Avliam and Connly, the only surviving commanders of cavalry with the recent deaths of Meborn and Tevlin. Representing the Sisterhood stood Lucella Sarelis, her meager assets of magantors belying her true stature among them, representing Queen Letha and the vast armies she was marshalling to their cause.

"As you can see, this is the last good ground between here and Notsu. Beyond this point is nothing but flat ground and little water," Torg explained, waving his hand from their point on the map to the walls of Notsu.

Water was the source of their greatest challenge in this campaign as it was for Morac before them. The surrounding hills had little water, though Torg had ordered more wells to be dug upon their arrival. Even when they were complete, they would not be enough for their armies. This, more than any other factor, forced their hand to move quickly off this position, which Torg rightly pointed out.

"Two thousand men of Notsu are marching with Dadeus' army. They know all the watering points within fifty leagues of their city. I will send word for those most knowledgeable to be sent ahead," Lorn said.

"That will help our supply caravans. The poor wretches have worked wonders to this point." Torg commended their efforts with their supply chains stretching as far away as Torry South and Maconia.

"What is the latest on Morac?" Lorn asked, moving on to the disposition of forces.

King El Anthar relayed the most pertinent information.

"A large host of Benotrists departed Notsu two days ago, marching due north by all accounts. We have tracked their retreat, keeping a respectable distance." King El Anthar stated the tidings that hastened Lorn racing ahead to their encampment.

"How many?" Lorn asked.

"Between thirty and fifty telnics, bearing the sigil of the 10th Legion," General Ev Evorn stated.

"That seems a generous number considering how many men of that legion we slew at Corell," Jentra said.

"We doubt that even half are from the 10th," Torg snorted.

"Then who are they?" Lorn asked.

"Likely elements of the 8th, 9th or 11th Legions, considering we slew or captured all their generals, while we have no accounting for General Gavis," General Bram Vecious said.

"If Morac reassigned them to Gavis, then what are we to believe by this movement?" Lorn asked, looking to each of them for an answer.

"They may be attempting to reposition before doubling back, striking us from the rear, though their lack of magantors would prevent them from screening their movements," General Valen said.

"It could be the first step in a full retreat, why else would Morac send away half of his strength," General Lewins said.

"They could be starving. We know almost nothing of their supply trains, but considering the difficulty of our own, that would be my guess," King Mortus opined.

"Then we must prevent the rest from escaping," Lorn said, eyeing the Kregmarin plain stretching north from the crossroads, covering most of their likely line of retreat.

"That might well be what Morac is planning, having us extend our necks before striking. He still has a considerable number of soldiers at his command," General Valen said.

"Without command of the skies, and lacking in cavalry…" Lorn paused, shaking his head.

"Should we delay, the rest may escape, and where will that leave us?" Lewins asked before answering his own question. "We will be left standing upon a dead city with our hands empty. We must take the rest of his army while we can."

Lewins' words gave Lorn pause. His father was once led astray at the Council of Corell, marching to the crossroads against General

Morton's advice, leading to the disaster at Kregmarin. He needed to be very careful. Should these armies be destroyed, they would certainly lose the war, but caution could be misplaced, costing them an opportunity that their victory at Corell has gifted them. They had driven Morac from the walls of Corell to here, giving him no respite to reorganize his broken legions until safely within the walls of Notsu.

"What tidings from Tro?" Lorn asked, the last he heard being the retaking of Gotto.

"We received this missive yester morn." Torg passed him a rolled parchment bearing the seal of Klen Adine.

"They are holding west of Gotto along the east-west road, waiting our decision. They currently have two telnics of Troans and twice that number of apes, their strength growing by the day. Matuzak is ferrying soldiers to Tro using merchant ships flagged from every realm that anchors at Torn. The Casians have lent their strength to the cause, with a fleet from Milito attaining Tro not four days ago," Dar Valen explained.

"I am not the only King here. I would hear your council." Lorn looked to El Anthar and King Mortus.

"We cannot stay where we are, and if we retreat, we leave Morac in possession of Notsu. He has depleted his strength by half. Now is the time to advance," El Anthar advised.

"Aye, that is the meat of it. We finish him, here and now," Mortus affirmed.

"What of Thorton? Has there been any sightings?" Lorn asked.

"None. Wherever he is, it is not here," Torg said, wondering what occupied the dangerous Earther.

"Captain Sarelis, what council do you offer?" Lorn looked to Queen Letha's captain of the guard.

"My Queen has committed to your cause, King Lorn. Her army shall soon strike Tyro in the west. The more his eyes are fixed here, and upon all of you, the easier her task will be," the proud woman declared.

"So it shall be. Once Dadeus arrives, we shall advance upon Notsu. General Valen, send word to our Troan and Ape allies west of

Gotto. Urge them to advance upon Notsu from the east. With three Swords of Light and a larger army, we shall take Morac and win this war," Lorn declared, his sentiment shared by them all.

* * *

Four days hence.
Notsu.

Morac stood upon the battlements of the north wall of the city, staring north where he once stood before these very walls offering parlay to the city after his victory at Kregmarin. He recalled treating with the city leaders under the flag of truce, demanding their surrender and the head of Minister Vabian for his insolent tongue, which the city elders hurriedly obeyed. Such was his power then, commanding six legions with King Lore dead, leaving so few to oppose him. He wondered where it had all gone awry? Here he now stood, trapped within this dead city, with the enemy drawing a noose around him.

To the east stood the Jenaii Battlegroup, taking position throughout the previous night. This morning his men awoke to see the wretched creatures staring back at them from beyond the east wall. To the west stood the Macon host, their standard lifting in the breeze, a golden crown upon a field of black, sigil of their traitorous king, who now aligned with Lorn, betraying his alliance with Nayboria. Most bitter of all were the forces arrayed to his direct north… the Torry 1st Army, their standard aligned before the main gate, a blue hammer and ax upon a field of white. Beyond their standard rose the sigil of the Torry King, a golden crown upon a field of white. Somewhere in that rabble was his nemesis, King Lorn, the embodiment of all that plagued him since first taking this city. First his sister defied him during the first siege, gathering enough allies to her doomed cause to turn back his great host. Then Lorn repeated her favor during the second siege, gathering another alliance against him.

He looked out across that deadly space to the forces arrayed against him, their numbers paling against their true power, their swords of light and the damnable Earther, wherever he was hiding.

Thoughts of Raven further soured his mood, thinking of the men he had slain, cutting them down in the thousands with such little effort. Victory would assuredly have been his had Raven not intervened. Though he could fend off his weapon's power, his army could not. He might have slain him if he could have gotten close, but atop the towers of Corell and without a magantor, it was nigh impossible. Here, however, on open ground, things would be different. Should Raven deign to open fire upon these walls, he would take one of the magantors he kept back, and fly straight for him, and slay him.

"Show yourself, Earther!" He spat, wishing to end his torment. Perhaps the Earther was wiser than he thought, hiding himself from destruction, or was he elsewhere, conjuring even more foul magic to plague him? The cruelest fact was that even if Raven revealed himself, he was likely protected by Terin or Elos. An even darker thought was the whereabouts of Dethine. Some of his men claimed to have seen him fall in battle, which meant his sword was lost, or in the Torries hands. If that were true, they had three swords to his one. He was confident that he could best Terin, but could he defeat Terin, Elos and another? His only solace was the strength of his position. With fifteen telnics of the 11th Legion, along with forty telnics of gargoyles, Notsu would not be taken by the forces Lorn assembled, not without destroying themselves in the process. He would also have the advantage of his gargoyles holding the high ground, something they had not had this entire campaign. They could easily spring from the walls and set down upon Lorn's men wherever they chose, even concentrating on one of the armies, before the others could join them, destroying them in detail, spread out as they were. For now, they held at a distance, likely to negate this very tactic, but could they do so indefinitely? Their supply trains were obviously strained, and could not endure a long siege, that meant they meant to attack, but when?

Thankfully, Morac's army was well supplied with food, the dying screams of a Notsuan echoing somewhere in the dwellings behind him, emphasizing that fact. There were other ways to feed fifty-five thousand warriors than strung-out supply trains.

* * *

The following morn saw the arrival of General Ciyon, leading the joint Macon-Torry army, drawing from the west, their column stretching to the horizon. His army now numbered fifteen telnics, accompanied by two thousand men of Notsu and most of the archers from Corell, along with their bundle bearers. Of the men of Notsu, almost half were former soldiers of the fallen city, the rest volunteers drawn from the citizens that fled the city before its surrender. Most spent the previous winter at Central City, organizing themselves into an army. Many of their number were men of Bacel who were elsewhere when their city fell. With their home destroyed they committed themselves to the liberation of their sister city.

Morac was again called to the battlements to witness the new arrivals drawing from the west, sunlight playing off their steel helms and mail like a million sparkling stars. He felt his heart sink at the impressive sight. When compared to his once-mighty host, such a display paled in compare, but his great army was gone, dead or fled, with the survivors holed up in this dying city. He could only hope to ever lead such a grand army again, which he doubted the emperor would give him. He doubted the emperor could even gather such a force again.

"More come every day," Kriton hissed, stepping to his side upon the west wall, setting his clawed hand upon the thick stone rampart.

"This is likely the last of them. There are only so many forces they can call upon," Morac said, his words failing to convince Kriton. He hated to be forced to lean on another, but he was growing more dependent on Kriton with every passing day. With all his Gargoyle generals dead, it was Kriton who had assumed the mantle of their commander, spending his days reorganizing them into discernable cohorts. Morac was aware of the unrest in their ranks, many yammering to abandon the city for home. Kriton quashed such sentiments, using the citizens of Notsu to focus their energy. Morac had sectionalized the city, cordoning off the districts, allowing the gargoyles to terrorize them in detail. Only the screams of the dying alerted those in different districts that something was amiss, but after nearly a year of brutal occupation, the ears of most had grown dull to the cries of those suffering.

"Our soldiers cannot allow them to further encircle us," Kriton said in the clearest and coldest voice Morac had ever heard him echo.

"What do you suggest?" Morac asked.

* * *

Macon encampment. Beyond the west wall of Notsu.

It was late evening when the revelry subsided, the men celebrating the arrival of General Ciyon, his men setting camp behind their lines before repositioning to the southern perimeter come the next morning. King Lorn visited the cook fires of the Macon army throughout the night, joining King Mortus as they circled amongst the men, lifting their spirits. General Ciyon soon joined them, the Macon soldiers keen to hear of the fall Besos, as they were far east of Corell when he returned to the palace.

Lady Ilesa was called upon to treat the wounded among the new arrivals, with most of the injuries incurred in accidents along the road. Cronus took upon the role of her personal guard as she treated the wounded, standing watch over her as she moved from man to man. He had spent the past few days along the Macon perimeter, while Terin guarded the Torry positions in the north, and Elos the Jenaii in the east, keeping a sword of light in every camp should Morac venture from the city. He kept a vigilant eye on the night sky as Ilesa knelt beside a wounded Macon scout from Ciyon's army, who was thrown from his ocran, his spine broken in the middle of his back. He stunk of urine and the food he had thrown up upon his tunic, his once-vibrant brown eyes dulled with exhaustion. He was barely conscious when she tore open his tunic, setting the regenerator upon his naked chest. Cronus stole a glance as the man was quickly restored, wiggling his toes with an elated glee, his paralysis healed.

"My lady, thank you." He wept, coming to his knees and kissing her hand.

"You are welcome, brave soldier." She smiled, cupping his face, planting a gentle kiss to his forehead before moving on.

She continued down the line of men, treating them in good

order, making her way in the closing darkness. Thankfully, most of the injuries were minor, requiring little of the device's power, leaving much of its charge when she finished. Cronus guided her back to the matrons' pavilion, neither saying a word for half their journey. Cronus, like Ilesa, was broken hearted, the death of Leanna dulling his tongue, with Ilesa sharing his affliction.

"Usually I am the silent one," she said, sensing the need to say something.

"My apologies, Lady Ilesa, I haven't been much company of late."

"For good reason, King's Elite Kenti." She sighed.

"Please call me by name. King's Elite is… too much."

"But it is a title you have earned, and earned well."

"Not so. I was fortunate in my friends and circumstance, my deeds growing beyond their proper place through legend. In truth, my part was much smaller." He recalled his actions at Tuft's Mountain, which seemed so long ago.

"I doubt that. My husband spoke well of you, King's Elite, and I believe his word over your own humility."

"Please, call me Cronus, and if you knew Kato, you would know he only spoke well of those he loved."

She smiled at that, though any mention of Kato made her want to cry. "Fair is equally done, please call me Ilesa, for Lady is just as brazen as King's Elite."

"Ilesa it shall be. Kato's gift to our people has spared much suffering. You operate it with such care and skill."

"You are generous in your praise. I am merely using it as it was intended. There is little skill involved. I use it to honor him." She could barely say his name without breaking. Her time was drawing close, the child within her nearing its gestation, and effecting her mood. She was more susceptible to emotions she could usually suppress, especially now.

"He would be happy if he could see you now."

She was quiet for a time, wondering what to say to that.

"Yes, he would be." She sighed, though he knew she meant to say more.

"I dream of her still."

"Leanna?" she asked.

"Yes. She speaks to me at times. It is almost so real that I believe her spirit still lives somewhere that I cannot explain." He hadn't spoken of this with anyone, until now. For some strange reason he felt eased by her company.

She was quiet again, his words having a profound effect.

"It is not just me then."

"Ilesa?"

She stopped, turning to face him somewhere between two cookfires, beyond earshot of the soldiers gathered around them.

"Kato speaks to me as well. He comforts me and sings to our daughter."

"Daughter? How can you be certain?"

"Because he says so, and Kato never lies." She smiled, her words sending pimples across his flesh.

"If they still live in some form, why can't we touch them? Why can't I hold her, just one last time," he said with his desperate green eyes.

"Because it is not our time, Cronus. It is the will of Yah, if one believes in our King's God."

"You are skeptical. So am I."

"Skeptical? No, but I have questions that are left unanswered."

"And they are?"

"If Yah is all powerful, why punish us so? He is either all good but not all-powerful or all-powerful and not all good. Too many good men and women have died in this war. What purpose do their deaths serve, and yet I am visited by dreams that speak otherwise. I must trust that Kato's death serves a great purpose that I may never know. For now, I shall honor him and serve our people with his wondrous device."

"Kato married well." He smiled, taking her by the arm, guiding her to her pavilion.

* * *

"No!" Cronus screamed, the gargoyle spear piercing his friend's side,

skewering his heart. He tried to intercede, but was frozen in place, his limbs disobedient to his will as the horrific scene unfolded. Men, Jenaii, apes and gargoyles were fighting all around upon unfamiliar ground, as if the whole world had assembled in that fell place, the fate of the war hanging desperately in the balance. He was there but not there, caught up in a vision that he had no control of, helplessly looking on as his world fell apart. Men he knew were all around, dying one after another, but none more precious than his dear friend, his heart impaled on that hateful spear.

"*NO!*" he screamed again, before jerking awake.

He found himself upon his bedroll within his small tent, trying desperately to shake the nightmare from his memory, but couldn't. This was no nightmare, or fevered dream, but a vision. No matter what he told himself, it was the same as his visions of Leanna. She was truly there, looking after him from wherever in the beyond she dwelt, and he wept whenever she faded, begging her to stay. They were pleasant visions, gifts from Yah, though he begrudgingly acknowledged him. Unlike those pleasant visits, this was terrifying, a cruel picture of what was to come to pass.

What was the reason? If he could not change what was to come, why show him? There had to be a reason, and Cronus was a man of reason, if nothing else. He had to save his friend, but how?

A sudden urge overwhelmed him, forcing him to his feet, his hand reaching for his sword lying beside his bedroll, strapping his belt about his waist, before reaching for his mail, drawing it over his chest, then fixing his helm. He exited his tent, driven by the power of his sword just as the horns blew, rousing the camp to arms.

HARROOM!

The horns sounded again as Macon soldiers raced all around him, taking up position. Cronus looked skyward, winged forms filling the starlit sky, drawing from the east. His gaze lowered to the walls of Notsu, where the creatures sprang from the battlements, pouring over its ramparts like a dark tide in a midnight sea.

* * *

"To arms!" King Mortus bellowed, drawing his sword across his chest, bracing for whatever might descend into his midst. His royal guard formed a circle around him as the first wave set down upon the men lined to their front.

"Kai-Shorum!" Gargoyle chants echoed in the dark, the creatures setting down upon raised spears and walls of shields. Only the light of dying cookfires illuminated grounds farther afield, the sound of clashing steel and dying men and gargoyles indicating the direction of battle.

Mortus looked on as a dozen gargoyles crashed down on the men off his left, taking them to the ground in a whirl of blood and crushed bones. Another crash off his right saw a dozen more of his men go down in a great heap, scores of creatures crawling over their mounds of flesh, biting and slashing at whatever they could find in the dim light.

Mortus ordered his guard forward, clearing the mound of dying men of their attackers. The guards to his left thrust swiftly between their shields, gutting a creature springing toward them. Others to his right cut down another before pressing on.

"Umphh!" a guard to his front moaned, collapsing under the weight of a gargoyle dropping into their midst. Mortus stepped forth, jabbing his sword into the creature's ribs. It raised its feral glowing eyes to his, hissing demonically, impaled upon his blade while clawing at him. Mortus drove forth, keeping his shield between the creature and himself, pushing it off his stricken guard while it thrashed and screamed. Once clear of the fellow, he twisted the blade, driving the creature to its back, while another guard hacked its wing and then its neck.

Mortus withdrew his blade, gaining his bearings just as another set down before him. Gathering his breath, he stepped forth, blocking a swing of its curved scimitar, his guards closing ranks beside him. Their welcome company was quickly waylaid as a dozen creatures set down all around them, some taking men from their feet, others impaled on upraised spears. Mortus backed a step, the creature to his front pressing forth, while another struck his shield, nearly taking him to the ground. He staggered, losing sight of either foe when a great light shone in his periphery. Gargoyle screams rent the air as Mortus backed a step, gathering his senses, following the golden hue of a glowing sword cutting down gargoyles in quick order.

It was Cronus, driving amidst the creatures, starlight playing off his sword, fueling its golden fire in blinding radiance. Even a lesser Sword of Light was a terrible weapon to behold, gifting its wielder great power. He watched as Cronus cut down gargoyles with effortless grace, clearing them from his path like a driving gale.

His guards gathered themselves, reforming a barrier around their king. Looking afield, he could see little in the distance but could hear the sound of battle raging all around them, clashing steel and anguished screams joining in a ghastly chorus. The glow of Cronus' sword grew dim as he drew away, moving on to other foes setting down afield.

* * *

Ilesa roused from her slumber to the sounds of war horns and her sister matrons screaming in terror, the echo of clashing steel drawing dangerously nigh. She gained her feet just as a creature tumbled into their pavilion, rolling onto its stomach, sprawling to lunge at her, her sister matrons drawing away to the tent's walls.

SLASH!

Their eyes winced before the brightness of the glowing blade lopped the creature's head off, sending it rolling to her feet, where she kicked it away, its dying tongue dangling from its lips. Standing in the entrance of the tent was Cronus. He looked to each of them, making certain they were safe before stepping away, disappearing as swiftly as he arrived.

* * *

Cronus moved among the encampment, cutting down gargoyles wherever he found them. He came upon men moving to and fro, lending swift aid where needed before moving on. There seemed no end to the enemy falling upon them, the sky pregnant with their winged forms, flowing over the west wall of Notsu in an endless stream. The following ranks passed farther overhead, assailing the soldiers of Ciyon's army camped to their west. He ran apace, following their shadowed forms in the night sky, his fell blade meeting them as they set down.

SLASH! SPLIT! THRUST!

He cut them down in swift order, losing sight of the greater battle, his mind lost to the sword. He thought of his soldiers that died at Costelin and Tuft's Mountain or in the dungeons of Fera, gaining justice for each of them with every gargoyle life he took. He thought of Arsenc, then Kato, and especially Leanna, raging madly at their loss.

Heavy cheers rang out as scores of riders drew from the north, sweeping into their encampments just as a Jenaii magantor drew from the south, Elos springing from its back, its driver passing overhead as the Jenaii warrior followed the glow of Cronus' blade, joining him in battle.

* * *

Guilen found himself half dressed, following Dadeus into the fray, jabbing madly at leathery wings flapping somewhere above him in the dark, only his shield protecting him from a glancing scimitar. He felt his blade strike something, dark blood oozing along his sword, the creature drawing painfully away, disappearing in the dark. He turned, losing sight of Dadeus as they grew separated, men and gargoyles mixing between them.

"Agghh!" a man cried pitifully off his left, a gargoyle dagger twisting in his eye, the creature now atop of him, driving the blade deeper into his skull.

WHOOSH!

A massive white blur swept down from above, snatching the gargoyle in its powerful black talons before passing on, the creature's screams growing fainter as it drew away.

"Terin!" Guilen called out to his friend, watching as he disappeared in the night sky, Wind Racer releasing his victim, the creature dropping like a stone with its broken wings.

Guilen collected himself, rushing to join his general.

* * *

Wind Racer rose high above the crowded sky, starlight illuminating the mass of leathery-winged forms below him. Terin took a breath, gripping his sword tightly before Wind Racer descended, cutting a swath through the gargoyle ranks. He followed his avian's course, striking out at whatever flesh fell within his reach.

SPLIT! SLASH!

He caught one creature across its left wing, the leathery appendage flying off his murky blade. He leaned to the opposite side as Wind Racer circled about, catching another across its feet, leaving it screaming in his wake. The powerful magantor swerved amidst the serried sky, snatching gargoyles from the air, crushing them within his talons one after another before soaring again above the fray. Terin took the respite to scan afield, trying to make sense of the madness with much of his view blocked by the waves of gargoyles passing below. He couldn't miss the bright golden and emerald hues of Cronus and Elos' blades flashing to his west, the pair seeming to work in unison. Scores of Torry cavalry swept down from the north while Macon cavalry swept around the periphery, cutting down strays and guarding the flanks. Far to the east, a telnic of Jenaii filled the sky but would be long to arrive. Beyond this, he could see little of the action below, the entire scene a disordered chaos. There was naught to do but kill as many as he could. With that he took a breath, riding Wind Racer into another dive.

* * *

Lorn swept into the Macon encampment like an ill wind, Torg riding upon his right, and Jentra his left, trampling gargoyles underfoot, skewering others with their spears while cutting a path to the Macon king. Lucas broke off from the relieving column, making safe the matrons' pavilion, circling the structure, with Ular sitting behind him, the Enoructan dismounting in a flourish as Lucas swept the area. Most of Lorn's elite were doubled up with an ape warrior sharing their saddles. Gorzak and his fellow warriors dismounted once the cavalry slowed to engage, jumping from their mounts with maddened war cries, hacking gargoyles to pieces with their axes and swords or smashing skulls with their hammers.

"You are a welcome sight, King Lorn!" Mortus bellowed, lowering his blood-stained sword, standing amidst a dozen corpses, an even mix of friend and foe.

"As are you, Father," he greeted him, his men fanning out around them. Torg dismounted, driving his sword into the back of a stirring corpse, making sure of it.

* * *

Terin gutted a creature as Wind Racer passed under it, snatching another in his beak, snapping it in half. The great avian angled left, avoiding a crowd of gargoyles coming straight at them, his talons finding another, crushing its wings before releasing it to its doom. Wind Racer sounded in pain, a gargoyle clinging to its leg, digging a dagger into his thigh. He faltered briefly as another managed to find purchase on his left wing, with Terin trying to reach it with his blade and falling short. Another clambered upon his tail, trying to claw its way toward Terin. Two more grabbed hold under the avian's breast, clinging desperately, and another three to his tail and legs. Terin thought to land so he could dislodge them, but Wind Racer ignored his command, soaring skyward instead.

Terin sheathed his sword, tightening his hold on the reins, wrapping them around his wrists as he sensed the warbird's intent, thankful his legs and hips were tied strongly to the saddle. Wind Racer ignored the creatures desperately trying to stab him wherever they clung as he soared high into the firmament. Higher and higher he flew, his powerful wings moving with determined power, throwing off the creatures clinging to them. Terin's eyes started to flutter, his mind spinning as he stole a glance to the east, where the sunrise threatened to break the horizon, before nothing, darkness taking him with the thinning air. Wind Racer continued straight up, the gargoyles falling away one by one, succumbing to the thin air of the airy heights. Once free, he dropped back down, bearing Terin's unconscious body to safety.

* * *

Cronus' slash split an arcing scimitar, slicing halfway through its wielder's chest, blood and bone flying off his blade. Elos halved another to his right before spinning around his back, lopping another's head. Unlike Terin before his power was stripped away and reborn to whatever it was now, Cronus was limited by his own endurance, forcing him and Elos to move at a measured pace. The power of the swords invoked another unique ability if their wielders were worthy, allowing them to work in unison with a natural grace. They moved across the battlefield, appearing where needed and when needed, moving on as swiftly as they arrived. The gargoyles feared their blades, but they lacked the power to invoke widespread panic in their ranks, unlike Terin at his zenith.

* * *

"Are they leaving?" Jentra asked, reluctant to lower his blood-stained sword though no gargoyle was near him.

Lorn's mount shifted as he turned about, his elite sweeping around him, having crossed the breadth of the Macon encampment before breaking through to the southern end. They found themselves on open ground, the walls of the city two leagues to their east with the dawn sky breaking behind its high ramparts. The heavens were soon illuminated in all their glory, revealing a near-empty sky. The others shared his confusion until their gazes shifted west, where the gargoyles seemed to have gathered beyond their rearmost positions.

Lorn thought to reform and brace for their imminent return but quickly realized they were withdrawing... withdrawing away from the city.

"Sire, look!" One of his Elite pointed skyward, where Wind Racer circled overhead before setting down in their midst, blood oozing from his legs and breast, with an unconscious Terin sitting his saddle.

Chapter 13

No greater love.

Thousands lay dead, wounded and dying across the battlefield, the sunrise revealing the carnage wrought by the gargoyle horde. Men lay writhing upon the ground, their innards spilling between their fingers or with their limbs hacked to pieces. The entire western perimeter of the besieging armies lay in desolation and disorder. Nearly one in three of King Mortus' 2nd Army counted among the casualties, and one in four of Ciyon's joint Macon-Torry army suffered likewise. Ilesa lamented the regenerator was only at half strength when the battle commenced, though beset as she was at the outset, there were few near enough to treat. By dawn she continued until it was fully drained, then paused to recharge the device as the wounded piled up before the pavilion, many dying waiting for it to be restored. Others could not be moved, their fellows watching over them until she could come to them.

General Bram Vecious went about reordering the Macon 2nd Army, with two of his telnic commanders slain in the battle, and eleven commanders of unit. He kept a watchful eye upon the city, wary of the city gates opening, making way for the Benotrists therein to finish what the gargoyles began.

The gargoyles were an even greater mystery. They swarmed over the city walls in unending waves, striking their encampments in force, only to continue west. The Torry and Macon cavalry gave chase, harrying the gargoyles while they continued west then north. They kept at a distance from the main body, as their magantor forces followed from above, dropping an occasional munition into their midst. It appeared the gargoyles were withdrawing to their homelands, forsaking the remaining Benotrists to their fate.

Gorzak's apes suffered their first casualty since joining the Torries at Corell, with Mucran, son of Muctar, taking a scimitar across his throat. Captain Sarelis and her fellow warriors accounted well of themselves, harrying the gargoyles throughout their retreat, most gaining their first kills of the detestable creatures.

Of the gargoyles, nearly five thousand perished in the assault. Their wounded unable to continue were slain by the besieging armies. No quarter was given the creatures, just as they returned none. The total that escaped to the north was difficult to count but likely numbered thirty-five telnics, the sum representing all that remained of the 4th, 5th, 6th, 7th, 12th and 14th Gargoyle Legions that had invaded the south. The surviving soldiers of these legions would never forget that Morac had brought them to such ruin and forsook him to his fate.

* * *

Torg was the first to help Terin off Wind Racer's back, his grandson slowly stirring, looking akin to a garment wrung out by a washer woman. Lorn could barely dismount before several others had already done so, helping Torg free Terin from his straps, guiding their weary champion to level ground, the boy staggering as if drunk.

"What ails you, lad?" Torg growled.

He then explained Wind Racer's affliction and unique remedy, which caused his attackers to fall asleep and drop off as the air grew light in the high altitude. Had it been daylight, Terin could only imagine what a sight he could have beheld. Not that he could have seen anything if it was daylight, since he suffered the same affliction as the gargoyles, saved only by the straps binding him to the saddle.

"Magantors are known for doing so in the wild when set upon

by lesser birds, and even gargoyles on occasion, but I have never heard of it with tamed mounts," Lorn said.

"If they had, we would never know since the act would doom any rider not bound in his saddle," Torg said.

"True," Lorn acknowledged. Magantor riders needed to be free to shift in the saddle, thus never binding themselves in place as Terin did. But by doing so, he was able to do things others were unable to, or would not risk doing, allowing Wind Racer to twist severely, or spin upside down, and now fly high enough into the firmament where the air was thin. Perhaps such risks were worth their gains, which was something for Lorn to consider.

As soon as Terin recovered, he saw to Wind Racer's many wounds, blood staining his white feathers along his legs, breast and tail. He couldn't determine their severity, though the avian seemed ill effected. Lorn assured him that Ilesa would see to him once the severely wounded were attended.

* * *

Morac stood upon the battlements of Notsu's west wall, looking on in disgust as the gargoyles moved north and west beyond the Macon armies, instead of south and east, where they were ordered to regroup and return to the city from the south. He was betrayed, whether by Kriton, who led the attack, or the rank and file, who abandoned him once beyond the walls. The greater meaning wasn't lost on him, that he was doomed. The men left to him were too few against the armies arrayed against them, their fifteen thousand men facing Lorn's vast host.

The city streets behind him were silent as a tomb, the sunrise doing naught to bring them to life. Only the sound of sandaled boots on stone streets echoed above the eerie silence. He needn't spare a glance to know its source. It was but one of many patrols his men conducted through the streets of the dead city, though they would find nothing amiss, for dead men stirred no trouble.

And so it was throughout the city, street after quiet street, the smell of rotting flesh drifting in the morbid air, drawing thousands of carka birds circling overhead. The foul birds were harbingers of death, eager to feast on the fallen.

It was Daylas who came to him, the only one brave enough to approach the Benotrist lord. The man was an able governor, administering the city since its surrender. Morac begrudgingly admitted the man's ability in command, having kept the city in good order, and securing his supply caravans, despite the difficulty in doing so with their lines of communication stretched dangerously across the Kregmarin. Those vital lifelines were now severed, leaving them to starve, trapped within Notsu's fated walls.

"They are gone, then?" Daylas asked, stepping to his side, placing the flat of his hand upon the thick rampart, peaking above the parapet, his gaze narrowed to the horizon where the gargoyles' retreating forms shrank in the distance.

"It appears so," Morac said, his voice dead of emotion.

"Your orders?" Daylas dryly asked. Their options were few, if any. There was no retreating from this place, not now. Gargoyles could fly over the enemy blocking their path, but those that remained were men, and men could not do so. Even now the enemy were building siege works to keep them in, leaving only the southern perimeter open to them to withdraw, but even that would soon close once Ciyon's army was positioned there. Even if it remained open, they could not risk it. They would have to move south and look for a way to maneuver north around these armies without being chased down. It was impossible, leaving only two options, to fight or surrender.

"We bleed them upon these walls as they did to us at Corell," Morac said before retiring to his quarters.

"As you command." Daylas bowed his head, knowing the truth of it. Surrender was not an option, not after what they had done.

* * *

It was late in the day when Cronus found Ilesa, watching as she moved among the wounded, her growing womb evident in the folds of her red matron gown. She knelt beside a wounded soldier with a gash running hip to hip, his eyes closed, having succumbed to exhaustion and shock long before she came upon him. The fellow was watched over by his friends, who were unable to move him to the matrons' pavilion, waiting upon her to come to him, which she could not do until all those with mortal wounds at the pavilion were treated first. Many more would perish if she moved about the battlefield treating men spread out over large areas, forcing her to first treat those gathered together before seeking out those spread out. She stopped several times to recharge the regenerator, watching painfully as men died waiting for it to restore.

Cronus watched over her as she worked, keeping at a distance to not be in her way, but close enough to protect her, along with the guards Lorn and Mortus assigned her. Whenever she finished with one patient, a sister matron would lead her to the next, guiding her as she worked. He was impressed with all the matrons and their ability to keep men alive long enough to be treated by her and to treat many injuries with what they had available. They were skilled in setting broken bones and the use of herbs to treat infections. Cleanliness was practiced vigorously, a lesson learned though ages of practicing their craft.

The soldier gasped, suddenly waking as she treated him, the wound to his belly closing as if never sundered. Looking upon Ilesa, the soldier quickly realized who treated him, thanking her profusely, his fellow warriors chorusing his gratitude. It was then Cronus realized the soldier was Torry, and his comrades who looked after him were Macon. He was likely one of many thousands moved from the Torry 1st Army to the Macon 2nd. The Torry 1st Army was similarly joined, containing as many Macons as Torries, the blending of their armies forging a special bond between their two peoples. There were drawbacks to such blending, the greatest of which was adjusting to different orders of march and command, as well as equipment, all while marching to war. The long journey from Fleace to Corell gave them precious time to accomplish this.

Ilesa greeted them kindly but gently disengaged, moving on the next soldier requiring her aid. Upon treating the next man, she was forced to wait and recharge the device, stopping in a small clearing away from her many guardians and helpers. He watched as she sat beside the regenerator on the matted grass, fishing a folded parchment from her breast. He watched curiously as she carefully opened and read it, its soiled edges proof that she had read it many times. Once finished, she wiped a lonely tear from her eye and folded the parchment, replacing it to her breast.

He watched as she silently sat there waiting upon the device, her gaze fixed ahead, though staring at nothing but a memory. He said not a word, respecting her privacy and broken heart. He watched over her for a time before stepping away, needing to call upon King Mortus and see where he was needed.

* * *

The Benotrist magantor riders remained as Morac's *guests* since General Gavis departed the city, confined to the quarters provided them while others attended their mounts. As scouts, the two men had no saddle mates, forgoing an archer for greater speed. They were completely blind to happenings outside Notsu's walls, though suspecting the sorry state of the siege, and the gargoyles forsaking their garrison. They wondered when they would be released to ferry messages for Lord Morac, eager to depart. Should they remain any longer, the option of leaving would expire, trapping them in this dying city. Each knew the dire straits they found themselves when their weapons were taken, and they were confined in their chambers under guard and far from the magantor stables.

It was late in the evening when they were roused from their beds and escorted to the stables, the large stone edifice near the vacant city forum. Large pillars surrounded the structure, supporting its massive roof with its circular platforms jutting from covered stables. They were surprised by the eerie silence of the city and the empty streets, streets that were always active even in the dead of night. They were greeted with a terrible rancid odor throughout their trek through the city streets before coming upon the stables. Passing before the north face of the city forum they spied a semicircle of pikes driven into the street in front of the ancient structure, with freshly severed heads adorning them, dead eyes staring back at them in the dim torchlight that alit the street. They quickly moved on, hurrying apace to the stables, their escort ushering them through its massive entrance, making their way to the stable roof above.

Lord Morac greeted them in the center of the stable roof, standing in the open circle surrounded by a dozen magantor stalls, which held only their two avians, which were saddled and waiting, tethered to their stalls. The stable had four launching platforms jutting from each corner of the structure, with a short tunnel leading to each.

"Leave us," Morac ordered the guards out.

"You called for us, Lord Morac?" one scout asked.

"You are to deliver this to the emperor," he ordered, ignoring the idiocy of his question, setting a sealed parchment in his hand.

"When shall I depart?" He asked his next foolish question.

Morac simply directed him to his magantor, where his weapons rested upon the floor beside the waiting avian.

The man quickly bowed and stepped away, taking up his sword and spear before leading his mount from its stall, following Morac's arm pointing to the northwest corner of the platform. Once clear of the tunnel, he took in the fresh night air upon stepping onto the open platform, gaining his mount, the bird strutting along the stone causeway, springing into the night air. He soared over the lifeless city streets before breaking over the outermost battlements, soaring higher into the heavens. He drew farther away, passing over the Torry and Macon encampments, the sound of horns below alerting them of his presence. The evening sky was soon filled with enemy warbirds soaring to give chase. He pushed on, urging his mount to outrace them, speeding apace through the night sky.

He was overcome several leagues beyond the city walls, arrows riddling both rider and mount.

As the rider succumbed, few noticed the second magantor passing over the south wall of Notsu, keeping a low silhouette before breaking higher, bearing two riders. Morac looked back one last time as the doomed city disappeared in the darkness, leaving his men to their fate.

* * *

The following morn found Governor Daylas in the former estate of Tevlan Nosuc, searching through the parchments in Morac's private sanctum for anything he might have left behind. His spies informed him of Morac's suspicious activity the night before but were late in telling him of his departure. Would the emperor truly overlook his failings after this disaster? Morac was twice defeated at Corell and now abandoned fifteen thousand soldiers to certain death, including himself. There were no more magantors to take Daylas from this place, and there was no hope of good terms should he surrender, Morac's latest antics saw to that. Once the Torry King learned of what they had done, there would be no mercy for them. He grew more frantic, finding nothing of value, not that it would do any good at this late time.

He gave up the search, throwing the stack of parchments across the chamber before looking up to the ostentatious fresco adorning the wall, depicting the battle of Kregmarin, displaying Morac in all his faux glory. Morac had commissioned a second fresco of his fabled triumph on the walls of the front atrium where every visitor to this grand estate could *admire* it upon entering. Morac's vanity was boundless, and Daylas cursed his name for betraying him to this fate. Daylas supplied his army, governed Notsu when no other could, and snuffed out treason wherever it took root, and what gratitude did he receive for his labors? To be left to die without even a word. Daylas' noted calm façade began to break, with the gravity of his dilemma becoming more apparent. He hoped to find something of value to offer the Torry King for his life, but there was nothing. Only Morac's remaining slave girls had any value, the poor creatures kneeling in the outer corridor as he searched the villa. He doubted Lorn would receive them in exchange for mercy. He could not even offer up the garrison; every soldier knew there was no hope for gentle treatment, for Morac saw to that before he fled.

"Madness." Daylas shook his head as he left the chamber.

* * *

The following days continued with the besieging armies tightening their hold upon Notsu. Ciyon positioned his army along the southern perimeter, cutting off the last avenue of escape for the defenders. The men of Zulon and Teso took up their place between Ciyon in the south and King Mortus in the west, while the men of Notsu positioned beside the Torry army north of the city. Lorn would see them among the first to enter the city, ensuring the good citizens of Notsu laud them with praise, seeing their own people leading the city's liberation.

A Notsuan commander of unit, Gleb Naruen, was the ranking commander among the few survivors of their once considerable army. Most of the men he now commanded were of citizen stock, recruited from the many refugees that fled to Torry North. Once encamped behind the Torry lines, Commander Naruen drilled his men relentlessly, preparing them to assault the city. He watched as they moved across the open fields in narrow columns, with shields interlocked forward, above and along their flanks, akin to an armored crustation snaking its way across open ground. It was a difficult formation to master, relying on group cohesion and practice, something that required time. The previous winter was much wasted in gathering these volunteers. By the time they began to form ranks, the Benotrist invasion forced them to war before they were fully trained. They were rushed into battle, skirmishing with the Benotrist invaders throughout the Torry heartland, before joining the siege of Besos, and then marching here.

Commander Naruen rode across the face of the formations, reminding them to dress their lines as they advanced, before galloping back to his observation position upon a low rise overlooking the drill, where King Lorn awaited him. The King took great interest in their progress, regularly observing their daily practice.

"The men are improving, Commander," Lorn greeted him upon his return to the observation point.

"Improving, Your Majesty, but with far too many mistakes," Gleb said, circling his mount about, coming alongside the Torry King to face in the same direction. The heated glare of the summer sun shone in his eyes, making the wearing of his helm most uncomfortable, but he dared not remove it, lest his men do likewise.

"Perhaps, but they are making fewer with every day of training," Lorn observed. Torg sat the mount upon his opposite side, sharing his opinion on the matter, with a dozen elite forming a perimeter around them.

"Yes, and hopefully less tomorrow. The sun is most unpleasant on my eyes, but I am grateful for the clear weather to train," Gleb said.

"True, but I would welcome rain to refill our cisterns, and ease our supply trains," Lorn added.

"Then we can give thanks for whatever the weather gives us, Your Majesty, though the men will gripe with either outcome," Gleb snorted.

"It is a soldier's right to complain." Lorn smiled.

"They take great pleasure in it," Torg snorted, having spent his life training warriors.

"Not to hasten the event, Your Majesty, but when might we assail the city?" Gleb asked.

"Soon. We have a few more surprises for the garrison before we commit ourselves," Lorn said.

"Very well. I will remind the men to double their efforts with these tactics," Gleb said, referencing the column formations that would be needed to advance along narrow streets with archers raining down arrows from every window and rooftop.

"And how fares the men's spirit, Commander?" Lorn asked.

"They are eager to reclaim our home, Your Majesty. Many have kin that still reside within the city." Gleb left unsaid the fears for said kin. The men had heard the rumors of the harsh treatment of their people. Many were sent north into slavery or slain outright by the occupiers.

"Hold firm, Commander. Soon you shall reclaim your ancestral home," Lorn reminded him.

* * *

One day hence.

The besieging armies cheered the arrival of thirty-five dracks, and their thousands of iron spears, which were quickly moved into position before the north and west walls. The smiths at Corell worked feverishly repairing many of the captured siege weapons, sending the greater portion of them to Notsu, the rest remaining at Corell. By nightfall they began targeting the north and west gates, and their surrounding battlements, the iron shafts punching holes through their weak ramparts, spraying stone fragments on the men manning the walls.

* * *

Three days hence.

The besieging armies again cheered as the vanguard of the ape and Troan army broke the eastern horizon, fresh from their victory at Gotto, and led by an ape commander named Horzak, a former captain of the 1st Ape Fleet. The thickly-built commander rode ahead of his army, following the Macon cavalry King Mortus provided to escort him to the command pavilion along the northern perimeter of the siege lines. With characteristic ape boisterousness, he rode through the cheering throngs of Torry soldiers, pounding his fist to his chest, a broad grin spreading across his face. His glee was further fueled by the sight of Gorzak and his fellow ape warriors who stood forward of the King's pavilion, hooting excitedly and shaking their axes and swords in the air while the Jenaii King and his attendants looked on with stoic indifference.

General Horzak dismounted and greeted his comrades heartily before following King El Anthar into the pavilion, where King Lorn, King Sargov and King Mortus awaited them, along with Lucella Sarelis, Gleb Naruen, and Generals Lewins, Valen, Ev Evorn, and Vecious, along with Torg and Jentra.

"Welcome, General Horzak." Lorn received him warmly, stepping forth to clasp the commander's forearm.

"Aye, King Lorn, Admiral Zorgon and General Mocvoran offer their friendship to your brave people," the ape general greeted him.

"And how fare your admiral and general?" Lorn asked.

"General Mocvoran has arrived at Tro with eight of his telnics. The rest of his army continues to be ferried from Torn. Admiral Zorgon holds Tro with what remains of his fleet and a portion of the Troan garrison. They are both reinforced by a growing force of Casian and Enoructan levies. As for my command, I've brought four telnics of apes and one telnic of Troan warriors from Gotto, where we lifted the siege with the aid of General Zem, who named me as his replacement until his return," Horzak explained.

"And where has your good General Zem gone?" King Mortus asked curiously.

"He has returned to Tro and his ship and sailed away."

"Sailed away?" Torg asked.

"Aye, but where to, I do not know. Here, this explains much." Horzak passed Lorn a parchment bearing the seal of the Troan magistrate.

Lorn opened and read it, holding closer to Mortus so he might read it at the same time.

"Magistrate Adine sends his regards and details the happenings at Tro. It seems a considerable force is being assembled at the port city, with more ships and soldiers arriving daily. Raven and the others arrived safely at Tro, and departed to complete repairs on their ship, though Klen Adine does not know where they went to do so. He further states he is aware of our situation and has arranged caravans of supplies to be sent from Tro, the first soon to arrive." Lorn shared the good news, which caused a chorus of relieved sighs from everyone, even the stoic Jenaii. If the Troans were so well stocked that they could afford to offer their excess, then things were truly turning to their favor.

"Does he state anything else?" King El Anthar asked.

"President Matuzak will soon arrive at Tro and asks that we commence a council of war upon his arrival," Lorn added, causing a hopeful smile on every face.

"Where shall we confer?" Torg asked.

"Here," Mortus declared.

"Here? We are in the middle of a siege," King Sargov said.

"All the more reason to end it. We take Notsu and hold our council in the city forum.," Mortus said.

"What of Morac? He still wields the *Sword of the Sun?*" Sargov asked.

"And we hold three swords of light. There will never be a better time than now. I say we take the city, slay whatever soldiers remain, and send Morac's head to his emperor."

"I agree." Lorn smiled, seconding Mortus' enthusiasm and plan.

"As long as you wait for my soldiers. We shall not be denied gargoyle blood!" Horzak bellowed.

"There are no gargoyles left in the city, only Benotrists," Jentra reminded the ape general.

"They'll do!" Horzak declared with a toothy grin that bordered insanity, giving the others pause. They rightly wondered who their new allies truly were. They saw what a handful of gorillas were capable of, but Horzak led four thousand, most of which were displaced sailors from the 1st Ape Fleet, each with bitter memories of their lost ships.

"We shall wait upon your army, general, before we attack," Lorn said.

"Good!" Horzak grinned.

With that they began to plan.

* * *

The evening grew late as Lorn and Mortus walked through the Torry encampment, their guards holding at a distance as they visited the cookfires of the men. The meeting with Horzak went longer than expected once the planning of the attack commenced. Every commander and King seemed to add valuable insight on the way to take a city, and the coordinating of such diverse forces. Men, Jenaii and apes had never fought as one, and required specific zones of responsibility once the city was breeched. Lorn felt reassured of their plan, humbled by the insight of so many accomplished warriors and kings. He recalled the lessons he learned during the siege of Mosar, particularly the chaos that ensued once the army was dispersed in the city streets, where command and control fell completely apart. He remembered fighting street to street with no sense of the overall situation. That was something he hoped to correct this time.

Visiting with the men at their cookfires was a welcome respite, listening to their stories and concerns, and where they haled. Mortus and Lorn visited with the men most of the nights of the siege, gauging their sentiments and morale. Their presence always lifted the men's spirits, knowing their kings shared the battlefield and hardships of campaign with them. These walks also gave the two men time to speak with each other as they moved from site to site.

"How fares your army?" Lorn asked of him as they stepped away from a cookfire, with the next some distance ahead, firelight illuminating the ground in between.

"Nearly half our casualties have returned to duty, most because of the efforts of our dear Ilesa," Mortus said, referencing the gargoyle attack.

"Yes, Kato's gift has been a wondrous boon." Lorn sighed.

"I wish I had known him as you had," Mortus said in all honesty. How strange, he thought, that he felt such sentiment. Had anyone told him before the siege of Fleace that he would befriend the Torry Prince, he would have locked them away for madness.

"I too wish that. He was a good man, and a better friend. Without his aid, I doubt we would have carried the day at Mosar."

"What is the old proverb? Victory is born of many fathers," Mortus recalled.

"Yes, and defeat but an orphan," Lorn completed the age-old phrase.

"Your Earth friend was but one of many fathers of that victory, if what I have leaned of it is half true."

"Yes. Terin was most helpful, and all the brave soldiers, both our own and our Yatin friends."

"And you," Mortus added.

"Perhaps in a small way. As a leader I simply pointed them in the direction to go. All the heavy work the men accomplished on their own."

"You did more than point. You led them to where they needed

to be, guiding them to their destination like a wandering star, while any experienced commander would question your judgement. It was your gift of foresight that carried the day, more so than the efforts of any one individual."

"Such foresight is a blessing from Yah, and not of my own effort. He bestows it upon those he chooses, often those who we would consider unworthy. Such was I, until he granted mercy to the odious child that I was."

Mortus heard this from Lorn many times now, trying to match the arrogant youth with the man who now walked beside him, and unable to do so.

"No matter what you consider your worth in his divine eyes, the fact remains that you are blessed by his generous gift of foresight and wisdom. What does he say to you now that we can make use of?"

Lorn stopped midstride, dim starlight illuminating his countenance, causing Mortus to stop as well.

"I have not had a vision since our victory at Corell, actually before then, during our march from Fleace. I have not heard his voice or seen his vision since. We stand before these walls of our own volition, not by his will or guidance." Lorn sighed, looking skyward to the starlit heavens, feeling as though he stood on the precipice.

"Notsu was the logical choice," Mortus reasoned.

"True. We are guided here because it made strategic sense to do so, and without Yah's guidance to direct us otherwise, we have little choice but to heed our own counsel. The problem that most concerns me is what path do we follow after we take the city?"

Therein lied their dilemma. Driving Tyro's legions from the south was one thing, but taking the fight north was far more difficult. One needed only to look north where the Kregmarin plain stretched endlessly to the Benotrist border to know the difficulty in such a task. No commander of any worth would suggest such a crossing, which left the question unanswered of what path they must follow.

"Do you trust your God to see you through to the end?" Mortus asked.

"Yes." He sighed.

"Then trust him in this. He has not spoken to you since Corell because taking Notsu was the obvious choice. All of your trials before this have forged you into a sound battle commander, one I am honored to fight beside. Yah has sharpened you into a lethal blade. If you have not heard his voice, you have either displeased him, or he trusts your wisdom, and there is nothing I have seen to indicate you have displeased him."

"Perhaps, but…"

"But?"

"I can't help but think of King Kal. He heard Yah's voice, and heeded his counsel and yet was destroyed, and his kingdom thrown down."

"There is one grand difference between you and King Kal, Lorn."

"In all candor, I can think of more than one." Lorn smiled in good humor.

"Since I knew Kal not, I cannot judge, but if the legends we were told are true, then Kal heard Yah's voice in those ancient days."

"The same as I," Lorn pointed out.

"Yes, but did anyone else in those days?"

This gave Lorn pause.

"Did any of his followers hear Yah's voice, or have visions?" Mortus asked.

"No one knows."

"Yes, no one knows, but what does your heart tell you? Mine tells me NO. If others heard his voice, then Yah would not have forsaken them to their doom."

"Perhaps, but what does this have to do with me?"

"Don't you see the difference? You are not alone in your visions. Yah has sent you help in many forms. He promised you the help of the chosen, the three men who were sent to help you, one that stands very near to us at this place." Mortus lifted his chin in Cronus' direction, where he stood watch just ahead with their other guards.

"True," Lorn conceded.

"And what of Jonas' visions? He has been given many since he was born to this world, using them to guide his path and Terin's as well. What of the Sisterhood? Captain Sarelis and her warriors all speak of what they saw in Queen Letha's throne room, especially

Deva. Is there one more unworthy to be given visions from Yah than her? Yet, I see no vitriol in her carriage. I cannot reconcile the woman she was with the woman she now is. For all that she lost, I would expect her to be bitter and broken, but she is filled with duty and devotion to your God."

Lorn hadn't considered that. Deva was changed, though Corry would never truly forgive her. No sane person would, unless they were forgiven themselves for their odious nature. He reflected upon his youthful arrogance, and the visions Yah gifted him to correct his path. Was he truly any better than Deva? No, he was worse. Deva was corrupted by her mother's wickedness. Lorn had no such excuse. His father was a good man, as was all his councillors, specially Torg, Jentra, and especially Squid. If an impartial judge weighed the greater guilt of Lorn and Deva, he would lose.

"I misspoke," Mortus said, drawing him from his painful thoughts. "There is one more unworthy to receive Yah's blessing than young Deva... and it is I."

"You were King looking out for the betterment of his realm. Your sin is that of duty and worry, not a flaw in your nature," Lorn said.

"You didn't know my heart, Lorn. I was just as foul as you claim to have been in your youth. All my life I have been plagued with dreams of you, dreams that Yah explained to you. Those dreams were visions gifted from Yah to bring us together. I could not see their true meaning, but I believe Yah blinded me from the truth so you might reveal them so powerfully as you did. Only such a display could turn me from my madness and unite us in cause and purpose. You see Lorn, many of us have been given visions from Yah to aid you in your destiny, and that is what sets you apart from King Kal. You have friends, and brothers, and armies that love you. Kal did not have such men to stand beside him."

Lorn regarded the Macon King for the longest moment, seeing in his eyes a friendship that was as strong as any he ever felt. He wished his father were here to share in this friendship, this kindred spirit that transformed both men so profoundly. It was the same friendship that manifested in their armies, each blended evenly with

Macon and Torry soldiers serving in every army, whether they bore a Macon or Torry standard.

Lorn placed a hand upon Mortus' shoulder, protected by its thick armor and mail.

"You are a great king and a better father but an even greater friend. I am honored to fight beside you." Lorn smiled, his eyes moist with emotion.

"Aye, lad, beside you to the end."

* * *

One day hence.

The next evening found Cronus walking among their cookfires, relieved of his duties of guarding the kings for a well-earned respite. He was surprised to find Jentra sitting alone beside a cookfire near King Lorn's pavilion, opening a well folded parchment to read by firelight, while sitting on his pack. It was a rare sight to see Jentra without Lorn or Criose's company, or even young Dougar, who seemed to gravitate to the seasoned warrior with natural ease. He thought to leave him alone, guessing he wanted privacy for once, but something within convinced him otherwise when Jentra lowered the parchment as if perplexed, shaking his head.

"Would you mind if I share your fire?" Cronus ventured, stepping from the shadows.

"For the hero of Tuft's Mountain, I would be honored," Jentra said, waving an open hand to the space beside him.

"If you knew what transpired that day, you would not quickly ascribe me such an honorary." Cronus smiled wanly, setting his own pack down to sit upon, noticing Jentra still holding the parchment in his hand, and not hiding it away.

"Bah, your humility is as misplaced as Terin's and our king's. From one soldier to another we both know the truth always rests somewhere in between."

"True enough. I didn't mean to bother you this fine evening, knowing you rarely have a moment of quiet," Cronus ventured.

"It is strange I hadn't noticed." Jentra spared a glance to his surroundings, surprised to find no one else around.

"You are usually our king's constant companion, and Criose your ever-vigilant shadow." Cronus smiled.

"Aye, even a blind man could see that. I sent Criose and Dougar to inspect our mounts some time ago, and then to fetch themselves some supper. The blasted fools would go hungry watching over me if I didn't intervene on their behalf." Jentra snorted, shaking his head.

"They are adherent to duty."

"Aye. I would growl at them more if not for all the poor lads have suffered. Dougar losing his kin as he did is enough to make a grown man weep. And Criose… well, you can guess what he suffered. Neither he or Terin speak much of what they endured in Guardian Darna's keeping."

"Somethings are best not spoken of," Cronus said, recalling all he endured.

"Aye." Jentra sighed, knowing of what he spoke as well as what he had so recently lost. He noticed Cronus looking at the parchment in his hands, and rightly guessed he was too considerate to inquire.

"I am not so good with words." Jentra sighed, referencing the parchment.

"Something you wrote?" Cronus asked.

"Aye. I received a correspondence from the lady Neiya, niece of King Mortus. She inquired of my safety and health, expressing her concern for my wellbeing. I took it upon myself to respond, and she wrote again expressing her pleasure that I am still well, and I again have penned this in response." He shrugged, lifting the parchment.

"You are fond of her?" Cronus asked, surprised to see Jentra show any romantic interest. Jentra was the most unapproachable man he had ever known, and he wondered what sort of woman could crack his iron veneer.

"She is a fine lady, and what she sees in an old soldier like me is beyond my limited understanding."

"You are not old, Elite Prime." Cronus smiled, speaking his official title.

"It's the wear more than the years, and we can forgo frivolous titles."

"Fair enough, Jentra."

"Aye, Cronus."

"Would you care if I had a look?" Cronus offered as Jentra handed over the parchment.

The missive read like a military order, with specific places and dates, detailing their movements and casualties in a painfully bland narrative. It was almost comical in a way, though Cronus was too polite to say so.

"What do you think?" Jentra asked, knowing if anyone knew how to speak with a lady, it was Cronus Kenti. Lady Leanna's reputable beauty was quickly whispered throughout the realm, as well as her tragic end. Once his mourning was ended, Jentra had little doubt that Cronus would find many a fair maid hoping for his hand.

"Well, the important thing is that you are responding to her. That shows your interest. I know very little of courting a lady, my Leanna being my first and only success in that regard, but I have learned a few things from her that might help you."

"What do you suggest?"

"Your missive is very detailed on our martial activities which, being a good soldier, you are practiced in saying, but a woman that expresses interest in a man, as she obviously does with you, would like a more... personal touch."

"Personal?" Jentra wasn't sure of that.

"Yes. Perhaps mention you were pleased to have been introduced to her. You can follow that with some small details about you she may find of interest, like your family and your journeys with our king. Maybe mention things you enjoy doing, or ballads that you find to your liking."

"Would that be appropriate?"

"You are already courting her, are you not?"

"Yes."

"Then it is more than appropriate."

"I should redo this. General Valen is sending a courier come morning, and I hope to get this to her hand as soon as I can."

"It shouldn't take you long to pen it."

"Should I include anything else?"

"No, start with that. Once she responds in similar fashion you can expand on what you said."

"Expand?"

"Yes. You can speak of your hopes and plans for the future, or things you are fond of, allowing her to share hers in kind. You will know what to say as she will likely ask you."

"Thank you, Cronus. I am not very good at these sorts of things."

"None of us are, Jentra, but you will get better. I think you and Lady Neiya will be a good match. You are still a young enough man to have many children, and I am certain our king would like that very much."

Jentra shook his head at that, not able to refute it.

"If you would be so kind as not to mention my writing to Lady Neiya with our king. Since it was his idea, he would be insufferable to learn that I found it favorable."

"I will remain silent. I know how our friends can torture us so." He laughed.

"We are agreed, very good." Jentra sighed in relief.

"I envy you in this, Jentra, experiencing courtship in its earliest phase. Those were pleasant days, then again, all my days with Leanna were pleasant." His voice trailed off.

"I am sorry for your loss."

"Thank you. I am thankful for the times we did have and the daughter she bore me. Without Maura I don't know how I could go on. Looking at her, I know a very large part of Leanna still lives."

"At least there is that. I look at all the men we have lost in this awful war, and I think of the mothers, wives and daughters they left behind. You are rare in that you lost your wife, and that she didn't lose you."

"If I could only have taken her place." Cronus sighed.

"Aye, every man of worth shares that sentiment, willing to lay down their lives for those they love." Jentra knew what Cronus endured was torturous, having to watch helplessly as his wife passed in his arms, with no power to save her.

"She comes to me at times," he said, taking Jentra aback, before elaborating.

"She speaks to me about our daughter and how she loves us, her presence a gift from her God, so she claims."

"Her God, but not yours?" Jentra asked.

Cronus was silent for a time, wondering about that. He was a man of logic and reason, trusting what he could see and hear over magical beliefs that he could not, but there were things logic and reason could not explain.

"I don't know, Jentra. I have denied Yah, thinking he is but of our king's fevered dreams, but after all that we have seen, I…" he struggled to find the words.

"Aye, I know. Only so many strange things can happen before you have to believe. I am not one for weepy confessions of faith and supplication, but I can logically believe that Yah is real, and Lorn's beliefs are true," Jentra said, looking to the starlit heaven, humbled before its majesty.

"You believe then?"

"I do." Jentra shook his head, still gazing skyward. It was then he knew that Yah dwelt within him, granting a peace he had never known.

For once, Cronus felt ashamed, for no matter the signs given him, he felt a shroud clouding his heart where Yah was concerned. He felt too much pain and loss to entertain his acceptance.

"I wish I could feel your faith, Jentra, to feel your peace, but…"

"But what?" Jentra looked to him now.

"Something holds me back. Part of me cannot reconcile it all, and another part is angry that if he is real, then why make us suffer so? Why take her from me?"

Jentra couldn't answer that and allowed Cronus to continue.

"Though I must admit he is real, as he confounds me with dreams of Leanna and nightmares of…" He regretted what he almost said, though Jentra knew there was more.

"Nightmares?"

"More like visions, visions so real and consistent, and repetitive that they must be from Yah."

"What are they?"

"It is always the same. My friend is slain by a gargoyle spear, and I am helpless to stop it. Nearly every night since we arrived here at Notsu I have been tormented by this vision, wondering the meaning of it all."

"This friend is very dear to you. I can hear that in your voice."

"He is. We have saved each other's lives many times, and I cannot bear to see him perish after losing so many others."

Jentra knew that was why Cronus approached him this night, and what troubled his mind.

"He saved your life, and you have saved his, each risking your own to do so, I assume," Jentra said.

"Aye." Cronus sighed.

"It reminds me of something Lorn often says. *There is no greater love than one willing to give up one's life for a friend.* You are a good man, Cronus Kenti." Jentra placed a hand on his shoulder, the two sharing a newfound friendship below that starry sky before the walls of Notsu.

* * *

It was late in the night when Lorn was finally able to sleep, despite thoughts of tomorrow's battle filling his mind. He was eager for this campaign to end so they could plan the invasion of Tyro's realm. The Benotrists holed up within Notsu felt more an annoyance than anything else. He wondered why they had rebuffed his offers of surrender or even parlay to discuss terms. They seemed committed to their own destruction. Regardless, he was determined to end this siege come the morrow. No sooner had he finally succumbed to exhaustion then he was awakened by a rather loud exchange outside of his pavilion.

Donning his cloak, he stepped without finding his guards blocking Deva from advancing. Her pained look gave him pause, knowing there was more to this than requesting a simple audience.

"Let her pass," Lorn ordered, seeing her lower her shoulders in relief as he waved her within. She was dressed only in a short tan tunic and sandals, forgoing armor or sword, as if she had recently been roused from sleep.

"Something troubles you, cousin?" Lorn asked, honoring her by acknowledging their kinship.

"I was awoken by a vision, Your Majesty," she addressed him formally, ever wary of her current station. Deva was not well received by her Torry hosts, with most looking upon her as the woman who enslaved their champion, offending the honor of the realm. King Lorn was more forgiving, knowing she was as worthy of redemption as he was, a sentiment most did not share.

"What vision have you been given?" he asked.

"We must forgo the attack tomorrow."

"Forgo the attack? We are on the brink of victory. The enemy are greatly reduced, outnumbered and starving, if the reports we have received are only half correct," he rightly pointed out.

"All you say is true, but the vision…" She paused, seeking the words to explain.

"I have received no such vision," he added, feeling something so momentous would deign a direct vision from Yah, and not through another.

"Why you have not, is beyond my understanding, Your Majesty, but the vision is real all the same. You must not attack come the morrow," Deva said with a voice nearly void of emotion, as if she were entranced. With that, she bowed and withdrew, leaving him with his thoughts.

He debated her words throughout the night, any hope for sleep beyond him now. Could he trust the word of Deva Estaran after all she had done? She was supposedly redeemed by Yah, but could that have been a false assurance? All logic and reason led to the attack on Notsu commencing come the dawn. How long dare he keep his army encamped outside these walls? Remaining in place incurred great risk as well.

Why would he be led here only to be denied by the word of Deva? No, it was decided. The attack must commence. He felt this to be the correct path, though Yah had been silent since Corell.

THE CHRONICLES OF ARAX

* * *

The following morn.

A blast of horns signaled the attack, the besieging armies closing upon the walls with the morning sun breaking the eastern sky. From the west marched the Macon 2nd Army, with seven and a half telnics arrayed for battle. General Ciyon's army assailed the south wall, fourteen telnics marshaling forth under the standard of a golden crown upon a field of black and white divided diagonally across its sigil. From the east came the four thousand ape and one thousand Torans marching over open ground with ten telnics of the Jenaii 2nd Battlegroup coursing overhead. From the north came the greater host of the 1st Torry Army, twelve telnics strong, spilt in half, each part flanking the two telnics of Notsuan soldiers marching upon the north gate of the city.

Notsu was mostly square built, with an outer curtain wall that ran seven leagues in circumference, with a wide moat dug below its forty-foot walls. A massive double doored gate was centered upon each wall, with raised drawbridges and iron porticus' protecting their reinforced timbers. The defenders manned the walls, their iron helms peaking above the ramparts at the vast host drawing dangerously nigh. The north and west gates spent the previous days under constant assault from the dracks aligned against them, the heavy shafts peppering the bulwarks around and above each gate, leaving large gashes torn from the battlements.

HARROOM!

The horns sounded a second time, bringing the advancing armies to a halt mid distance to the city walls, well within archer range, but the Benotrists wisely held their aim. Scores of Torry, Macon, Jenaii and Sisterhood magantors flew overhead, fire munitions dangling from their saddles. General Dar Valen coordinated the attack, saving his munitions for this assault. The flaming projectiles were difficult to produce and transport, and needed to be used judiciously. The large avian soared high above Notsu, keeping beyond archer range, though a few ballistae managed to bring down two of the warbirds as they angled lower, dropping their munitions upon the city walls. Lorn looked on from where his mount stood before his disciplined ranks, watching as fires ignited along the north wall. He could see men flailing behind the stony battlements, flames licking their backs and arms.

The armies held in place as the Jenaii approached the east wall in force, soaring high enough to test the Benotrist archers that saved their aim for them.

HARROOM!

Horns sounded again, heralding more Jenaii, a telnic each assailing from south, west and north, approaching each gate of their respective walls, while the greater host of the Jenaii assailed the east wall, focusing on the gate and its supporting bulwarks. Amidst their airy ranks came Wind Racer, driving straight for the north gate, his powerful wings pounding the air like claps of distant thunder.

* * *

Terin leaned in the saddle as Wind Racer sped toward the north gate, his hair trailing his steel helm, slapping poor Cronus in the face, where he sat behind him.

WHOOSH!

A ballistae shaft grazed Wind Racer's left wing, the avian dipping below its path before correcting, with another passing under his breast. Terin held on, leaning to one side and then the other, Wind Racer swerving through a hailstorm of arrows, while Jenaii swarmed the skies around them. Several struck true, dropping the winged warriors from formation, arrows piercing wings and limbs, with one taking a Jenaii through the throat. Cronus watched as the warrior dropped off their right, hitting the ground after a steep plunge. Notsu's north gate loomed prominently ahead, its battered ramparts still holding despite the dracks' unceasing barrage. Benotrists still manned the battlements, with nearly twenty archers crowding the turrets flanking the gate, sending shafts into the encroaching foe.

Terin watched as dozens of Jenaii passed over the north gate, setting down upon the battlements, nearly half skewered by Benotrist spears. A flurry of clashing steel sparked where the survivors set down, most cut down by Benotrist blades jabbing from every direction. Twenty more soon followed, breaking left, concentrating on the east turret, where the north wall met the jagged battlements jutting above the raised drawbridge. Terin lost sight of the melee, winged Jenaii forms obscuring his view. Dozens more swept over the north gate, breaking right to assail the west turret, Benotrist archers thinning their ranks before being overcome by their numbers. Hundreds more followed, sweeping onto the battlements above the gate as Wind Racer set down in their midst, Terin and Cronus springing from his saddle.

SPLIT! THRUST! SPLIT! SLASH!

They cut into the nearest foe, breaking blades, and cleaving men in two. The Jenaii swarmed all around them, sweeping the Benotrists from the ramparts. Arrows spewed from the rooftops of the structures behind the north gate, where Benotrist archers took up position. Dozens of Jenaii staggered or dropped all together, feathered shafts piercing wings or vitals, before they raised shields, fending off the unexpected barrage. Hundreds more followed, passing overhead to assail the enemy bowmen, penetrating deeper than they had planned. Terin and Cronus raced down the nearest stairwell, with scores of Jenaii following them below.

SPLIT! THRUST!

Terin cut down a Benotrist rushing up the stair to meet them, catching him unawares by the startled look in his eyes. They fought their way to the base of the stair, stepping in the open behind the north gate, greeted by dozens of angry Benotrists armed with swords and spears.

SPLIIT! SLASH!

Terin broke left and Cronus right, taking them by surprise with their intrepid charge, the swords fueling their power and boldness. The Benotrists staggered briefly, taken aback by the sight of their comrades dropping in quick succession before dozens of Jenaii joined the fight, swarming around Terin and Cronus like a cleansing wind.

Seeing the enemy dead or fleeing south deeper into the city,

Cronus disengaged, gathering a group of Jenaii to commandeer the gate.

* * *

Elos led the Jenaii telnic assailing the west gate, swerving through the air, dodging arrows and ballistae, his Sword knocking others awry as he swept over the battlements, setting down upon the wide causeway atop the gate.

SPLIT! SLASH!

He cut down the nearest sentry, his blade cleaving an upraised shield and the arm holding it. He slipped around the stricken warrior, taking another across the chest, moving before ascertaining the damage, the blow taking the man from his feet, dropping where he stood.

Dozens of Jenaii warriors dropped dead from the sky, many striking the causeway where he tred, arrows feathering their limbs and vitals, one with a ballistae spear driven through his lower chest, the stricken warrior writhing briefly before expiring. Elos blocked such sights from his mind, moving dutifully apace, his every step executed with practiced grace, cutting a swath through the disordered defenders. Scores of his brethren set down around him and swarmed the adjoining turrets flanking the gate. Elos shifted, knocking an arrow aside, stealing a glance over the inner parapet, looking east where Benotrist archers were perched atop the rooves of the nearest structures, firing into the following waves of Jenaii passing overhead. Elos could barely discern what followed with the morning sun shining in his eyes as the Jenaii swarmed the rooftops, the sound of clashing steel and dying men echoing above the din.

The Jenaii above the gate kept within the shadows of the reverse parapet until the Benotrist archers to their east were silenced, their comrades sweeping over the adjoining rooftops. Once the rate of arrows winnowed, they moved apace to the nearest stairwell, or sprang over the parapet, setting down behind the west gate, where they were met by a unit of Benotrist warriors, greeting them with a wall of shields and spears, cutting down many in the confined space.

Elos followed his comrades over the parapet, setting down upon the street below, dodging a spear thrust between a wall of shields, the Benotrists driving the Jenaii back from the gate. Elos slashed at the encroaching shield wall, snapping spear tips and blades with every swing. He pressed his own attack, cutting large gashes in the formation, his fierce countenance bathed in the glow of his emerald blade. His bold attack fueled his comrades resolve, many falling in around him, though their smaller shields were poorly matched against the Benotrists' larger square ones. Men and Jenaii cried out, dozens dropping on each side, spears and blades taking their toll in that confined space, the high ceiling and narrow causeway affording little space for the Jenaii to fly overhead without being skewered. Eventually fissures broke in the shield wall, the Benotrists yielding ground before being overwhelmed.

Once clear of enemy, Elos ordered the porticus raised and drawbridge lowered, his fellow Jenaii holding the gate and its surrounding area while the Macon 2nd Army advanced into the city.

* * *

The south gate fell soon after the west, the Jenaii telnic eventually overtaking the defenders, while the east gate succumbed to the ten telnics of Jenaii passing over their ramparts and much of the adjoining wall.

BOOM!

The entire east gate was awash in flames as soon as the Jenaii seized it, flames erupting through the half open gate after the porticus was lifted and drawbridge lowered. Flames swept the adjoining stairwells, spilling out onto the battlements above, as well as the turrets flanking the gate, engulfing scores of Jenaii warriors. Dozens more sprang from the walls, their wings alit as they fled the battle.

BOOM! BOOM! BOOM!

More fires erupted along the length of the east wall, as if every cask of munitions was gathered there for that purpose, the Benotrists saving them solely for the Jenaii. Nearly one in ten of the Jenaii attacking the east wall was wounded or dead, terrible blasts sending the rest in disarray. King El Anthar swept through the heavens above upon his mighty magantor, his stoic gaze sweeping the length of the east wall, flames leaping above its outer parapet. He swept lower, meeting his wavering army in midair, drawing his blade, pointing it toward the city and the structures beyond the beleaguered wall. He sped onward, his warriors following his path forward over the wall and beyond.

The great host of apes shouted their war cries, following the Jenaii toward the east wall, with the Troans beside them, racing for the open gate which was engulfed in flames, the bodies of friend and foe flopping throughout the tunnel of the opening beyond.

* * *

The north wall.

HARROOM!

Lorn gave the signal for advance, signaling the Notsuan ranks forward through now open north gate, the Torry army following in their wake. Commander Naruen ordered his Notsuan cohorts into a column formation as they neared the gate, suffering few arrows from the winnowed ranks of Benotrist archers manning the adjoining lengths of quickly emptying walls. The Notsuan soldiers' hearty cheers grew deathly quiet as they passed over the drawbridge, and through the gate, passing between the Jenaii warriors guarding the opening, the winged warriors regarding them respectfully. They continued on, Gleb Naruen ordering them to break off into three columns, one east, one west and the third south.

They marched in good order through the wide avenue of the city that ran due south where the city forum rested at Notsu's center, before continuing straight to the south gate. The other great causeway bisected the city crossway, connecting the east and west gates, again meeting at the city's center where the central district of the city rested. They drove south unmolested, with nary a soul in sight, while the Jenaii sprang from rooftop to rooftop, watching their flanks.

King Lorn followed in their wake, passing through the north

gate, Wind Racer catching his eye, circling overhead like a watchful sentinel. His empty saddle meant Terin and Cronus were loose somewhere in the city. General Lewins followed his king through the gate, ordering his army up the nearest stairwells, sweeping the wall in each direction from the north gate. Lorn dismounted, following them to the battlements above to gain a better view of the city, Torg and Jentra guarding his flanks. Clearing the stairwell, he was greeted by the ghastly carnage of the east wall, where billows of black smoke obscured the sun, their noxious fumes carrying into the city from the prevailing winds. Even from afar, he could see hundreds of Jenaii warriors struggling amidst the flames, while thousands more passed deeper into the city.

Lorn shook his head sadly, knowing his plan to hold the outer walls before advancing in force was quickly coming undone. The last thing he wanted was an all-out assault through the deadly narrow streets, where casualties would needlessly mount. No plan ever survived the sting of battle, and fighting through the confines of a city made the task doubly difficult. The Jenaii were to take and hold the east wall but were now forced to pass over its heated walls, seizing the next line of structures. That plan was soon waylaid when a series of explosions erupted along the adjoining rooftops, more fires igniting scores of dwellings and barracks west of the east gate. Hundreds of Jenaii succumbed to the tactic, many flying off through the air, caked in flames, or dropping into the streets below. By now King El Anthar signaled a withdraw, pulling back beyond the wall, while the apes held outside the east gate, waiting for the fires to die.

Lorn ordered a messenger to halt the Notsuan advance, keeping them several blocks south of the north wall while they ascertained their overall position. By the time the missive was sent, they had already advanced another block, sweeping away the few soldiers in their path. It was all too easy, and Lorn's order was poorly received, but Commander Naruen relented all the same. The Jenaii shadowing their advance held up on the rooftops to either side of the Notsuan columns, keeping a watchful eye on their surroundings.

From Lorn's vantage point, he could barely make out the happenings along the west and east walls, and could see nothing along the south wall, the city obscuring his line of sight. Two of General Valen's magantors set down upon the battlements above the north gate to ferry missives to the other commands. Lorn immediately set them out to the El Anthar, Ciyon and Mortus' commands to inform of his position.

Mortus' army had already seized the west wall, his men fortifying in place, as Ciyon's army did likewise along the south wall. To the east, the Jenaii reformed outside the city walls, waiting for the fires to die before returning. The Torries and Macons fortified in place along their respective walls, sweeping away the last vestiges along the adjoining causeways, waiting upon the Jenaii to resume their advance before pressing deeper into the city.

* * *

With the advance into the city paused, the Notsuan columns found themselves in the vulnerable position south of the North gate along the central avenue. The men along the flanks formed shield walls, wary of any movement from the adjoining structures, most of which were plain stone edifices with flat rooves where scores of Jenaii were perched, watching carefully for any sign of the enemy. Commander Gleb Naruen grew impatient waiting for the order to advance, knowing his men were inexperienced soldiers, lacking discipline to hold in place for long. They seemed prepared to jump at anything that moved. His greatest fear was his column breaking, drawn off by any distraction, whether fleeing or attacking, leaving the rest of the column exposed.

Such fears repeated in his mind as Benotrist soldiers began to emerge south of their position, hundreds forming into shield walls across the breath of the avenue some three hundred paces ahead.

"Close ranks!" Gleb ordered his men, extending his line across the width of the wide street, matching the length of the Benotrist line. The Jenaii along the rooftops pointed out movement to their east, likely a second column of Benotrists attempting to flank them.

* * *

The plight of the Notsuan columns was quickly relayed to King Lorn, who stood atop the battlements above the north gate. The original plan was for all attacking armies to seize each wall first before advancing together into the city, but the Jenaii were still absent on the east wall, and the Notsuans exposed forward of their lines. He feared repeating the costly battle of Mosar, his army bleeding as they fought street to street, where all order was lost to thousands of individual melees. Despite such fears, he ordered his men forward.

Horns sounded their advance, the first columns advancing along the Notsuan left flank, preceding the sounds of battle waging in the streets ahead.

"All columns forward!" Lorn ordered, knowing the battle was joined.

All along the north wall, Torry units advanced, as more soldiers of the 1st Army passed under the north gate, entering the city.

* * *

"Kai-Shorum!"

The Notsuan lines faltered at the sound of Benotrist war cries as soldiers spilled out of the structures along the west side of the avenue, while the greater host advanced north upon their position. Dozens of Jenaii warriors sprang from the rooftops, dropping down upon the Benotrists emerging from the buildings, bringing their full weight down upon them, breaking necks and shoulders as their boots stuck their heads or backs, crumbling most to the ground, before springing back into the air before their fellows could strike back. Many were skewered before able to do so, Benotrist spears driven through their middle. The bold Jenaii tactic strengthened the Notsuan column, giving their commanders time to dress their faltering ranks.

Commander Naruen ordered the right half of his columns to advance into the buildings where the Benotrists were spilling from, while sending his left to brace for the Benotrist flanking attack from the east. His forward ranks remained in place, awaiting the Benotrists advancing to meet them, now closing within one hundred paces.

"Hold!" he ordered, standing behind his shield wall, watching the enemy advance.

Within moments the Benotrist column smashed into their front, swords and spears jabbing fiercely between their shields, while arrows passed overhead.

* * *

Torry infantry flooded the adjoining streets, commanders struggling to keep their formations tight as they advanced. King Lorn joined the center most column racing south along the main thoroughfare to directly aid the wavering Notsuan ranks. He followed three units of infantry, with Jentra and Torg guarding his flanks, and Criose, Ular and Lucas close behind. The way ahead was a cacophony of fire and death, with smoke billowing above rooftops to either side of the street, while men battled along the broad avenue.

Up ahead, the Torry front ranks were strongly met by columns of Benotrists, the sound of clashing steel and iron echoing over the din.

CRACK!

Torg snagged Lorn by the collar of his mail, pulling him back as the structure to their east began to falter. Criose rushed forth, grabbing hold of Jentra as the tall granite columns lining the face of the edifice buckled, spilling onto the street, with the roof of the structure collapsing atop of it, crushing dozens of Torry soldiers beneath the massive stones. Men cried out in agony, limbs broken and trapped beneath the ruble, powdery debris choking the air, billowing above the street in a thickening cloud.

CRACK!

Another structure began to falter farther north, before collapsing into the street, crushing dozens more beneath its crumbling weight.

* * *

Two streets west of the Notsuan columns.

Terin and Cronus followed the Torry column marching south through the adjoining avenue, the street far narrower than the central causeway the Notsuans traversed, with small stone dwellings lining either side. There were no Jenaii to guard the rooftops above, or to scout ahead. The way was eerily quiet for several blocks, before coming upon a prominent crossway, before the advancing Torries were met by a host of Benotrists spilling out from dwellings on each corner.

Terin raced to the fore, skirting the left side of the Torry column, before bursting east along the adjoining street, smashing head long into a Benotrist shield wall.

SLASH!

He cut into the approaching wall of iron, blood spraying off his blade before slashing again, caving the center of the formation. Cronus passed to his right, slashing in kind, his fell blade blunting the Benotrist line. Before the enemy could react, Torry soldiers filled in around Cronus and Terin, exploiting the confusion.

* * *

Gorzak led his small ape contingent in King Lorn's wake, trailing the Torry King as the structure dropped in his path, Lorn's visage obscured in clouds of debris. He raised his twin axes, bellowing an ape war cry, leading his brothers forth as the second structure dropped where they had been. They raced southward, ignoring the cries of the wounded in their wake, and the rising din up ahead. They continued through the settling powdery cloud, coming upon the disordered Torry ranks, and the sound of clashing steel drawing ominously nigh.

Jentra staggered to his feet, coughing up dust while struggling to clear his eyes. He found Criose laying at his feet, his left leg bent at an unnatural angle, with bone peaking through his sundered calf, his screams rending the foul air. The man had saved him, pulling him back from certain death, and taking the blow intended him.

"Good lad," Jentra said proudly, squatting at his side, while ordering the nearest soldiers to attend him before seeking out Lorn.

He found the king bent over with his hands upon his knees, coughing up debris, with Torg standing watch before him, sword drawn and ready.

"Here they come!" Torg declared, stepping forth as a host of Benotrists emerged through the debris, dozens passing overtop the rubble from the east, while many more swept into the street around it, emerging from all points east.

The Torry Master of Arms gave them no time to climb down from the debris, cutting the legs out from under the first to come near, standing atop a slab of broken granite while Torg hacked his right ankle. Torg stepped aside as the fellow face planted into the street, before hacking his sword arm as he lay at his feet. Torg moved on before finishing him, lifting his shield to glance a hurried strike from the next fellow approaching the edge of the rubble above, swinging madly at Torg's head below. Torg swiped his feet as well, the force denting his left greave, breaking his ankle. Torg moved back, the fellow dropping atop the rubble above, writhing in pain.

Jentra closed ranks beside Torg, meeting a Benotrist jumping into their midst, his shield blunting a hurried sword thrust, his counter taking the man's sword arm at the wrist.

By now Lorn was at their side, parrying a spear, before gutting a man attempting to jump upon them. The sound of men flooding the street off their left forced them to back away from the rubble, as the surviving Torries north of the fallen structure closed ranks. From their vantage point, Lorn could not see what was happening south of the ruble, only the sound of clashing steel and shouting indicating the battle happening there. The Torries formed a shield wall to receive the throngs of attacking Benotrists.

"YAHHH!"

The sound of gorilla war cries rent the air, with Gorzak leading his eight fellow apes into the fray, his twin axes cutting into the Benotrist mob. Lorn couldn't spare a glance northward where the apes were fighting, with far too many enemies between them. He could not see Carbanc, son of Hukok, brain a man with his war hammer, or Huto, son of Hutoq, lopping heads with his sword. Nor could he see Ular and Lucas fight in tandem somewhere in between, the Enoructan champion dodging blows and striking opponents with fluid grace.

"PACKAWW!"

Torry magantors passed overhead, bearing fire munitions, depositing them into the enemy midst far to their south, where a great host was gathered.

* * *

Eastern siege lines of Notsu. Jenaii encampment.

General Valen kept a magantor in reserve to move Ilesa where she was needed, her first stop being behind the Jenaii and ape siege works. She immediately ordered the wounded gathered in one place, and began to treat them, nearly all victim of terrible burns. She cried silent tears for these brave warriors, most refusing to cry out in pain, their stoic nature refusing to relent. The casualties were in the hundreds and would quickly drain the regenerator. Thankfully it was early in the day, and she could recharge it once it was drained.

* * *

The Macons advanced from the west gate, Elos and the telnic of Jenaii crowding the west gate preceding them along adjoining rooftops, scouting ahead. News was quickly relayed to them of the falling structures. King Mortus ordered his men to slow their advance and search and clear structures along their path.

Ciyon's army pushed on from the south wall, his men clearing the structures as they advanced, their telnic of Jenaii bounding rooftop to rooftop, mirroring their path, while keeping a vigilant eye north, where towering structures of Notsu's central district rose imperiously into the morning sky.

* * *

Terin cut through the edge of the Benotrist formation, swerving left to the north side of the east west street, Cronus following at his heels, before passing through the open archway of the nearest structure, following a retreating Benotrist. He dipped below an arcing blade, the northern steel glancing across his shield. He made a shallow arc with his own sword, adjusting to the dim light as he pressed on, feeling his blade strike something soft, blood flying off its murky tip. Cronus followed close behind, breaking left as he entered, meeting a hurried thrust before cutting down his foe, the golden hue of his blade illuminating the chamber.

SPLIT! SLASH! THRUST! SLASH!

Terin moved apace across the floor, the chamber's dim light growing brighter by the moment. He moved right across the open space of the structure, striking down men in quick order, while Cronus swept in the other direction. Both circled back, coming upon each other as the last foe dropped, their blades crossing path, Golden light meeting Terin's murky blade, with specks of green flickering along its length whenever they drew close.

They paused to catch their breath, taking stock of their surroundings. The chamber had a high domed ceiling above an open floor, portending some sort of municipal structure, perhaps the atrium of a council forum or magistrate, or even a warehouse of exotic goods, which would have been displayed for the wealthy customers of the city. Whatever its purpose, they could only guess. They saw several corridors breaking off from the chamber into the back recesses of the structure. They thought to ignore them and rejoin the battle in the streets outside, but something drew them hither.

They advanced across the floor, deciding on the nearest corridor, centered in the back wall. Taking one step therein, they were met with a rancid odor, strong enough to give them pause. The terrible scent grew intensely as they advanced, becoming almost unbearable, Terin's cheeks growing pallid with every step. Cronus fared little better, following a step behind, keeping his sword at the ready. A series of doors lined either side of the corridor, and they passed through the first they came upon along the left. Within the small room they were met by a gruesome sight, several heads set in the middle of the floor in various stages of decay, the rest of their severed corpses piled along the side of the chamber.

They immediately withdrew, searching the next room and finding it much the same. Two more rooms continued with the grisly finds, with even greater numbers piled in their center. They were soon joined by others storming the structure as the Torry columns pressed the enemy beyond their position, sweeping the Benotrists ever eastward. Terin and Cronus withdrew, rejoining the battle in the streets outside, thankful for fresher air, their fellow Torries following their exit.

* * *

Dadeus Ciyon joined Telnic Commander Gorin Houn, trailing the forward ranks as they swept north along the broad avenue that ran from the south gate to the central district of Notsu. They were weakly met with unit sized elements attempting to slow their advance, their shield wall driving the enemy before them with relative ease. Dadeus raised his shield, deflecting an errant shaft fired blindly into their ranks from a rooftop to their front right, the archer that sent it quickly overcome by Jenaii racing ahead, bounding rooftop to rooftop. Dadeus didn't spare a glance to the archer tumbling from atop the structure, his broken body impacting the unforgiving street below.

Commander Houn ordered his trailing units to sweep the buildings to either side of the street as they advanced, wary of the tactics that waylaid their brothers advancing from the north gate. Dadeus was thankful for the competent Houn, the man an able commander who was assigned to his command from the Torry 1st Army. Because of his ability, Dadeus gave him the most important axis of advance, driving due north from the south gate. His other telnics marched north through the adjoining streets, paralleling their advance.

"General!" Guilen shouted from behind, alerting him to a messenger making his way to them through their crowded ranks, marked by green feathers adorning the man's bright helm, signaling the ranks to allow him to pass.

"What have you?" Dadeus asked, keeping his eyes forward, trying to see over the sea of iron helms before him.

"Bodies, General!" the man said, his face ashen.

"Bodies? Speak sense!" Dadeus admonished.

"Bodies in every dwelling and structure we have searched," the man elaborated.

"Whose bodies?" Dadeus asked, tearing his eyes from the front to look at him.

"We don't truly know as yet, but most likely the people of Notsu. We are finding them in piles in every place we have entered."

"Get word to our Jenaii friends, have them relay these finding to the other commands!" Dadeus ordered, pointing out the winged warriors guarding the rooftops to either side of the avenue.

The man hurried off just as Guilen reached his shield overhead of Dadeus, deflecting another errant shaft that somehow fell in their vicinity. Dadeus gave him a broad smile, thankful for his friend's timely intervention.

* * *

Lorn managed to reorder his broken column, clearing every dwelling and structure along the rubble strewn street, before advancing deeper into the city, reinforcements swelling his ranks. He inwardly groaned as they were caught up in fighting street to street, and dwelling to dwelling, losing all sense of order and command. This was his greatest fear, the repeating of the costly battle of Mosar that bled his army so terribly. His plan of a slow, methodical advance had degenerated into chaos, playing into Morac's hands. They circumvented the debris, sweeping south and east, marching ever forward toward the center of Notsu.

They passed over several cross avenues, many empty, and some strongly reinforced, forcing them to halt and engage. More than once they were aided by the Notsuan column spilling into the cross streets from the west, while they advanced from the east, crushing the enemy between them. Lorn met briefly with Commander Naruen, the Notsuan general looking well used by this point in the day, blood staining his mail, with vicious scratches along either side his helm, proving he came close to death several times this day. They agreed to continue their advance upon Notsu's center, returning to their respective avenues of approach.

It was late in the day when they eventually came upon the central district of Notsu, its impressive structures towering above the rest of the city, with large citadels spiraling into the heavens. With most of their fire munitions spent, their magantors circled above the city, their archers targeting wherever the Benotrists gathered, firing into their midst from safely above. Lorn could see where the magantors circled above, guiding him to the where the Benotrists were concentrated.

His column came upon a broad open space with a great fountain at its center, surrounded by the city forum, magistrate, and amphitheater, and several other impressive structures he could not identify. Gathered in this open space was gathered several thousand of the enemy, formed into a defensive circle, their spears leveled between their shields. The open space was paved with close fitting stones and mortar, with dozens of streets converging upon it from every direction. The sounds of clashing steel and dying men echoed from the west side of the Benotrist formation, where the first telnics of King Mortus' army arrived.

Wasting no time, Lorn ordered his column to advance into the enemy from the northeast, driving forth, with Gorzak and his apes following close behind, and Torg and Jentra guarding his flanks. They remained behind their shield wall as they two armies collided. Within moments, the Notsuan column arrived from the north, then Terin and Cronus' column from the northwest.

"Kai-Shorum!" Benotrist war cries echoed over the din, with thousands more emerging from all the adjoining structures, many racing down the wide, stone steps of the city forum, rushing madly into the fray. Others spilled out of the amphitheater, pouring through its many archways, engaging the Torries and Macons wherever they found them. Hundreds emerged from the magistrate, resting along the northwestern face of the open area, many stumbling unexpectedly into Terin and Cronus' fell blades. Thousands more emerged from all the structures circling the area, their war cries building into a deafening crescendo.

The advancing columns held in place, waiting upon their rear echelons to fill in around and behind them, strengthening their lines before advancing. The Benotrists swarmed the forward ranks of the Notsuan column, pressing the center of their shield wall. Gleb Naruen ordered reinforcements forward to stem the tide, before his lines bowed further. His green soldiers lack of experience was balanced with desperation, each fighting to survive with nowhere to withdraw. The men lacked the training to rotate their forward ranks in combat, causing the men manning the shield wall to quickly tire, succumbing one by one. Fissures started to spread, quickly filled with charging Benotrists. The Notsuans fought desperately to stem the tide, giving ground grudgingly.

Deva ordered her driver to fly lower, readying an arrow as they passed over the center of the Benotrist army, loosing her shaft in their clustered ranks. They circled overhead as she fired arrow after arrow into their gathered midst, unable to miss. Her sister riders joined in the tactic, with Captain Sarelis leading her contingent with skillful grace. Dar Valen ordered his riders to follow their tactic, along with the Macon and Jenaii magantors.

WHOOSH!

A Benotrist heavy spear whipped past a Sisterhood rider, the shaft grazing its left wing, causing it to shift violently, several feathers fluttering off as the projectile passed. Lucella Sarelis trailed the nearly stricken warbird, looking south and west to the source of the attack. There upon the roof of a towering structure rested a ballista, its crew readying another heavy spear, shielded from ground view by sturdy sandstone battlements. She ordered her charges forth, closing upon the foe from several directions, until a flash of emerald light gave her pause, where Elos' familiar form could be seen approaching the crew from behind, dispatching them in quick order. Lucella led her warbirds in a sweep of the area, looking for any other ballista they might have missed.

* * *

Terin and Cronus again broke free of their column, meeting the Benotrists charging down the steps of the magistrate, cutting down the first ranks before they reached level ground. They split shields and blades with ease, lopping heads and limbs, or cutting men in half as they went. Terin's blade grew darker with every kill, the blade swallowing the light around it, while Cronus' burst in ever strengthening brightness, nearly blinding his foes with its golden light, strengthened by Terin's blade. Terin was nearly invisible to his foes, catching most by surprise, with few raising a blade before he cut them down. Whenever Cronus' sword drew near, specks of blue light flickered across his blade, allowing his foes to see him but do little else, their sword arms paralyzed as if frozen in place. They forced the Benotrists back, before joined by a unit dispatched from their column. The reinforcements drove the Benotrists through the entrance of the magistrate, holding them in place with leveled spears between their shield wall, freeing Cronus and Terin to move elsewhere where needed.

King Mortus' men pushed from the west, driving the enemy back into the open space of the city square, their Jenaii scouts swarming the rooftops above, overlooking the open ground below. The emerald glow of Elos' blade danced along the battlements of the city forum, his fellow Jenaii struggling to keep pace.

From the south, the first elements of Ciyon's army began to arrive, pressuring the enemy wherever they emerged from the adjoining streets. The entire scene was still an even run affair, with thousands of Benotrists crowded across the open space, with many more spilling out of the surrounding structures. The Jenaii accompanying the Torries in the north, and Ciyon in the south, converged upon the rooftops above, joining Elos' warriors drawing from the west. Hundreds of the enemy spilled out onto the rooftops, contesting the Jenaii for control of the battlements overlooking the unfolding battle. Dar Valen's magantors swooped down upon the enemy wherever they emerged on the rooftops, snatching them in their talons, dropping them beyond the battlements.

* * *

Lorn trailed his shield wall, keeping a vigilant eye as the enemy pressed their front and left flank. They were heavily outnumbered but kept a tight formation as reinforcements continued to fill in behind. Jentra guarded his left, and Torg his right, with Ular and Lucas not far behind. Jentra wondered Criose's fate, having left him in others care far to their north. The man had saved his life, risking his own to do so. They found themselves staring out across the sea of soldiers crowding the city square, which was more akin to a giant circle, the battle spilling out into a dozen adjoining streets. Stealing a glance to the top of the structures surrounding the crowded circle, they spied the clash of steel and arrows spewing back and forth along the rooftops and battlements above. A constant stream of magantors soared overhead, their archers firing ceaselessly into the enemy's midst.

With a sudden surge, their entire front advanced, the Benotrist shield wall giving way. Lorn wondered the cause of the unexpected shift, until a line of flames erupted across their front, the sound of his soldiers screaming piercing the air. It was a trap, a line of oil spread out across the ground, waiting for them to advance upon before being set alight. The flames were not unusually strong or high, but they caused the shield wall to falter long enough for the Benotrists to exploit.

"Kai-Shorum!" the enemy shouted, the war cries reverberating along the front, before charging into the flames.

The Torry shield wall bowed and cracked, dozens of fissures expanding with the Benotrists slipping through. The flames broke up the Benotrist formation as they advanced, no man willing to stay in place with flames licking their sandaled feet, but the damage was done. Both sides degenerated into hundreds of separate melees. The men separating Lorn from the front melted away, many withdrawing in any direction they were able, while most hurried forth, engaging the enemy where they found them.

Torg stepped forward of Lorn, blocking a slashing sword with his shield, reaching his blade underneath, slicing the inside of the man's arm in a fluid motion. He shifted around the stricken foe, engaging the next as the man's sword clanged off the stone street.

Lorn barely had time to react as Torg cut down the second man, managing to jab him repeatedly in the side, before crushing his knee with his boot. He didn't bother finishing either foe, before advancing upon his next. Lorn recovered, following after the Master of Arms and Commander of the Elite, finishing his kills as Jentra followed at his side. Benotrists swarmed all around, coming upon them in an unending stream. Lucas appeared off their right, knocking one to the ground with the flat of his shield, before Ular slipped around him, hacking the man's sword arm, while Lucas gutted him. Ular spun around his friend, taking another approaching Lucas' right, catching him unaware, his blade finding purchase above the left hip.

Lucas shifted, blocking another hasty strike with his shield, driving back the attacker with a hurried jab, before a furry arm passed overhead.

CRUNCH!

The man cried out, Carbanc, son of Hukok, planting his hammer in the man's skull, his fellow apes filling in around them.

Jentra guarded Lorn's left, blocking another strike, before disarming the man's sword, his following move driving him back, finishing him soon after before another was upon him. Lorn stepped to Torg's left, parrying a strike intended for the old warrior, who was onto his fourth kill, moving amongst them like a starving Lincor. If Lorn had time to spare, he would stop and watch Torg move about the battle space, shifting from blunt force to fluid grace, each opponent determining his method. Whenever they came upon him in greater numbers, he shifted, stacking them to one side while finishing the closest, leaving the others to his comrades. Lorn found his third kill an easy mark, the man's attention drawn to Torg, not seeing Lorn coming at his side.

And, so it went, with all of them drawn into a hundred separate battles with commanders struggling to reestablish their lines. There seemed no end to the enemy, with more and more breaking through, charging in every direction. Lucas dropped another, with Ular guarding his back, before switching places. Gorzak accounted well of himself, spinning his twin axes in a dizzying flurry with a maddened glee in his eyes. His fellow apes were equally charged, instilling abject terror in their foes. A sudden howl escaped the lips of Gullor, son of Gummor, a Benotrist spear piercing his throat, making him the second of Gorzak's warriors to fall in battle. His death fueled his comrades' rage, each tearing into their foes with unnatural strength.

Another surge pressed their left flank, scores of Benotrists crashing through what remained of their shield wall in that direction, opening the entire front to chaos. The enemy no longer came in twos and threes, but a massive herd, met only by those who stood to post, buying time for their comrades to rejoin the battle.

"Kai-Shorum!"

The Benotrists shouted, a near dozen fixing Lorn in their sights with leveled spears, rushing forth in a maddened charge. Lorn turned, blood dripping from his sword, having finished another foe. He had little time to register his eminent death, hoisting his shield and readying his blade to receive them.

SMASH!

A sudden blur of silver and blue crashed into the lead attacker, taking him from his feet, followed by a flurry of jabs and slashes, dropping two more in quick order. There between him and death, stood Jentra, wielding his blade like the master swordman he was. He cut down another as Lorn hurried to his side, the enemy coming upon him all at once. Lorn rushed to his left, engaging another as Torg finished the enemy he was previously engaged with, freeing him to join them.

"Agghh!" Lorn heard the awful scream, finishing his foe before turning about.

There upon the ground was Jentra with a Benotrist impaled upon his sword while two others drove their spears through his gut, standing over him, twisting their shafts free to stab him again. Lorn moved with unnatural speed, cutting down the first, causing the second to back away. Lorn drove forth, knocking his spear away, then taking his wrist before he could draw his sword. He drove him to his back, hacking his legs, then his middle, working his way around the prone and wounded man. He didn't stop until his arms were chopped, and a dozen blows delivered to his head and breast for good measure, blood spraying the King's face, giving him the visage of a tortured spirit.

Torg moved past him, striking another, with Ular and Lucas guarding his flanks. Thunderous roars echoed over the din, heralding thousands of gorillas swarming from the west, flooding the circle. Above this black tide soared the great host of Jenaii, together sweeping the enemy before them. Lorn looked on as the enemy drew away like water retreating from the shore. His gaze found Terin and Cronus beside Torg, with a dozen bodies at their feet. He hadn't seen them emerge out of nowhere just as Jentra stepped forth to save his life.

With the enemy dead or dying all around them, Lorn hurried back to Jentra, quickly finishing the Benotrist still impaled upon his sword, the man writhing on the ground beside him. Lorn killed him swiftly, dragging him away from his friend before kneeling at his side. Jentra looked up at him, his eyes staring through the slits of his helm, before Lorn eased it off his head. Lorn quickly tore a strip from his own tunic to dress his friend's wounds, but it was nearly useless, blood issuing from his lower stomach, his innards bulging to spill out.

"No!" Tears welled up in Lorn's eyes, knowing their time was short unless Ilesa was close by.

"Lorn, I..." Jentra lifted a bloody hand to him, touching his face, his eyes going in and out of focus, his body wracked with pain.

"Hold on. Give Ilesa time to find us. Please hold on," Lorn begged of him, his heart breaking at the sight.

"I don't know if I can. Forgive me."

"Forgive you? You saved me. It is I that beg forgiveness for bringing us here," Lorn said, tears squeezing from his eyes.

Jentra just shook his head, refuting that.

"You are my king and my brother, and I would follow you to the ends of the world and beyond," he said, before coughing up blood.

"Don't give up, Jentra. Stay with me. Give Ilesa time," he begged.

"I..." Jentra winced in pain, trying to form the words he so wanted to say, but Lorn spoke for him, needing him to know what he meant to him.

"You are my greatest friend, Jentra. I could have done nothing without you. You are my friend, my brother, and my right arm. You need to live; do you hear me? You need to live and wed a woman worthy of you. You will have many children and they will wed my children, and we will grow to be old men, with our grandchildren gathered around us while we tell of the battles we fought, and the adventures we shared." Lorn forced a smile for Jentra's sake, despite the tears now pouring off his cheeks.

Terin and Cronus stood near, looking on as the battle drew away from them, before Torg scolded them to move on.

"You've a battle to win. You haven't the luxury to say goodbye." Torg pointed them across the way, where their armies were pressing the enemy on all sides. With heavy hearts they moved on, each wishing they could say something, but such was war. Bearing swords of light, they knew every foe they killed meant life for one of their own. Lucas and Ular followed them, disappearing into the mass of ape, human and Jenaii soldiers sweeping the enemy before them.

Torg remained, standing watch as Lorn held onto Jentra, while sending runners to find Ilesa, though doubting if they would reach her in time.

Jentra's eyes were growing heavy, but he managed to pull a parchment from beneath his mail, handing it weakly to Lorn, blood smearing across it, Lorn receiving from his shaking hand.

"Please give that to Lady Neiya. I missed sending it with the currier this morn. Tell her I am sorry." He coughed again.

Lorn had nothing to say, remembering Kato's last missive to Ilesa.

"You are the greatest king to have ever lived, Lorn, greater than King Zar, King Lore and King Kal. I am proud of you," he managed to say despite the pain wracking his body.

"I love you, my friend," Lorn said with watery eyes.

"And I you, my friend." Jentra sighed, his eyes drawing dully open.

There in the center of Notsu, Jentra died, and Lorn wept.

Chapter 14

As Jentra lay dying in Lorn's arms, the others swept the Benotrists before them. Torries, Macons, Notsuans, Troans, apes and Jenaii pressed upon them from all directions. General Ciyon's men cut their escape southward, his army converging on the center of Notsu behind their shield walls. Men of Teso and Zulon joined them, cutting down the enemy like grain before a scythe.

Jenaii warriors swarmed the rooftops and battlements of the surrounding structures, slaying every Benotrist to a man. Magantors coursed overhead, their archers firing into the Benotrists ever shrinking pocket. Deva fired her one hundredth arrow, loosing her shaft into the mass of enemy squeezed in the city's central square below. Her driver circled above, before breaking north, giving space for the other magantors crowding the serried sky. She looked on as the great mass of ape warriors swarmed from the east, smashing the Benotrists shield wall like hammers to clay. A sea of furry arms snatched shields from the Benotrists' grips, tossing them overhead while their fellows caved chests with hammers or axes. Others simply used the shields as blunt objects, smashing them atop their foes. The ferocious tactics exposed many to counter thrusts, Benotrist swords gutting gorilla warriors in equal numbers, but the damage was done. The entire western face of the Benotrist shield wall gave way, with apes pouring through.

From on high, she could see the glow of Cronus' sword as he

moved through the enemy ranks, hundreds of Torry and Macon soldiers following in his wake. Terin was beside him, though difficult to see, his visage fading and appearing throughout the battle, with no rhyme or reason. He was in one place and then another, though never far from his friend's side. The Benotrists were given no quarter, any attempting to surrender cut down with impunity. The sound of clashing steel and screams of the dying echoed hauntingly above the city.

Deva felt numb to it all, watching sadly at the unfolding horror, knowing this was their lot, to suffer in victory or defeat until the bloody end of the war. How many would endure to the end? Precious few was her only guess.

* * *

King Mortus and Elos paused at the steps of the ruling forum, briefly regarding the pikes driven into the street, where sat the rotting heads of Morac's victims, their identity obscured by decay. They continued up the steps, hundreds of Macon soldiers clearing the way before them. They passed through the entrance, traversing the high stone corridor leading to the inner rotunda, passing between the crafted columns lining either side of the wide causeway. Soldiers stood in close ranks to either side, holding position as the Macon monarch passed.

Though warned of what to expect, Mortus was taken aback upon entering the rotunda, where the Council of Notsu governed the ancient city since its founding. Passing through the arched entryway brought them upon the upper part of the circled chamber, with rows of stone benches lined along its circumference overlooking the center platform below. The forum was akin to a large bowl, with the benches circling the open stone circle below. Men of greater standing and distinction would always be seated upon the lowest benches, nearer the stone circle where debates were held. Along the far side of the circle rested high backed chairs where would sit the ruling forum, forming a half arc around the platform.

Staring down upon the stone circle, Mortus and Elos were met with a gruesome sight. There before each chair was driven a pike through the stone floor, upon which rested the heads of the ruling forum, preserved with tar coating their flesh, with enough decay to give them a ghoulish appearance. They descended the nearest stair which passed between the rows of empty benches, joining the telnic commander who sent runners to warn the King of what he discovered. The commander saluted Mortus with a fist to his heart as the king and Elos stepped onto the center platform.

"It is the same as we have found throughout the city, Your Majesty," the commander said as Mortus examined the heads of the once proud council. Every dwelling they came upon they were greeted with the heads of the citizens of Notsu. They had yet to discover any surviving citizens, believing the entire populace had been put to the sword.

"This would explain why they fought to the death." Mortus shook his head. After this atrocity, they would expect no quarter.

"This is the same everywhere you have looked?" Elos asked, regarding the scene with his usual stoic resolve.

"Everywhere," the commander answered.

"Why does this one stand apart?" Mortus asked, stepping toward a pike placed off to the side, with no chair representing a place upon the council.

"We believe that is General Meborn," the commander said, regarding the missing commander of 3rd Torry Cavalry.

"Send a runner to King Lorn. He should know of this," Mortus ordered.

"Yes, my king." The commander went about it as Elos examined what remained of Commander Meborn.

"There is still one thing for us to discover," Mortus said.

Elos gave him a curious look.

"Where is Morac?" Mortus asked, pounding his right fist into his left hand.

* * *

Ilesa labored without respite, working her way along the line of wounded Jenaii warriors, having to recharge the device twice before healing the last. The brave warriors regarded her fondly, bowing their heads in respect as she moved on. She bowed in kind, impressed by their stoic resolve while enduring such agony. Burns were terrible wounds, and without Kato's gift, could not be healed. It was another reminder of what he meant to their cause. She shook such thoughts from her mind lest she cry. Thinking of him tore at her heart. They had known each other for such a brief time, but she felt she had known him all her life. His memory comforted and hurt her at the same time. Her only solace was healing others with his device, for it kept her mind occupied and brought joy to others. Every soldier she healed, in turn mended her heart, if ever so slightly. In time she hoped it would heal her fully, allowing her to think of Kato without crying.

She put that thought from her mind as she moved location, climbing into the saddle of her escort magantor, the rider helping her into place behind him before taking to the air. She went from there to Notsu, looking on with horror at the scene below. The streets of the city were covered with wounded and dying soldiers. Looking below they came swiftly upon the center of the city, where thousands more lay strewn across the vast open space of the city square, with more looking dead than wounded. They set down upon a space that was cleared for them, with a wall of soldiers forming a protective ring around their new location as they set down. She lamented the slow recovery process of the regenerator, knowing many of their soldiers would die this day waiting for it to recharge.

She went to work as soon as her tired feet hit the ground, thankful that they had brought the first wounded to her new location, saving her the time of seeking them out. Her voice caught in her throat as the first face she saw was King Lorn, kneeling beside Jentra, whose eyes were lazily open, staring at nothing… dead. She felt suddenly weak, losing the will to even stand, but steeling her heart for the task before her. She had failed them, her king and Jentra, failing to arrive on time, but there was no accusation in King Lorn's tired eyes as she knelt beside them wishing she could do a miracle that was beyond her mortal power.

Lorn gave her a smile, gently squeezing her shoulder before stepping away, leaving her to her work. It was a subtle gesture, but grand in its meaning.

*　*　*

The former estate of Tevlan Nosuc.

Governor Daylas leaned back in the chair, swirling the wine in his goblet, wondering how it came to this. He was surprised with how long it took for the Torries to discover him. A flax-sized element now surrounded the table where he sat, with leveled spears as if he were a threat.

Fools, he laughed to himself. The poison he took was starting to take effect, and he would leave this world so very soon. He would not give them the satisfaction of killing him or the opportunity to torture him. He did wonder why they hadn't seized him as yet but accepted their caution as a fortuitus boon, one last favor from the Fates before he died. He was mildly surprised to see a commander of rank enter the room, before recognizing the four braided cords adorning the shoulders of his bright golden mail, marking him a general.

"I stand at a disadvantage, General. I do not know your name," Daylas said in good humor. He was known for his bland demeanor, which suited him as an administrator. With death now encroaching, he threw off his controlled facade, speaking his mind.

"I am General Dadeus Ciyon, commander of the Torry-Macon unified army. Who am I addressing?" Dadeus asked as Guilen took up position to his right.

"A loyal servant of the empire would never divulge anything of use, but fortune smiles upon you, Dadeus Ciyon, for my loyalty is spent." He smiled, downing the contents of his goblet.

"Your name?" Dadeus asked more firmly.

"I am Daylas, former governor of this now-dead city, and member of my emperor's elite, though such titles are now rendered meaningless."

"The kings will have questions for you. Take the governor into custody," Dadeus ordered his men, which caused Daylas to chuckle.

"Something humors you, Governor?" Guilen asked, nearly drawing steel, wary of Daylas' strange behavior.

"Your kings will receive no answers from me, and neither shall either of you in the next few moments." Daylas grinned sadly.

They took his words as a threat, all of them backing a step to the door, half expecting the roof to fall upon them.

"Peace, my dear friends, you are in no danger from me. The only threat I pose is soiling myself as I expire, which thankfully shall be soon," he said lifting his goblet to indicate the source of his demise.

Dadeus ordered his men to call for Ilesa, hoping to save the wretch for further questioning, but doubted there was time to do so. Even if there was, many men would die waiting for her to return to her duties. He would still risk it, for the information Daylas possessed might save many more.

"You have only a few moments, General Ciyon, so ask what is most pressing to you." Daylas smiled.

"Where is Morac?"

"Ah, our absent Lord. He took to flight, forsaking us to your benevolent mercy, leaving in the dead of night after our gargoyle friends hastily departed. You did not know this? Of course, you were distracted by the other magantor he sent out, drawing your attention while he slipped away to the south. He is likely at Nisin now, planning another debacle, unless our good emperor sees reason and removes his head. Though removing his head is quite difficult considering the sword he wields."

"He is gone?" Dadeus growled.

"Gone." Daylas tossed his goblet on the floor, flapping his hands mimicking Morac's flight.

"Why did you murder the people of Notsu?" Guilen asked, his voice laced with disgust.

"Not a decision I can claim, but I was an accomplice, though a very unenthusiastic one. Our absent lord and his gargoyle friends thought it a suitable recourse considering the state of things, in particular your approaching armies. Of course, they committed these foul deeds, leaving us few who remained to suffer your wrath. I believe our dear *Lord* Morac planned this, using the murder of the citizens to stiffen our soldiers' spines. The men were well aware what fate awaited them had they surrendered, so they fought to the death."

"All except you," Dadeus accused.

"You would be correct if I somehow survive the next moments." Daylas shrugged, his eyes growing heavy.

Dadeus and Guilen looked on, wondering what to ask as Daylas continued.

"Take heart, my dear fellows. I have spared the city's water springs for your noble cause, one last order of my departed lord that I have refused. With that I must bid farewell," Daylas said, sagging weakly in his chair, his eyes going out of focus, dying where he sat.

Another soldier entered the chamber shortly after, informing Dadeus of the discovery of a few slave girls detained in the cellar of the estate, the only apparent survivors of the city.

* * *

The day grew late as they went about clearing the city, moving district to district, street to street, and structure to structure. The Notsuan soldiers wept at the sorry state of their city, their once vibrant home now a graveyard. The soldiers would go long stretches of finding nothing, before coming upon pockets of stern resistance, or stumbling upon snares or collapsing dwellings. They quickly learned the signs to look for, making their way across the city. It would take days to count the dead and missing, and to heal the wounded, so great were their numbers.

In the heat of battle Terin was struck by an arrow to his thigh, bleeding profusely before taken to Ilesa to be healed. He was never wounded in battle before this day, the power of his sword and Kalinian blood protecting him. Whispers began to circle wondering if his power was corrupted or gone altogether. He quickly recovered and rejoined Cronus, helping clear most of the streets. After fighting throughout the day, they retired for the night, with Terin taking up quarter in the home of Tevlan Nosuc, where Lorn, Mortus and

El Anthar established their temporary headquarters. It was nearing sundown when Cronus returned to King Lorn's pavilion north of the city to safeguard its contents and personnel before they could be moved into the city the following morn. He was overcome with exhaustion as he approached the site, greeted with salutes from the soldiers left to guard their encampments. Upon reaching Lorn's pavilion, he was greeted by Dougar, the young boy having spent the day attending the king's affairs.

"King's Elite Kenti." Dougar bowed his head, pleased to see Cronus return. He longed to hear news of the battle, having spent the day attending his duties beyond the city walls. He desperately wanted to join in the fighting, but Lorn ordered him to remain where he would be safe. It was a strange sight to see a child so young wearing sturdy mail over a gray tunic, with greaves and a matching helm that he kept on throughout the day, prepared for any threat that might emerge from the city gates.

Cronus froze upon seeing him, forgetting that he was here.

"Dougar, it is good to see that you are safe and well," he said, forcing a smile for the boy's sake, fearing how he would receive the news of Jentra.

"We have looked for the enemy all day, King's Elite, but they have not emerged," he said, standing at attention, holding his small fist to his heart, saluting like a seasoned soldier.

"Be at ease, Dougar, and when we are alone, please call me Cronus." He knelt before the boy, reaching out to remove Dougar's helm, knowing it weighed upon him, freeing his mop of hair in the evening breeze.

"I have polished the king's second blade, and knives, and oiled his leathers, as well as Jent… Elite Prime Jentra's," he corrected himself, unsure if he should reference Jentra so familiarly. He noticed the strange look crossing Cronus' face upon him mentioning Jentra. He was very perceptive of such things, and his heart started to race.

"Dougar, you know we are at war, and sometimes things happen that we cannot help," Cronus began, his heart breaking as the boy's face began to fall, his every word stinging like a lash.

"Is the king well? Is Jentra?" he asked, his voice laced with worry.

"The king is alive and well. The city is taken and the enemy put to the sword, but…"

"No!" Dougar shook his head. He knew that tone, having heard it when he learned of his mother and father dying.

"Jentra saved the king, but took many blows to do so, blows intended for the king. We could not heal him in time. I know he was fond of you, and I am so very sorry for having to tell you." Cronus felt like weeping himself as the boy stood there, tears pouring down his cheeks. Dougar wanted to flee, to run away and cry in private, but lacked the strength.

"He can't be dead. He promised he would train me to be a soldier," he said with the saddest voice Cronus had ever heard. There was more to this than Jentra training him. Though it was Lorn that brought him into their circle, it was Jentra that spent the most time with him, showing Dougar a tenderness he couldn't show to the men, or anyone for that matter. Jentra was more a father to him than anything else, and Dougar loved him dearly, more than anyone else. It was another blow to the poor child. He had steeled his heart when his parents died, fearing to suffer such pain again, until that bright sunny day when Lorn drew him into his world, daring him to love again. Now his heart was shattered.

Cronus drew the boy into a fearsome hug, knowing the pain he suffered. He had lost his own parents when he was a child, then his uncle, his brother Arsenc, and finally Leanna. He was crying now, holding the boy to his chest as Dougar's tears broke more heavily, fueled by Cronus' embrace. He wrapped his small arms around Cronus' neck, weeping uncontrollably. They held each other for the longest time, two souls sharing their sorrow, each drawing strength from the other. After a time, they finally relented, pulling apart.

"I will train you to be a soldier, Dougar." Cronus ruffled his hair.

"You will?" he asked, his hope tempered with the reality that Cronus might die also.

"I will."

* * *

Three days hence.

The city lay in ruin, its once-beautiful streets now filled with rubble and marred with gore and blood. The main thoroughfares were littered with fallen debris. Nearly every dwelling contained the grisly remains of its former citizens. The allied armies continued the work of clearing the streets and rooting out the remaining Benotrists, wherever they found them. Nearly all were dead, but a patrol would stumble upon a small group from time to time as they cleared the city. Most of the seriously wounded were treated by Ilesa, with many hundreds more awaiting treatment for lesser wounds. Their armies hurried clearing the dead with the carka birds circling the skies above, awaiting the promise of carrion.

It would take many more days to get a full accounting of the fallen, but the number was certainly above six thousand. The Notsuan contingent lost more than five hundred, a heavy sum for their meager size. Commander Naruen struggled reordering his ranks with so many commanders of unit slain, and his men scattering throughout the city to search their homes, checking upon their families. It was a painful and often fruitless endeavor, with many of the murdered citizens slain in dwellings not their own. Before the end, most of the citizens no longer dwelt in their own homes, Morac's legions confining them to the poorest sections of the city, using their dwellings to house their troops.

The apes lost nearly six hundred of their warriors, though killed many times that number. The Jenaii suffered most of their losses at the outset, with the munitions exploding along the length of the east wall. Most of their casualties were wounded, the majority suffering burns, which Ilesa healed during the battle. Lorn was thankful for Ilesa, her presence with Kato's device preventing their death toll from rising much higher than it did.

Lorn found himself standing in the central atrium of Morac's previous residence, the former home of one Tevlan Nosuc, staring at the fresco adorning the circled walls depicting the Battle of Kregmarin, matching the one adorning Morac's private sanctum. A neutral observer might appreciate the intricate details the artist painted in every portion of the work. Lorn felt nothing but regret and pain looking at it, especially the visage of his father's head held aloft in Morac's outstretched arm. Yah called out to him, drawing him from the precipice he found himself, looking over the dark abyss threatening to consume him. He lacked the strength to destroy the foul fresco that surrounded him and would not let others destroy it for him. Looking upon it was a reminder of his own folly, and until he could reconcile it, the painting must remain.

King Mortus and King El Anthar allowed him his grief, working with the others to reorder their forces, while he mourned Jentra. Had he only listened to Deva's warning, Jentra and so many others would still be alive. Was he any different than his father, who failed to heed General Morton's warning about marching east, and then to Kregmarin, leading an entire army to their doom?

It was Cronus who interrupted his morose thoughts, entering the vast chamber despite his own orders not to be disturbed.

"My king," Cronus said, stepping to his side, both looking at the dreadful scene painted above and the triumphant demeanor depicted in Morac's countenance.

"Cronus." Lorn thought to ask why he was disturbed, but something held him back. Perhaps such a rebuke was too similar to his old self, the self-serving prince who Yah transformed into the man he now was. Despite his moral transformation, he thought how easily one could fall back into their wretched selves.

"I've had dreams of late," Cronus said, wondering where to begin and deciding with that.

"Dreams or visions? Dreams possess the firmness of clouds, without cause or purpose. Visions are direct in their message, leaving little doubt of their aim," Lorn stated dryly, steeling his emotions lest he break.

"A vision then, for it is clear and repeats itself constantly, even when I am awake." Cronus decided to draw upon the king's curiosity with his own torment rather than speak of what troubled Lorn.

"What is the nature of this vision?" Lorn asked, keeping his eyes upon the painting, pretending it was of interest.

"A friend dying by a gargoyle spear while I stand helpless to stop it. When this shall occur, I do not know, nor is the place familiar. If I were to guess, it happens not far in the future, somewhere in Tyro's realm. My guess could be wrong."

"This friend you see, you do not name him, or is it her?"

"No. I sense I should not reveal the name. Why this is so, I do not know."

"I understand. This friend is dear to you, I sense."

"He has saved my life, and I have saved his, many times over now, I no longer keep count."

He. Lorn mused at that, greatly narrowing the individual in question.

"I do not know what I am to do with this vision, but there is something I am missing. I tell you this not for you to find the answer, for that I must come to on my own. I thought you should know that I shared this with Jentra on the eve of the battle. We spoke that night on many things, but in this his words struck true."

"What did he say?" Lorn still couldn't look at him, guarding his heart by looking at the painting.

"He remembered something you had said to him, something only a true friend could understand. *There is no greater love than one willing to give up one's life for a friend.*"

Lorn froze at Cronus' words, recalling the words Yah once told him. Cronus' next utterance would break his heart.

"I don't believe Jentra sacrificed his own life for his king. He did so for his friend."

Lorn hung his head, feeling his world coming apart, while feeling the love for his friend that he had never confessed.

"Do not be ashamed, my king, for you would have done the same for him, just as you have done before. You honor him by doing what you must to win this war. Jentra knew this, and so do you."

"No greater friend." Lorn sighed, finally looking to Cronus, who placed a hand to his shoulder, comforting the king.

"There is one more thing that he said."

Lorn silently waited for the answer.

"He took your God for his own."

With that, Cronus thrust his fist to his heart, and stepped away.

THE CHRONICLES OF ARAX

* * *

It was the following day when Lorn busied himself with his duties, returning to matters at hand before they decided the greater plans for the war. The casualties gave them pause, realizing they could ill afford many such engagements. The thought weighing their minds was what to do next? Defeating Morac's legions in the south was one thing, but invading the north was something far more difficult, if not impossible. Fortunately for Lorn, such decisions would wait until their current situation was thoroughly resolved. Their armies still required provisioning, which strained their supply caravans. Just as Daylas said, the city's underground water springs were untainted, much to their relief.

Lorn called for Deva, asking if she had any further visions, but she had none since the eve of the assault. He well knew these things came about unexpectedly, and in an irregular pattern. It was both reassuring and frustrating that others now had visions gifted by Yah, as it alleviated all the burden from falling upon him, but it in turn made him dependent on others. Some of the visions were personal in nature, with no apparent value to the greater cause, but it was wrong to assume so, he reminded himself. Yah would not invoke visions without value to his overall aims. He was a God of small things as much as grand ideals. In some ways the small things mattered most, for they brought him the greater joy.

Greater joy, he mused, wondering what joy there was in Jentra's death. He wanted to scream at Yah for taking him, before relenting. Who was he to question the creator? He was just a man, and a very weak one at that, but a man all the same, one with a heart that was broken. Losing Jentra was akin to losing his sword arm. This was foremost on his mind as he traversed the city square, passing the great fountain centered in that vast open space where days before the enemy host had gathered. Most of the dead were cleared, dragged outside the city to be burned. Even now the stench drifted back over the city walls with the shifting dry winds. There were still thousands of bodies laying across the city, and he could only guess how long it would take to clear them all. Hundreds of soldiers still labored in the open square, saluting as he passed, thrusting their fists to their hearts as he returned the gesture. The men still looked upon him fondly, though he half expected them to blame him for the debacle in ordering the attack.

Suddenly the crowd drew away to the north side of the square, drawn by an altercation among the men. He moved to investigate.

"Make way for the king!" his guards shouted, clearing a path for him. He found Lucas atop another soldier, striking the man in the head, before being pulled off by Ular and two other members of the elite.

"What is the meaning of this?" Lorn asked, his gaze shifting between Lucas and the bloody-lipped soldier upon the ground, the crowd forming a circle around the entire scene.

Neither spoke, with Lucas glaring at the man, his labored breath preventing him from speaking. This was out of character for Lucas, who was good-natured and easy-tempered. The soldier he assaulted struggled to his feet, wiping the blood from his mouth with the back of his hand.

"Lucas?" Lorn repeated, demanding an answer.

"He talks too much, Your Majesty," Lucas said, offering no more than that.

"What did you say?" Lorn asked the man.

"I meant no offense to our champion, Your Majesty. It... well... I said we cannot rely on him to win this war for us, for his power is failing him. If the rumors are true, we can guess why this is happening, though I did not blame him for it," the man tried to explain.

"Blame him for what?" Lorn asked, his eyes narrowing severely.

"Tell him!" Lucas growled.

"We... well... we have heard the rumors that he is the grandson of Tyro," he confessed, feeling the king's gaze upon him.

"Where did you learn of this?" Lorn asked.

"It is spreading throughout the army, Your Majesty. Where it began, I do not know. We all know what Champion Caleph has done for us, for all of us, but we are not blind. We can see his power failing. He was struck by an arrow in the battle. It was quickly healed, but it struck him all the same. That never happened before his capture at

Carapis. We cannot help but ask if Yah is forsaking him," the soldier managed to explain, feeling many hard stares along with nods of agreement, such was the division among the men.

And there it was, the awful truth of Terin's heritage laid bare for all to see. How they had kept it secret this long was a miracle unto itself, but Lorn knew this would eventually happen. It was the arrival of the Sisterhood warriors that accelerated the tale, all of them having seen Terin invoke the power of Yah in Queen Letha's throne room, where his unique heritage was revealed. Lorn knew the truth needed to be shared with the army at some point, but there was never a good time to do so. That moment was now upon them, and considering the state of things, it couldn't be at a worse time.

"Is it true, Your Majesty?" another soldier asked, a chorus of nods joining the sentiment in needing to know.

"Terin Caleph is the blood of King Kal and has a unique heritage that is not easily explained, nor appropriate in a heated debate. I want every commander of unit and telnic of the 1st Army gathered in the city forum. We shall explain this to them, and they will share this tale with all of you," Lorn said, ordering the men to disperse and return to their duties.

* * *

The Forum of Notsu.

Nearly every commander of unit and telnic of the 1st Army gathered as ordered in the forum, along with many commanders of the Macon, Jenaii, ape and Troan armies. Kings Mortus, Sargov and El Anthar stood behind Lorn upon the stone circle at the base of the forum as he addressed the assemblage. Terin stood uncomfortably off to the side of the platform, with Cronus and Dougar beside him, looking down as if ashamed. He knew this day would come and dreaded it. Though most of his friends already knew this awful truth and accepted him despite it, he knew the rank and file might not be as understanding.

"Hold your head up, Terin. You have nothing to be ashamed

of," Cronus whispered, keeping his eyes to the crowd above. Terin obeyed, steeling his heart for what was about to be revealed to the realm as Lorn began.

"I stand before you this day to address the rumors spreading through our ranks. It is wiser to address them directly and prevent the truth from degenerating into a thousand rumors and directions, with few bearing any truth at all. The story of Terin Caleph goes back to the days of King Kal…" Lorn began, the entire assemblage leaning forward on their benches, hanging upon his every word, so riveting was the tale. And, so he told Terin's story, revealing many details that even Terin was ignorant of, Lorn's knowledge likely inspired by Yah.

And, so the men listened, taken aback by the strange and winding tale of the boy who stood before them, their champion and comrade. He was the blood of Kal, of Tyro and of Torg, who stood beside Lorn, his face a mask of stoic indifference, though anyone could see the pride he had in his grandson. No one could truly reconcile the fact that Terin was the blood of Tyro and Torg, torn between two realms and two men who were diametrically opposed to one another. The questions of Jonas' whereabouts were also addressed, causing even more questions as to his loyalty, which Lorn explained.

"The blood of Kal cannot abide loyalty to gargoyles or their allies. Jonas can never align with his father without sealing his doom. Such is the blessing and curse of Kal's blood," Lorn explained.

"What of his power failing him, Your Majesty?" one commander of unit asked, regarding Terin.

"Yah has not failed him, as our friends from the Sisterhood have witnessed." Lorn looked up to Captain Sarelis, who sat upon the upper benches above with Deva and several of her warriors.

"What of his wound, and his sword growing dim in battle, Your Majesty?" Another asked.

"Since Yah has revealed himself through him, we must believe there is a reason for why his power has been changed, or even weakened. Perhaps it has nothing to do with Terin at all, but with us," Lorn said, with Terin turning sharply to him, wondering at that.

"With us, Your Majesty?" the same commander asked.

"With us. Do you think Yah will grant us victory simply by us following Terin's immense power into battle? What role would we serve in this? What faith would be required of us? None at all. Would Yah free us from the gargoyle curse simply by us following Terin into battle? He granted Kal such power, and when the men of old were called upon to follow him into battle, they forsook and betrayed him. Perhaps Yah is testing us and testing our commitment to the cause by dimming Terin's power." Lorn's words were having their intended effect, the men seeing things from a different perspective.

"Then what are we asked to do, Your Majesty?" another asked, eager to do what was expected of him.

"In time he will show us. For now, we must wait, and put this city back to rights," Lorn said.

This was not well received. The last thing the men wanted was inaction. They needed a sense of order and direction in Lorn's plan. Waiting here until called upon by Yah was unbearable.

"What is the reason for our champion's gift if he cannot use it?' Another asked.

It was then that Deva stood from her bench, making her way to the floor below, every eye eventually drawn to her as she came to stand beside the king. The men were all aware of who she was, and her role in Terin's captivity. She steeled her heart, suffering their judgement without recourse. She knew her guilt and would not deny it, such was the burden she must bear.

"I am Deva, daughter of Darna, former Guardian of the Sisterhood. It was my mother and I that brought about Terin's fall, and the weakening of his once mighty power. Many of you know what happened during his captivity, but none know the full truth of his suffering," Deva began, telling them of everything from his capture at Carapis to the sundering of his power at Caltera, and its miraculous reawakening in the Queen's throne room, along with her own transformation. Many gave her a murderous look, but they quickly eased realizing she was no longer the same creature.

"...It was then, when he granted me mercy, that I was struck by Yah's incredible power, so intense that it sent me to the floor, writhing in its embrace. Visons flashed before my eyes, of things past, present and future. It was here where I saw myself in your esteemed company, debating the course that lay ahead. Though Terin is the blood of Tyro, he is also the blood of Torg Vantel, the blood of Kal the mighty, but most of all he is your champion. You need him beside you in order to carry the day, but you also must play your part, men of the Torry Realm," Deva said, her terrible gaze sweeping the assemblage.

Terin looked on, unable to reconcile the woman who enslaved him to the woman who now spoke on his behalf. She was clearly not the same person. It was then he was struck by the truth that she was the same person, but with a new spirit, one touched by Yah.

"AGGHHH!"

A terrible scream issued from Deva's throat, reverberating throughout the rotunda in a screeching crescendo. Terin looked on as she dropped to the floor, her eyes clouding over as if touched. Lorn and Torg went to help her but were thrown back by an unseen power. Soon others among the assembly began to scream, dropping where they stood or slumping over where they sat, sharing her affliction, adding their screams to hers in a deafening chorus. Lorn gathered himself, staggering to his feet, the screeching cries akin to daggers twisting in his ears. Torg steadied him, the old warrior beating him to his feet. All around them men, women, apes and Jenaii were afflicted, nearly one in ten of the total assembly, including Lucas and Mortus.

"What is the cause of this?" Torg asked warily.

"Yah is speaking to them," Lorn said.

Chapter 15

She swam in darkness, her mind a maelstrom of leathery flesh and vicious fangs curving menacingly nigh. They came upon her from every direction, swarming over and around her like a stream of horror flooding its banks. She rose into the air, her vision expanding above the swarm below, bringing the full weight of their number into focus. The land below was afflicted, covered in an unending black mass of living flesh, leathery wings shifting atop each other like insects crawling out of their nest. Gargoyles stretched to the horizon in each direction, gathering their strength in unknown numbers, the source of their power a mystery to her untrained eye.

Her eyes grew dark, feeling herself pulled away, carried aloft to an unseen fate, before plunging into the bowels of a subterranean realm. Her eyes sprang open, finding herself amidst a massive cavern, its high stone ceiling strangely alit, as if for her own purview, to reveal all the sins of the foul place. The cavern floor was a mass of white leathery flesh of wingless gargoyles, each clawing at the air with sightless eyes, each screaming into the fetid air, their haunting shrills echoing off the cavern walls. Her spirit drifted amid the throngs of hideous creatures, struggling to lift herself above the sea of agonizing flesh. She felt herself break free, lifting in the air before clawed digits dragged her back, digging into her ankles.

"NO!" she screamed, kicking herself free before again ascending, her body lifting as if it were ethereal, drifting higher into the chasm, seeing what lay below in its ghastly horror. There, upon the floor of the vast

cavern a mass of white-skinned gargoyles gathered in the hundreds of thousands, wingless and sightless, and slighter of stature to their black-skinned kin. Many had bulging wombs, expanding as they gave birth to their wretched spawn, their get either black and winged or white and blind, male and female birthed into a hellish void.

"Come back to us, Deva," Terin's voice called out, drawing her from the abyss.

She opened her eyes, finding herself in Lorn's arms, with Terin and Cronus kneeling beside her as she lay upon the floor of the forum. Dozens of gasps echoed in the air as the others similarly afflicted awoke from their visions. She looked to Lorn, then Cronus and back to Terin, her body shaking uncontrollably.

"What did you see?" Lorn asked.

* * *

Council of war.
The former home of Torlan Nosuc.

"I know what I saw!" Mortus slammed his fist upon the table, the image of the gargoyle horde repeating itself in his mind.

"There couldn't be that many. We have destroyed nearly all their gargoyle legions. All the survivors of Corell can't number more than fifty telnics. Those in Yatin number less than thirty. What else do they have but garrison dregs and…" King Sargov tried to reason, but the Macon king was having none of it.

"I saw them, the same as all the others. There were countless thousands swarming across the land in an endless stream," Mortus growled, giving the others gathered about the table a withering look. He was joined by Lorn, Sargov and El Anthar, along with their many commanders and allies, including the Notsuans, Troans, Sisterhood and apes. Their royal elite and warriors of renown gathered about, all standing around the table with a map of greater Arax unfurled across its surface.

They were all confounded by the visions that many had, especially Deva's, which was greater than the others. The afflicted were not confined to the city forum, but all across Notsu, striking one in ten of their entire army. They all claimed to have seen the same thing, a massive gargoyle host swarming over the land, land unfamiliar to any present, but that all who saw it somehow knew was in the north.

The silence that followed was deafening. Lorn stared at the map, lost in thought. If what they saw was true, and he knew that it was, it presented a nigh impossible challenge. They needed to invade the north if they harbored any hope of final victory, but if the result of Notsu was any indication of what they could expect in the north, he couldn't see a way to do it.

"Can you say again what you saw, Deva?" Captain Sarelis asked, standing across from her at the table. Deva sighed, resigning herself to repeating the dreadful vision, looking back to her captain, who stood intently between King Mortus and Torg Vantel.

"I believe it was a breeding ground, a massive cavern where their species are spawned," she said, going on to describe the unique nature of the female of the gargoyle species, wingless and sightless, hidden from the eyes of men through the ages.

"That would explain much," Torg said, scratching his chin. They often wondered how gargoyles reproduced, wondering if they sprang from eggs, or were asexual, though their male appendages always put that theory in doubt.

"What does it mean? These visions must have a purpose," Gleb Naruen, commander of the Notsuan contingent wondered.

"Could it be a warning of what awaits us in the north?" General Lewins asked.

"Or a warning of what shall happen if we don't invade the north. We must prevent them from respawning," General Ciyon countered.

"How, General Ciyon? Look at the losses we have incurred taking this city, where we greatly outnumbered them, and we had three swords of light to their none," General Bram Vecious, commander of the Macon 2nd Army asked.

"I do not know, but there must be a way." Ciyon sighed, placing his hands flat on the table, staring intently at the map.

"What say you, King Lorn? If any here hold Yah's counsel, it is you," King Mortus asked, looking over at his son by marriage, standing upon Torg's opposite shoulder.

"I have received no vision or even the slightest insight to his mind on this. I am forced to lean upon the visions of others for reasons that are kept from me. Perhaps it is a test of my faith, or it serves a purpose I don't yet see. As this is so, I can only guess the meaning of what they saw. Is the vast horde of gargoyles in their visions a portent of things to come, a harbinger of what will come to pass if the gargoyles are free to spawn a new generation? Or is the horde a vision of what now exists, a great host held in reserve for the purpose of destroying any invader of Tyro's realm? Relying only upon reason, I must ask why was Deva shown the breeding grounds, while the others saw only the horde? I believe the breeding grounds are a warning of what shall come to pass if we do not end the threat ourselves, leaving it instead to our descendants. We could stay where we are, leaving the north to its current master. We could spend the next twenty years unifying all the lands south of the Plate Mountains into a powerful alliance not seen since the days of Kal," Lorn said, this last suggestion finding favor with many gathered around the table, by the look on their faces. He hated to dash such hopes, but he needed them to see the alternative.

"Though I favor the idea of ending this war and living out my days in peace with my wife and child, such a vision contradicts all that Yah has revealed to me to this point. Yah did not bring us to this juncture only to leave the gargoyles in place to plague our future. Mankind failed Yah in the days of Kal, failing to follow their rightful king in vanquishing the gargoyles for all time. That is the task before us, and the sole purpose for our current unity. Should we falter in ending the gargoyles, our unity will shatter, just as it did in the days of Kal. We must invade the north," Lorn declared.

"But how?" King Sargov asked, looking despondently at the map, wondering how they could move an army across the Kregmarin, let alone lay siege to a castle the size of Nisin or Fera.

"I do not know," Lorn answered honestly.

"Then what shall we do?" Sargov asked.

"I shall ask the one who does know," Lorn said, stepping toward the door.

"Who shall you ask?" King Mortus questioned.

"Yah," Lorn said, giving them a look before stepping without.

* * *

Lorn stood upon the terrace of the grand estate, looking at the starlit sky, calling upon his God to answer. How small he felt before the majesty of creation, wondering how a creature so small as him could call upon the master of all that he could see? Despite the friends and armies that surrounded him, all allied to his cause, he felt alone. He thought of Jentra and all the times his old friend stood at his side. He never realized how much he needed him until he was gone.

"I miss you, my friend," he whispered into the night, wondering if Jentra could see him now, from wherever Yah placed him.

He wondered why Yah took him of all people. He understood why his father was taken, though painful it was, but Jentra? What purpose did his sacrifice serve?

He saved your life, you fool, he reminded himself. He felt horrible, knowing he was the cause of it. He lowered his head, bereft of strength, feeling his world torn apart.

Torn apart? He scolded himself for such self pity. He was blessed beyond measure. Had not Yah delivered Corell from destruction? Did he not help him unite with King Mortus? Did he not grant victory in Yatin? Did he not rally this great army to his cause? Did he not gift him the most beautiful woman to be his wife?

"Forgive my forlorn mood, Yah. Even your most stalwart servants are prone to our human failings. I am grateful for all that you have given me. I ask only that you bless Jentra's spirit, wherever you have sent him. I owe him my life, but so much more. Tell him… tell him I love him, that he is my brother, more so than any other, and that I am lost without him. He always complained about my wild decisions and strategies, though faithfully committed himself to executing every one of them. I now stand without his guidance and call upon you to guide me."

Lorn paused, his gaze sweeping the starlit heavens as if Yah might answer from any point in the sky.

He felt a heaviness come upon him, forcing his eyes to close before finding himself standing above an ancient battlefield. There below stood a man of great power, wearing a cuirass of silver and gold blended together in a bright sheen. His helm was black with a plume of blue feathers running along its top. His greaves and vambraces were gold and black, sparkling like the surface of a dark sea. Though he stood above him, he could see into his eyes, eyes so vibrant he wanted to turn away but couldn't, drawn by his determined gaze. He felt comforted by the man and feared him all the same. Before the warrior stood a horde of gargoyles, baring their fangs, wanting to strike but fearing to draw near him. He then realized the man stood alone, his friends and comrades abandoning him to face the enemy. The gargoyles wavered, torn between their desire to kill him and their fear of him.

"Kal," Lorn whispered, knowing he was the warrior who stood in defiance of the enemy host. The vision faded, replaced with the long-suffering history that followed, century after century of the realms of man beset by the gargoyle curse, before his own visage appeared upon the same place as Kal stood before, facing the untold strength of the gargoyle race. He was arrayed in silver armor over his sea blue tunic. Yet, he did not stand alone. Beside him stood so many that he could not fully count their number, King Mortus, Terin, Cronus, Raven, Elos and countless others, all his brothers in arms. There stood Queen Letha and her vast host, with men of Yatin, Casia, Tro and Jenaii. Ular and many Enoructan joined with apes and Earthers, all joined to his cause. As Yah promised, he was not alone. He thought of each of them and smiled, before realizing what he would suffer to spare their lives. The vision expanded revealing the greater host arrayed before them, and the gargoyle breeding grounds behind them, placing his army in between. What was the meaning of this? What was the vision telling him?

He was struck by another vision, all his friends and comrades falling in battle, their corpses withering before the passage of time, leaving only bones picked clean by carka birds circling lazily overhead.

"No!" He shook his head, trying to shake the image from his mind. "There has to be another way," he pleaded. It was clear the final price of deliverance was the lives of all he held dear. The south was saved for now, but to preserve the future of Arax, a sacrifice must be offered… their army. If they were willing to lay down their lives, then Yah would give them victory.

"There must be another way, Oh Yah," he pleaded again, looking from star to star for the answer.

No greater love.

A voice answered back, repeating Jentra's words, words he learned from Lorn, who learned from Yah, and were passed to Cronus who said them back to Lorn. There was no greater love than one willing to lay down one's life for a friend.

"Or friends." Lorn sighed, the answer clear to him now, as clear as a bright summer day.

"Show me what I must do, Oh Yah, and I will give my life as you ask, if you would spare my friends."

He was struck by another vision, nearly taking him from his feet. His eyes welded shut, refusing to open as the image took shape in the murky depths of his vision before bursting into focus… Deva.

It was then her screams rang out from the far side of the estate.

* * *

Lorn found Deva upon the floor of the grand atrium, cradled in Guilen's arms with Terin and Cronus kneeling beside her. The others from the war council were gathered around them, all refusing to leave the estate until Lorn's prayer was answered, when Deva was suddenly struck by her latest vision, her eyes turning pure white as she screamed. The others parted as Lorn knelt beside her, waiting upon her to awake. By the look of his face, they knew he was connected to her, each holding their tongue until the situation calmed. After several moments her screaming ceased, the color returning to her eyes as she came to.

Deva looked disoriented, wondering why they were all gathered around her, until remembering her vision, which suddenly filled her mind in its full detail, causing her eyes to fix upon Terin and then Lorn.

"What did you see, Deva?" Lorn asked, the others crowding closer to hear what she would reveal.

"You know what he is asking of you," she said, her cryptic answer causing the others to wonder what Lorn had seen.

"I do, but not the full cost. My vision revealed you as the conduit to his instruction. What did Yah reveal to you, Deva?" Lorn asked.

"Your sacrifice is not sufficient. Yah demands his chosen join you on your journey," Deva said, her tone void of emotion, as if she were entranced.

"His chosen?" Cronus wondered at that as Deva looked first to Terin before shifting her gaze to many others gathered about the chamber.

"I can see them," she said.

"See who, Deva?" Lorn asked.

"The chosen."

* * *

They stood there deep into the night, contemplating what Deva had revealed. They were not kings, warriors or men and women of renown at this moment, just a band of comrades brought together by something greater than themselves. Ironically, it was the ever-stoic King El Anthar that spoke first, his serene voice soothing to tired ears.

"For so few to be chosen, there can be no hope for victory unless Yah wills it."

"That seems the point." King Mortus shrugged, his once-fiery spirit tempered by his new faith. He was not the man he was when Lorn approached the walls of his capital. He resigned himself to what must be done, no matter the cost.

"Is this truly the only way?" Dadeus asked, not pleased with the choices before them.

"We hold no hope of invading the north without sacrificing our entire host. Yah is granting us this one choice, if we who are chosen are willing to stand," Lorn said.

"My king, you are asking the rest of us to remain idly here while you give up your lives? How can we agree to such a thing?" Cronus shook his head.

"We sacrifice some of us or all of us, Cronus. What else would you have us do?" Lucas asked, standing across the circle they all formed in the grand atrium, divided by those chosen, and those tasked to remain at Notsu.

"We are all soldiers, Lucas. I would not see you march off to certain death while I sit here doing naught," Cronus growled.

"It must be as your king says, King's Elite Kenti," Deva said, standing the opposite side of the circle from Cronus, among those chosen to follow Lorn into oblivion.

"You are asking that I stand aside and allow my friends and king to die so that I might live. There is no honor in that. Why not ask that I go and those with more to live for remain?" Cronus was looking at Terin, knowing Corry would be heartbroken should he die.

"You have a daughter who needs you as much as any who needs us, Cronus," Terin reminded him. The two friends shared an anguished look, neither wanting to die but not willing that others die in their place.

"No greater love, Cronus." Lorn smiled sadly, reminding him of Jentra's words.

Cronus stood there, his heart breaking at what Yah was asking of them. He thought of his own vision, which had no correlation to what was now decided. It made no sense. He looked over at Torg, who stood with him among the unchosen, seeing the anguish breaking on his craggy face. What were his thoughts on remaining here while his grandson marched off to war?

As if he could read Cronus' thoughts, Lorn called upon Torg.

"You have been most quiet, Master Vantel. I would hear your counsel."

"There is the matter of who shall command in your absence, my king, as King Mortus is among the chosen?" Torg asked, first looking to King El Anthar, who stood beside him among the unchosen.

"My daughter stands as acting regent of Maconia," Mortus said.

"And she stands as regent of the Torry realms with Princess Corry as her co-counsel. But I shall inform them both that you hold final say in the defense of the realms," Lorn explained.

"And I charge you with the same responsibility for Maconia, General Vecious," Mortus added, regarding his commander of 2nd Army.

"What of myself, Your Majesties? Do I follow Master Vantel or General Vecious?" Dadeus Ciyon asked, as he commanded a joint Macon-Torry Army.

Lorn and Mortus shared a look, the Macon monarch allowing Lorn to decide.

"You shall be the balancing vote should they disagree, Dadeus," Lorn said, knowing full well that Vecious and Torg were more likely to agree on matters than Dadeus.

"I think it best we rest while we have some dark left to us," Mortus advised, for dawn was not far off and the morrow would bring much work.

* * *

The following morn came all too soon, the streets of Notsu coming alive with activity. By then, every soldier in their armies was aware of the visions that afflicted so many of their comrades the day before, as well as Terin's unique origin. The commanders of every unit in the Torry 2nd Army relayed the tale of Terin's heritage to their men, which was almost forgotten after the visions struck so many. They all knew it was a sign from Yah, and to a man, nearly all of them wanted to be among the chosen, even if it meant certain death. Such was the bond of their armies, each willing to be part of something greater than themselves.

The armies took turns marshalling their soldiers into formation, allowing Deva to inspect their ranks, calling out those chosen by Yah. Besides King Lorn and King Mortus, Lucas was chosen, while Ular was not. Of the apes, only Huto, Carbanc, Krink and Gorzak were chosen, each having fought at Corell, before joining the attack on

Notsu. Elos was chosen along with eighty of his fellow Jenaii. Among the Sisterhood, Deva and two of her sister warriors were chosen, with Lucella Sarelis not among them, much to her chagrin. Criose, Cronus, Ular and Ilesa were among the many not chosen, along with Dadeus and Guilen. Only sixteen hundred were chosen, including a handful of Troans, Notsuans, Zulonians, Tesoans and Sawyerans, along with an even split of Torry and Maconia, giving representation to all the armies gathered at Notsu.

Few knew the route of travel they would undertake to enter Tyro's realm, but most could guess it was somewhere to the far west. Many of the chosen already departed, ferried to a destination west by Dar Valen's magantors, able to take a few at a time. The first took to the air at sunrise, namely commanders of rank as well warriors of renown. Nearly an even dozen of the Torry elite were chosen, and an equal number of the Macon elite.

Lorn stood back as Deva inspected one of the last formations, a unit from the Macon 2nd Army, finding seven among their ranks to add to their total. He summoned Lucas as Deva worked her way through the last row, standing beside the great fountain in the center of the city square.

"Your Majesty." Lucas greeted him with a fist to his heart, which Lorn returned.

"I know you wish Ular would join us, considering the great friendship you have formed, but alas, such is our lot."

"If we do succeed, I will be glad that he lives," Lucas said honestly, knowing those who were chosen were likely to perish.

"And you would rather go without him than lose him beside you." Lorn shook his head at the man's bravery. Such was the attitude of all who were chosen. Lorn ordered that no man was forced to come. If one was chosen, they could stand aside, with no shame cast upon them, but none refused. It was those who were not chosen that objected, each begging to join their comrades, feeling ashamed to remain behind.

"The others feel the same, my king. It is strange really that I am at peace knowing what fate likely awaits us." Lucas smiled wanly, resigned to his fate, yet with a joyful heart.

"Yah is filling you with his spirit, fortifying your heart for the journey ahead."

"I believe you have the right of it, Your Majesty. Despite the wonders I have seen, I never truly understood until now."

Lorn smiled at that, feeling much the same, learning to trust in Yah's guidance with every passing step. He placed a hand upon Lucas' shoulder, directing his gaze to Deva as she finished with the last row.

"We have a long journey ahead, Lucas, one that is fraught with peril. We are few and the dangers are many, but there are those among us we cannot spare. Deva has become very important, for she has been chosen by Yah to reveal his will to us, and therefore must be protected. I would trust this task to you," Lorn said, taking him aback.

Lucas shook his head at the madness of it all. Deva was Terin's captor, their enemy just a short time ago, and now she joined them, transformed into Yah's acolyte. Was there ever a transformation so profound as that?

"She has truly changed." He sighed, trying to reconcile the creature he knew at Bansoch with the woman standing before them.

"She has. Does this surprise you? If so, then look no further than King Mortus, who was once our enemy and is now our brother in arms. Look to our Yatin allies, who were our ancient foes, and now fight beside us. Look no further than your king, who was once a wretched creature and is now under the mercy of his creator. She is a new person, Lucas, and one I would see kept safe."

"I shall guard her with my life, my king." Lucas thrust his fist to his heart, avowing it so.

* * *

Terin stood upon the outcropping of the magantor stables, overlooking the city square below, where gathered many of the departing, each bidding farewell to their comrades. He could see Lucas and Ular clasping forearms, wondering if they would ever meet again. Elos stood farther off, bidding farewell to his king. King Mortus and King Lorn greeted their commanders, trusting them with defending their realms. There were many tearful goodbyes, friends and brothers in arms wondering if they would ever see one another again. On the far side of the open square, he spied Guilen and Deva embrace, each tearfully bidding adieu. He thought of his former mistress, wondering how Yah had transformed the wicked woman into whatever she was now. He wondered if that was the purpose of his enslavement all along, to bring her into Yah's fold? Couldn't Yah have invoked such power in anyone?

Fool, he reminded himself, knowing Yah could have given his own power to anyone as well. Who was he to decide Yah's servants? He was just a man, a boy really, and his life held no greater worth than any other, not in Yah's eyes. As it stood, his own power was even less unless he could restore it to its former glory, which he could not. That decision was Yah's, and they all must submit to his will in order to see this through. If successful, it would likely mean they would all perish. Thinking of that gave him a pang of guilt with Deva, knowing their encounter led her here, preparing to march to her death with the rest of them. She deserved better after changing her heart. It was hardly a reason for anyone to come to Yah if his most faithful servants needed to die in order to win. He regretted thinking that, knowing Yah was far wiser than he, and if he asked them to undertake this journey, there had to be a reason. If he had learned anything during his enslavement, it was to trust Yah's will, that and of course, patience. He now had enough patience to last his lifetime and hoped Yah did not require him to learn more.

His thoughts then shifted to Corry, wondering how she would receive all this. Not good, he sighed. She would be certain to voice her displeasure and try to order him to remain. It would matter little, for they were following a path none could turn from, not even him, and not even his king.

The midday sun shone overhead, its clear sky a good omen for travel as he stroked Wind Racer's neck, the large avian nudging his beak against his chest, returning the affection.

"One last ride, old friend," he said, more for his own sake. Once the chosen were assembled at Rego, they would proceed afoot, but he would leave Wind Racer at Corell. He would not have him die as well in this adventure.

"I thought to say goodbye before you leave," Cronus said, stepping onto the platform.

Terin turned, smiling at his friend's approach. It was one of the farewells he dreaded most, this and Torg and, at last, Corry. He stepped from Wind Racer to embrace his friend. They held one another for the longest time before parting.

"I shall miss you, Cronus. I wish for your company on this journey, but not at the cost."

"This is madness, Terin. We should all be going together, all of us marching as one, and if we must all die in the end, so be it."

"Is it not better for few of us to perish than the whole? I go gladly knowing my friends are safe." Terin gave him a brave smile, though even Cronus could see through it.

"There is no guarantee of victory even if you few go. Isn't that what Lorn often said, that even if you follow Yah's will, victory still wasn't ensured?"

Terin thought to say it was different this time, that all they endured to this moment led to this path, where only Yah could deliver them, demonstrating his power for all the world to witness, but decided against it. Cronus was in no mood to listen to such. He needed to make these last moments with his friend memorable.

"I cannot say what path is right, Cronus, but I can say that I was fortunate in my friends. I am thankful that of all the men I could have met on the road to Rego that day, it was you. You are my closest friend and my brother in every way one could be. Thank you for everything." Terin embraced him one last time, his eyes growing moist, fighting back the tears that would soon break.

Torg watched the exchange from the shadows of the stable, waiting for them to separate and for Cronus to depart before advancing, saying his own farewell. He stepped forth, placing a hand atop Terin's head, his grandson feeling torrents of emotion pouring off the old warrior.

"I don't care what your God says, you come home, boy."

Terin wrapped his arms around Torg, taking him by surprise, hugging him tightly, tears running down his cheeks.

"I love you, Grandfather," he managed to say through his tightening throat. Unlike their last farewell when he departed for Yatin, this felt permanent.

With that, Terin climbed into the saddle, Wind Racer strutting forth, springing off the platform into the midday air. Torg watched as he circled the battlements of the stables one last time before passing over the city's west wall, disappearing into the horizon.

Chapter 16

Corell.

Queen Deliea sat her husband's place within the council chambers, overlooking maps of the Torry and Macon realms, looking for the site of their new capital. Corry sat at her side, detailing the advantages and disadvantages of each Torry location, with Chief Minister Monsh and Ministers Antillius and Thunn providing their own keen insight. The Macon high minister Orton Lorvius provided an equal acumen on the Macon sites of interest. Deliea had taken to her role of the Torry Queen, exuding the deepest respect for her adopted home and possessing deep knowledge of its rich history and geography. She was surprised by the acceptance of her new sister by marriage, Corry showing little sign of animosity for her taking her role as her own. Deliea was well aware of the affection the Torry people for their princess, and the stories that spread of her brave defense of the realm through both sieges of Corell. Even now bards sang of her bold adventures, including her rescue of their beloved champion from the Sisterhood, and her defiance of Morac during their parlay, and her blood-stained sword defending the battlements of Corell. She knew Corry cared for none of that, only for the safe return of Terin and her brother, and all the others she so loved.

"Tuk sits upon the confluence of the Nila and Monata Rivers, joining both greater Maconia and Torry North. It is also strongly guarded by the lesser Cress Mountains, cradled between its lower peaks running along this line." Corry pointed out Tuk's strategic position guarding the eastern border of Torry South.

"All points in its favor, but its proximity to Zulon would be seen as a threat to our ally," Chief Minister Monsh pointed out.

"Such is the detriment of any city we select that rests between our three realms," Deliea reasoned, giving encouragement to Corry's suggestion, as Teso and Zulon rested inconveniently between their realms.

"We could offer our own capital city, as Fleace rests an equal distance between Torry North and South," Chief Minister Lorvius said.

"Yes, but not in a direct line as the Monata valley connects Torry South with Sawyer, not her sister realm of Torry North," Deliea said, having debated that very point with herself since given the task of establishing a new capital for both realms.

"Turlis would be a fine choice, my queen. It stands at the confluence of the Nila and Stlen Rivers, and rests at the far western end of Torry North, and nearly equal distance between Cagan and Corell, and closer to Fleace than either of them," Torlan Thunn, the Torry Minister of agriculture said.

"Such a location presents the same difficulty as Tuk, posing a direct threat to Teso, which makes any decision nigh impossible, as Teso and Zulon sit between our realms." Chief Minister Monsh sighed, shaking his head.

Corry sensed Deliea had another location in mind, noticing her gaze intently drawn to the map, wondering which point drew her interest.

"Is there a site you are considering we have not discussed, sister?" Corry asked.

"Our kings, my father and your dear brother, have commissioned me with this task, trusting in my wisdom to select a location that would symbolize our unity. Our child shall inherit both realms one day, and his capital should represent the highest endeavors of his rich heritage. As such, we should look beyond our current cities, each loyal to their own native leanings. As this shall be a new kingdom, an empire really, it should have a new capital city to inaugurate our union, one to distinguish our realm from what came before. It should also pay tribute to the past. The site I intend does not compare to the grandeur of Fleace, or the immense size of Cagan, or is strategically placed as Central City," Deliea said, giving Corry a knowing smile, touching her finger to where she was leaning, drawing a chorus of interest from the others, especially Squid.

"Tarelia?" Corry raised a curious brow.

"It is naught but ruins, my queen, and remote from all centers of power and commerce," Chief Minister Lorvius pointed out. The ancient holdfast rested along the northern shore of Lake Monata, shielded by the Arian Hills, separating it from Torry North. Its closest neighbor was Sawyer, another state independent of their union.

"True, but it is protected from all enemies, as we only share control of Lake Monata with Sawyer and the Jenaii, both staunch allies. Its remote location limits undue influence upon the decisions of the crown, making the throne a fair arbiter of disputes, especially from competing regions of influence and commerce," Corry reasoned, knowing the pressure competing interests placed upon the crown when holding court. Deliea hadn't thought of that advantage, pleased her new sister pointed it out. Deliea had held court for three days since Lorn departed for Notsu, finding the task nigh impossible in balancing justice and the law. She was ever grateful that Corry stood beside her throughout, offering sage counsel.

Deliea noticed Squid's unusually quiet demeanor, his tired eyes indicating he hadn't slept, but the mention of Tarelia sparked an obvious reaction, drawing his gaze intently to its place upon the map.

"Minister Antillius, I would have your counsel on the matter," Deliea asked, knowing her husband's fondness for the elder statesmen.

"I have visited the ruins of Tarelia, my queen. Its fabled walls and watchtowers are but broken rubble of a long-dead civilization. The site is isolated from all of our lands, though it appears close upon a map. No one has dwelt there in over a thousand years. But despite these detriments, I can think of no better place." Squid's easy smile waylaid any misgivings she harbored.

The others had little response, Squid's simple eloquence disarming their arguments, leaving them surprisingly in agreement.

It was Corry who brought teeth to the proposal, calling upon the royal engineers from Central City and Fleace to collaborate upon this grand undertaking. Armies of masons, geographers, and carpenters would need to be recruited, as well as untold logistical support and thousands of laborers. Most of such labor was committed to the war effort, which would slow the construction, but planning could commence immediately.

The meeting concluded, leaving Deliea pleased with the result. She and Corry asked Squid to remain as the others filed out, drawing the minister aside as the door closed.

"Something troubles you, Squid. The worry is evident upon your face," Corry observed.

Squid sighed tiredly, scrubbing his face with his hands.

"I have had dreams of late." He sighed.

"Dreams are not uncommon," Deliea said, knowing there was more to this or Squid would not have begun so.

"There are dreams, and there are…" He tried to explain.

"Visions," Deliea finished his thought.

"Yes, that is the right of it. I have had visions so… detailed, and repetitive, that I can only ascribe them to a future event."

"The details of said vision?" Corry asked, not wishing to remain ignorant of what he saw.

"It was many things, all jumbled together in a chaotic mess, but some stood apart, giving structure to what I saw. I saw Deva calling upon me, drawing me away as if I rode a current, obedient to its mysterious course," he began.

"We should have slain her at Bansoch," Corry nearly spat at the mention of her name. She couldn't understand everyone accepting her into their ranks as if her sins were not her own.

"You are free to feel so, my dear, but are we not all indebted to Yah's mercy? Even one as her can find purpose among Yah's servants," Squid said.

Corry nodded, swallowing her anger and allowing Squid to continue.

"Beyond this, I saw a great battle, greater than any I have ever partaken. You were there, Corry, and Lorn, King Mortus and countless others, so great that I could not name them. I was there also, standing among our armies, gathered upon the heights of a great valley, one morbid and foul with legions of carka birds circling above, waiting upon our death. We stood in ordered ranks, waiting upon a great host of gargoyles pouring over the land in numbers so great that they stretched to the horizon. I saw Jenaii, Yatins, Macons, Torries, the Sisterhood, along with apes, Enoructans and Earthers, all fighting together against the gargoyle horde. But…"

"What else did you see, Squid?" Corry asked, sensing the dread in his tone.

"I saw most of us dying in that valley, so many I dare not count."

"Was Terin among them?" Corry asked.

"Was Lorn?" Deliea asked.

"I could not see, both falling beneath the shadow of their numbers."

They both paled, feeling their flesh pimple. There was no uncertainty in Squid's tone or demeanor, his voice poignant and prophetic. He could see the effect of his words, and regretted speaking so openly, but what choice had he? There was no simple way to reveal his vision while omitting its greater impact. If what he saw was true, most every one of them would die on some distant battlefield.

He quietly rose and stepped without, leaving the queen and princess sitting there in silence, contemplating everything he revealed. It was a somber reminder of the war that would not end, despite the recent respite they were gifted. After the breaking of the siege, a sense of normalcy returned to Corell, with Deliea holding court, and the ongoing efforts of cleansing the palace and its surrounding lands. The air was almost breathable again, and the awful stench of so many gathered in such proximity starting to wane. Deliea and Corry both oversaw the import of access aloma powder, the cleanser becoming scarce during the siege. Food stores were replenishing and the dead buried or burned. The castle itself was beginning to regain its luster, the smoke- and blood-stained walls and battlements returning to their ordered state.

Squid's vision made them consider the uselessness of their efforts. They sat there for a time, neither saying a word. Was it all vanity? Was there a point to all their planning and stewardship? What choice had they but to do so, with the battlelines now far beyond them, and so much to oversee in Lorn's absence. Corry wanted to pick up her sword and follow the others into battle but knew her new sister needed her counsel. She knew the difficulties in ruling her native land, let alone one you are unfamiliar. If Deliea made bold decisions it would be seen as presumptuous, if she only made superficial ones, it would be seen as weakness. Despite this, she received the love of their people, having rode alongside her husband and father to the relief of Corell. By remaining at her side, Corry was instrumental in continuing the mutual goodwill of the new queen and the Torry people.

"What think you?" Deliea finally asked.

"One vision does not portend disaster, but considering the man who dreamt it gives me pause. I think we should take time to determine the truth of it." Corry sighed, concealing her fear that what Squid saw was correct.

It was then a message runner appeared, bringing news of the battle at Notsu including a lengthy list of the fallen, including Jentra. This grim tiding was followed by nearly one in ten of the garrison being struck by visions, each crying out in their sleep from the terrible sight they saw, each matching Squid's vivid description. It was three days after that Terin arrived, preceding the many chosen who were enroute to Corell, before continuing west.

* * *

Wind Racer set down upon the northeast magantor platform, attaining Corell ahead of an encroaching storm. Word of Terin's arrival spread like grassfire on a windy day. Soldiers saluted as he passed or shouted his name as he followed his escort through the corridors of the palace. He returned their affection, though the strains of his journey played heavily on his face. Corry did not wait upon him, rushing instead to meet him as he approached the council chambers where the others gathered to receive him. She came into his arms in the middle of the long corridor, the guards politely looking away as their princess and their champion shared their embrace. She clung to him, pressing her forehead to his own, the beat of her heart sounding audibly in their ears.

"You have been missed, husband." She sighed, pulling briefly away to look into his eyes. She could see the fatigue weighing his countenance, though he tried to conceal it from her discerning gaze.

"And I have missed you." He smiled, pressing his lips to hers.

They shared a long embrace before relenting, neither wanting to let go.

"We received word of the battle not three days ago. How did we lose so many?" she asked, looking worriedly into his sea blue eyes.

"There is much for us to discuss," he said as she led him to the council chambers, where waited the ministers of both realms, Queen Deliea and their commanders of rank.

* * *

Terin waited upon their response after relaying the events at Notsu, standing at the head of the table with Corry at his side. She was visibly displeased hearing of Jentra, and of Deva's role in revealing Yah's revelation, but put no voice to her objection. How could one argue with the will of Yah, especially with so many experiencing his visions. Her neutrality was tested once Terin explained the *Chosen*.

"The number chosen by Yah will march upon Fera, as he has ordered," Terin said.

"March upon Fera, how?" Commander Balka asked.

"We shall gather at Rego, and from there march north through the wilderness and untamed lands, crossing over the Cot River and circumventing the Mote Mountains. It will be a long and arduous trek," he further explained.

"You said less than 2,000 were chosen from the army, or was it a 1,000? For so few to march upon Fera is madness. Even with your sword you shall be overwhelmed. What then shall befall us?" Chief Minister Monsh asked.

"Terin, I too have had visions. I saw great armies arrayed for battle, facing untold hordes of gargoyles. I saw many of our friends and comrades gathered there, far beyond the paltry number you claim are chosen," Squid said.

"What you saw was what would be unless..." Terin paused, wary of revealing this part to Corry, who was staring intently at him, waiting upon his next utterance.

"Unless?" Deliea asked, not liking where this was leading.

"The vision reveals the cost of defeating the gargoyles for all time, with nearly everyone Squid saw perishing in the effort. Yah claims that most will die, but victory will be given, but offers an alternative to spare the loss of so many," he said, still holding back the vital part.

"What alternative?" Corry asked, growing impatient.

"The Chosen. If those chosen by Yah are willing to march forth of their own free will, he shall spare the rest."

"And the fate of said Chosen?" Deliea asked, her breath growing heavy with every word.

Terin simply nodded, not needing to explain, the implication hanging ominously in the air before Corry exploded.

"You are to die then? Is that the choice before us? You expect us to remain behind while you march into oblivion?"

"If we all march, then we all shall perish. Is it not better for a few of us to die, than all of us?" he asked.

"There is no guarantee of victory if you do this. What then? Tyro will have your sword to add to Morac's. What hope have Elos and Cronus against them?" Deliea pointed out.

"Elos has been chosen, my queen," he said.

"Then your failure shall doom us all. Both *Swords of the Moon* and the *Sword of the Sun* against Cronus and Tosha's blades?" Corry let that possibility linger in the air.

"Unless Cronus is among the Chosen as well," Deliea said.

"He is not." Terin sighed, lowering his head.

"And what does he say of this?" Corry asked, guessing Cronus' response.

"He feels much as you," Terin said.

"Of course he does. Do you know what you are asking? Seeing

all of you march off to Notsu was difficult enough, but this? This is certain death."

Terin sat there, with no words to assuage her anguish.

"Perhaps you should discuss this between yourselves while we plan for King Lorn and King Mortus' return," Squid sagely advised.

* * *

She sat upon their bed, staring at the wall, her mind a turmoil of emotion. Terin sat beside her, oblivious to the comforts of their quarters. There they sat upon rich furs and calnesian sheets, with a glowing hearth along the near wall. A large window rested off their left, overcast concealing the night sky. His sword rested upon a chest near the bed, with his helm and mail sitting the floor below it. How he longed to be here, to enjoy one last night with his wife after suffering the privations of the road, yet such happiness was ruined by what lie between them… his fate.

He was dying inside, wanting to hold her, but fearing she might explode if he touched her. She sat there with waves of anxiety and anger pouring off her. She was like a serpent, coiled to attack.

"Corry, I…" he began, but she was having none of it.

"Do you know what you are asking?" she said, refusing to look at him.

"I do."

She turned to him, her eyes moist with pregnant tears.

"No, you do not. What if it were I that was to march off and die so you might live? What would you do? How would you feel?"

He had no answer for that.

"Your silence confirms what you would do. What use is my life without you? Remember what you said when you believed I had died during your enslavement? You despaired of life. My feeling is no less."

"I can't live in a world without you, Corry, that is why I am going. If Yah demands my life to preserve yours, then I shall pay it," he said, his heart breaking with the sadness in her eyes.

"You won't live in a world without me because you won't live at all."

"Perhaps Yah will show me mercy. We must trust in him."

"You mean trust in Deva. We are to take the word of your mistress after all she has done?" And there it was, her true feelings on the matter laid bare.

"She is not the same person as before, Corry. Whatever she is now, it is not the same. Looking into her eyes is to gaze into a consuming fire. Yah is using her as his vessel. Perhaps that is why I had to suffer, to bring about this transformation." He ignored her referencing Deva as his mistress, refusing to let any words Corry might use to anger him.

"Does it not strike you that the woman once smitten with you claims your God demands you accompany her into oblivion? Am I the only one to question her intentions?"

"I will not waste what time we have defending the likes of Deva Estaran. All I know is Yah speaks through her. As far as her intentions, I sense nothing from her but guilt. I have forgiven her, but that was for my own sake more than hers. Yah has taken that bitterness from me, which could not be done without my releasing it freely. There is no room in my heart for anger and revenge. There is only room for you, and you have filled every part of it." He reached out, running his hand along her cheek.

Curse him, she inwardly moaned, hating how he so easily disarmed her ire. Even when she wanted to be angry with him, she couldn't when he looked at her with those sea blue eyes.

"How do you know this will work, with so few of you marching to face the enemy?" she asked with a calmer voice.

"It was something that Jentra said to Cronus the night before he died."

"What was it?"

"It was something Lorn once told him, claiming it was from Yah. He said there was no greater love than one willing to give up one's life for a friend. The next day Jentra did that very thing. Lorn would have fallen had Jentra not placed himself in the enemy's path. That is what Yah asks, asking if we who are chosen are willing to lay down our lives for our friends."

"And what of us who are not chosen? Should we stand aside

and allow this? Do you know what you are asking? What life shall I have without you? We are joined as one, Terin, and you would sever that. I will not wed another should you die. I will die old and alone, lamenting what might have been. Is that the life for me you would surrender your own for? You are not giving up your life for me, you are surrendering the life we now have for a grave for you and loneliness for me. I would rather fight together than die apart, if that is the only way we can come through to the other side together."

"What if you are chosen?" he asked, not having considered that.

"Then we march to our doom together."

"Then we should wait and see if you are chosen before continuing this debate," he offered.

"Very well," she agreed, touching her lips to his.

* * *

They had little time to wait as King Lorn arrived the following day, borne by General Valen's magantor, with Lucas, Deva and Elos following after, along with King Mortus. Many others were ferried to Corell by magantor, while the greater host traveled by ocran, sharing mounts with their cavalry, or huddled in empty supply wagons and carts. It was the first leg of a long arduous trek, before continuing on to Central City, Rego and then the wilds beyond.

Queen Deliea formally received them in the throne room, greeting her husband and father upon their return. Lorn met her halfway up the dais as she descended to greet him, before sweeping her into his arms, violating all decorum, the eyes of the court looking on amusedly. Deliea raised no objection, pleased that she invoked such passion in the man she loved.

"I am grieved for Jentra's loss, my love." Her smile eased as he set her down, knowing it conflicted him.

"No greater friend had I. Thank you for sharing my grief." He smiled, lifting her hands to his lips, kissing them gently.

"You are my king and my husband. We share each other's grief and pain." She freed one hand to cup his cheek, searching his eyes with her own.

"He penned a parchment for your cousin. I promised to deliver it. Would you see it done?" he asked.

"Of course." She closed her eyes, knowing the pain the Lady Neiya would feel for his passing.

"We have much to do and to discuss," Lorn said, stepping aside, revealing his entourage waiting behind him, Elos, Deva, Lucas and her father.

Deva paused at the base of the dais before breaking off from the others, walking straight for Squid, who stood among the ministers off to the side of the chamber. Squid nearly backed away as she drew near, her eyes locked to his as if entranced. She stopped before him, placing a hand to his cheek, her touch sending a tendril of energy across his flesh.

The guards took a step to intervene, but Lorn ordered them back, knowing what this meant.

"He is chosen, Your Majesty," Deva declared, her intense gaze waning, her shoulders sagging as if taxed.

Those gathered in the throne room gasped, taken aback by the spectacle, though they were warned of the process. Corry stood high upon the dais beside Terin, waiting to see if she would be chosen as Deva moved across the chamber, touching two members of the royal guard, before finding Aldo, Chief Minister Monsh's scribe, proclaiming him among the chosen. Matron Dresila was also selected, lending to the belief Yah intended for her to bring Kato's regenerator. The last among those gathered in the throne room to be chosen was Tessa the seamstress, whose tale was sung by Galen on the eve of Lorn's coronation. Since that night she was called upon to attend every gathering in the throne room, set in a place of honor. Like many of the chosen, she accepted the call cheerfully, honored to be among them. None of the chosen held any illusion what was asked of them, knowing certain death awaited them at journey's end. Despite this, none voiced complaint, or thought to shirk their duty. It was surreal for those looking on. Where was the fear that must take them? Nowhere it seems. It was as if Yah removed the fear from their hearts, or supernaturally strengthened their resolve.

Corry quietly raged, knowing she was not among them, the

quiet truce between her and Terin breaking with this cold revelation. Was she to remain while her husband, brother and so many she held dear walked into oblivion? She lost her mother when she was a child, and her father at Kregmarin. She and Terin had not had children as yet, and if he died now, they never would. She would not wed another if he passed. She could not do that. There was no one but him. She stood there in that crowded chamber, never feeling so alone. She felt Terin take her hand, squeezing it tightly as they looked on, their faces masks of indifference. Oh, how she loved him, knowing his heart was breaking with her own. She wanted to be angry with him, to shout and scream, but couldn't. Unlike the others, she sensed no glee or joy with him, only resigned duty. He knew life without her was meaningless and accepted his fate as the price to save her, though knowing it would kill her all the same. There was no recourse for a broken spirit, as he well knew when he thought her dead, that lie of Deva's rending his heart.

And so it went, with the garrison brought into the throne room one unit at a time for Deva to inspect. Lorn left the undertaking to Lucas and the others, calling upon his commanders and King Mortus for a council of war. There was little to truly discuss, other than revealing his succession plans, both he and Mortus leaving their respective realms in Deliea and Corry's hands, each acting regents until Lorn's heir reached maturity. When asked what would happen should the child die, Lorn assured them of Yah's promise that the child would live and unite their realms. Deliea listened as her husband and father discussed their imminent departure, masking her angst with her queen's face. She recalled something her late mother once said of the regal duty of presenting strength to the realm even when you are dying internally.

* * *

Terin followed Corry to the nursery nestled within the confines of the Royal apartments, where she found Maura in the arms of her wet nurse. She had just been fed and was slowly falling asleep in the wet nurse's swaying arms. Corry relieved her of her duties, taking the child in her arms. She and Deliea had taken turns watching over Cronus' daughter in his absence, as well as Galen, who spent many a night singing to the child.

"She is beautiful." Terin smiled, running a finger along her little cheek as Corry rocked her in her arms.

"She is family now, our family. Deliea feels much the same. She will want for nothing and will bask in our love," Corry said, feeling her own world falling apart. This was her only sanctuary in the coming storm, the love for this child a balm to her own pain.

"Thank you," Terin said softly.

"We are much the same, little Maura and I. We both lost our mothers, and our fathers have gone to war. I only hope her father returns safely to her, unlike my own." She sighed.

"I wish I could give you a child of our own, Corry."

"We have one last night to try. If not, then our bloodlines end here. We would have born lovely children, but such is the price Yah asks of us." She tried not to sound bitter, but there it was.

"A heavy price," he sighed. A part of him was tempted not to go, to remain with her forever, but he was the blood of Kal, and of all the chosen, he was the most important, as Deva and Lorn had explained. Besides, he had disobeyed Yah once and would never do so again.

She hated that he agreed, wishing he wouldn't so she might lash out. The damnable misery of it all was that they both were right. She hated what they were sacrificing, and he needed to go to save the realm and all that they loved. What was he sacrificing? She thought of his parents, knowing their fate was likely tied to his own. His entire family would be lost if things went as she foresaw. He deserved more from her than her selfish arguments.

"I am sorry for troubling you, my love. I don't wish to be angry with you, blaming you for something that is beyond us, beyond any mortal reach. If this is our last night together, then let us treasure every moment." She smiled at him.

"I am the one who is sorry. I hate to lay this worry upon you. Your love is the greatest gift I have ever known." He closed his eyes, pressing his lips to her forehead, never loving her more than now.

With that, she called upon the nearest maid to take Maura, then led her husband to their bedchamber.

* * *

King Mortus joined her upon Zar Crest, the night sky ablaze with starlight, the previous days rain giving way to a clear night sky. Her back was to him, her dark hair lifting in the summer night breeze. She wore a silver gown, her left hand running over her growing womb, though little could be seen as yet. He hated what he and Lorn were doing to her, but the fate of so many rested upon their willingness to obey Yah's will.

"A lovely night." He smiled, stepping to her side, placing a hand upon the stone parapet. He wondered if the spot he stood was where General Bode met his end but put such thoughts from his mind as his daughter turned to look upon him.

"You did not search for me here to speak of the weather, Father," Deliea remarked.

"True, I did not. We haven't had a moment to ourselves since my arrival, and I…" He struggled putting thoughts to words. Of course, what words could he speak to assuage her anguish?

"Do not trouble yourself with apologies or false assurances, Father. We both know we have no choice but to follow Yah's bidding. The greater good demands no less. I will not have you burdened with guilt for leaving me. Once you begin this march your mind must be singularly focused on the task ahead. I would have you remember that you are loved and be a comfort for Lorn in my absence." She smiled, though it was painfully forced. She had the same conversation with Lorn before coming here. Like Corry she would not waste her last evening with her husband in useless arguments on matters they could not change. He was currently attending to vital matters of state, before he could join her in their bedchamber, partaking of each other one last time. It was soul-crushing, the euphoria of their victory at Corell replaced with this dreadful despair. She needed to be strong for him, and for her father, who looked a broken man about to topple. She reached her hand to his cheek before coming into his arms, hugging him fiercely, clinging desperately as if she were a small girl again.

"I love you, my child," he said past the lump in his throat, stubborn tears running down his cheek.

"And I love you, Father." Deliea wept in kind.

* * *

The following morn found Terin in the magantor stable, bidding Wind Racer farewell with Corry beside him. They would continue their journey on ocran, at least as far as Rego. Perhaps he would see Vonto, his faithful mount he had left in Squid's keeping before he departed for Molten Isle to rescue Corry and Tosha so long ago. He hoped the beast would remember him. It was only fitting that he took his last journey with the mount he began his adventures with so long ago, but relented of such a notion, knowing it would only condemn poor Vonto to share in his fate.

"I shall miss you, old friend," Terin said, running a hand along Wind Racer's neck before the avian gently nudged him with his beak, returning his affection.

"He should be with you, Terin. The Torry Champion should have greater mobility for the battle ahead," Corry said.

"I can't take him where we are going. I would have him stay with you and be your mount. Would you do that, Wind Racer?" he asked his friend, who seemed to understand what Terin was asking.

Corry wiped a tear from her eye. This all felt so wrong. Wind Racer belonged alongside him. It was another reminder of the finality of it all.

HARROOM!

Horns sounded from the courtyard, signaling their soon departure. He didn't have much time now, taking her into his arms one last time, kissing her farewell.

"I shall look for you above the main gate," she said as their lips parted.

"If Yah is merciful, I shall return to you," he said, forcing a smile.

She cupped his cheeks, staring intently into his sea blue eyes.

"Promise me that you will do your utmost to live and return to me. No matter the odds or the cost, promise me you will fight with all your strength, guile and wits to come back alive."

"I promise."

There upon the magantor platform of Corell, Corry kissed her husband farewell, wondering if it was their last embrace.

* * *

Deliea joined Corry upon the outer battlements of the north wall, overlooking the main gate. The mid-morning sun warmed the right side of their faces, heralding a beautiful summer day spoiled by the grim sight below where Lorn and Mortus led their column through the main gate, with nearly a hundred riders in their company. Most of the chosen were still enroute from Notsu, but Lorn and Mortus marched on ahead of them, preparing the way. Corry found Terin riding beside Elos, his silver helm resplendent in the morning sun. She felt her heart sing and cry at the sight of him, singing for her love and crying for his departure, the current of war again taking him from her arms. The standards of the kings lifted in the breeze at the head of the column, crowns of gold upon fields of white and black, the sigils of Lorn and Mortus. Deliea and Corry watched as they rode forth before breaking west, disappearing into the Zaronan Forest.

"What think you, sister?" Deliea asked, neither voicing their true thoughts on the matter with each other… until now.

"They were insistent that we not follow." Corry repeated Lorn and Mortus' strict orders.

"We should obey them, then?" Deliea asked, her gaze remaining in the distance.

"Yes. We should not follow them." Corry gave her a knowing look.

"Agreed."

"We have much to discuss before I depart for Notsu," Corry said.

"Agreed." Deliea smiled.

Chapter 17

Notsu.

Torg Vantel stood upon the steps of the ruling forum, watching the activity in the city square below. Men, apes and Jenaii hustled about their appointed tasks. He was impressed with the order they restored to the city. In a short time, they cleared the dead and rubble, repaired the city walls, and restored places of commerce and exchange. These measures were essential before Notsu's exiles could return, but even now many venders and merchants began establishing roots in the city, under the watchful authority of Gleb Naruen, the Notsuan commander named acting governor until a new council could be formed. When such a council would be placed, only Yah could say.

Probably never. Torg shook his head at the futility of it all. He couldn't help but feel all their efforts were as useless as a spit in the wind. Did anything they accomplished matter in the end? The fate of the war now rested on their friends' sacrifice, if what Deva and Lorn said was true. Where did that leave them? He knew where it left them, sitting here in this dead city sitting on their collective asses doing nothing. He wasn't alone in that sentiment. Despite their efforts in restoring the city, their army felt the same. He could see that in their eyes and hear it in their whispers whenever they thought he wasn't listening.

"How fare you this morning, Master Vantel?" General Bram Vecious greeted him upon ascending the wide steps of the forum.

"As well as any other," Torg snorted as the Macon commander stopped beside him, turning to spare a glance to the activity below. The two men managed to work well together ordering the armies and reestablishing the basic function of the city. Ciyon was to be the balance between them, but the two grizzled warriors seemed to agree on most things, while Ciyon found himself differing.

Bram grinned, appreciating Torg's blunt response, not certain if *any other* was a reference to other mornings or other men. It didn't really matter. It was the closest Torg came to saying he was happy to see you.

"Things are progressing faster than I anticipated," Bram said, pleased with the state of the city.

"The soldiers have performed well, and busywork keeps their minds occupied, though that will soon come to an end. Even we won't keep them from growing weary of sitting here," Torg aptly described their situation.

"Aye, they are eager to join the fight, and we have no fight to give them."

"General Ciyon disagrees," Torg said.

"Dadeus is full of vigor. He is young and bold, fancying himself akin to a great commander of old. He would have us march across the Kregmarin to give battle, against all good sense."

"The enemy will do us no favors by returning south to give battle, straining their supply lines, and we should do them no favors by marching north, suffering the same fate. So here we sit staring at each other across that damnable arid plain. Not to mention we lack magantors and cavalry to scout ahead should we choose to do so," Torg pointed out, considering their magantors and cavalry were currently ferrying the *Chosen* westward, save for General Connly's 2nd Torry Cavalry, which remained with their command.

"True, but it doesn't make this any easier. The men are growing restless."

"Aye, even our Jenaii friends are in agreement on that, and our Teso and Zulon allies."

"I overheard King El Anthar speak of it, wondering the wisdom of doing naught while the true battle is elsewhere," Bram said.

"It is good that he feels so, for any advance could not happen without him, but it doesn't change the problem we face. It's not if we should intercede as much as HOW we should intercede. Even then, the king was adamant that we remain here, defending the south."

"True, but our ape allies might invade on their own," Bram said, watching two of said apes wrestling on the near side of the great fountain, their argument sparked by some minor disagreement. Such was the nature of the gorillas.

"If they don't kill each other first." Torg shook his head as one of Captain Sarelis' magantors passed overhead, returning from its morning scouting mission. With all the Torry and Macon magantors occupied with the Chosen, only the Sisterhood and Troan magantors remained. The Jenaii spilt their warbirds between helping ferry the Chosen and remaining at Notsu. No matter their number, Torg was thankful for their presence.

"The sun is nearing its apex shortly," Bram observed, sparing a glance skyward.

"Unfortunately," Torg snorted, knowing another commanders' call was scheduled at that time, as it was every day. It would likely be more of the same, the apes clamoring to march north, while Ciyon concocted a new strategy to win converts to his plans, leaving poor Torg and Bram trying to speak sense to them. Ciyon's latest plan involved sending a naval force up the Veneba River, assailing the enemy upon the lake, supported by the Jenaii telnics who could fill the decks of said boats. Even if successful, the tactic would be little more than a nuisance to the enemy. Only a concerted attack across the Kregmarin would draw the enemy's attention, and such an attack could not be agreed upon.

"Master Vantel!" Criose shouted, drawing his attention to the western sky, where approached a flock of magantors. Criose acted as his personal guardian, given this task by King Lorn upon his departure, the man constantly standing watch behind him and shadowing his every move, much to Torg's annoyance.

A flock of warbirds was a common sight, but this one was unique by the size and color of its lead mount… Wind Racer.

* * *

Cronus made his way through the corridors of the former estate of Tevlan Nosuc, greeted by saluting soldiers as he passed, each thrusting their fists to their hearts as he returned the gesture. Young Dougar followed at his side, his shorter legs struggling to keep pace. The boy had been his constant shadow since King Lorn departed, trusting him in Cronus' care. Cronus thought the boy did a fair job of watching over him, reminding him to eat and fetching whatever he needed, oftentimes before he knew he needed it.

"Do you think it is true?" Dougar asked as they passed through the main atrium where the Battle of Kregmarin was distastefully painted upon the surrounding walls. Cronus wanted nothing more than to remove the offensive reminder of their king's murder, but Lorn ordered it not be touched. *Leave it for posterity to determine its fate*, Lorn had said. A part of Lorn that took offense was overruled by the part thinking his people needed a reminder of what they were fighting for. Cronus agreed on that part, for every time he looked upon the fresco it made him even more eager to kill the enemy.

"We'll find out soon enough," Cronus said, referencing the rumor of Princess Corry arriving at Notsu.

That rumor was further validated as Cronus came upon Havis Darm and Dalin Vors standing guard outside the council chambers, their distinct blue tunics and silver mail marking them members of the elite. The two former magantor riders were named to the elite after the first siege of Corell for saving Princess Corry's life during the final assault. They were also among her favorite elite, often taking positions of prominence guarding her. Their presence meant she was likely waiting within. Cronus greeted both men, ordering Dougar to remain with them before entering the chamber.

* * *

"Welcome, King's Elite Kenti," Corry formally greeted him upon his entrance, waving him to a place beside her at the table, where stood the commanders of rank among the Macon, Jenaii, Torries, Sisterhood, apes, Notsuans, along with kings Sargov and El Anthar. He was surprised to see Galen standing upon her other shoulder, the minstrel having accompanied her upon her journey. Torg stood opposite them, the gruff commander of the elite's impassive countenance concealing his opinion on her presence. He wondered the purpose for her journey, which she immediately addressed.

"I have come at the behest of our esteemed queen, who shares my opinion on the matters we are to discuss. Before we commence, what is the state of the remaining Chosen in the city?" Corry began.

"The last of the Chosen departed three days past, most having attained Surlone shortly after, before marching further west, Your Highness," General Lewins said, referencing the former Notsu holdfast that was being refurbished nearer the Torry border. Surlone was now a vital resupply point on the road joining Notsu and Corell.

"Very good. What I speak of is for your ears only. Let your subordinates draw their own opinion of any actions that follow this council, but do not divulge what we speak of with them," she began, giving pause before continuing.

"As you are aware, our king and King Mortus have embarked upon a long, arduous trek which shall lead them into the heart of the enemy, somewhere along this line," she said, running a pointer along the map to either side of the Mote Mountains.

The others gathered about were not certain of Lorn's route of travel between Rego and Fera, though passing either face of the Mote Mountains was the likeliest path.

"I am aware of the King's orders for you to remain behind to guard the south, but he also has placed his authority over the realm in the hands of our queen and myself. While Master Vantel and General Vecious have full authority over military affairs, your queen and I have final authority in the direction of the Macon and Torry realms, authority we shall not use to coerce either of your cooperation. That stated, I would ask that you agree with our assessment of our situation and act in accordance with our wishes." Corry looked to both commanders, as well as Dadeus, who stood off to her left beside Guilen.

"And your wishes, Your Highness?" Dadeus asked curiously.

"Our King asks that we remain behind while he and the Chosen march upon the heart of the enemy… here," she said, pointing out the approaches of Fera in the far eastern regions of the Benotrist Empire. "With most of Tyro's legions destroyed or weakened, the nearest available legion, beside his many garrison forces, is the 13th Benotrist Legion positioned at Laycrom. The remnants of the legions that escaped to our direct north are still near Nisin and its surrounding regions. It would be a great boon for our king if we could draw the eyes of these legions elsewhere, leaving only the garrison of Fera for our Chosen to deal with. As we speak, the Macon, Torry, Yatin and Sisterhood navies are gathering great strength to assail Tyro in the west, bringing much infantry to bear. This should suffice in occupying the 13th Legion. As for the legions in the east, those that survived Corell and departed Notsu, it should fall upon us to keep their eyes and swords fixed to the east," she stated.

"Though I agree with your sentiment, Your Highness, it does not change the difficulty in crossing the Kregmarin Plain," General Vecious explained.

"That is where you are mistaken, General Vecious. We do not need you to cross the Kregmarin to attack the enemy. We only need the enemy to *believe* that you are going to," she said.

"Thus keeping their eyes upon Notsu." Dadeus smiled, appreciating the strategic mind of the Princess.

"A wise alternative, but still difficult. Any foray across the Kregmarin, or elsewhere in the east would require the movement of large portions of our armies to convince the enemy we pose a significant threat," General Lewins said.

"And even if we stage large forces to our north, feigning invasion, it won't matter if the enemy does not see them. Their magantors must be committed to scouting said approaches," Bram Vecious pointed out.

"I leave that to you. You are all generals of great renown, and together should find a way to achieve these aims," she challenged them.

THE CHRONICLES OF ARAX

* * *

Corry left the commanders to discuss the plan forward, stepping into the outer corridor, ordering Cronus to follow her, her guards and Dougar following at a distance as he guided her to the chambers prepared for her.

"Your daughter grows stronger with every passing day, Cronus." She smiled slightly, regarding him from the corner of her eye as they walked.

"Thank you for watching over her, Your Highness."

"It is the least of the debt I owe to her parents. Maura shall always have a place at court, and should anything happen to you, I shall adopt her as my own, though our queen has made the same vow."

"You are kind to say so."

"And you are unusually reserved considering the state of things, Cronus Kenti. What think you of our King's departure? I know it doesn't sit with you."

"Am I so transparent?"

"No, I simply know your mind. You are as displeased with this endeavor as I am, remaining behind while those we love fight our battle," she nearly spat.

"On that we are agreed, but I see no way forward, though your plan is at least doing something to shape their battlefield to our favor."

"Yes, but I would prefer a more direct approach upon the enemy, and I cannot see a way of doing that." She hated admitting that, wishing to change the cruel facts before them. The Benotrist border was simply too far, and across hostile lands that would kill many of their soldiers before ever reaching the other side. Any serious attempt to cross the Kregmarin would only deliver the survivors up to the enemy upon crossing.

"I agree." Cronus sighed. She sensed a strange acceptance of this fact in his demeanor, or was it something more?

"Something troubles you, I sense," she said.

Cronus stopped midstride, causing her to do so as well, the others holding in place several paces behind to give them privacy.

"Though you do not seem as troubled by recent events as I first believed, there is something more. Whatever could it be?" she asked, regarding him studiously.

"Before much of our army was struck with visions, I too had visions, but nothing of the sort shared by the others," he began.

"But you were not among the Chosen," she stated.

"Though every one of the Chosen had visions of some nature, not all those with visions were chosen," he rightly pointed out.

"I hadn't considered that. Now what of this vision you saw, and why does it trouble you?"

"This whole matter of the Chosen facing the enemy on their own does not match what I saw," Cronus said, going on to explain his own vision of the future, with himself and so many others not chosen standing with those who were, facing untold hordes of gargoyles in battle. He spoke of his friend slain by a gargoyle spear, the vision so real he knew it to be true.

Corry was silent, struck dumb by this revelation. She thought it misplaced, considering all that the others had seen, but looking into Cronus' eyes convinced her of the truth of it.

"Of course, none of what I saw matters unless a different way forward presents itself," he conceded.

"It is all so strange." Corry sighed, not sure what to believe.

"After all we have endured since the start of this war, we should have expected this. Come, let me take you to your chambers. Though protocol suggests we place you in the most grandeur apartment on this estate, we found a more appropriate chamber for a princess of the realm," Cronus said as they continued on.

"Something was inappropriate in the master's suite?" she wondered.

"Morac used it as his private sanctum during his stay, decorating its walls with most unseemly frescos that you would find in poor taste." Cronus referenced the lewd frescos painted upon the walls of Morac's private chamber, along with the second rendition of Kregmarin tastelessly displayed upon entering.

"In poorer taste than the abomination displayed in the main

atrium?" she wondered, referencing her father's severed head held aloft in Morac's hand, the scene one would see upon entering the estate.

"Yes." Cronus sighed.

"Your Highness! Master Vantel asks that you return to the council chamber!" Criose said with labored breath, having raced after them, blocked by her guards still holding at a distance.

"What ails Master Vantel?" she inquired rather harshly.

"There is sorcery about, Highness," Criose said.

"Sorcery?" She lifted a brow at that.

"The Earthers have possessed the chamber."

* * *

Upon returning to the council chamber, Corry and Cronus were greeted by the sight of a large hovering disc the size of a man's fist floating above the table in the center of the room, far larger than the diminutive discs the Earthers used before. The disc maintained a constant circling motion, its murky surface matching the hue of its surroundings, quite useful in masking its existence, except for now as it declared its presence. The others gathered about appeared taken aback, save for the stoic Jenaii and boisterous apes who all displayed ridiculous grins, and of course Torg, who simply stood there with his arms crossed, staring down the mysterious object. Torg's steely composure was explained as a familiar voice emitted from the object.

"*Welcome back to the party, Corry, now we can get down to business.*" Raven's voice echoed strangely from the object, proving this iteration was far stronger than Brokov's previous disc.

"Rav?" Cronus made a face, not having seen this technology from his friends before.

"*Yep, it's me, Cronus. Glad you can join us.*"

"How are you speaking?" Cronus asked.

"*Just another of Brokov's toys he brought online. It's a lot better than the last. We have a few other surprises in store for my father-in-law too. If that doesn't put a smile on your collective faces, then you're a bunch of idiots.*" He chuckled, with a few asking what the term *father-in-law* meant, until Cronus explained it.

"Now as I was explaining while Criose went to fetch you, Lorken is on his way to you as we speak. He should arrive in a couple of hours unless he falls off the air ski, which, knowing him, is a real possibility." Raven again chuckled, most of the others still wondering what an air ski was.

"Lorken isn't the clumsy one," Brokov's voice interjected, setting the record straight.

They heard a gentle thud, wondering the source as Raven pushed Brokov rather forcefully, the sound of his body hitting the wall the source of the sound they heard.

"Enough, Raven!" Tosha's voice echoed over the comm. *"Haven't we had enough fights lately?"* she growled.

"Your Highness, you are well?" Lucella Sarelis asked, pleased to hear Tosha's voice.

"I am well, Captain Sarelis. How fare our sisters?" Tosha asked regarding their warriors, which Sarelis briefly detailed.

"And you are with Captain Raven on his ship?" Lucella asked.

"Yes, I am, along with a multitude of others," Tosha said with an annoyed voice.

"We'll cover all that later. Right now, let's talk business," Raven said, retaking the comm. The others gathered around the table tried to form a mental picture of what was happening on the other end of the communication and failed miserably.

"And what matter do you wish to discuss, Raven?" Corry asked, using his familiar name, much to the surprise of the others. She had long given up on him addressing her formally.

"The upcoming invasion. We are going to need you to begin marching north real soon," he said as if that was a simple thing.

"Raven, we cannot advance in force without…" Cronus began, before Raven cut him off.

"We got you covered, Cronus. Don't worry about all that other nonsense. All you need to do is begin marching in the next couple of days, and we'll help you with the rest. That's why we sent Lorken. He'll help with the technical issues you'll need, as well as a little comic relief." Raven laughed at his own joke, the others still not following what

he was saying, before Brokov again nudged Raven aside, explaining things in a way they could understand.

"*What our simpleminded Captain is trying to say is we can resolve your resupply problems, scout farther afield than any of your magantors could dream of, and locate all your enemies long before they could engage you. All you have to do is march north in a straight line,*" Brokov said, receiving another nudge from Raven by the sound of the scuffling they heard through the comm, followed by another scolding by Tosha and Kendra, who most did not recognize.

"Are you two fighting?" Corry asked, not at all amused.

"*They are always fighting, along with the rest of our new crew members,*" Tosha answered back, the annoyance evident in her voice.

"*Stop making a big deal over it,*" Raven said, taking back the comm. "*You guys just hold tight and wait for Lorken, and we can start making plans.*"

"And what plans are you referring? I assume it is more than merely walking straight into enemy territory as brazenly as you suggest," Corry asked.

"*That is precisely what he is suggesting,*" Tosha answered back.

"*Oh, and tell Ular we need him back aboard. We saw him somewhere around there, but lost sight of him,*" Raven added, his request seconded by Brokov, who explained that Lorken would ferry him to the *Stenox* before again rejoining them at Notsu.

"How long have you been observing us?" Cronus asked, the others wondering the same.

"*Just a couple of days with our smaller discs. This one has been there since yesterday. We kept it well hidden until we got the layout of the place, and since we saw Corry arrive, we decided to drop in on your little meeting,*" Raven explained, before Orlom somehow managed to squeeze himself in over the comm.

"*It's good to see you, Coach,*" he shouted happily, with Cronus and Corry looking to Torg, indicating to the others who Orlom was referring.

"You are most kind, Orlom. It is good to hear you." He shook his head, causing Corry to smile at the scene.

Chapter 18

Tro Harbor.
Weapons room of the Stenox.

"I hope this plan you idiots came up with works," Kendra said, standing over Raven and Brokov's shoulders as they sat at the consoles, staring at the various screens, displaying visuals from each disc. The restoration of these observation platforms was one of many new systems Brokov installed after visiting their isle.

"Of course it will work. The boy genius over here has thought about everything," Raven said, jerking a finger toward Brokov.

"Raven, my love, you are talking about moving more than one hundred thousand warriors across vast distances, relying on nothing more than the power of this ship and the tools you gave Lorken. Should you falter, they will all perish," Tosha said, touching a hand to his shoulder.

"Did you just call me *my love*? That's a first." He looked back at her over his shoulder, wondering if someone switched faces with his wife.

"Idiot." She slapped him alongside his head.

"That's my girl," he said, reassured she hadn't hit her head on something, which earned him another slap.

"True love, what a lovely sight." Brokov shook his head, causing Kendra to smile. If there were ever two people who deserved each other it was Tosha and Raven, and he meant that in the worst way possible.

"I'll be glad to have Ular back to help with all this stuff," Raven said, trying to follow what was happening with each of the visuals playing across the screens.

"What's the matter, Rav, don't like doing real work for a change?" Brokov quipped.

"Real work? Who do you think landed us safely on this planet with our busted ship?" Raven growled.

"Lorken," Brokov said dryly.

"He was just there for comic relief. I was the lead pilot. And who traveled all the way across northern Arax, bringing Cronus safely to Tro? That was me. While you were sitting here in comfort. I had to sleep on the ground, ride through the rain, and wipe my ass with…"

"Alright, spare us the visuals. I knew you would bring that up." Brokov made a face.

"Brokov does have the right of it, Raven. What exactly do you do on this ship other than sit the captain's chair and pretend to order everyone about?" Tosha asked.

"There's more to it than that, Tosh, and you are one to talk. What exactly do you do when you sit on the throne?" Raven looked back at her over his shoulder.

She rolled her eyes, recalling the first time they had this argument, and the many times since.

"Besides, once we win this war, there will be plenty of work for all of us," Raven added.

"What sort of work?" Tosha asked.

"For one thing, we still haven't explored the rest of your planet. When we landed here…"

"Crashed here," Brokov corrected him.

"Landed. When we landed here, we first noticed your continent and picked the isle far enough off shore to avoid immediate contact but close enough to explore the mainland. We didn't have time to check out the rest of the planet before we set down."

"Set down? Have you seen the ship?" Brokov refuted his description.

"You're alive, aren't you?" Raven pointed out.

"Boss did good," Orlom interjected, having surprisingly said nothing for the longest time.

"At least your sidekick agrees." Brokov jerked a thumb over his shoulder at Orlom.

"Orlom is a very intelligent member of our esteemed crew, with a keen sense of observation." Raven gave the young gorilla a thumbs up, causing Orlom to grin widely.

Tosha shook her head, wondering how Raven instilled such loyalty in the young gorilla. She recalled their recent visit to Torn Harbor and the reception she had received from President Matuzak and nearly every ape she encountered. They looked upon her with hearty grins and deep respect, impressed by her *antics* in wedding Raven. She feared they would receive her poorly considering her and Raven's strife-filled past, but they curiously considered it a positive. She couldn't even take offense at their referring to her as *Lady Raven*. She appreciated their friendship and was taken aback by their warm reception, especially the kind treatment they offered her sons. She longed to remain with them, hugging them fiercely when she took them into her arms. She strongly considered remaining with them, her maternal protectiveness overriding her duty, but eventually relented. There was nowhere safer at the moment than the Ape Republic. She would help her husband win the war and then return for her children. Once again Raven's voice drew her from her musings.

"As I was saying, we have a whole world to explore and map," he said.

"You believe there are other lands beyond the sea?" Kendra asked.

"We spotted several during our descent, but only got a cursory glance before landing. Whether anyone lives on them, who knows," Raven said.

"The Jenaii claim to have come from across the sea, from a land far to our south," Tosha said.

"Then we should start there. Might be a good idea for Elos to join us to bridge the cultural differences in case any of his people still dwell there," Raven said.

"You pronounced his name correctly. Very impressive." Brokov's sarcasm received him a punch in the arm, referencing his mangling of Elos' name every time he spoke it.

"He could always do so. He enjoys the twisting of everyone's name," Tosha said.

"That would require a level of deception and cleverness that Raven doesn't have." Brokov smiled, shifting to avoid another punch in his arm.

"You two are worse than children. How did ever you manage your affairs before us?" Tosha scolded them, sharing a knowing look with Kendra.

"We managed quite well before all this female interference," Raven said, receiving another gentle slap to the head.

"Don't even think of doing that with me," Brokov warned Kendra, who sported a devious smile on her lips watching Tosha and Raven.

"I wouldn't dream of it, my love." She leaned down to kiss the top of his head.

"Why don't you do that with me instead of all that slapping?" Raven asked Tosha, observing their interaction.

"Because, you large oaf, every time I say something kind, such as *my love*, you make a stupid comment," Tosha growled.

"A slap to the head is better than a kiss, boss. It means she really likes you," Orlom said in all seriousness.

"She must like you a lot." Brokov smiled, before something caught his eye on the center viewscreen. He reached out to the console, expanding the image, revealing a line of ships bearing the red anchor upon a field of blue, sigil of the Casian city of Milito.

"Where is that?" Kendra asked, leaning over his shoulder to get a better look.

"Twenty leagues south along the coast. It looks like the rest of the Casian 2nd Fleet is ready to join the party," Brokov observed, counting twenty warships among the group, along with a hundred merchant vessels, their sails full with the wind. The remaining sixty ships of the Casian 2nd Fleet were already anchored at Tro, along with numerous merchant vessels used to transport the 2nd Casian

Army, twelve telnics in all, ready to join the Troans, Enoructans, and apes in the campaign ahead. The Casian army bore the same sigil as the fleet, the red anchor on a field of blue. It was Casian custom to assign sigils to all naval and army cohorts designated to one city. As the Casian League was in truth a loose confederacy, each city state held autonomous control over local affairs, keeping its own sigils to designate their ships and armies, though each were manned by men drawn from across the League. It was mainly foreign adventures and trade alliances that required submission to the authority of the ruling council at Teris. As the ruling council approved a declaration of war upon the Benotrist Empire and Nayboria, Milito directed all their forces to the battles in the far north, leaving the other Casian cities to face Nayboria.

"I guess we should inform Matuzak and Klen," Raven said, swiveling his seat around to stand up, making his way to the door with Tosha following close behind, wearing matching earth garb as her husband, with her sword of light riding her left hip and a laser pistol upon her right. Her time aboard the *Stenox* was changing her in both subtle and obvious ways. Orlom followed on their heels.

* * *

THUD!

Raven stepped back, trying to step onto the stern of the first deck, when a furry body dropped at his feet.

"Ugghh!" the gorilla moaned, shaking the blurriness from his eyes before gaining his feet, ready to reengage his companion, a smiling Gorbad who stood at the portside rail, before Raven's hand snatched him back by the collar of his boiled leather mail.

"Easy, Darpak, we got more important things to do," Raven said, pushing him toward the starboard rail before advancing onto the exposed section of the stern, Tosha and Orlom following close behind.

"Aye, boss!" Darpak said, giving Raven an Earther salute, his furry hand touching the corner of his thick eyebrow. Raven returned the salute, finding the whole scene surreal. Darpak and Gorbad were their newest recruits, joining them at Torn Harbor, where they met with Matuzak, before bringing him to Tro ahead of his fleet.

"No sparring without Argos or myself," Orlom reminded the two gorillas as Raven and Tosha ascended the ladder to the second deck.

"You are not boss, Orlom," Gorbad argued, giving Orlom a shove. Before Raven cleared the ladder, the two of them were already rolling about below.

"Knock it off, guys, we got work to do," Raven said without stopping to see if they obeyed before stepping onto the bridge, where Zem stood awaiting them.

"Captain," Zem greeted him, pleased to speak his rank, while considering himself a general.

"Lieutenant," Raven said, using Zem's Earther rank over his Araxan one.

"Very funny. I will remember that one day when we return to Space Fleet, and I receive my proper rank," Zem said.

"Good luck with that," Raven said, taking his seat in the captain's chair, while Tosha posted beside him, looking out over the bay, the *Stenox* sitting in the middle of the vast harbor.

"Zem has earned his rank as general, Raven. Perhaps if you were a little kinder you would have more friends." Tosha slapped his shoulder.

"What are you babbling about? Zem and me are great friends." He gave her a look.

"I was named an honorary member of his family, as well as his father's favorite son," Zem said. She sensed humor in his deep, metallic voice.

"Truly?" she asked amusedly, Raven's silence on the matter proving it true.

"Yes." Raven shook his head while raising Brokov on the comm.

"*Yes, Rav,*" Brokov answered back, remaining below to monitor the visual feeds.

"Where are Arg and Matuzak today?"

"*The magistrate or the forum. If you can't find them there, just ask Klen.*"

"Thanks. Zem, would you do the honors?" Raven waved an open hand toward the helm.

"I believe our new crew member wants to demonstrate her ship handling." Zem stepped aside, giving Tosha the helm.

"You letting her drive the ship?" Raven didn't like that idea.

"I can handle your little ship well enough." She slapped his shoulder before taking her seat.

"Alright, see if you can manage parking it along that stone pier in front of the harbor magistrate." He waved a hand in the general direction.

"This isn't that difficult," she said, increasing speed as the ship lumbered forth, before shifting into a smooth glide.

"Just don't speed up too fast or Orlom and the boys will take a tumble off the back of the ship."

"Then they better hold on, and if not, they could use the bath," she quipped.

There before the forward viewport of the *Stenox*, the southern shore of Tro Harbor was alive in all its splendor. Galleys and warships bearing the flags of many lands crowded the piers, most notably the 2nd Ape Fleet and the 2nd Casian Fleet, each bringing to bear thousands of soldiers of both the Casian and Ape 2nd Armies. The Troan Fleet boasted fourteen warships from their original fleet and another six converted from merchant galleys. There were more than a thousand Enoructan warriors now gathered at Tro, paired with five hundred Dorun mounts, the large aquatic mammals a now familiar sight in the city. Beyond this great host were thousands of volunteers flocking to the harbor from the surrounding lands, including expatriates of Gotto and its tributaries.

The entire ensemble was breathtaking in its strength and diversity, and Tosha couldn't help but wonder what her father was thinking attacking Tro to begin with. The might of this army was one thing, but bringing it to bear was another, which was where the Earthers would prove most helpful.

Tosha handled the ship with surprising skill, easing the hull alongside the pier.

"Not bad" was the closest Raven came to admitting she did very well.

"Not bad indeed." She gave him a look, following him and Zem off the bridge.

* * *

Notsu.

While Raven and Tosha sought out President Matuzak, Lorken circled the city of Notsu before sweeping over its north wall, keeping above the range of any sentry that wasn't expecting him. The last thing he needed was a spear or arrow sent his way by some solider taken by surprise. The sentries manning the wall looked on in dismay as the strange object passed overhead, craning their necks as it sped toward the center of the city. Lorken spotted only one magantor patrolling the skies above the city, but it seemed oblivious to his presence, its rider looking south as he sped toward the former estate of Tevlan Nosuc, guided by the readout on his display console, sent by their recon disc.

"Hope they cleared space for me to land," Lorken said, ducking below the clear shield affixed to the front of the ski, a crude but effective means of keeping dust and bugs off his face. The only thing they hadn't thought of was a means of keeping all that crap from smearing across the shield. The shields on Earth simply dissolved any debris on contact, removing such an inconvenience. It was another thing to place on their to do list.

He angled lower, skimming above the rooftops, wooden slat roofs giving way to tall pillared structures, before passing between towering citadels. There ahead lay the large manse of Tevlan Nosuc, resting prominently along the city square, or more like a circle, Lorken mused. He spied dozens of soldiers manning its upper battlements, and several warriors standing forward of its large open doors, the gateway to the residence, presiding above a wide stone stair leading to the street below. He quickly recognized Ular standing among the warriors guarding the entrance and Cronus' familiar mane lifting in the summer breeze beside him. They were obviously placed to guide him to the location. Examining the width of the open doorway gave him an idea. Seeing no sense in setting down on the street or upon the rooftop, he decided on a more direct approach.

Lorken swept down, skimming just above the street level, the crowds gathering below backing away as he passed overhead, staring and pointing in awe. Not one spear was raised or arrow loosed as he went, making him believe the were informed of his imminent arrival. That guess was confirmed as Cronus and Ular ordered the men around them to make way as he drew closer, the air ski slowing down as he passed above the wide steps, stopping before the open doors and between his friends. The ski hovered silently as Lorken stopped with Cronus upon his left and Ular his right, and an open doorway directly ahead.

"I thought you might fly that thing straight inside." Cronus smiled, greeting his friend with a hand to his shoulder.

"No point in walking more than necessary. Which way to the council room?" Lorken asked.

"Just inside, at the end of the central passageway, down upon the right," Cronus said, pointing his left hand through the open doors.

"I'd give you both a ride, but I have all this stuff in the way." Lorken smiled, nodding his head behind him, where was bound numerous objects in a large bundle.

"What is all of this?" Ular asked with his watery voice.

"The gifts of the magi." Lorken grinned.

"We can walk." Cronus smiled, leading his friend inside, somehow guessing what he was referring.

*　*　*

Once Cronus raced ahead of Lorken, he ordered the guards standing post outside the council chambers to stand aside, allowing Lorken to glide into the chamber, air ski and all. Those gathered therein were not as surprised by the strangeness of it all as they should have been, most growing used to the Earthers' strange tools and antics. Few in the chamber had met Lorken before then, finding his dark complexion a point of curiosity. His demeanor, they soon realized, was much like Raven's.

"I see you decided to bring that all the way in here." Corry gave him a look as he stopped just inside the doorway, before advancing to him, embracing her friend as he dismounted.

"It's easier for me to hand these things out without carrying them," Lorken said, returning her embrace. The others looked on, taken aback by Princess Corry's familiarity with the large Earther, before remembering her close friendship with the entire *Stenox* crew. Torg reminded all of them that it was Lorken who joined Corry in rescuing Terin from Darna's dungeon. It was also Lorken who helped rescue Cronus from the dungeon of Fera. His legend was every part as grand as Raven and Kato's, and here he was, coming to aid them in the task at hand.

"Things?" Corry asked, following his gaze to the bundled objects resting on the seat of the air ski.

"Gifts from our crew that you might find use for," Lorken said loud enough to draw their collective attention from staring at him to what he was about to give them.

He proceeded to give them three more tissue regenerators, which he would demonstrate how to use to Ilesa, who he was interested in meeting. He provided detailed maps of the Kregmarin Plain and its adjoining regions, including the most recent locations of all Benotrist and gargoyle forces south of Nisin, curtesy of Brokov's observation discs, which scouted all the lands to their immediate north over the last several days. Torg lifted the finely crafted maps, impressed by their intricate detail. Lorken gave them water purification equipment, and water source locators, each drawing curious stares until he expounded their use.

"These will restore tainted wells. These will show you where to dig new ones without first breaking the soil. They are real good time savers," Lorken explained, drawing gasps from the council. If true, they could easily overcome the greatest difficulty in passing over the Kregmarin.

"How is this possible?" General Vecious asked, wondering if it was true.

"The Earthers are workers of magic, my friend," General Lewins reasoned.

"No, General, their wise men have simply mastered things ours have yet to conjure," Captain Sarelis corrected him, receiving a nod from Lorken confirming her analysis.

"Good to see you again, Lucella," Lorken said, recalling his visit to Bansoch.

"And you, Lorken of Earth." She saluted him with a fist to her heart.

"I have two of these for you, but they should be used very carefully," Lorken said to Corry, handing over two laser rifles.

Corry received them with heartfelt gratitude, taken aback by the considerate gesture.

"By careful, I mean they should only be used by those who have an aptitude for them. Whoever you choose should be paired with whoever has your magic swords in the off chance Thorton sends a blast in their direction. Speaking of magic swords, where are Terin and Elos?" Lorken asked, looking around the room, not finding them.

It was Cronus who explained what transpired with the attack on Notsu, and the death of so many, as well as the visions and the Chosen. For some reason word of this had not reached the *Stenox*, or even Tro, an oversight that made little sense considering the importance of it all.

"They just up and left, planning to march into the heart of Tyro's realm?" Lorken asked in disbelief.

"That is the heart of it." Torg sighed gruffly, disliking the situation as much Lorken.

"Then why not follow and help them?" He asked the obvious question.

"We were ordered to not follow them. They are to advance on their own volition, alone. None are to follow them," Corry said bitterly, hating this more than any.

"Then why are you all here if you aren't supposed to do anything?"

"We were told not to follow, but nothing was said of advancing on other fronts, or threatening to advance, as we were planning until Raven interrupted our council," Corry explained.

"Well, we figured you were planning a full invasion and figured to coordinate with our own. Since we aren't actually following them to Fera, that means Nisin and the eastern half of Tyro's empire are fair game." Lorken smiled.

"Fair game?" more than one asked, wondering the reference.

"We were planning to demonstrate along this entire front, keeping the enemy's eyes to the east and perhaps reducing the forces our friends would face," Cronus said, stepping toward the map displayed across the table, sweeping his hand along the Benotrist border from the foothills of the Plate to the shores of Lake Veneba.

"But now Raven asks that we truly invade the north, forgoing our planned diversion," Corry said, looking to Lorken to explain.

"That's why I'm here. I need to take Ular back to the ship since we are short on qualified crewmates, freeing me to return here and move things along," Lorken said.

"Move things along? Even if we can overcome our resupply issues crossing the Kregmarin, we lack sufficient forces here to invade the Benotrist realm," General Lewins said.

"If you march north, we can drop two armies on the northern coast," Lorken said, tapping the map near Pagan Harbor.

"What armies?" Torg asked.

"The 2nd Ape and 2nd Casian Armies."

"The last we heard, only a portion of the 2nd Ape Army had reached Tro. As far as the Casians…" General Lewins began to say.

"The entire 2nd Ape Army currently sits at Tro, and the Casians will all be in position by tonight. From there it is simply a matter of sailing up the coast and dropping them at Tyro's doorstep. While they do that, you march your armies across the Kregmarin and let Tyro decide which direction to attack."

"It might work." Torg scrubbed his chin with his left hand, looking over the map.

"Once I return from the *Stenox*, I will head north with an advance team and prepare the watering sites your king used guarding these hills," Lorken added, indicating the place where King Lore met his end.

Corry looked on that hateful place, imagining the final moments of her father's life, picturing the very image displayed in the outer atrium with Morac's gloating face holding aloft her father's head.

"I should be able to identify many other watering points along that entire route that haven't been explored. Oh, almost forgot," Lorken said, returning to the back of the ski, fishing out a handful of small devices, handing them out to the Torg and many of the others gathered about, bringing a knowing smile to Corry's lips.

"What are these?" King El Anthar asked, examining the device in his hand.

"Comms," Corry said, her face blossoming with hope, before explaining to the others their potential significance.

* * *

Lorken departed for the *Stenox* immediately after arriving, returning Ular to help with their new crewmates, before again returning to Notsu, where he would stay with their army throughout the campaign. He arrived the following morn, this time parking his air ski in the atrium of the estate of Tevlan Nosuc. Before settling upon the floor, he hovered his ski halfway up the wall, after fishing an assortment of paints from his pack.

Several guards looked on as he went about altering Morac's fresco, sharing one of two reactions to his creative choices, half turning away offended, the other half smirking deviously. By the time he finished, Corry and Torg were alerted to his arrival, entering the atrium just as he set the ski upon the floor.

Torg recalled his first interaction with Raven, trying to reconcile his personality with Kato's, wondering how two men from the same world could be so different. He wondered if the other Earthers were more inclined to Kato's respectful and resigned nature or Raven's outlandish antics and blunt speech. Looking upon Lorken's artistic endeavor, that question was answered. There, the wall of the atrium, where once stood Morac in glorious triumph, holding aloft King

Lore's severed head, now displayed Morac sporting a pair of generous breasts and holding aloft… a phallus. To further expound his intent, Lorken had altered Morac's jaw, drawing it disproportionately agape as if to receive the item in question. To Torg's surprise, Corry took no offense to the outlandish display.

"A true masterpiece," Corry said in a deeply serious tone.

Torg simply shook his head, wondering how the Earthers had so easily corrupted their beautiful princess.

Chapter 19

Nisin, the Red Castle.

Nisin castle rested between the headwaters of the Reguh to the west and the Tur River Valley to the east. Its blood red stone towers rose imperiously above the Nisin Plain, matching the fell hue of its crimson walls. The outer walls rose over a hundred and ten feet, connected by twelve turrets, with two to each face, and four resting at inverted angles to each corner of the palace. The inner walls mirrored the outer walls, rising another thirty feet, with a wide causeway between them, similar in design to the battlements of Corell. Behind the inner walls stood the inner keep, with four towers rising from its upper roof, spiraling high into the firmament, and magantor platforms jutting from its sides. Like Corell, a large opening rested between the inner battlements and the inner keep, opening to the courtyard below. Upon its highest citadel, the fabled tower of Vatar, flew the sigil of the Benotrist Empire, a black tower upon a field of red.

Davin Gorel, regent of Nisin, sat the ancient throne of the fabled holdfast. A Benotrist of high standing, he was named regent of the mighty fortress after leading the expedition to seize it during the waning days of the Benotrist revolution. He was so named by Tyro himself, the emperor honoring him for his fell deeds and many victories. As regent of Nisin, he in effect ruled over the eastern half of the empire. Silver tainted his once-dark mane, showing the years that cruelly took their claim. He was a stout-built man with discerning blue eyes, wearing burgundy robes over a golden tunic. Ten members of the Benotrist elite stood guard upon his flanks, hands resting on their sheathed blades, ready to draw at a moments alarm. He sat his throne, treating with General Gavis, who stood rigidly below as if cut from stone, regarding Davin Gorel with mismatched gray and black eyes, and a vicious scar running from his left ear to chin.

"Greetings, General," Regent Gorel received him, always wary of Gavis' mercurial temperament.

"Greeting, Regent Gorel," Gavis curtly replied. He had traveled far since taking flight from Notsu, marching his beleaguered army across the Kregmarin before attaining Nisin. He was most wary of the enemy's intentions, knowing the fate of the empire rested upon the precipice. Tro was a hopeless situation, the vital port city growing in strength with every passing day, apes and Casians now flocking to their cause. The Earthers had apparently survived Morac's blundering attack, though the emperor's pet claimed ignorance in directing the attack upon them. Their hopes of Prince Lorn being drawn into conflict in the south proved false, with him now firmly entrenched at Notsu with the Macon king beside him. Their only ally remaining in the south was Nayboria, but for how long? The latest reports from that front were equally disastrous, and he doubted King Lichu would last the summer. It was only a matter of time before the enemy gathered the strength and courage to invade. The one great mystery was Lord Morac. The latest rumor placed him at Notsu with the remnant of the 11th Legion, but other reports reached their ears claiming he stole away in the dead of night. As poorly as Gavin thought of Morac, he thought even less of Regent Gorel, a vicious, cunning sycophant who attained position through flattery over battlefield prowess. Gavis knew the truth of Gorel's victories in the revolution and his taking credit for the abilities of his subordinates.

"You stand as the only surviving general of our southern expedition. The emperor would hear your account of events there," Gorel said, implying that he would act as the emperor's ear on the matter.

"We marched into a trap, set upon by the might of the southern realms, now allied in purpose, as well as the Earthers, who brought great destruction upon us. That is my account. Any failings of said expedition fall upon our commander, as none of my suggestions gained purchase in his ears throughout the campaign. If *Lord* Morac wishes to refute my claim, he can stand to post and rebuke me," Gavis challenged. If Morac was present, this challenge would surely draw him out, and if not, then he either went crawling to the emperor directly or forsook their cause.

"Peace, my friend. Lord Morac has not appeared to give account. His whereabouts are a mystery, though there have been... rumors." Regent Gorel lifted his open hands to placate the cantankerous general.

"His absence speaks loudly to either his demise at Notsu or his cowardice. Either path leads to your final authority on matters of state in the east from this moment forward unless the emperor deigns to intervene. If this is so, we must prepare the realm for the inevitable," Gavis said, his tone carrying the undercurrent of ill omen.

"The inevitable?" Davin asked.

"Invasion. The south will march upon us, on that you can be certain. We must prepare the realm for battle."

"The garrisons of Pagan and Nisin were both reduced by half, their strength given to fill out the depleted ranks of our legions, legions now destroyed before the walls of Corell. My garrison has been further thinned by the insufferable rebellion that has sprung up across the east," Davin said, revealing their collective weakness.

"A man holding a wall is worth three attacking it. Our numbers shall suffice in that regard. What we need is Lord Morac's sword to counter the Torry Champion, and our own Earther to match theirs," Gavis said.

"As for Lord Morac's whereabouts, I can provide no clarity, but we are not lacking for an Earther." Davin smirked, though overlooking that Thorton's presence meant his power in the east was subordinate to the second-ranked member of the imperial elite.

* * *

"From this valley they say you are leaving
I shall miss your bright eyes and sweet smile

THE CHRONICLES OF ARAX

*For they say you are taking the sunshine
That has brightened my pathway awhile..."*

Ben Thorton sat in the corner of the palace tavern, listening as Ella sang, his back to the wall while nursing a northern ale, the strong brew a rare indulgence for the large Earther. He hadn't partaken alcohol since arriving upon Arax until returning to Nisin, learning of the attack upon the *Stenox*, wondering if any of his old friends had perished from Hossen Grell's stupidity. This terrible news was followed by the events of Corell, when he learned Raven survived, destroying much of Morac's army before the walls of the Torry palace. Any hope of Tyro bringing Arax under his sway was now waylaid. All his efforts to bring these people out of their dark ages went for naught. Most damnable of all was the attack on the *Stenox*. There was no recourse for that. He sat there in silence, trying to drown his failures in ale and failing in that too.

He looked at Ella, who stood in the center of the floor surrounded by tables of drunken soldiers, her beautiful voice contrasting the stale air and foul company that surrounded her. She sang the ancient ballad he had taught her, the *Red River Valley*, to perfection, most of the words matching the rhyme of their original English dialect. He remembered the last time Jenny sang that refrain, smiling at him from across the pilots' lounge of the *Stalingrad*. She followed that with his favorite song, *The Yellow Rose of Texas*. It seemed so long ago now and yet felt as if it was just yesterday. Time was a fleeting thing, its current twisting reality, jumbling one's memories. How he missed her, her gentle voice able to sooth his tortured soul. She was everything to him, and now she was gone, leaving him with only a memory. Was that all that life truly was, a memory? Was it simply an amalgamation of a lifetime of experiences, both good and ill, which you recalled precious few? Once you died it was gone, leaving only those who knew you and the memories they still recalled of you. That was Jennifer now, living on only in his memory. Who would remember him when he passed?

Perhaps Ella, he thought, regarding her alluring beauty as she stood in the center of the stone floor, torchlight playing off her silken black hair, her gray eyes returning his stare with a gentle smile. Would she remember him, and if so, would it be fondly? Did he even look upon her fondly in return? His heart felt cold as ice, a frozen relic of a long-dead life. He would never love another, that he was certain, so why did he save her? Was it merely her voice that reminded him so much of Jenny? Was it a simple act of charity, one surely to count for naught in the grand scheme of things? Or was it merely a small humane act to remind him he was still human after all? No, he didn't believe in psychological undertones. Such things were the musings of idiots. He was a man of hard facts and reason. As a man of reason, he knew Tyro had lost this war. There would be no Benotrist victory, nor a unified Arax. Should his people ever discover this planet, their disunity would hand over their sovereignty to a bunch of bureaucratic lickspittles and grifters. The Earth diplomatic and bureaucratic corps were populated with such lowlifes. He could see it now, the Araxan people relegated to mere oddities as if they were children requiring re-education and oversight by self-appointed pansies.

Maybe they wouldn't find them, that possibility giving him hope for these people. But then the problem of their backwardness still remained. They needed to advance but without wars that would devastate their population. The damnable misery of progress through the ages was its reliance on war, for need drove innovation. None of that mattered now, not for him anyway. All he could do is pick the time and place to die. With that, he downed his tankard. Looking at Ella reminded him of one last gesture he could do before passing. She was helpless without his protection. Her beauty might spare her life but not her freedom or virtue. He knew how the men looked at her, like a starving man looks at a steak. He had no doubt that if he had died hunting Alen, Regent Gorel would have placed his collar around her lovely neck, claiming her as his own. He needed to find someplace for her, somewhere safe.

The silence of his companion sitting beside him made him almost forget he was even here. The boy didn't say a word, sitting at his table, his wounded right leg resting uselessly below the hem of his tattered tunic.

"You're a quiet one, I'll give you that," Ben said, eyeing Alen out of the corner of his eye.

"There is nothing to say." Alen looked down at his wrists resting on the table, heavy manacles connecting them. Since his capture, Thorton kept him close, making him wonder his purpose. He had expected to be slain at any moment or tortured for the amusement of his captors but so far… nothing. He knew the palace regent had demanded him to be tortured for information and then put to death, but Thorton denied him.

"There is always something to say. You just need the courage to say it."

"Kill me and be done with it. There is no life for me now, no life worth living. But I doubt you would be so merciful. I know why you spare me Regent Gorel's wrath."

"You do? Enlighten me," Ben said, pushing away the empty tankard.

"I will be taken before the emperor for torture and judgement. You forget that I lived at Fera most of my days until Raven set me free. I have seen the punishment given to Tyro's enemies. I expect no quarter or mercy… or hope."

"A drink for the boy!" Thorton called out to the bar wench, who hurried to obey.

"I care not to partake." Alen tried to refuse him, but Ben was having none of it.

"Afraid you'll divulge information? No need to worry about that. You have no information I care about, so enjoy a brew and try to forget your troubles for one night," Ben said as the girl returned with an overflowing tankard, foam cresting its wooden lip as she set it down.

"Why do you show me kindness?" Alen asked warily as Ben pushed the ale into his hands.

"Because you're the only bastard in this place as miserable as me. Drink up."

Ben didn't miss the looks the other patrons sent his way, wondering why he kept the prisoner in his company. None dared ask why, one look from Ben Thorton stripping their courage. Only Zelo dared question Ben's motives, the two becoming trusted companions, if not friends. The gargoyle stood at the bar on the far side of the tavern, keeping a watchful eye on Ella, as well as any trouble that might stir. He and Ben shared knowing glances throughout the night. The Benotrists gathered there looked equally warily upon Zelo, noticing the laser pistol hanging from his right hip, tied down to the thigh of his thick trousers. He was the only gargoyle to wear trousers, as Ben advised, considering the need to tie down his holster.

By then, Ella finished her song, taking requests from the patrons for another, deciding upon a local favorite that she knew called the *Merchant's Daughter*. As she began to sing, a runner appeared, bearing a message for Ben from General Gavis. Ben called Zelo over to the table.

"Keep an eye on the kid and the girl until I get back," Ben said, handing the folded parchment to his comrade.

* * *

Ben found Gavis upon a lonely stretch of the outer battlements, the nearest sentry fifty paces to their east, the weary soldier staring into the night sky, fighting the boredom of his duty.

"You wanted to talk, General?" Ben asked, stepping to his side, resting the flat of his hand on the parapet, their position offering a generous view of the southern approaches of Nisin even in the closing dark.

Gavis was not one to mince words or laud praise like a slavish lickspittle. He hated court officials and false pleasers, and sensed Ben's similar affinity in this regard. The two only met twice before and shared few words even then, but Gavis detected in those few encounters Ben's blunt speech and disdain for pampered court officials.

"I would have words beyond the ears of others," Gavis said, his battle-scarred face visible in the pale moonlight.

"You picked a stupid place for that. Gorel probably has spies in the stone works of this floor, let alone eyes on every tower and battlement surrounding us."

"Even those ears can't hear the words I whisper," he said so lowly even Ben could hardly make them out.

"Then what troubles you, Gavis?"

"I would hear your counsel and ask for your aid."

"Can't give you the second unless you explain the first, so start talking."

"I have seen the enemy forces arrayed against us, their great number but a portion of what they shall gather. We have little hope of defeating them unless they dare venture here, and even then it shall be a close-run affair. I departed Notsu with whatever force I could gather under my authority, authority granted by the emperor himself…"

"Authority you arranged by messenger after fleeing Corell." Ben decided to let him know that he was well aware of how Gavis usurped Morac's authority on that delicate matter.

"I…" Gavis stuttered, appalled that his subterfuge had been uncovered.

"Relax, Gavis, I don't hold it against you. If you hadn't informed Tyro of what truly happened at Corell then Morac would have kept you and all your men at Notsu, and we know what that would have meant. It was rather sneaky of you but necessary. Why don't you tell me what really happened at Corell?" Ben asked, setting Gavis' nerves at ease.

And so he did, explaining Morac's many blunders, including allowing Hosen Grell the latitude to alter Ben's specific instructions regarding the ape fleet and the *Stenox*. Those foolish actions led to Raven being at Corell and decimating their legions at the critical juncture of the siege, first sending them into disarray and then decimating them in battle. The end result was the destruction of their army, with only his battered telnics escaping Notsu before the noose closed upon the rest. Add to the grim tidings that Gavis was the only surviving commander of legion and the loss of Dethine's sword, and Ben had a more apt description of the disaster.

"I now command less than forty thousand men, gathered from the remnants of the destroyed legions. I have word that the surviving gargoyles departed Notsu soon after I did. If we can unite both their telnics and mine, along with our garrison forces, we can hold the eastern empire, checking the enemy from advancing. But should we face their armies, and their swords of light and your Earth friend's weapons, even our numbers will count for nothing. What I need is you to match them and Morac's sword to match their champion, though I do not even know if he escaped Notsu."

"He did, if the reports are true," Ben revealed.

"So Gorel speaks true. He said much the same."

"Gorel and the truth are unlikely friends, but he's heard the same as me. The most credible sighting was from Farange. The commandant there claims he spent a day as his guest before pushing on, likely heading west to Fera," Ben said, naming the holdfast of Farange, resting along the northern foothills of the Plate Mountains to their immediate south.

"He seeks audience with the emperor," Gavis snorted, scrubbing his face with his hand.

"Or he is on the run, not wishing to show himself. The problem with that is there is only so many places he can hide."

"If true, then we face a difficult path. How can we contest the Torry Champion, or the Jenaii Champion? And there are the Earthers."

"Do you want the truth, or do you want me to tell you happy lies?" Ben asked lightheartedly.

"The truth, Emperor's Elite Thorton," Gavis said.

"Spare me that frivolous title. Call me Thorton or Ben or nothing at all. The truth is, Gavis, there is no way forward for victory if they march their army here. After that stunt in Tro Harbor, my people will refurbish their ship and return with a vengeance. No coastal city is safe. They will level them all and sink our navy while they're at it. What that truly means is the empire is doomed. If I were you, I'd take your forty thousand men and march back to Fera and advise Tyro to make peace. Maybe he can negotiate keeping part of his realm."

"He will never do that. He would lose credibility with our people, and besides, our enemies will not relent until the gargoyles are exterminated."

"Credibility is second to power. If Tyro makes peace, his people have no recourse but to accept it. As far as the gargoyles are concerned, they have already fled the eastern empire. Our latest reports show Kriton leading them west as well. You need to follow them. If you can join your strength with the 13th Legion at Laycrom, you can consolidate your position and reestablish firm areas of control. Staying here will soon be untenable if what I think will happen, does."

"Will you march with me?" Gavis asked, hoping to sway him.

"No. If my old friends come here, I will meet them. There is no other path for me now. The die is cast." Ben sighed.

Gavis guessed the meaning of the phrase by his tone.

"My army is camped to our east. I will consider your advice," Gavis said, turning to leave when Ben called out to him.

"When you see Tyro, tell him not to be like me, too proud to bend."

With that, Ben turned back to the parapet, looking beyond the palace walls, his mind lost in thought.

Chapter 20

He crossed over the confluence of the Morga and Reguh Rivers, forsaking any plan to stop at the cities that dotted their riverbanks, his magantor sweeping overhead, obedient to his determined purpose. Morac lifted his chin, savoring the northern air upon his face, glad to be free of his troubles, if even for this brief respite. He forgone stopping at Nisin along his flight, or seeking out General Gavis, or even Kriton, fixing his aim westward to the nameless hills, and the possibilities that lay beyond.

The midday sun rested high above, bathing him in its warm glow. How he longed for the comforts of his pavilion, and the tender flesh of his comely slave girls, but they were gone, and he vowed to restore his fortunes, no mater the cost. He angled south and west, following the course of the Morga. Somewhere to his north rested the port city of Mordicay, where the Reguh River emptied into the northern sea. He thought to go there instead, rallying the garrison to his cause as they were still loyal to his reputation, having none of their muster sent to bolster his legions in the south. He knew full well what reception he might receive at Pagan or Nisin, the soldiers pilfered from those garrisons having met a grisly end before the walls of Corell. He thought to gather new levies loyal to him, but knew they must be untainted by the rumors he knew were spreading across the realm. He knew Gavis despised him and would speak invectives to the emperor's ear, poisoning Tyro against him. He needed to stay ahead of Gavis, and the rumors, and be first to address the emperor before others spoke lies of him. This deep-seated fear forced him to slay his magantor driver, silencing his tongue concerning his actions at Notsu. Fortunately, the avian accepted his command, a fortunate boon amid his recent defeats.

He wondered where Kriton had fled, the large gargoyle leading the remnant of the gargoyle legions from Notsu. The last he learned was of them crossing the eastern face of the Plate Mountains, before breaking west. What was Kriton's plan? Did he mean to abandon the war in the east for their homeland? Would he seek out the emperor, trying to gain his ear before others spoke of his own failures first? Kriton betrayed him as much as any other, forsaking Notsu with the remaining gargoyle host just as Gavis had done with the majority of their Benotrist levies. What weak excuse would he give Tyro for his actions?

Such musings quickly soured his mood, filling him with a bitter resolve. He pushed on, pondering his options as the lands passed swiftly below. Should he venture to Fera, or elsewhere? He was reminded of a recurring dream, one so visual that he believed it prophetic. He was standing upon open ground, a great host of his native realm surrounding him, facing the Torry Champion and the Torry King, leading a paltry cohort against them. He felt great power coursing his veins, strengthening his resolve, and fueling his courage. It would be upon that open ground he would strike down his enemies and claim a crown of his own. But why would he face so few of the enemy? Were they decimated in battles before then? Was that paltry few all that remained of their once-vast host? The more he thought on it, the more he was resolved to see it to fruition.

He knew it was his destiny to gather his countrymen to this grand cause, to bring an end to the Torry realm, their allies, and their king and champion. He would have Terin's sword for his own, and Elos' as well. He would sire many sons, giving the blades to them one day, planting the seeds of a new empire… his empire.

Reassured by his vision, Morac pressed on, a delighted smile touching his lips.

BENJAMIN SANFORD

* * *

The northeastern foothills of the Plate Mountains.

Kriton stood upon a fat rock on the hillside, overlooking the rows of campfires where his beleaguered telnics huddled. There were many thousands of them spread out across the open ground below, nestled between the foothills upon which he stood and the dense forest to their immediate north. They marched without rest since fleeing Notsu, abandoning Morac to his fate unless he too came to his senses and fled if he was able. There was more to Kriton's motivation than forsaking a hopeless cause. He was beset with dreams, dreams shared by every gargoyle in his company, which he found equally unsettling. It was more of a calling than a dream, instilling an impulse to return to their ancestral lands. It was strikingly similar to their mating call, the one time each generation was called to the mating grounds where the strongest among them won the right to breed. The mating season had already passed eight years before, birthing the next generation of gargoyles to wage war upon their enemies, a generation even larger than their own. Was this dream a call for them to prepare that generation for battle? Their offspring were still too young for battle, making him doubt the intent of his dream. To call upon them was a dangerous and desperate tactic for if they perished, their race was doomed. Who would sire the next generation if they were slain?

Unlike his comrades, Kriton had a second dream, one so vivid, he doubted his sanity. He recalled the strange vision as if it happened before his very eyes.

Sails, dark sails rising upon the masts of a thousand ships, or was it ten thousand, he could only guess as they dotted the sea as far as his crimson eyes could see. They sailed over cold waters, with images of gargoyle maidens cast upon their bows, surf breaking upon their naked breasts as they broke the waves. Hundreds of thousands of gargoyles crowded their serried decks, clad in bright iron mail and helms, their crimson eyes staring back at him with knowing kinship. Each vessel was identical to its sisters, sleek-hulled with a single row of oars to each side, worked by rows of human slaves and gargoyle lasses, whose blind eyes stared hauntingly forward, their white irises matching their pure white flesh, their bellies swollen with gargoyle young. Unlike the human slaves, the gargoyle lasses were unchained, their place on the oars a matter of practicality. The humans were pitiful specimens, diminutive in stature and spirit, bred to this sorry purpose.

Onward the armada sailed, traversing the wine-dark sea like ghostly phantoms conjured from a human's darkest fear.

Kriton pondered the meaning of it all, wondering if this was a vision of a time long ago or the present? Or could it be the future? Was this a portent of an age to come where his descendants are driven from the shores of Arax, seeking sanctuary across the sea? If true, then where would they find so many ships to bear their numbers? And where would they go? What awaited them beyond the sea? According to legend, the Jenaii came from across the southern sea before coming to Arax, setting ashore at the mouth of the Elaris. Would that be their destination? It made little sense if that far-off land was still populated with the hateful Jenaii. So where then could they flee?

As if in answer to his question, Kriton felt his eyes cloud over, his mind awash with swirling visions. He felt himself lift into the air absent his body, looking down upon his mortal flesh where it still stood, statue still, staring vacantly forward as his spirit was carried aloft. The world shrank below him as he ascended, the hillside becoming little more than a small mound before reducing to a speck in his suddenly clear vision. His senses were vibrant, illuminating the world in full clarity as he sped north and west, the rivers and forests of the empire passing below like points on a map. He soared through the firmament, coursing the wind to heights unimagined, the mountains and rivers below seeming insignificant as he drew higher. The land soon gave way to open seas stretching endlessly to the horizon. He continued north and west passing over endless water, time and distance losing all meaning until towering peaks broke the horizon. He continued onward, the distant shore coming boldly in view.

There below he spied the far-off land with an inlet bay fed by a wide, deep river, with a ring of mountain peaks forming a protective arc in the distance. Foreboding forests stretched to either bank of the river and its many tributaries. Beyond the forests, the land transitioned into arid plains, with cracks and gorges cut into its landscape, before giving way to ominous foothills with jagged slopes, each mere shadows of the towering peaks beyond. His vision lifted to airy heights where the gray and black slopes peaked below crusted snowcaps, with pointed summits jutting prominently above.

His vision lowered to the base of the mountains, where rested large openings that seemed cut from the rock by a fell power, each an entry way into massive caverns beyond. He drifted lower, drawn into one of the cavernous openings below, passing into the subterranean realm. Passing into the underground realm, his eyes beheld its mysterious wonder, as if the walls of the vast cavern were alit like the sun, affording his mortal eyes clarity. The cavern was deep and wide, stretching beyond his sight like an endless sea. Upon this stone floor waited countless legions of gargoyle lasses, their bellies swollen with young, their shrill voices joining into a hypnotic chorus echoing off the cavern walls.

> *The time of our reckoning has drawn nigh*
> *The time of our ascension has drawn nigh*
> *Vengeance, mutilation, death chants cry*
> *Flesh of man, flesh of Jenaii*
> *Devour the favored sons of Yah*
> *Slay them child lass and all*

Their chants repeated without cease, fueling Kriton's spirit and renewing his strength.

His eyes sprang open, finding himself standing upon the foothills overlooking their camps. Was it a dream, a fevered delusion of a tired mind, or did it portend something more? No, it was real, as real as the flesh of his sharped nose. The truth was as clear as the starlit sky above. Somewhere beyond the northern sea was a far-off land, a place where his race could flee and build anew. It was distant and unknown to human eyes, a perfect sanctuary for the gargoyles to escape and husband their strength until they were strong enough to return to Arax and destroy the humans completely. Instead of fighting and struggling to survive, they could claim a home shielded from human endeavors, giving them time to build a true empire, one powerful enough to grant them final victory. That was their purpose, their calling, to gather their numbers and find a fleet to carry them. A large smile painfully stretched his lips, a rare gesture alien to his nature. He knew what he must do.

* * *

Telfer, the Purple Castle. North Yatin.

Crisnak awoke from his fitful dream, sweat pouring off his leathery face, his crimson eyes springing open, finding himself abed. Was it all a fevered delirium or a message, one so vibrant he dare not question? The gargoyle commander of flax climbed off his cot, his clawed feet scraping the stone floor of the barrack. It was still the dark of night, with most of his comrades soundly sleeping in the large chamber. A few suffered in their sleep, their winged bodies tossing and turning about in their bunks or cots. He donned his mail and sword, making his way to the outer corridor and the battlements above.

Stepping onto the outer ramparts of the east wall, he was met with a blast of fresh night air, a stark contrast to the stifling confines of the crowded barracks below. He was not alone upon the outer wall, finding dozens of others similarly afflicted, each coming here to clear their troubled minds. The sentries standing watch became accustomed to the sight, with scores of soldiers gathering upon the battlements each night. Many hundreds had already abandoned the palace altogether, stealing away in the dark of night over the past ten days, fleeing for home. More would flee this night, and Crisnak understood why, considering the beguiling nature of the dream they all shared. He wondered when he would break, with only his duty to his rank keeping him from running.

Even without the dream to fuel their desertions, the sorry state of the garrison tested their collective resolve. After taking the castle, most of their brethren marched south to Mosar with General Yonig, leaving the unfortunate ten thousand to remain here in place to guard the Yatin fortress. Once word reached them of Yonig's demise, along with most of their comrades, their spirits lowered further. There was now little hope for victory in Yatin without significant reinforcements, which were clearly not coming. They were now tasked to hold Telfer at all cost, denying the enemy an avenue of advance. Soldiers could only endure so long before other thoughts crept upon their sense of duty.

Then there was the dream itself. Each night many were visited by the same vision, the image of their gargoyle lasses calling them home, though it made little sense considering the mating time was still many years off. Perhaps it was not a mating call at all but a summons to gather their kind for one last battle or to safeguard their ancestral lands, particularly their breeding grounds.

Crisnak thought to step off the outer battlement, spreading his wings to take flight, drawn by the call of their gargoyle lasses. He resolved to remain at his post, struggling to balance his duty to his oath with his duty to his nature. Eventually his nature would win. Three days later he slipped over the wall unseen, taking flight northward, to the Benotrist Empire, to his ancestral lands, to home.

Chapter 21

King Lorn approached Central City with a heavy heart, its fabled walls running across his line of sight in an impressive arc from the southern bank of the Stlen River to his immediate north, to the northern bank of the Pelen to his south, before arcing in a circle back to the joined river downstream. Even from afar he could descry the towers of Leltic Palace peeking above the east gate, though it would not be seen again until one advanced far into the city, its impressive size obscured by the structures lining the causeways of the Carn-Ro, the main thoroughfare circling within the city walls.

He fondly recalled the countless times he entered the city in Jentra's company, his faithful friend always riding at his side, voicing his displeasure with Lorn's every action but following him all the same. He wished he could go back and tell his friend what he meant to him, how he couldn't have done the simplest task without him at his side, let alone win countless battles and three campaigns. That was the damnable misery of war, losing your dearest friends without having time to say goodbye. He discounted the few words he shared with Jentra at his passing, the brief utterance a poor substitute for what Jentra deserved. A part of Lorn died with Jentra that day, a very large part, and he struggled reconciling it with his faith in Yah.

Why him? Lorn lamented. Was it so he would know the pain of war, and why it must be avoided once this war was ended? Was it to remind him that life was precious and to value it above all when he would rule this land? How could that be when he was marching now to sacrifice himself and those in his company to save their friends? Was Jentra's death but a symbol of what this great company must do for the greater good? Or was his death simply the price of battle, where one is taken and another left alive by no determination other than chance? Whatever the reason, he missed his friend.

No, he reminded himself again. There was a reason for Jentra's death.

"No greater love," Lorn whispered, a wan smile touching his lips. It was this simple statement that now portended much more. It was the very essence of the choosing, the honor bestowed upon those who are called to sacrifice themselves for the world. He would soon join his friend in the afterlife along with the brave souls in his company. He was proud to be among them but sad for their collective fate. They still had much to live for, and most fought for so long that they deserved the reward of peace at the conflict's end. Alas, this was not to be. He thought of Terin and the loss his sister would feel for his passing. She deserved better than this, but such was war. He thought of his father by marriage and newest friend, Mortus. He was finally free of his tormenting visions that plagued him throughout the years and now marched beside him into oblivion. Then he thought of Deva, who rode behind him. She had turned from her selfish ways, redeemed by Yah to this great purpose. He wished he could give her reprieve, a second chance to prove herself throughout a long life.

Commander Torvin, commander of the city garrison, awaited him ahead, his silver hair clinging to his scalp as he removed his helm, sitting his ocran, the beast shifting slightly as Lorn approached. A sizable escort accompanied the commander, standing off to either side in ordered ranks, their bright cuirasses and helms resplendent in the midday sun. Behind the commander the road was open to the east gate, which opened to receive them, with throngs of people lining the streets beyond, eager to greet their new king and his impressive company.

Though the city had long outgrown its ancient walls, with structures advancing in every direction, the way was clear for several hundred yards beyond the east gate. Lorn's advance guard broke right or left, posting beside Commander Torvin's escort as Lorn drew nigh.

"Greetings, King Lorn, Central City awaits your eminence," Commander Torvin received him, dismounting to kneel.

"Remain mounted, old friend. Time is fleeting and urgent is our quest." Lorn waved off the formality.

"Very well, Your Majesty. The city is yours. The people are eager to see their new king. Your legend precedes you."

"Rumors often grow men greater than they are, Commander. If you could see to the lodging of my company, I would be most grateful. We still have far to go, and the comforts of our capital shall be the last we enjoy, I fear."

Commander Torvin wondered at that, having only heard the barest detail of their quest from General Valen, who preceded the king, allowing Torvin time to prepare for his coming.

"My steward has prepared accommodations for all of them. He awaits just within the city gate. I must inform Your Majesty of other recent arrivals that seek audience," Torvin said.

"Who?" Lorn made a face.

"Men of Yatin, nearly three hundred, all arriving but two days past. They seek to join you on your quest, claiming to have been *Chosen*. I asked the meaning of the reference, but they insisted that the Torry King would know of what they speak," Torvin explained, his contorted face indicating his curiosity.

"Lady Deva shall treat with them, if you could gather them in one place," Lorn said.

"Aye, the amphitheater would best suit such a purpose," Torvin said as another party of riders drew up alongside King Lorn, led by a man of renown clad in golden mail and helm over a scarlet tunic.

"Commander Torvin, I present my father by marriage and dear friend, King Mortus of Maconia," Lorn formally introduced them.

"Your Majesty," Torvin greeted him, bowing in the saddle.

"Commander, a beautiful city you command," Mortus returned his good manner.

"Leltic Palace is prepared for you both," Torvin said, his gaze drawn to the others trailing the Macon King, counting numerous Jenaii and several apes among them.

* * *

Terin waved to the crowds gathered to either side of the Carn-Ro as they rode through the city. He would rather have entered quietly, avoiding accolades that only embarrassed him. He was not one to relish such praise but returned their affection with a genuine smile and enthusiastic wave. Aldo rode beside him, the minister's apprentice feeling even more unsuited to public adulation. Unlike Terin, he was new to such adulation and knew he only received it by being in Terin's company.

"I should have been with the advance party or further to the rear of the caravan," Aldo lamented, desiring the attention even less than Terin.

"That is foolish talk, Aldo. You are properly placed beside me," Terin said, holding a half-dozen voli given him by a young maid upon entering the city, their sweet fragrance a pleasant respite from the odor they incurred upon their journey.

"It is you they cheer, my friend. I am simply a minister's apprentice, one they could not name if given a thousand lifetimes. It is the Champion of the realm they wish to greet."

"You are the apprentice to the Chief Minister and would one day be the king's highest counselor. Your fame will be far and wide, Aldo. Everyone will know your name, and those who are wise already do." Terin looked over to him, still taken aback by his change in attire. He now wore the vestment of a warrior, with polished mail over a white tunic and a sword riding his left hip. It was a stark change from his long apprentice tunic and cape.

"You are kind to believe so, Terin, but it matters not, for that future is no more." Aldo smiled wanly, knowing they would not live to see those far-off days when he would rise to the Council of Ministers.

Terin wished to say something to that but was bereft of words.

"Forgive my morose spirit, Terin. It is unbecoming. The people rightly laud you for your great deeds. You are right to repay their adulation with equal glee. I too am fond of you." Aldo smiled gently, reminding Terin why they so easily became friends.

"You are no less worthy of their praise, Aldo. You will long be remembered for this journey." He smiled back.

"I don't think…" Aldo tried to disavow that notion, but Terin was having none of it.

"Bards shall sing of the minister's scribe who took up a sword and marched into certain death for the sake of his friends and realm. Nearly everyone in this grand company is a warrior. Those few who are not shall be lauded most for their courage," Terin said, thinking of Tessa the seamstress as well, who marched in their company, or Dresila the matron, who would always be remembered by her guild for undertaking this quest.

Aldo had nothing to say to that, thankful for Terin's kind words. There was some truth to that as those who stand apart are often more easily recognized and acknowledged. He prepared to thank Terin when his friend broke off from the column, handing one of the long-stemmed voli to a young girl standing among the crowd, clutching her mother's skirts as the army passed. Her eyes brightened as he reached down from his mount, handing it to her before riding on. Aldo smiled at the scene, marveling at his friend's kindness. He wondered if the young girl would remember this small gesture. One day, when she grew older, her mother would surely tell her it was the Torry Champion who handed her a flower, before he rode off to war and likely his death, joining the chosen in their sacrifice. He thought of what Terin was losing beside his life, for they spoke much during their journey, where his friend shared his deepest most desires, all surrounding his dearest wife, the Princess Corry. Their time together as husband and wife was terribly brief before the war drew them apart. Aldo thought the Fates cruel for sundering them from each other after enduring so much. Now Terin was likely to die, and Corry set to mourn what might have been. Aldo thought of his own misfortune, wondering if he would have wed. It was but another mortal pleasure he would never know. What would be kinder, to have never loved or to have loved so strongly and have it ripped away?

Aldo shook such sentiment from his mind for it only saddened him. Yah had given them this choice to join this quest, and they should march gladly, knowing what they were saving by doing so. With that, Terin drew up alongside him as the column advanced into the city.

* * *

Two hundred and ninety-three Yatins assembled in the great amphitheater in the heart of the city. Each stood in ordered ranks, an odd mix of civilians and soldiers, with some as young as fifteen years, or as old as sixty. Most were men, though a few women counted among their number. Their leader was a commander of telnic from the 2nd Yatin Army, Yarlo Gilain, native of Mosar and devotee of Yah. It was Gilain that formerly received Deva upon her entrance to the amphitheater, having first made her acquaintance when the delegation from the Sisterhood arrived at Mosar after the fall of Emperor Yangu.

"We meet again, Guardian Deva." Gilain greeted her with a fist to his heart.

"I am simply Deva, Commander," she said, sparing a glance to the stands above that circled the arena, the late-day sun dipping below its high western wall, casting a shadow across the center of the open area where they stood.

"As you wish, Mistress Deva. I am told you are ordained by Yah to determine his Chosen. Each of my people have dreamt of this moment and journeyed here to join King Lorn in his holy quest," Gilain said, leading her to the first row.

Lucas remained at her side, her diligent guardian, protecting her throughout their journey. He found her quiet demeanor difficult to gauge, often mistaking her humbled spirit for coldness. He struggled reconciling the quiet woman walking beside him with Terin's tormentor. Her transformation in Queen's Letha's throne room was monumental. He had not known her before then, muting his awe of the change Yah had wrought, but he could clearly sense its significance. He watched as she approached the first person in the forwardmost row, a young man wearing the purple tunic and dark mail of a Yatin soldier. He removed his helm as Deva approached, standing rigidly at attention as she placed her hands to his face. Her eyes clouded briefly, drawing upon an otherworldly power, before relenting, the color returning to her irises.

"He is Chosen," she simply stated, causing the young soldier to sigh in relief. She moved on without saying anything further, taking the next in hand and repeating the process. And so she went, working her way along each row and column, confirming each of them. Strangely, not one was rejected, as if Yah instilled in them the drive to endure the journey, where the false believers were dispirited along the way. Commander Gilain thanked her profusely, but she refused his gratitude, reminding him they each served Yah and to acknowledge him before her mortal vessel.

Dusk was upon them as Lucas escorted her from the amphitheater, leading her to the palace where King Lorn awaited them, making their way through the busy streets of the central district. The entire city was celebrating the King's arrival with merchants upon every street hawking their wares and bards on nearly every corner stringing ballads of the King's renown. There was music and festivities in every street they passed, making Lucas wonder if the people knew what was truly happening. Did they not know that the Chosen were likely to not return, that they were marching to their deaths? Deva sensed the cause of his morose spirit, looking at him from the corner of her eye as they walked.

"They do not understand, Lucas. Forgive their ignorance and be glad they can partake such merriment. The times ahead are difficult enough without reminding them of the true cost we must bear," she said kindly, taking him aback with her gentle voice.

"You read my thoughts so clearly. Am I so transparent?" he asked in good humor.

"Your thoughts are no different from the rest of us. I am constantly admonishing my own self pity." She sighed.

"Self pity, you?"

"Yes, does it surprise you?" She smiled wanly.

"You serve Yah with such fervor I have not seen the merest doubt in you."

"I serve Yah most fervently, but I am still human. I have the same dreams and fears as you, Lucas of the Torry Elite. I still think of the possibilities that life might offer if I didn't die on this quest. I question why we are marching to our deaths and how that serves Yah's will," she sadly reflected, her vulnerability surfacing.

"What is it exactly that we are to do when we reach Fera? Are we to fight or to give ourselves over to the enemy?" Lucas wondered.

"I do not know." She sighed.

"But you are Yah's oracle. Has he not told you?"

"I am his instrument, but I have no more insight to his will than you. I do not know what shall become of us, only that we must undertake this journey."

That wasn't reassuring, he thought, his disappointment visible in his demeanor.

"I am sorry that my words bring you no comfort, Lucas of the Torry Elite," she said with sincerity.

"Please, I am simply Lucas. We shall be spending most of our time together on this long journey. It will be tedious for you to use my full title every time we speak, Mistress Deva," he said.

"Fair enough, Lucas, then I am simply Deva. Though I am a mistress of the blade, that too is needlessly stated with our every interaction."

"Deva it is, then." He smiled.

"And Lucas. Of course, if I am a mistress of the blade, you are a master as the men tell it."

"Not truly. I am a fair grappler, but there are many better swordsmen than I, and even grappling, I can name several better still," he said, thinking of Ular and Terin.

"Perhaps I can test your skill with a blade during our journey and assess your renown for myself?"

"Bargain struck, Deva." He smiled just as they came upon the palace entrance, the guards opening the forward gate for them to pass.

* * *

The festivities continued into the night throughout the city and the royal castle, with revelers gathered in the great hall of Leltic Palace. Famed bards and musicians gathered in the grand chamber, entertaining the king and his many companions. There they were joined by General Fonis and many court officials, each treating with their new king and his father by marriage. Lorn urged Mortus to join him in dancing with the highborn ladies of the city, especially Enora Fonis, the daughter of the Torry general. The Macon King was impressed by her enchanting beauty and gentle charm. Lorn had told him of his plans for her nuptials, having told Deliea the Macon groom he intended Enora to wed before he departed Corell. He only wished he could be there to introduce Enora to her intended, but such was their fate.

Of all his companions, it was the apes that drew the most interest from his people. Gorzak and Krink found themselves dancing with one maiden after another, managing to not step on any of the ladies' feet throughout their endeavor. Carbanc entertained several of the gathered warriors by juggling his ax and hammer, the large ape managing to do so without losing a finger.

The Jenaii received more subdued interest, the people looking upon them with deep reverence but feared approaching them as their stoic demeanor gave them an otherworldly aura. Elos politely engaged with his host, coming to understand the human need for interaction.

The Lady Enora Fonis had danced with two of the apes and many of the Torry and Macon warriors among the chosen. She danced with Mortus, finding his fatherly charm similar to her sire's. He inquired of her friend, the Lady Illana Ornovis, whom he was to wed. She extolled her friend's many virtues, reassuring him that she would make a fine queen of Maconia. After what seemed her hundredth partner, she again found herself dancing with King Lorn, the Torry monarch taking an unusual interest in her this night.

"Your behavior is most peculiar, my king. Might I inquire what strikes your fancy?" she asked as they moved across the floor.

"I must confess, my Lady Enora, that I have found a match for you, if you are so inclined." He smiled mischievously.

"A match?" She wondered at that, trying to hide the concern twisting at the corners of her lips.

"As you know, many of our warriors have wed maidens from Maconia, and in turn, many men of Macon have wed Torry maidens. Many more are still to do so, though the war hinders our efforts."

"Indeed, as I have spoken with King Mortus concerning the Lady Illana. They will make a fetching couple." She smiled, wondering why her words found little purchase as Lorn's face fell with her utterance. She then recalled what was asked of them, forgetting that King Mortus was unlikely to survive the quest before them, nor would Lorn.

"They would," Lorn said sadly. They were quiet for a time before he spoke again, directing their thoughts to more pleasant matters.

"Once our party continues north, I would ask that your father arrange transport for you to Corell."

"Corell? Is this where I shall meet this mysterious suitor for my hand?" She smiled suspiciously.

"In time. Unfortunately, his duties currently keep him from court. My queen is expecting you and shall formally introduce you. You may refuse the match if he is not to your liking, but I would ask that you give honest effort. He is equally concerned with the match as you are, but I would ask that you trust my instinct. Perhaps it will not come to fruition, but there is little lost in the attempt."

"If it pleases my king, I will give this man his fair due."

"My gratitude, Lady Enora." He lifted her hand as they danced, kissing it.

Enora smiled at that. She had known Lorn all her life, spending many winters at Corell with Princess Corry and Lady Ornovis. If he was eager for her to meet a Macon warrior, then he must be a fine choice.

"It is I who should be grateful, my king, for all you have done and for what you are sacrificing on this journey."

"It is a small price to pay if all goes as Yah has promised." He smiled wanly.

"Your lives are far more than a small price," she whispered, her eyes growing moist as she thought of that.

"True, but I would give my life ten thousand times over to spare you who remain. Everyone in my company feels the same. They are good men and women, every one of them." He sighed, stealing a glance of King Mortus dancing with Tessa the seamstress. The elder woman had won the hearts of many and danced with the spirit of a young maiden as they moved across the floor.

Good men and women. He smiled at that, proud of those in his company.

"When shall your journey continue?"

"Tomorrow Deva shall inspect the members of the 2nd Army. I do not how many she will find among them. We shall leave the day after, though many more are still making their way here from Corell," he said. There was yet another matter he must attend before departing Central City, to call upon the House of Celen and give his condolence to Leanna's mother and father, and to inform them of their granddaughter's well-being. It was one last gift he could extend to Cronus before he went north.

* * *

The late evening found Terin upon the upper battlements of the palace, overlooking the city where the Stlen and Pelen Rivers merged below, the lights of the nearby wharfs reflecting off their tranquil surface. It was a beautiful night but wasted without Corry to share it with. His gaze drifted north, wondering what fate would befall them in the lands beyond. He thought of his parents who were somewhere in that broad expanse, wondering if they lived or died.

"I thought I would find you here all alone, lost in thought," Squid said, stepping to his side, placing the flat of his hands upon the parapet.

"It is a beautiful city." Terin smiled, comforted by his old friend's presence.

"There are grander cities across the face of Arax, adorned with great wonders and higher walls, but there is no place fonder in my heart than here," Squid said proudly of the city he called home.

"I should savor its tranquil beauty, for we shall find no such equal going forth." Terin sighed.

"There are greater things than beautiful places to strengthen one's heart," Squid reminded him. "I have found throughout my travels and many years that the company I keep has proven a greater comfort than the places I have been. Good fellowship can make any harsh place a comfort, while even the grandest residence is but an empty tomb when filled with men of shallow worth."

Terin conceded that sentiment, recalling his many journeys and the friends that made them bearable.

"You are a good man, Squid Antillius. My father was fortunate to know you, as am I."

"Your father would be proud to see the man you have become. He is the finest man I have ever known, and that speaks well of his character considering the other great men who I call friend."

"He feels the same for you, Squid. He often spoke of you, sharing wonderful tales of your friendship and adventures. They made for good stories before bedtime, filling my head with tales of far-off lands and adventure. I wonder where he is now, and if he is well?" Terin looked northward once more, contemplating the answer.

"I cannot be certain of his fate or that of your mother, but my heart tells me they are well. It is not something one can know for certain, but I feel it quite strongly. If any man can face the Benotrist emperor and live to tell the tale, it is Jonas Caleph."

"I sense it also, as if his fate and ours are intertwined," Terin reflected with a faraway look.

"Perhaps. The future is ever shifting with multiple possibilities. Yah's hand is in this, and what kind of servant would I be to doubt his wisdom now? Come, there is much to celebrate this night. Let us not waste this time mourning what has yet to transpire. I have a surprise for you, my boy." Squid drew him way from the battlements to rejoin the festivities below.

"Surprise?" Terin wondered at that.

"Yes, as you know, I have arranged for Vonto's upkeep since you departed here for Molten Isle. He has been stabled at my country estate, but the caretaker shall bring him here on the morrow for you to visit him."

Chapter 22

*Thirty leagues southeast of Terse,
along the northeastern coast of Arax.*

ZIP!

A thick beam of purple light issued from the bow of the *Stenox*, sweeping over the calm surface of open water before striking the portside bow of the lead warship. Benotrist sailors jumped overboard as the laser swept along the hull, gutting the ship bow to stern. Before the next ship in line could raise alarm, the *Stenox* shifted aim, taking that vessel amidship, cutting it in half. The laser stopped while Brokov shifted aim, targeting the third galley in the Benotrist column.

Raven sat the captain's chair, watching the battle from the comfort of the bridge, with Tosha manning the helm and President Matuzak standing at his side. It was the third squadron of Benotrist vessels they had encountered since departing Tro, each numbering between fifteen and twenty vessels, this one bearing the sigil of the 4th Benotrist Fleet, while the others bore the standard of the 3rd. Before Raven returned from Corell, Brokov sank nearly two dozen Benotrist vessels along the approaches of Tro.

The *Stenox* sailed ahead of the fleet, clearing the sea lanes from Tro to Terse, while never straying too far from their growing armada. Most of the Casian and Ape warships were stripped of their armaments, making room for transporting more soldiers. It was a calculated risk, relying on the Earthers to engage the enemy warships. As long as the strategy held, all the fleet had to do was sail along the coast until they reached their destination, with the port city of Terse marking the first leg of the journey.

"You'd think they'd turn tail about now," Raven commented as another burst of purple light streamed from the bow below their viewport, striking the fifth ship in the column, the blast cutting away the top of the bioar above the main deck. Tosha expanded the visual, watching as the ship's masts toppled over, crashing into the jumbled mess of the main deck. Dozens of sailors lay strewn across the ship's top deck, many with their feet severed above the ankles, victims to the laser's path.

Tosha gasped, her heart breaking for her father's men, but such was war. She would be forever torn between her father on one side, and her mother and Raven upon the other. War was cruel work, and Raven was correct in that the only mercy was its swift end. He told her this repeatedly in recent days, quoting a famed general from his people's ancient past. She hated that it was so but understood as the trailing vessels turned hard to starboard, making for the distant shore, a line of gray and brown running the breadth of the western horizon.

"They have learned the lesson of the others," Matuzak snorted, watching as the ships rowed in all haste for the shore. The first squadrons they came upon after departing Tro tried to first engage the *Stenox*. After half were sunk in quick order, the rest attempted to flee north, only to be cut down in detail. The second squadron met a similar fate with the last ships in the column rowing for shore, with two managing to beach their vessels. Brokov blasted away their sterns once they beached, crippling the ships for good, the *Stenox* leaving them stranded along the coast. This squadron didn't wait for half their ships to be sunk before heading straight for shore, wisely forsaking any notion of fleeing north.

Tosha looked back to Raven, wondering what he would do. He couldn't leave them at their back, but would he slay them all before they could attain the shore? It was almost murder how easily they sunk her father's ships.

"Let them beach their ships, then cripple them," Raven said into the comm.

"*You sure about that?*" Brokov's voice echoed back.

"It's a long walk home from here, and I doubt they'll make it before the war is over," Raven said, looking at Tosha, his mercy gaining favor in her countenance.

"*Fair enough,*" Brokov answered.

They looked on as the ships pushed for shore, only for them to halt halfway when the laser had gone cold, wondering if the danger had passed.

"Brokov, remind them we are still here," Raven said.

A burst of green light issued from the portside bow, striking the largest ship in the column, a heavy trioar, likely the flagship of the squadron, the blast punching a hole through its portside stern along the waterline. The tactic had the desired effect, the entire column lumbering forth with all haste. Brokov held fire until they all beached along the shore, most caught shy of dry ground. A few hurried blasts with the smaller lasers hastened their disembarking, Benotrist sailors clambering over the sides of their ships before rushing up the beach. Brokov gave them a few moments before opening fire on the beached vessels, blasting away their sterns and cutting long gashes along their hulls. The *Stenox* continued on with Zem playing *Anchors Aweigh* over the ship's comm, causing President Matuzak to grin with approval.

* * *

By nightfall, the *Stenox* was back with the armada, the combined fleets dropping anchor before sunset. Tosha joined Raven atop the lookout deck, the clear starlit sky shining brightly overhead, casting her face in its pale light. Only the torch lights of the surrounding vessels illuminated the night air, dotting the surface of the sea like the cookfires of a vast army. There were countless ships, a collage of Casian trioar and bioars, along with Troan galleys and the entirety of the 2nd Ape Fleet and the remnants of the 1st Ape Fleet. Even Kaly managed to equip three of his own ships, packing their hulls with Troan soldiers and hired free swords, and a cohort of cavalry. Every morning the *Stenox* would scout ahead while the armada sailed north, skirting the coastline at a fair distance to avoid running aground. The sea lanes south of Terse were notoriously dangerous and the coastline barren, explaining the few settlements between Terse and Tro. Each night the *Stenox* would return, taking up position in the center of the armada where the commanders would meet to discuss the next day's order of movement, usually upon *Gorn's Roar*, the flagship of the 2nd Ape Fleet. Accompanying the armada were the Enoructan contingent and their dorun cavalry, the bottle-nosed creatures swimming alongside the flanks, scouting for shoals and shallows that might rip open a ship's hull. At night many of their warriors would climb aboard a ship and bunk for the night while others circled the armada, patrolling for any danger that might present.

Below deck, Ular and Zem conducted diagnostics on the ship's engines and weapons systems while Argos and Orlom instructed their new recruits on the operation of the ship's food processor, before partaking a generous meal. General Matuzak was still aboard the *Gorn's Roar*, coordinating with the fleet admirals on the order of movement and reviewing landing sites once they entered Benotrist waters. Brokov and Kendra were fast asleep in their cabin while Raven and Tosha took the night watch.

"You were merciful today," Tosha said, looking over at him where he stood at her side, resting his thick forearms on the low wall of the lookout deck.

"They aren't rejoining the fight anytime soon. Maybe we can end this war before they do," Raven said, thinking about the Benotrist sailors stranded along the barren coastline. President Matuzak sent an envoy to the survivors, advising them to release their oar slaves, promising them free passage overland. If not, he assured them the Earthers' magic would slay them where they stood. From what he learned, they followed Matuzak's suggestion as hundreds of freed slaves were spotted soon after, making their way south along the shore.

"All the same, you could have killed them all. It is what you have done before, and I wonder the change?" she asked, sensing the difference in his demeanor. Of course, she was different as well, as she stood beside her husband, clad in tight-fitting Earth garb with a laser pistol riding her right hip and her sword riding her left. Her clothing matched his, from the black boots to the black trousers, shirt and jacket. She would never admit that she found the clothes comfortable and to her liking, seeing no need to boost his ego by agreeing with his tastes.

"I've killed enough men in my life. I don't need to kill any more than necessary." He sighed.

"Truly? That doesn't sound like the Raven I have known." She smiled.

"Yeah, well… the old Raven could be an ass at times." He snorted, shaking his head, causing her to laugh.

"To be fair, I too have been so afflicted, especially when you entered my life." She ran her hand along his shoulder.

"You can say that again," he said all too seriously, earning a playful slap from her.

"You needn't agree so readily." She rolled her eyes.

"You can take it, you're tough, which is another reason I like you." He gave her a playful nudge in return.

She smiled at that. Of all the men she had known in her life, there was none like him.

"I keep thinking about what Lorn said to me that night at Corell," he said, looking out across the sea.

She recalled him speaking of it, of Yah's bringing Raven and the others to her world to help Lorn against her father.

"Lorn spoke of redemption, how men are inherently wicked, and naming himself the worst of us all before Yah redeemed him. I guess that was in my mind when those sailors were trying to beach their ships. Maybe during their long walk home, they can find redemption." He sighed, wondering when he had become so weak.

Tosha wondered at that, remembering her hatred for Deva, demanding her head when Terin showed her mercy. Had she her wish, then Terin might not have been restored and the glory of Yah would not have shown before her mother's court. That simple act of forgiveness transformed her and all who witnessed it that night. She hated looking back to the person she was before, recalling her antics with Raven at Fera and the times thereafter. If Raven had changed, she had changed so much more. Deva too changed, perhaps more than any of them, transformed by Yah for a great purpose.

"I keep thinking of Jentra. I didn't know him long, but he seemed a good man, and I expect Lorn misses him quite a lot," he added. Lorken had relayed the news to them once he returned to Notsu, figuring he would like to know that. He died taking the city, if what Lorken said was accurate.

"He died saving Lorn's life. I am certain Lorn misses him. They were always the best of friends," she added.

"Best of friends." He shook his head.

"You are thinking of another pair of friends, I surmise."

She had the right of it. He thought of Thorton constantly, dreading what he must do.

"I have to kill him." He resigned himself to that grim reality.

"If Lorn can be redeemed, and myself and you, and Deva, why not Ben?" she asked, wishing to add her father to that list of possibilities, but not voicing such hope.

"He killed Kato."

"And Kato tried to kill him, from what you said. Did you not say that Ben tried to wound him, but Kato stepped into the blast, taking the blow to the heart?"

"That's what one of the survivors claimed, but who really knows, and I doubt Ben will give me an excuse. He is too stubborn. He'd rather die than admit to a mistake. I know him too well." Raven shook his head.

"Stubborn? That reminds of someone I know." She smiled, nudging his shoulder.

"I can't be that stubborn if I let you wrap me around your finger." He gave her a look.

She smiled at that, knowing what he meant as he had used that phrase before.

"I tried the stick but only the carrots work with you." She nudged him, using one of his phrases.

"Yeah, and what a carrot it is." He gave her body an appreciative look, earning him another slap to his shoulder.

"You're incorrigible." She rolled her eyes.

"You like me that way. I wouldn't want to bore you."

"You have many faults, husband, but boring is not one of them."

"I don't know, boring sounds pretty nice about now. I can't think of anything better to do when this war is over than to sit on the stern and cast a fishing line, and spend my life doing nothing."

"It doesn't suit you. Your restless spirit would revolt after one day."

"Probably. Nice thought, though. At least you're here now to liven things up," he said with a stupid smile.

"Yes, someone has to keep you alive."

"I haven't died once in all my travels, with or without you."

She shook her head, wondering how his mind came up with half the nonsense he said.

"You haven't had anyone shooting back at you before, except at Fera. My sword will protect you as long as I am at your side."

"Yeah, those swords come in handy. Just be careful where you swing it. Don't know if it can cut through the ship, but no point in finding out," Raven warned. The swords' power was a mystery. Brokov had analyzed Terin's, Elos' and Tosha's blades, unable to identify their properties. Whatever made up their constitution was from elements unknown to any periodic table in the ship's archive. Only the covering to the swords' hilts was made of a known material, a blend of ancient steel, the rest the product of the ancient star that fell to Arax if the legends were to be believed.

"I will be careful, but you must not wander far from my side when we set ashore." She poked him in the chest, emphasizing that point.

"Fair enough, partner." He took her in his arms, kissing her below the starlit sky.

Chapter 23

Plain of Kregmarin.

Corry stood upon the hillside where once stood King Lore's army, surveying the surrounding landscape covered in bones picked clean by carka birds and bleached by the sun. The gray sky shrouded the battlefield, casting a grim aura over the barren plain. She wondered if her father stood upon this very spot, or one of the other nearby hillsides where the entire army was encamped? She thought to ask General Valen when he returns, the magantor commander currently scouting the lands to their north and west. Tens of thousands of Benotrist and gargoyle skeletons gathered at the base of the surrounding hillsides, particularly along the north facing slopes to her front, where stretched a line of palisades, their weathered remains a grim reminder of what transpired here. The Torry corpses were easily discerned by their lack of skulls, which the gargoyles had removed to adorn the pikes that ran from this fell place to the walls of Corell. The line of macabre trophies still lingered in places where the carka had not taken their fill, and the posts remained soundly founded. She would order them taken down wherever they camped, and the heads given proper burial, though the greater task of clearing all the remains would have to wait until war's end.

"Your father would not have you see this," Torg said with an unusually soft voice, stepping to her side, his eyes sweeping the low ground below, where King Lore likely met his end.

"I need to see it. I will not turn blindly from Morac's crime. I will burn this sight into my memory," she said icily. She stood upon the hillside like a warrior queen of old, with bright silver mail over a white tunic and polished greaves running north to her bare knees. Her helm rested in her left hand, freeing her golden tresses in the summer breeze.

"Aye, stubborn to a fault, just like me," he snorted.

"Stubbornness is no vice in the grim work we are tasked, and cowardice no virtue. I see the world for what it is, not for what I wish it was. How fare the men?" she asked, looking north where the first cohorts of the Macon 2nd Army began their march, forming the vanguard of their vast host.

"Their spirits are up as far as I can sense, though much of that is to our ease of march to this point. Your Earther friend has done much in that regard." Torg looked behind them to the many watering points Lorken had restored, and the many other new sites he managed to locate and their men put into action. All of that was done before the army reached this point, and now they were preparing to move on. He spotted Jenaii camped to their west, their winged forms coming to and fro, passing through the air with regularity. General Ciyon's army drew up along their east, preparing to follow the Macon Army in the order of march. The Torry army held the center, camped between the circle of hills behind them. Beyond them marshaled the ape contingent, including General Horzak's small force and the late arriving 3rd Ape Army, led by General Vorklit, whose soldiers marched from the Talon Pass to Notsu, before joining them on this campaign. Their ranks were further bolstered by the Troan, Teso and Zulon contingents, all camped nearby.

"Yes, he has been most helpful. Has he contacted you since this morn?" she asked, keeping her gaze northward, trying to visualize how the battle unfolded here, as if she could see Morac's columns assailing the hillsides in their thousands.

"Aye. He has already established watering points ten and twenty-three leagues north of here. We should find our advance elements already there waiting for us, sitting atop generous reserves of water. The farthest point was already operational upon his last contact. He should already be far north of that point, seeking the next stopover for our army. These shall be most useful during battle." Torg said, removing the comm from his satchel, eyeing the small magical tool with a measure of respect and curiosity. He could only imagine their benefit coordinating their armies during battle, negating the need for runners or visual signals.

"Yes, as well as telling us the location of the enemy for hundreds of leagues," Corry said without turning to address him, her gaze still fixed northward. She referred to their constant communication with Brokov aboard the *Stenox*, who relayed whatever sightings his scouting discs found. His unique reconnaissance constantly surveyed the areas between Notsu and Nisin. As it currently stood, there were no Benotrist or gargoyle forces of significance between those points, other than paltry border garrisons. General Gavis was currently near Nisin, and the gargoyle horde that Kriton led was nowhere to be seen, its last sighting placing it west of Nisin nearer the Plate foothills.

"With nothing stopping our advance, it appears we shall invade the north," Torg said, never imagining such a thing was possible.

"Yes, we shall bring our strength to bear, and draw Tyro's eye to something other than Lorn's small band making their way to Fera. I wish I could do more, but must take the steps before us, each leading to our final objective… to give Terin a better chance than certain death," she said icily, determined to give her love whatever help she could muster.

Torg remained silent, understanding her grief, for they both loved that boy, and so many others that accompanied him into oblivion. Wind Racer seemed to agree, nudging her gently with his powerful beak, standing at her other shoulder. Corry surprised Torg by wrapping her arms around the great avian's neck, embracing him as a lone tear squeezed stubbornly from her eye, the two bound by their love for Terin. Torg's heart broke for her. She was the strongest woman he had ever known, facing down Morac's legions with steel in her heart and nerve of iron, yet Terin had revealed her vulnerability, stripping away her iron façade and exposing the tender heart hidden within. It was only when she was alone with Torg would she lower her shield, revealing a weakness she would never show anyone else. He placed a gentle hand to her shoulder as she kept her embrace with Wind Racer. She looked to him from the corner of her eye, her love for the old man shining through her moistened gaze.

* * *

Forty three leagues north of Kregmarin battlefield.

Cronus held tight to Lorken as the air ski sped across the arid plain, dust swirling past their forward shield. He struggled keeping the sand from his eyes whenever the ski swept close to the ground, raising dust with its powerful motion. Lorken swept around a large boulder the size of a cottage, angling east for several moments before circling about, setting down on the dry, cracked landscape, the gray sky keeping the sun from their backs as they dismounted. Lorken lifted his seat, fishing the geological analyzer from the compartment below it, while Cronus scanned the horizon for any sign of trouble while his friend went about his duties. It was a mystery how the Earthers' equipment worked, and Cronus could only stand aside and marvel with the ease with which Lorken scanned the surrounding landscape before finding what he was looking for.

"Over there." Lorken pointed out a shallow rise to their immediate east, the ground somewhat discolored around it. Cronus fell in step beside his eager friend, walking briskly for a hundred paces before stopping. Lorken swept the analyzer in a wide arc, its readings feeding him what he wanted to know.

"Success?" Cronus asked, though the answer was obvious by Lorken's reaction. He had accompanied him on every watering site scouting trip since leaving Notsu, their task made easier by the disc floating high above beyond Cronus' sight, which gave Lorken a general area to search, leading them to the likeliest water sources.

"Success. Hand me the marker," Lorken answered, with Cronus handing over the tubular device no larger than his fist. Lorken placed it into the ground, before activating its beacon. It would send a signal to the advance team, which Lorken outfitted with a tracker, leading them to this spot. He also gave them many tools to help dig out the wells. It was a methodical and effective process, preparing watering sites where the army could camp throughout their march north. Water and food were the essential requirements for any army attempting to cross the Kregmarin. Each soldier was outfitted with thirty days rations to carry on their backs, leaving to Lorken and the advance teams to provide the water. So far, the plan was working, and there was no sign of the enemy for hundreds of leagues.

"You make this too easy." Cronus shook his head. It seemed the Earthers managed to remove their greatest problems with little effort. He could only imagine what a whole world of Earthers were capable of.

"It's just technology, Cronus. Our people spent just as many years as your people struggling with the problems you face before learning how to solve them," Lorken said as they made their way back to the air ski. They would return to the main encampment, two watering sites behind, where the army would be arriving in force before nightfall.

"Knowledge is power, and your people have it in abundance."

"We do. It reminds me something a great thinker long ago, a Greek philosopher I think, who said that *wonder is the beginning of wisdom*. It is that inane desire to learn and discover that drives men to achieve and advance, each man's accomplishments building upon what came before. This technology we share with you was passed down to us from thousands of years of human achievement. Perhaps when this war is over, we will share all we know with your people and make a better world."

"You would surrender your advantage if you did this. Would you and the others take such a risk?"

"That has always held us back, fearing to give such power to untrained hands. Our weapons are inherently dangerous, but our tools can be immeasurably helpful. Technology is like a two-edged blade, able to do great good and harm with equal measure. We will have to proceed very carefully, and slowly, advancing your people methodically through the stages of development. It won't happen overnight, but it will happen. Besides, we won't live forever, and will pass on what we know before old age takes us. Of course, that all depends on us winning this war first, which I like our chances." Lorken grinned, his good humor not having the desired effect as Cronus' face fell unexpectedly.

"Something wrong?" Lorken asked, stopping short of the air ski.

"I would ask a favor, Lorken," Cronus said, almost crestfallen.

"I will try to grant it if I can. What is it?"

"Ask Raven to remain on the *Stenox* for the duration of the war." Lorken made a face, wondering the reason.

"You must trust me in this. He must not set ashore with the army he is taking north," Cronus implored.

"Alright, but he might not listen."

"I only ask that you try."

"Can I ask you why?"

"I cannot say, and I ask that you simply trust me in this."

Lorken didn't know what to think, for it was an odd thing to ask. Cronus' demeanor changed so dramatically in this; it must be caused by something far greater than either of them could grasp. It reminded him of the intuition some pilots had in battle, averting their star fighter just before an enemy blast took them, sensing the danger in some strange manner. If it was anyone other than Cronus asking this, he might have disregarded it outright, but if there was one attribute Cronus possessed above all others, it was his honor.

"I will do what you ask, Cronus, you have my word."

* * *

Army encampment ten leagues north of Kregmarin battlefield.

Lorken and Cronus returned before dusk, just as the trailing cohorts, the 3rd Ape Army, began to set camp along the southern perimeter. Tomorrow they would lead the vanguard to the next watering site, each army rotating in the order of march. The camp was bustling with activity despite the gathering dark, and no sources of wood to set a cookfire. The men would live on hard rations until they crossed the Kregmarin. The commander's pavilion was provided with enough torches to illuminate its spacious interior, where gathered King El Anthar, King Sargov and Generals Lewins, Valen, Connly, Vecious, Ciyon, Horzak, Vorklit, Ev Evorn and the commanders of the Teso, Zulon, and Troan contingents. Torg and Corry presided over the grand assemblage, relaying the latest scouting reports from Brokov.

"The way is clear to the border." Torg reported Brokov's findings, stretching his hand across the map, sweeping from their current location to the northwest, and across the Lesser Veneba, the southwestern tributary that fed into Lake Veneba. Though it showed prominently on the map, the Lesser Veneba River was easily fordable, with its banks only cresting in springtime. Morac had erected a bridge over it during his invasion, but it was torn down by General Gavis during his withdraw.

"And the river?" King El Anthar inquired.

"Its banks have receded and will be a shallow crossing. We plan on sending a team of engineers forward to rebuild the bridge, but it is unnecessary for our advance, only for our supply caravans that follow," Torg explained.

"And the greater Veneba?" General Ciyon asked, pointing out the larger tributary resting northwest of the lesser, which ran from the foothills of the Plate Mountains in the west into Lake Veneba to the east. It was the most significant obstacle in their path, with two stone bridges resting thirty and fifty leagues upstream from the mouth of the lake.

"Both bridges remain intact with small contingents of Benotrists manning their garrisons," Torg informed them.

"Are they not aware of our advance?" General Bram Vecious asked.

"From what Brokov has observed, no," Torg replied.

"They will surely attempt to destroy the bridges once they learn of our approach," King Sargov said.

"Not if we take them by surprise. Lorken has a plan for that, and will begin implementing it in the coming days," Corry reassured them.

* * *

Lorken and Cronus set down beside the matrons' pavilion, the only other site provided with torch light in the camp. They found young Dougar standing post at the entrance, the boy saluting them with his fist to his chest. Cronus returned the honor while Lorken patted his helm, their affection puffing the boy with pride.

"You make an excellent guard, Dougar. The matrons are well served by your vigilance, though I think you can remove this for now and rest your weary head." Cronus smiled, gently tapping his helm.

The boy happily did so, setting it aside as the two men stepped within. Since Jentra's passing, Cronus took him underwing, giving him small tasks to perform each day to build his confidence and instill discipline. Lorken had joined in the effort, taking Dougar aside each night, teaching him useful skills or sharing interesting stories that captured his imagination. He promised to take the boy aboard the *Stenox* one day, if they survived that is, though Lorken always spoke of their possible demise with good humor, as though he didn't believe it. His optimism and gentle ribbing of his friends was infectious with those around him, especially Dougar.

Just as they did every day upon their return, Cronus and Lorken sought out Ilesa, to see if she had encountered any problems with the tissue regenerators and to check on her welfare. It was little secret their protectiveness of her, considering she was Kato's widow and late in her pregnancy. Their suggestion for her to remain behind met with stubborn resistance, with Ilesa reminding them of her duty. Lorken suggested removing her to the *Stenox*, where she would be safe until the baby was born, but she refused, insistent that she needed to stay. She had grown fond of Lorken, appreciating his concern and his loyalty to her late husband, and she held Cronus in deep regard, understanding the pain of his personal loss.

A cursory glance across the pavilion found the other regenerators fully charged, having cleared all the wounded that were brought to them. Most of the injuries of late were twisted ankles and torn knees during the march. One of General Connly's riders was thrown from his ocran deep in his patrol, breaking his neck, thus dying before they could reach him. That was the only death the army suffered since departing Notsu. Ilesa was ever careful to spread the regenerators out along the order of march, only coming together when they converged at day's end where the army set camp.

Standing along the side of the pavilion were Criose and a soldier named Culn Davorin, drawn from the ranks of the Macon 2nd Army. Each of them was selected to carry the laser rifles Lorken had given Corry. Each day Lorken would take them aside to instruct them on their use. Once Lorken scouted ahead, they were tasked with guarding the Matrons. Once the army crossed the Benotrist border, they would be deployed in the forward area where they would be of great use. It was almost unfair the advantages the Earthers brought to the army, and Lorken intended to make them more unfair with the way he intended to use them. While he took them aside, Cronus drew Ilesa from her labors, where she busied herself with unnecessary tasks which he rightly guessed served her desire to feel useful, never giving herself a moment of rest.

"Working yourself to exhaustion will do us greater harm than good, Ilesa. You must take advantage of these peaceful nights, saving your strength for the battles ahead," Cronus gently scolded, seeing the weariness in her eyes.

"I could make a similar claim upon you, Cronus. You work without cease." She returned his sad gaze.

"That is my duty as a soldier, but you are heavily burdened with child, and we must look to your safety."

"The child is safe, Cronus."

He held his tongue, catching himself from saying something he would regret. He couldn't help but think of Leanna and feared a similar fate for Ilesa. Leanna had had the benefit of resting each day leading up to the birth, whereas Ilesa was pushed to exhaustion. She could see what was on his mind by the pain on his face.

"I will have a regenerator nearby at all times, Cronus, should anything unfortunate transpire," she said.

"That is no guarantee, Ilesa. Things happen that are unforeseen, especially in battle."

"Your concern is appreciated, Cronus, but I MUST march with the army."

"Why?"

"…" She had no words to answer him, guarding her thoughts with her silence.

"Very well." He sighed, knowing when he was beaten.

"You are a good man, Cronus Kenti," she said as he turned away, feeling the torrents of anguish pouring off the man. She hated dismissing his concern, but one day he would know her purpose.

Chapter 24

Thirty leagues north of Tenin Harbor, along the Yatin coast.

Admiral Onab stood at the prow of his flagship *Devastator*, a sturdy built trioar that weathered the battle of Carapis, leading their surviving warships from the enemy armada. That dreaded battle seemed a lifetime ago, the fortunes of war souring with every passing day since. He managed to retreat to Tenin Harbor, gathering the remains of the 2nd, 5th and his own 7th Benotrist Fleets into a consolidated armada of 63 warships and the Magantor Carrier *Morbus*, its once mighty contingent of warbirds reduced to six magantors. That once sizable force was further reduced as he fled Tenin, suffering a Torry-Macon magantor attack upon his fleet exiting the harbor, once word reached him of a massive armada approaching from Faust. The grim tidings were confirmed when his magantor scouts spotted a massive fleet of Torry, Macon and Yatin warships drawing nigh, along with long columns of infantry marching along the coast bearing the sigils of the Torry 4th and Yatin 1st and 2nd Armies.

That ill tiding was followed with most of the gargoyle garrison of Tenin abandoning their post, fleeing north. A similar thing transpired at Telfer, with nearly half the garrison having deserted their posts in a moon's time. By last count, only five telnics remained to hold the Yatin fortress. Tenin harbor was in far worse position, with only nine telnics remaining to hold the city. Though more than Telfer, the harbor needed a far larger force to defend its miles of low walls. With the approaching Yatin, Macon and Torry forces converging upon the vital port city, there was little choice but to abandon it. Admiral Onab needed to preserve what remained of the three Benotrist Fleets that fought at Carapis, and the Magantor Carrier *Morbus*. He was informed that Admiral Plesnivolk's 1st Benotrist Fleet was moved to Tinsay, joining Admiral Zelitov's 8th Benotrist Fleet. He needed to join his strength to theirs to protect the Benotrist coast from the approaching enemy. He had already lost six of his sixty-three warships in recent days, suffering Torry magantor strikes to four of them, and another two colliding at night, breaching their hulls.

Admiral Onab looked out upon the peaceful sea, thankful for its calm water to ease their escape. The enemy armada was less than a day to his rear, making haste to catch him. His last scouting report placed the enemy armada between 150 to 200 warships with two magantor carriers with full complements of warbirds, far too large for him to delay, let alone engage. His only hope was in his swift withdraw. General Torab had already declared Tenin an open city, his remaining gargoyles fleeing once Onab's ships put to sea. It was a bitter end to a Yatin campaign that once was all but won.

Onab breathed the fresh sea air, a sweet taste to any old sailor, trusting his survival to their tall masts and sails full with the wind. If they kept their speed and good weather, they would reach Tinsay before the enemy caught them. That hope quickly died with what he saw emerging along the horizon.

There upon the horizon sailed the might of the Sisterhood Navy, the 2nd and 3rd Fleets bearing the sigil of the Federation, a fiery sword upon a field of black. Their full strength would soon come into view, a combined 130 warships, nearly all bioars with two trioar flagships for each Sisterhood Admiral.

"Your orders, Admiral?" Onab's aide asked, rushing to his side.

"Attack," Onab sighed, his voice faltering as he faced his doom.

And so it went, the fleets engaging in a series of skirmishes, the Sisterhood fleets refusing a full engagement until the Torry, Macon and Yatin armada drew into range two days after, crushing the Benotrist fleet between them.

THE CHRONICLES OF ARAX

* * *

Five leagues north of the Yatin-Benotrist border along the coast.

Queen Letha strode ashore, sunlight playing off her golden armor and helm, the surf kissing the hem of her short red tunic as she trudged through the sand. Two telnics of infantry held position along the ridgeline ahead, their shields interlocked, facing east to whatever awaited beyond. The queen's royal guard strode forth along her flanks, their shields in their left hands and spears in their right, racing ahead to form a wall of protection as Letha made her way up the beach, their silver armor and black tunics contrasting her gold and red.

The 1st Sisterhood Army began to disembark early in the morn, finding little resistance as they stormed the beach, planting their standards upon the rise ahead, a black spear upon a field of white, their sigil lifting in the midday breeze. General Na, commander of the 1st Army, received the queen as she ascended the slope, saluting with her fist to her breast.

"Welcome ashore, Oh Queen!" General Na greeted her, her green eyes staring through the narrow slits of her golden helm.

"General, how fares our position?" Letha asked, forgoing cordial chatter, her mind singularly focused on the task at hand. They were in a precarious position, their paltry force unable to resist a strong counterattack until more of the army was offloaded from their transports. Letha spared a glance to their surroundings, spying their soldiers in ordered ranks along the ridgeline overlooking the beach and a thousand more positioned to their immediate east, forward placed upon a second rise overlooking the flat ground beyond that ran nearly two leagues before bleeding into the Layvon Forest. A narrow road traversed the flat ground running north to south, the coastal causeway connecting the Benotrist Empire to the Yatin Empire. A second and much larger road connected the two empires farther east, shielded by the Layvon Forest along its length. It was that larger causeway that Yonig had used to invade Yatin, the Layvon concealing his approach, catching the Yatin border garrison unaware.

Letha could see no enemy formed to greet them, the way clear to the forest and each direction north and south, as far as she could see. Behind her, her ships dotted the sea, three hundred galleys of every sort, from merchant ships to fishing vessels and cargo galleys, all packed with the soldiers of the 1st and 3rd Sisterhood Armies. To their north sat the might of the 1st Sisterhood Fleet, one hundred and twenty warships, guarding their flank should an enemy fleet approach from Tinsay. Admiral Nyla stood upon her flagship, *Melida's Fist*, a powerfully built trioar resting at the center of her fleet, staring northward with her hands upon her hips, daring the enemy to approach. The Sisterhood warships waited with their sails furled, and anchors dropped, their red stained hulls reflecting off the surface like a sea of blood. Letha looked north beyond her fleet, trusting that the enemy was nowhere in sight, as their latest scouting patrol reported. Bolstering the 1st Fleet was the magantor carrier *Velima*, and its full complement of twenty-five warbirds. She thought to send the carrier with their southern fleets in their expected clash with Admiral Onab and the Benotrist fleets at Tenin, but that force already outnumbered Onab, while their position here faced many unknowns.

"We are in a precarious position, my queen. Should any force of size emerge out of the forest to our east, they will throw us back into the sea," General Na stated the grim reality they faced until they could unload more soldiers.

"How soon before you begin fortifying our position?" Letha asked.

"When the fourth telnic sets ashore, I shall order them to begin. I dare not start before then," General Na warned.

"Aye," Letha agreed. The last thing a commander wanted was her soldiers digging fortifications when the enemy attacks, catching them with their heads down and backs turned.

"I hope to begin before nightfall, but we are captive to the tide." General Na looked sourly to the small cove below, where only six ships at a time could moor to offload their soldiers. The cove was a half-circled inlet with a small fishing village lining its shoreline, its few residents abandoning their dwellings once the Federation armada appeared.

"Offloading our soldiers is our highest priority. Do you have a timeframe for its completion?" Queen Letha asked.

They discussed this very thing in every war council, the time contingent on the weather and the skill of each individual ship crew.

"If the weather holds, perhaps two days, maybe three, my queen," General Na conservatively estimated. Letha knew the general always underpromised and overdelivered, but landing so many soldiers in so small a cove was highly irregular.

"May Yah grant us the weather and time to see it done before the enemy bestirs himself. General Jani shall be ashore in the next offloading," Letha informed her.

"I shall hold command until she arrives, my queen. I will prepare her pavilion as soon as practical," she replied. General Jani was the supreme commander of all Sisterhood armies and garrisons, and with two of their three armies crowded upon the ships offshore, she held command authority of the expeditionary forces.

"Very good. I ordered two units of cavalry to be offloaded along with the supreme general. Their scouting range will be most useful before we advance inland. The magantor patrols from the Velima reported no enemy land or sea forces in either direction along the coast up to twenty leagues. That leaves only what we might find with the Layvon Forest," Letha said.

"And if we find nothing there?" Na asked.

"Then we fortify our position, retake the Yatin border posts, and await our allies."

* * *

Three days hence.
Yatin Benotrist border.

Queen Letha led ten telnics of the 3rd Sisterhood Army to retake the Yatin fortress resting atop the forested vale that once guarded that fallen empire from Benotrist incursions. Her soldiers moved among the trees, using the forest to shield their approach before stepping upon the open ground surrounding the ancient fortress. The fact they could draw so near without raising alarm was a testament to the Yatins' unpreparedness when General Yonig caught them unawares during his invasion. Any suitable defense required the clearing of all avenues of approach, especially trees that hadn't been cut down for eight decades. Yonig hadn't bothered correcting that mistake since the lands north of the fortress were his own.

The morning sun alit the low battlements of the fortress, where stood a handful of Benotrist guards to receive them, the rest spilling out the south gate to flee, forsaking the fight to Letha's large army. She ordered her telnics to envelope the fortress, sending two telnics to the east and two to the west, circling the pitiful structure in a desperate state of disrepair. Before she could order a full assault, the garrison surrendered, opening the gates to her soldiers. She was surprised to find only eighty-six defenders, all Benotrist, with nary a gargoyle in sight. They were taken captive and removed to their landing sight five leagues north, where waited the other half of the 3rd Sisterhood Army, and the full muster of the 1st. When asked the whereabouts of the gargoyles, the captive Benotrists claimed they had fled northeast, abandoning their posts. They spoke of similar happenings at Tenin and Telfer, the gargoyles beset by strange dreams calling them home, fleeing over the foothills of the Cress Mountains to their immediate east.

Letha expected to stain her sword of light with gargoyle blood, but the battle with the creatures would have to wait. For now, she would garrison this fortress with a small force and return to her encampment north, where she would await the Macon, Torry and Yatin armada, along with her 2nd and 3rd Fleets, and the Yatin and Torry armies making their way north after taking Tenin. Once their might was joined, they would march in force upon Tinsay, assailing the harbor from sea and land.

She did not know the happenings to the far east at Notsu or of Lorn's fated march upon Fera, but for her in the far west, the Benotrist Empire was about to fall.

Chapter 25

Fall of Nayboria.

The period following the first siege of Corell came to be known as *the time of woe* in Nayborian lore. The first blow was the decimation of the 1st Naybin Army during the breaking of the first siege of Corell, reducing its strength to three telnics to guard the northern border. King Lichu again committed his champion Dethine to Morac's second siege of Corell, leaving his homeland exposed to Jenaii adventurism, resulting in the disastrous Battle of Elaris and the destruction of the 4th Naybin Army and the halving of the 3rd. Their misfortunes continued with the death of their champion at the breaking of the second siege of Corell and the loss of their sword of light. With their armies decimated and their sword lost, they were woefully exposed to Casian aggression, leading to the fall of their port city of Naiba with the Casians destroying their fleets and seizing the city with their 1st and 3rd Armies before advancing up the Naiba River with their navy while their armies advanced along their banks.

Rumors of their plight spread across the realm and their neighboring lands, incurring revolt within their vassal regions and invasions from the wild lands to their north and east. The greatest incursion was from the independent city state of Barbeario, which sat astride the overland routes to the Ape Republic. The ruling archon of Barbeario sent a force of five telnics to plunder the Nayborian northeastern provinces, attacking just as the Casian armies reached the capital of Plou. The Barbeario invaders were further aided by the revolts spreading throughout the region, drawing the already crippled 1st Naybin Army away to put down the rebel factions when the Barbeario army crossed over the upper Naiba. With the 2nd Naybin Army sitting at Plou, holding the capital against the approaching Casian armies, King Lichu remained at Non, the *Yellow Castle*, the fortress constructed by the Tarelian kingdom of old. There he sat with seven telnics of his garrison and the five remaining telnics of his 3rd Naybin Army when a large force of Jenaii approached from the west.

* * *

King Lichu stood upon the upper battlements of the palace, looking out in the distance at the Jenaii host gathering along the horizon. They held at a distance, fortifying in place and beyond the range of the famed Nayborian longbows and ballista. The Nayborian king was nearing his sixth decade, silver tainting his once reddish mane. He wore the vestments of his regal station, rich burgundy robes over a long golden tunic and sandals. He contemplated when to don his warrior's garb, wondering when the enemy planned to assail his walls. With most of the Jenaii far away in the north, he knew they couldn't have brought more than a full battlegroup. Could twenty thousand Jenaii do here what ten times that number of gargoyles could not do for Morac at Corell? The Jenaii were better flyers than the awkward gargoyles, who could barely attain the outermost battlements of any of the great fortresses. The Jenaii could easily assail Non's highest battlements, let alone its outer walls which rose ninety feet above the grounds below.

King Lichu lamented his position, wondering how all his plans fell to ruin. The fate of his realm always hung upon the battle of Corell, which he fully committed his greatest assets and treasure, but to no avail. That decision only hastened his eventual fall, and how swiftly that fall came. His commanders had no sage counsel for his plight, other than to hold in place. They could not call upon the 2nd Army without forsaking Plou, thus surrendering half the realm to the Casian curs. What then might they achieve even with the 2nd? They could not lift the siege without attacking across the open grounds surrounding the palace, playing to the Jenaii strength and their weakness. He needed the Jenaii to bleed themselves upon his walls, but that didn't seem likely by their current behavior. They seemed content to starve him, isolating his twelve thousand men within these walls, where his stores were desperately thin. With the countryside in flames, in open revolt or in enemy hands, there was no hope of renewing his stock upon the next harvest, even if he could break the Jenaii's lines. His armies were destroyed or decimated, his navy sunk, and half his realm overrun. It was only a matter of time now, for even a blind man could see it.

Such thoughts weighed upon him since receiving the missive from the Jenaii commander earlier that morn, calling upon him to surrender.

"What shall you do, Father?" his daughter's soft voice asked, standing at his side.

He shook his head, keeping his gaze to the horizon as she touched his hand, interweaving her fingers with his own, the gesture reminding him of what he must preserve. He turned, regarding her comely face and fierce green eyes that looked upon him with such innocence to break his heart. He couldn't look at her without knowing he had failed her, failed her and her younger siblings, and their mother. He led the realm to ruin, aligning with Tyro to destroy their age-old enemies. Tyro's legions were crushed, and the survivors thrown back, now lacking the strength to threaten the south for a generation, or longer. The southern realms were now free to fall upon Nayboria, feasting upon its bones with impunity. Should he refuse? To what end? Nothing would change his fortune in the coming season. His realm had fought the Jenaii since General Plou toppled the old Southern Kingdom, becoming the first king of Nayboria over a millennium ago. His people fought bravely for fourteen centuries against the hated winged warriors only for him to lead them into ruin.

"I do not know, Felicia," Lichu bitterly said, struggling to reconcile what he needed to do with what he wanted to happen.

"The terms are generous," she reminded him.

"Generous?" he questioned. Was there ever a term more subjective than that?

The Jenaii guaranteed the survival of his children, including his infant heir. In return, he was to surrender the garrison. The Jenaii would garrison Non with a strong force, giving them a permanent dagger to the throat of his realm. They would cede all lands up to one hundred leagues north of the port of Naiba to the Casian League. In return, the Jenaii and Casians would aid his armies in vanquishing the Barbeario invaders, restoring order to the realm. His wife and children would remain at Non as guests of the Jenaii garrison until suitable matches could be made from the seeds of old Tarelia, which he was to assume were families from Sawyer or Torry North. Eventually his future heir would wed a child of the Jenaiis' choosing, whereupon the fortress would be returned to his realm. Such promises of restoration would be many years after his passing. The final act of submission was that he and ten members of his imperial elite were to be taken north to bear witness. What they were to witness was not revealed, and he thought it most peculiar.

He could refuse this offer, but his family would surely be put to death and his line ended. He was proud but not a fool. Looking one last time into her soulful green eyes forced his hand.

"I will agree to their terms." He sighed, running his hand along Felicia's beautiful face.

The royal standard blowing above the tower of Plou was lowered, the garrison opening the gates to the Jenaii, thus ending the Nayborian campaign.

Chapter 26

Rego.

The chosen assembled north of the city, preparing for their long march into the wilds. They partook the comforts of Rego in recent days, savoring the last vestiges of civilization before venturing into the unknown while awaiting their stragglers to arrive. Their numbers swelled to 2,734, with Deva having found fifty-seven among the men of Rego, adding them to their host. The city received them warmly, the populace having endured Yah's visions prior to their coming, each understanding the sacrifice required of the chosen.

Terin looked back to the city, imprinting the sight of its high wooden walls into his memory, recalling his first visit to Rego, the day he first met Squid Antillius and the Earthers. It seemed just yesterday and yet so long ago. He entered Rego a naïve boy, oblivious to the role appointed him and the greater world as well. What would that boy think if he was told all that would transpire? He lifted his gaze, looking upon the clear summer sky, resigning himself to the journey ahead. He was but one of many gathered north of the city, preparing to disembark. There they stood, Torry, Macon, Troan and Yatins, soldiers from every realm. They were joined with Jenaii, apes, and men of Notsu, Rego, and Sawyer. Three from the Sisterhood joined them, most notably Deva, who stood beside Lucas, her ever-vigilant guardian, her arrogance replaced with humble devotion to something greater than herself. There was King Lorn and King Mortus, the two standing forward of the gathered chosen, their once-resplendent armor replaced with simple gray mail, greaves and helms over plain gray tunics. The others wore the uniforms of their native realms, though the elite were clad as regular soldiers, including himself.

He looked down to the plain sandaled boots of brown leather he wore, matching the hue of his plain tunic. His mail and armor were weathered gray, built for sturdy use and practicality over aesthetics. The only objects he possessed that proved he was more than a simple soldier were the swords riding his hips, the *Sword of the Moon* upon his left and the blade Torg had forged for him which rode upon his right. Though born to wield the *Sword of the Moon*, it was Torg's blade he treasured more. He wrapped his right hand about the hilt of the sheathed blade, feeling a connection to his grandsire. He wondered where he was at this moment. Was he still at Notsu, or had he returned to Corell? He could only wonder at the pain the old man suffered knowing his daughter and grandson were now lost to him, along with so many others. He hoped Torg had many years left to him for the new queen's sake and for Corry, for they would need his counsel.

Corry, he thought bitterly, longing to see her one last time, to hold her and never let go. He wanted to weep but dared not among his companions. What was life without the one you loved? She was his everything, his other half. Part of him died every time he thought on it, thought of what he was losing, but what choice had he? If Yah demanded their sacrifice to save everyone else, he could not refuse him. If he refused, then Corry and he would die anyway, or their unborn children after them, doomed because he wasn't willing to pay the price now. The men of Kal's day refused their duty, condemning mankind to two and half thousand years of suffering. How many had perished since then, slain by gargoyles in the cruelest manner, all because the men of old failed to obey Yah's will? They now had a chance to rectify that sin, and he would do his part, though it came with great cost… everything.

He tugged on the straps of his heavy pack weighing his back.

Every member of their esteemed company was similarly laden, bearing as much food and provision as they could carry. They forsook their magantors and ocran, going forth on foot as the path would narrow for many parts of the journey. The burden would lighten as they progressed, as they ate from their stores. He wondered if they would have enough for the entire journey, but scolded himself for doubting. If Yah called them to undertake this journey, he would see them to its completion, and deliver them to whatever fate awaited them at journey's end.

He saw Matron Dresila moving among the chosen, seeing if any required her attention before they departed. He was thankful for her joining their company, the Earthers' healing device giving him a sense of reassurance. Many calamities awaited them marching through the wilds, where the land itself conspired against them. What terrible fate awaited those who were injured along the way should they have to leave them behind in the middle of nowhere? That grim possibility was waylaid with the regenerator. He admired the elder matron, who bore her own pack without complaint, refusing others who offered to bear it for her. Seeing her stand among them without complaint shamed Terin for his own self pity. He looked from one face to another, committing each to memory. They each had a story to tell, their sacrifice no less than his own, each willing to lay down their very lives for everyone else. They were his brothers and sisters, in spirit if not in flesh, and he was honored to stand among them.

He shared a knowing look with Elos, who stood a fair distance to his left among his fellow Jenaii. The two champions had shed much blood together, with Elos coming to his aid time and again. He thrust his fist to his breast, saluting his friend, who returned the gesture.

"Once again your adventures bring you to Rego, where we must embark upon a dangerous journey," Squid said, standing at his side, the elder statesman dressed in similar armor and attire as his former charge, his shoulders weighed by the heavy pack he bore.

"To Fera." Terin sighed, his journey bringing him full circle, departing Rego for the *Black Castle*, though this time by a direct, albeit a more dangerous route.

"This time you are bringing more friends," Squid said in good humor.

"Aye, that I am." He smiled, placing a hand to Squid's shoulder.

It was then all eyes went to King Lorn, who raised his hands, directing them north, taking the lead with King Mortus beside him. The others parted, giving him space to walk between them before falling into step, following them north, beyond Tuft's Mountain, beyond the headwaters of the Nila and across the Cot River, beyond the Mote Mountains to the very gates of Fera.

Chapter 27

Fera. The Black Castle.

Tyro stood at the window of his private sanctum as the morning sun broke upon the Feran Plain. He looked to the horizon where the barren landscape met the green edge of forest and farmlands that rested beyond. Many of his gargoyle legions once camped upon that barren plain, despoiling the land for many moons beyond their departure. It still bore the scars of their presence, once-vibrant fields now twisted and overturned like trees uprooted from a storm. Though his allies since the revolution, the gargoyles were destructive creatures, eating the land itself if they lingered too long in one place. The legions that once camped here met their demise at Kregmarin and Corell, dying before the white walls of the distant holdfast in great number, if the tidings he received were true. How powerful he once was, sending massive armies against his enemies in many directions, only to be blocked, driven off or outright destroyed at every turn. He contemplated his failures, scolding his foolishness. This was not the revolution, where he oversaw most of the strategic and tactical planning of every battle, personally leading his soldiers into the fray. He was emperor of the largest empire Arax had ever seen since the days of Kal. He needed to lean on others to carryout his plans, others less wise, or worthy than himself.

Tuft's Mountain was but the first of many blunders. Yatin was the next, but not for lack of leadership. His mistake was not fully supporting General Yonig throughout the campaign. Had he committed his legions to that campaign, rather than invading Torry North, Yatin would have been overrun in a fortnight. His legions would be standing upon the doorstep of Torry South. A gentle push would have toppled King Lore's southern realm, keeping the Macons from ever coming to accord with the Torries. Torry North would then be surrounded on three sides. He could have simply squeezed them over the years, slowly breaking their spirit until they toppled altogether. Or he might have allowed Morac to assail Torry North as he did, but with himself leading the legions, and wielding the *Sword of the Sun*. Morac could have wielded one of the lesser swords, and between the two of them they would have taken Corell in a well coordinated attack. Terin could not have stopped both of them, and if he spared King Lore's life at Kregmarin, he could have leveraged his ransom with the surrender of the fortress. Instead, he allowed Morac to blunder his way through the campaign and blundered himself by allowing him to renew the campaign, stripping the empire of even more men and gargoyles to see it done, only for him to lose.

His legions had lost in Yatin, at Rego and twice at Corell. Now he was threatened with invasion. He held the latest missive in his hands, having read it thrice over, wondering if it was true. His wife had landed a great force upon his shore, threatening Tinsay. A large Torry, Macon and Yatin force swept his remaining forces from Yatin, the gargoyles melting away like ice on a summer day. They would be certain to join with Letha's army and march upon Tinsay. To the east things were just as dire, a great force of Torries, Jenaii and Macons marching north across the Kregmarin, while the Earthers' ship destroyed his fleets wherever they found them. His dream of an empire stretching the breadth and length of Arax was now gone. His empire in its current state was now lost to him. He needed to shrink his current borders, consolidate his remaining armies and reestablish a defendable position in order for his people to survive. This meant one unavoidable fact… The Benotrist Empire was fallen.

Perhaps he could establish a Benotrist Kingdom within the current borders of his falling empire, if he could hold off complete destruction. The enemy could not bring more force to bear than his own, preventing them an easy victory. And how long could they remain in the north before their armies succumbed to starvation and weather? His wars brought him many enemies, enemies determined to end him and his people, but their zeal would wane with time and sacrifice. In truth, he still outnumbered the armies marching against him, so long as he didn't lose any more because of incompetence. To prevent that, he needed to consolidate his armies and withdraw far off garrisons, bringing those soldiers here.

Most concerning were the reports of gargoyles abandoning their posts, drawn away by strange dreams of their nesting grounds. Regula, his loyal second and oldest friend, revealed what was transpiring, the calling had come, summoning them to their nesting grounds, though it came many years early. It was to come but once in a generation, the last one being but eight years before. Since his victorious revolution over the hated Menotrists which birthed his empire, Tyro had uncovered the original nesting grounds the gargoyles used during the reign of Kal, with vast caverns large enough to birth and shelter untold thousands. He restored the sacred lands to his gargoyle allies, lands that were taken from them with the rise of the old Northern Kingdom established by the ancient Tarelians. This calling bore watching for it could not have come at a more inconvenient time; he needed his gargoyle allies in the fight to come.

Beyond the concerns for his crumbling empire, Tyro was beset by dreams of his own, so vivid in detail to convince him of their truth. He found himself standing upon a mountain overlooking a severe precipice with his arms outstretched and incredible strain contorting his face. In one hand he held his empire, the culmination of all his labors and endeavors, while the other held his family. He lacked the strength to bear them both, their combined weight pulling him over the precipice. The dream repeated itself, visiting him night after night, tormenting his sleep. Why must he choose? It made little sense. Why couldn't his blood join with him, helping him bear the weight of his empire? Couldn't they see he needed them? Couldn't they see why he had done what he did? Did they not know the crimes the Menotrists inflicted upon his people? Who would have protected the Benotrists from their oppressors if he had not done so? Where was their justice for the crimes committed against them? How many more centuries would they have suffered if not for his intervention? Only his empire protected his people, and he wished his son could see that. Was his empire truly worse than those that preceded it? Mankind was ruled by one cruel master after another, petty monarchs who were unworthy of loyalty or obedience. At least he earned his crown. It always came back to the gargoyles, which his son could not abide. He earned his crown and empire by toil and blood. Was he to throw all that away because the rest of humanity hated his allies? If Joriah couldn't see reason, then perhaps his granddaughter could. He wished he had known Terin, wondering how different things might have gone if the boy was raised in his household, but that was beyond him now. All he could do was disarm the boy and lock him away somewhere safe.

 He sighed tiredly, looking one last time to the horizon before turning toward the door. He had a sparring session with his son, a routine which they partook daily. He stopped at his bed, where sat his steel helm, drawing it over his head, before testing the hilts of his swords that rode his hips, drawing them briefly from their scabbards, their distinct golden hue brightly emitting from their blades. He drove them back into their sheaths, extinguishing their otherworldly light. Once in the arena he would use blunted training swords, keeping these blades secret lest he have need of them. Only Joriah knew that he possessed them, as he was unable to hide them from his Kalinian blood. He paused before stepping into the outer corridor, feeling the weight of his mail, greaves and helm. Since the grim tidings of his recent defeats, he hadn't worn the robes and vestment of his high station, making a habit of wearing a warrior's garb. How long had it been since he was martially attired? Too many years to rightly count. He forged his empire wielding a sword and leading armies. He lost it trusting others to do so in his place and would restore it by reassuming that role. Tyro was a warrior before he was an emperor, a warrior that was never bested, or known defeat. The only man able to defeat him awaited him in the training arena, the very man that could not render him harm. That irony was never lost on him. With that, he stepped without.

* * *

Jonas waited upon his father in the arena, keeping his mind from his troubles as he tested the training blade. Unlike his father, he kept his Sword of Light hidden in his bedchamber, traversing the corridors of the palace with his common blade in his scabbard. He noticed his father bearing both of his wondrous blades at all times now, wondering what brought about this measure of caution? Had he received ill tidings of late? It seemed the only explanation. His father also wore armor nearly all the time as well, forgoing his rich robes and heavy crown. He wondered at that, knowing something troubled him greatly. Despite his crimes and evil deeds, Jonas still loved him, conflicting him with shame and guilt for doing so. He reflected on that, trying to reconcile the two brutal facts, his love for his father with the hatred he felt for his many deeds. Most troubling of all was the pain he saw in his father's eyes. He couldn't let him die until those eyes again shined with his former glory, but how? What he wouldn't give to save Tyro's soul, to see him fight by his side, father and son, against the true foe of mankind.

Jonas looked up, beseeching Yah's mercy and guidance, as if the deity stood upon the ceiling of the arena awaiting his prayer.

What must I do, Oh Yah? What must I do to save him? Jonas sighed, his heart breaking. Whenever his father gave him hope that he could change, like freeing Cronus' companions into his care, he followed with abhorrent decisions to solidify his rule. While Tyro doted upon his granddaughter, he ordered many of his subjects to be put to death. Jonas wasn't blind to the fact that this was war, but his father didn't hesitate to condemn his enemies, refusing to show the slightest emotion when ordering their death. And was it truly Jonas' place to save him? Could he? No one could save a man's soul but the man himself. All Jonas could do was light the way. Besides, he came here to protect his wife and child, a task requiring all of his attention and strength, but he couldn't help but think beyond this, wishing to spare his father as well. He beseeched Yah daily, waiting patiently for an answer that didn't seem forthcoming.

"Your shield, Master," Safed Corlen said, interrupting his musings.

"Thank you, Safed," Jonas said, taking the shield from his hands. The two shared knowing looks, with Jonas hating having to present himself with such airs. Safed returned to his place beside Tarlan and Geornon, standing off to the side in the loose sand. They were attired in the brief tunics of palace slaves, with the hateful collars affixed to their throats. They had suffered more than any man should, enduring gelding and beatings without cease while toiling dawn to dusk until coming into Jonas' keeping. When he received them, they were sullen and dispirited, contemplating ending their lives to escape their misery, but Jonas implored them to soldier on, reminding them that they may be freed if Jonas' plans come to fruition.

What hope is there if we obtain freedom? We can never wed and sire children. We shall die old and alone, forgotten by our kin for the shame we bear, they argued.

You can be restored, Jonas said, explaining the Earthers' wondrous gift to their people. He would see them to freedom and see them restored to their former glory, his words kindling something that was lost to them until that moment... hope.

And so they followed Jonas' lead, playing the part of dutiful slaves under the watchful gaze of their Benotrist jailors, biding their time until Jonas could deliver them. Their calm demeanor was short-lived once Tyro entered the arena, preceded by his imperial guards who fanned out to either side of the entrance.

"Your eminence," Jonas greeted Tyro, saluting him with his blunted training sword raised before his face as his father drew nigh.

"Joriah," Tyro greeted him in kind as a servant hurried forth, presenting his training blade, which Tyro took a few practice swings before a second servant provided a shield.

They spoke not a word as they began, circling each other in the loose sand with measured steps before engaging. The others looking on had grown accustomed to their unnatural speed and skill, the two moving in accordance, their feet shifting with no wasted motion. Jonas forsook his restraint, giving his father his full measure as he promised. Tyro deflected his forceful thrusts, his feet shifting as he moved. Jonas maneuvered around him, testing his balance before striking, nearly driving him from his feet. They continued their dance of steel before Jonas touched his sword to Tyro's side, ending the bout.

Tyro acknowledged the win, retaking his starting position. And so it went for much of the session, the two engaging in an endless train of bouts, with Tyro managing one victory to Jonas' ten, and even doubting if that lone accomplishment was not given him. The two finally paused, neither saying a word as they discarded their shields for a second blade. They briefly tested the weight and balance of their second blades, spinning them slowly before reengaging in a flurry of strikes, sparks flying off their blunted steel. In this, Tyro held his own, though Jonas gained upon him with every passing day. It would anger Tyro if any other beside Jonas bested him, but he recalled something his father once said, *the only man who shall ever celebrate your defeating him is your father*. As much as he came to despise his mighty sire, he understood the truth in that. He wanted his son to be better than he was, and he wondered if his own father would have looked upon his accomplishments with pride even though he brought his Menotrist kin low in doing so? Did not a part of him celebrate Terin's many fell deeds even though they came at his expense? If only Jonas aimed higher than to live in obscurity. If only he desired what Tyro desired, to forge an empire to pass onto his heirs, and bring glory to their bloodline. All his son spoke of was bringing glory to his God, denying his inheritance. He had so much to give his son, but Jonas wanted none of it. Even the sword he gifted him meant little, considering Jonas could have claimed it on his own if he truly wanted to at some point. No, it was Jonas who was giving him gifts that he truly desired, crossing swords in this arena and sharing his child's love.

He was so lost in his thoughts he didn't notice the sword flying off Jonas' left hand, leaving him one blade to his two. He drove him back with a flurry of strikes, Jonas managing to fend him off with uncanny speed and skill before finally relenting, winning him their first bout. Such a swift victory was a rare occurrence when sparring with Jonas, even with two blades, which he trained every day for all his life, and Jonas only sparingly. Jonas was the finest swordsman Tyro had ever known, far better than himself, and it was more than his Kalinian blood. He had a natural affinity for sword handling. If Jonas had one weakness in this regard, it was that he fought honorably where Tyro fought with every advantage he could find, no matter how underhanded. Though every time he tried to use unorthodox means when sparring with Jonas in order to teach him such tactics, his son was able to see it coming and countered accordingly.

Jonas responded by taking the next three bouts, impressing his sire with his ability to master two blades, though he wondered the practicality when using one was far easier, and easier was better when chaos ensued. In true combat, chaos always reigned, with heavy doses of fortune and misfortune. Tyro managed to take two of the last five bouts before ending their session early once Larus Braxus, Castellan of Fera, appeared at the entrance with urgent tidings for the emperor.

* * *

Morac waited in the center of the throne room, standing upon the red-mirrored stone floor, its reflective surface akin to a bloody sea. He gazed to the ceiling above where torchlight alit the jewels embedded in its black stone, mimicking stars on a midnight sky. He regarded his own soiled attire, his golden helm marred and battered, the ape skull affixed to it broken away above the nose. His cuirass was dull and battle-worn, while his blood-red cape was soiled and ripped at the left shoulder. He thought not to come, to avoid the emperor lest he be condemned for his failures, but he retained enough pride to show his face. He heard the rumors before presenting himself, rumors of a new favorite gaining the emperor's affection, a Torry no less. The need to know who the man was drove him to appear here more than anything else. Did Tyro mean to take his sword and give it to this stranger? To a Torry? It made little sense with the information he was privy, which meant there was more to this than he knew. And if Tyro meant to take his sword, who said he was obliged to obey? He wielded the *Golden Sword*, the greatest of the swords of light. Such a blade would not leave his hand unless he yielded it, and he would not yield it.

His eyes were instantly drawn to the figure emerging behind the throne clad in warrior's garb. Realization struck him as he recognized the warrior to be the emperor, taking him aback with his martial presence. Morac advanced several paces and removed his helm and knelt as Tyro sat his throne.

A painfully long silence passed before Tyro ordered him to his feet. It had been a long time since they last saw one another, shortly after Terin and the others escaped Fera, when Tyro sent Morac forth at the head of his legions to conquer the Torry realm.

"When last we parted you led a great army. Now you stand here alone."

"I failed," Morac bitterly confessed, refusing to offer weak excuses, which the emperor despised.

"I have heard what transpired from many lips. I would hear it from your own," Tyro ordered as Morac told the tale from the Battle of Kregmarin to the sieges of Corell, the attack upon Tro, and his flight from Notsu.

"...Once the gargoyles abandoned us, our situation was untenable. I could not save the ten thousand men that remained there but could not remain and risk the loss of the *Sword of the Sun* to our enemies," he finally explained, before expounding his decision to come directly here rather than Nisin to reconfigure the empire's armies in the east.

Another long silence followed as Tyro considered his options. Despite his cruelty to his foes and the harshness of his rule, Tyro possessed one noble virtue... loyalty. He was loyal to his kin, his people and his friends, no matter their sins and shortcomings. He was known to take the heads of poor commanders, such as General Vicon after the Battle of Tuft's Mountain and Admiral Mulsen for his subterfuge initiating the invasion of Yatin. But if commanders were loyal lieutenants, he would show leniency, and Morac was almost his son, as he had raised him since the death of his father Morca during the early years of the Benotrist revolution. Though he would show mercy to those who were loyal, they still needed to be reminded the price of disloyalty. He motioned his herald hither.

The man stepped forth from the side of the chamber, bearing a short metal pole with a severed head adorning it, a clear glaze covering its dead flesh, preserving the man's likeness for Morac's purview. He quickly recognized the black beard that only natives of the Lone Hills possessed, and the identity of the dead man whose vacant eyes stared unnervingly back to him.

"Hossen Grell," Morac said evenly, his voice masking his beating heart.

"Yes. He thought it wise to alter my plans for the attack upon Tro. I instructed Thorton on the objectives I desired to achieve in the attack, but our dear Hossen altered that plan to the detriment of our cause, which in turn helped destroy your army at Corell. The Earthers were not to be attacked until the war with the Torry realms was concluded. Be assured that I reward loyalty and punish treachery," Tyro said with an eerily calm voice.

Morac wondered what became of Hossen after he departed Notsu. It seemed agents of the emperor brought him to Fera to answer for his failure.

"My loyalty is yours, as always, my emperor. How might I serve?" Morac asked.

"Queen Letha has landed a great host upon our western coast, south of Tinsay. The Torries, Yatins and Maconians are marching north through Yatin to join her. I am sending you to Laycrom, where you are to lead the 13th Legion and fifteen telnics of the city garrison, bringing them here," Tyro ordered, taking Morac aback by ignoring his defeat at Corell. This strange order presented a myriad of other questions.

"Should I not lead them to Tinsay and throw back this invasion, my emperor?"

"No, I have sent Draken to oversee the Tinsan Campaign. I am entrusting you to bring our more significant forces to bear. See that it is done."

"As you command, my emperor." Morac bowed, a thousand more questions filling his mind, wondering the emperor's strategy.

Chapter 28

Lower bridge. Thirty leagues from the mouth of Lake Veneba, along the Greater Veneba River.

Corry paused at the south end of the great bridge, staring at the awesome structure built over a thousand years before, by the old Eastern Kingdom that once ruled this land. It still stood the test of time, strongly anchored into the river with a series of stone arches, spanning nearly six hundred feet across this gentle stretch of the Greater Veneba. It was wide enough for three wagons to cross side by side, with a stone parapet running along its impressive length. Tall porian and lupec trees encroached the riverbanks on either bank upstream, with thick foliage and underbrush between them to mask anything that lay beyond. The stretch of riverbank to either side of the bridge was stripped bare, providing a clear field of view in all directions, especially from atop the watch towers overlooking the north end of the bridge. The towers rose imperiously above twin stone fortresses flanking either side of the north end, their outer walls rising twenty feet above the bridge.

Corry's gaze drifted to the east tower, where the royal sigil of the Torry Macon alliance graced its summit, a golden crown upon a field of white and black. The blue helms of the Jenaii warriors manning its walls stood out in the midday sun.

"An inspiring sight, perhaps I shall pen a ballad of this momentous event," Galen said, standing at her side as another column of soldiers marched across the bridge, a contingent of General Ciyon's third telnic, as their standard indicated.

"You should have no lack of inspiration, Galen, and even more so by journey's end," she said, looking skyward as another magantor circled high overhead before breaking north, its dark brown feathers marking it a Benotrist scout. Corry ordered their own magantors to remain safely south, conceding the skies to their foes. The Benotrists quickly discovered their warbirds' absence, emboldening their patrols as of late.

"The second I have seen this day," Galen said, following her gaze to the enemy warbird.

"They are quite fearless at that height, knowing they can outpace our Jenaii warriors should they challenge them," she said.

"They have done as you hoped, Your Highness," he quipped.

"For now. Let us hope their generals act in accordance." She needed the Benotrists to see them crossing the Veneba River in force, drawing their eyes south, away from the landing sites Raven and the Earthers were leading the Ape and Casian fleets to. The latest report from Brokov indicated a large concentration of Benotrist soldiers encamped west of Nisin, bearing the standard of the 10th Benotrist Legion. It was that force she wanted to march south to oppose them, allowing their allies to land along the coast weakly opposed.

They watched the men cross over the bridge for a time before catching sight of several riders approaching along the southern bank of the river, emerging from the tree line upstream. She recognized General Connly's familiar face at the head of the small column of cavalry, the rider to his left bearing his standard, a rearing silver ocran upon a field of green. The commander directing the armies across the bridge halted the columns of infantry, granting the cavalry space to cross over to the opposite side, where stood Princess Corry and Galen.

"Hail, Your Highness," General Connly greeted her, thrusting his fist to his chest, his ocran's hooves coming to a stop before her.

"General Connly, what tiding have you?" she asked.

"We have taken the western bridge, and General Vecious is leading his army across it," he reported, regarding the second bridge resting twenty leagues upstream of the first. Both were built during the age of the old Eastern Kingdom, each of a similar design, with fortifications upon their northern ends, guarding the way north from a southern incursion.

"Casualties?" she asked warily.

"Six of the enemy, none of our own. We took thirty prisoners, the rest having fled long before our Earth friend attacked," Connly answered.

"Nearly the same result as here," she said, recalling Lorken's exploits taking the bridge from the north side with Criose and Culn, each armed with laser rifles, while Lorken sped overhead upon his ski, firing into the fortresses guarding the bridge. The defenders quickly yielded, suffering just three casualties before surrendering. What was most curious was the weakness of the garrisons. Did they not think to oppose their crossing into Benotrist lands? Everything now depended upon the 10th Legion moving south to confront them, thus aiding the landings upon the northern coast. As yet, there was no sign of enemy forces anywhere near the two bridges.

"I sent half of my cavalry across the west bridge to scout ahead. I shall lead the other half north from here, sweeping the lands north and west, meeting the other half at the gathering point we selected," Connly said, regarding the place that Brokov advised for their first encampment beyond the bridges, nearly twelve leagues to their northwest.

"Very well, General," Corry said as he saluted before seeing to his men.

She released a measured breath, looking again to the north side of the bridge, and the lands beyond. She felt pimples raise across her flesh, considering the gravity of this moment. They were invading the north, bringing the war to Tyro's realm. She thought to savor the significance of that, but her thoughts went to Terin, wondering where he was at this moment. She let her feelings of him swiftly pass, lest they sweep her away. She looked to the north, focusing upon what she could control. They needed to advance and engage the enemy, knowing every Benotrist and gargoyle they slew was one less Tyro could throw at the *Chosen*.

"May Yah protect them." She sighed before climbing onto her mount and riding across the bridge.

* * *

Eighteen leagues west of Nisin Castle.

General Gavis, commander of the 10th Legion, looked over the unsealed parchment bearing the sigil of the emperor for what seemed the hundredth time. Tyro ordered him to return to Fera with his legion. It was ironic that he was commanded to do what he already planned to undertake. He had moved his legion west of Nisin in recent days, ignoring the instructions of the regent of Nisin, who demanded he march south and oppose the armies crossing over the Veneba River. Regent Gorel's orders degenerated into pitiful pleas, beseeching his aid in the battle soon to come.

Fool, he mused, shaking his head at Gorel's lack of vision. There was no stopping what was to transpire. The eastern half of the empire was fallen, and their only hope to save what was left was to consolidate their armies in the west. He guessed that Tyro gave the garrisons of Nisin and Pagan similar orders, to forsake their positions and flee west, sparing their soldiers from certain defeat. He doubted Gorel was wise enough to heed that order. Thorton was correct in both his advice to march west, and the idiocy of one Regent Gorel. He thought of his last conversation with the Earther, remembering his advice for the emperor, and wondered where he was at this moment. The latest missive from his spies at the court of Nisin claimed Thorton had departed a short time ago, taking his gargoyle companion, the girl Elena and the captured rebel. He recalled his cryptic answer about his coming fate as if resigned to what he expected to transpire. It was unfortunate, for they needed him alive and with them for the battles ahead, for only he could counter the other Earthers and their incredible power.

"Your orders, General?" his nearest aide asked, standing beside his saddled mount, presenting Gavis the ocran's reins.

"We march," Gavis ordered, climbing into the saddle, drawing his sword and extending it to the west where stretched the open road running to the horizon and beyond. Behind him gathered the strength of his reconfigured 10th Legion, their ranks now swelled to nearly forty-two telnics with survivors of the Corell campaign and local garrisons joining the muster.

"Kai-Shorum!" the men shouted, their war cry echoing along their columns as they lumbered forth, following their general west.

* * *

The Benotrist coastline.
Twelve leagues northwest of Pagan Harbor.

President Matuzak stood upon the bridge, scanning the shoreline ahead through the viewport of the *Stenox*, observing the first ships offloading their troops. The *Stenox* rested just offshore, keeping a watchful eye upon the coastline in each direction. They preceded the armada to this position, their shipboard lasers striking several targets of interest along the shore along with a lone merchant galley skirting the coast, its masts now peeking above the surf where it went down off their left. The dorsal fin of a dorun crested the waves off their right, the surf battering the chests of its Enoructan riders. Nearly a hundred Enoructan warriors already set ashore, attaining the dunes overlooking the beach, their silhouettes visible atop the shallow heights. Beyond the dunes stretched a low flat plain, a perfect place to assemble the army once they completed the landings. Brokov's discs scouted further inland, scanning the area surrounding the landing site in each direction. There were a few civilians in the area traversing the coastal road that ran some two leagues inland, shadowing the shoreline. As yet, no one had discovered their arrival, and by the time they did, they will have landed most of their armies and secured their position.

"Well, Mr. President, what do you think?" Raven asked him, sitting the captain's chair to his left.

"A splendid day, my boy," he said, reaching out his furry hand, ruffling Raven's head like he was a wee tot, the gesture causing Tosha to smile, standing at Raven's opposite side while Ular manned the helm.

"Then we should get you ashore before the first ships finish unloading," Raven said, gaining his feet.

"Where are you going?" Tosha asked, her smile faltering, knowing that look in his eyes.

"Going ashore with Mr. President. He wants to be in the first wave," Raven said, pushing past her toward the door.

"But why are you going?"

"I can't let the President go by himself."

"What about Cronus' warning?" she asked, recalling what Lorken had told them, Cronus' concerns giving her pause.

"I'll be alright. We can't worry about what might happen, and besides, I'm going to have to go ashore sometime before this is all over with." He shrugged off her worries.

"Then I'm coming with you."

"No, you're not. You need to stay and help Ular man the bridge."

"I'm coming!" she growled, stepping close to him, balling the collar of his black shirt in her fist.

"Alright, Eisenhower, let's go." He eased her hands off him before leading them off the bridge, where Orlom was waiting atop the lookout deck, asking where they were going as they stepped onto the stern.

"Can I come, boss?" he asked with his stupid grin.

"Why not, everyone else is. Can I trust you flying one of those?" he asked, pointing at the two new air skis resting on the stern of the 1st deck, the product of Brokov's industriousness as of late.

"Aye, boss." He grinned.

"Alright, you take the President, just don't crash or he'll bash your head in."

Matuzak stood beside Raven, pounding his right fist in his left hand to emphasize the point while Tosha rolled her eyes with the stupidity of it all. No wonder her husband and the apes were the best of friends, they all acted like children.

* * *

It was nearly dusk and only a third of the ships were offloaded. Raven and Tosha stood upon the dunes overlooking the shore as another unit of Casian soldiers made their way up the beach. The landing area accommodated up to six ships unloading simultaneously, the process encumbered with the tide and the need to ferry the soldiers ashore after loading them into smaller landing boats which dropped them off in the shallows before pushing off again to fetch the next group. Offloading their cavalry contingent would be even more difficult. It was a slow, methodical process and would take through the next day to complete, if not longer.

"Welcome home," Raven said, wondering how she felt on that matter while looking out across the sea, where the masts of their great armada stretched to the horizon. It was a sight to behold, and a miracle that they reached these distant shores without losing one ship. Much of that was due to the *Stenox's* weather forecasting, allowing them to navigate around any trouble.

"You needn't remind me." She sighed.

"You feel guilty, don't you." He guessed her anguish.

"The Benotrists are my kin, Raven, and by extension, our children's kin as well. I don't expect sympathy considering their actions as late, but they are my people, and here I stand, leading an invasion of their realm."

"I know, it stinks having to fight someone you love," he sighed, his gentle tone taking her aback.

She knew what he was thinking, wondering if he would have the stomach to face Thorton and kill him. It was constantly on his mind, and by extension, upon hers as well. She reached out and took his hand in hers, and he surprised her by letting her without one of his flippant comments. They stood there quietly, watching one group of soldiers after another make their way ashore as the sun dipped low in the west.

* * *

In the coming days the armada disembarked the 2nd Casian and 2nd Ape Armies, along with the Troan expeditionary force. President

Matuzak gathered the great host and began the march upon Pagan Harbor, riding at the head of their armies with the Casian General Motchi, and the Ape General Mocvoran, presenting a united front as they advanced upon the Benotrist port city. News of their advance quickly spread, sending the ancient port into panic. Thousands of citizens began to flee east, or southeast, skirting the Tur River upstream. Most sought shelter in the surrounding hills while others with the means traveled farther to Gostovar, the key trading hub linking Pagan to the coastal free cities of the east, though it was recently sacked by rebels before order was restored. Many others remained at Pagan, placing their hopes in the Benotrist garrison to hold the city. It wasn't until the enemy armada appeared that those hopes dimmed.

Raven sat the captain's chair of the *Stenox*, scanning the harbor as they drew near. Pagan was an impressively-built port city, resting at the mouth of the Tur River, which emptied into the northern sea. A line of breakwaters lined the approaches of the city, the most prominent shielding the western half of the bay where the largest docking areas were built. The city had grown along both sides of the bay, with a massive bridge connecting the two halves of the port just upstream and within its protective curtain walls. The native population were not Benotrist or even Venotrist, but the descendants of the Verunium people whose federation ruled the Tur River valley after the fall of King Kal. They maintained their wealth and position through the centuries by aligning with the kingdoms and empires that came to rule in the northeast. When Tyro's empire quickly expanded east, they sent emissaries offering union in exchange for favorable trading privileges, strengthening their hold on the trade routes to the coastal cities of Filo, Terse, Corpi and Bedo, and especially Tro. In return, the city submitted to the empire, naming a Benotrist general as regent of Pagan, who wed a daughter of every ruling family, gathering an impressive number of wives to begin his rule. The current ruling regent was equally as avaricious, taking numerous wives and concubines that dwelt in his palace, whose towering minarets graced the western shore of the bay, where the sigil of the empire graced its summit, a black tower upon a field of red.

"Let's see if they are going to do this the hard way or the easy way," Raven said, watching a small flotilla emerge from the port, navigating the breakwaters that crisscrossed the approaches of the bay, bearing the sigil of the 6th Benotrist Fleet. He wondered how many ships the 6th had left considering the trail of sunken wrecks the *Stenox* left in its wake since Tro. That held true for the 3rd and 4th Fleets as well, as Pagan was home port to all three. By now they had to know the reputation of the *Stenox*, and the futility of confronting them.

"We shall soon know," Tosha said, standing at his side, attired in her traditional uniform armor and black tunic, her black hair trailing her golden helm in corded braids. Her sword rested her left hip and a dagger her right, forgoing the laser pistol and Earth garb she had grown accustomed.

"We'll try doing it your way, Tosh. You know these people better than me." Raven shrugged, admiring the fit of her tunic and the way it displayed her shapely…

"Eyes up here." She slapped him upside the head.

Ular looked back at them curiously, his hypnotic eyes blinking rapidly. Despite his lengthy time in their company, he would never grow accustomed to their antics. He simply looked back to the control panel of the helm, accelerating forward of the armada as the Benotrist flotilla emerged from the breakwaters, the lead vessel raising a blue flag upon its forward mast.

"I guess we do it your way," Raven conceded, noting the guarded smile touching Tosha's lips.

* * *

Palace of Burrs Galenta, Regent of Pagan.

Tosha entered the throne room of the palace, flanked by Raven and Argos, comforted by the wide berth given them as they traversed the corridors of the castle. The throne room was richly decorated with white marble floors and stone columns liberally spaced along the chamber, supporting its domed roof. The dais at the end of the chamber was modest, a quarter the size of her mighty sire's at Fera but impressively adorned with finely woven tapestries upon its walls. Regent Galenta sat the throne, adorned in emerald robes over a silver tunic, the crown of regency nestled in his thick dark mane. He was surprisingly young, barely attaining his third decade, his slender form swallowed by his wide-set throne. His green eyes followed her as she drew nigh, while tearing away to regard her imposing companions every few moments.

"Princess," Burrs Galenta received her.

"Regent Galenta," she answered firmly, displaying not the slightest fear in his presence, her tone laced with firm authority.

"I am uncertain of the proper protocol receiving your eminence, considering you stand among our enemies, Princess. Should I kneel or demand the same of you?" Burrs warily asked.

"I stand before you as the Second Guardian of the Sisterhood and rightful heir to my mother's throne. My father's throne is not mine, but that of my son's. Since the Federation has declared war upon my father's realm, it falls upon me to answer that call. As you are fully aware, a large host of Casian, Ape and Troan armies will be at your gates before the sun sets on the morrow. Your people need not suffer the destruction these armies and the vast armada that waits outside your harbor can visit upon them."

"You would threaten your own father?" Burrs' eyes narrowed severely.

"I would beseech my father to see reason. He has waged war upon the nations of Arax with impunity. There is little recourse to avoid the destruction of our people but to surrender. The Ape ruler is among their vast host and offers generous terms to your city. I have bargained on behalf of your great city to win the most favorable of terms. Should you refuse them, I dare not think of the suffering the people of Pagan shall endure," she proclaimed.

"You would have me surrender my garrison without one sword yet raised against it?"

"You needn't suffer a grievous wound to see the folly of resistance. My husband stands before you. Know that his vessel can rend your walls in mere moments, allowing our armies to march over their rubble and take the city with ease. What is left of your fleets shall be equally destroyed before our first warship breaches the harbor. These are not idle boasts but cold truths that I have witnessed time and again," she warned.

He hesitated to respond, and she pressed her advantage.

"There is no relief army coming to save you. As we speak, an army larger than the one approaching your city is crossing the Veneba River and will attain Nisin in less than a fortnight. General Gavis is retreating west, forsaking Regent Gorel and the eastern half of the empire to their fate. You and your city are on your own," she stated.

"How can you know this?" he asked, doubting the truth of her words.

"We see all, Regent Galenta, just as we saw you share your bed with your second wife, Queen Neha, last eve. Once you partook of her pleasure, you sent for your fourth wife, Queen Letena, who rested on your chest as you held her in your left arm. Do you require that I reveal more?"

"How can you know this?" he asked, his face ashen.

"As I claimed, we see all."

"If I do as you ask, I would be attainted, branded a traitor of my oaths. On what ground can you claim otherwise? You stoke rebellion against your sire and think you innocent of that charge? What has transpired to bring about such a change in you, princess?"

"Yah."

"Yah?" He made a face.

"The ancient deity of King Kal. He revealed his glory in my mother's court, convincing us of his truth. He calls upon us to heed his will, to fulfill our ancient oaths."

"Ancient oaths? What oaths are these?"

"To vanquish the gargoyles, the sacred duty entrusted to Kal and all of mankind."

"Even if there is truth in your words, how can I forsake my vows to a Benotrist emperor, one who has raised up our people from bondage?"

Tosha could not answer to that, understanding the man's plight, for she felt it herself.

"What if you swore an oath to Tyro's true heir and eldest grandson, one who shares your Benotrist blood?" Raven asked.

"You mean your sons by your union with Princess Tosha," Burrs said warily.

"No, not our son, our nephew."

"Nephew?" He made a face.

And so Tosha revealed Terin's heritage, of his Kalinian bloodline and the task anointed him by Yah. Most especially, she revealed his parentage, marking him Tyro's true heir, one who could not claim his rightful throne unless the gargoyles were destroyed. Regent Galenta leaned back against his throne, overwhelmed by what Tosha revealed. How could it be that their greatest adversary, the hated Torry Champion, was in truth their emperor's true heir? He was of Kal and of Torry, but also Benotrist. Was he touched for believing this incredible tale? Deep within he knew what they said to be true. Should he reveal his own troubling dreams, dreams plagued by the creatures the empire was allied with? Should he speak of a great battle between mankind and gargoyles and the terrible future that might await them all? What was his own sense of honor when weighed against such? There was one possibility, and the princess offered it so plainly, he need only take it. He could reconcile his dishonor by swearing his oath to his emperor's heir and not the armies that were at his gate.

"And these generous terms you speak of?" he asked.

* * *

The following morn.

When President Matuzak arrived at Pagan, the city gates opened to receive him. The garrison stood down as the 2nd Ape and 2nd Casian Armies entered the ancient port. Kaly, who led the largest contingent of Troans and hired free swords, rode upon Matuzak's right as they passed through the west gate, taken aback by the warm reception the populace offered, young maidens throwing voli petals in the air as if they were liberators and not conquerors. He was surprised to find Raven waiting for them as they traversed the main thoroughfare, leaning casually against the pillar of a structure off their left as if he hadn't a care in the world.

Matuzak halted the column, easing his ocran to the side of the wide avenue, with Kaly and the Casian General Motchi upon either flank.

"What is this?" he bellowed, wondering why Raven was standing by his lonesome, the surrounding crowds apparently oblivious to his presence.

"It's about time you fellas showed up," Raven said.

"About time? Not all of us sailed here, lad," Matuzak growled.

"Might I ask, why are you standing here all by yourself?" Kaly asked, wondering why the Earther didn't fear for his life in the city.

"Not much else to do. Besides, I needed some fresh air."

"Fresh air from what?" Matuzak asked.

"You'll find out." He shrugged, jerking his thumb down the avenue where stood the regent's palace with a strange standard gracing its highest tower. Gone was the black tower upon a field of red, sigil of the Benotrist Empire. In its place was an azure sword upon a field of silver.

And so it came to be that Regent Galenta proclaimed Terin as the champion of the Benotrist people, swearing loyalty to the emperor's true heir, raising a standard that bore his new sigil. The people were told that the emperor was to be betrayed by the gargoyles, and his true heir was leading a great host to save the realms of men, including their own. It came to be that the populace had suffered troubling dreams of late, tormenting them with visions of gargoyles feasting upon their flesh and swarming over the land. The dreams intensified before their arrival, weakening their resolve when faced with Matuzak's army and the great armada appearing off their coast. The people's enthusiasm to declare for Terin was greatly fueled by Tosha's appearance at the court of Pagan where she bore witness to Yah's anointing of Terin at her mother's court. As Second Guardian of the Sisterhood, she proclaimed Terin champion of her mother's realm, a title now extended to his Benotrist kin who were willing to pledge him their allegiance. And so, despite many of their kin having perished in the war to this moment, the people of Pagan declared for Terin. Their decision was further reinforced by Morac and Gavis' abandonment of the eastern empire.

Tosha was received by the populace with great pomp and ceremony as befitting a princess of the realm. The palace was filled with hundreds of court officials, affluent citizens and nobles of all sorts, gathered to celebrate their new alliance and treat with the emperor's daughter.

Thus was the state of the palace as President Matuzak and the allied generals passed through its storied gates.

* * *

The following days found the Casian, Ape and Troan armies gathered in the port of Pagan, where their ships offloaded needed supplies while the city augmented their food stores. Tosha and Regent Galenta oversaw the naming of a ruling council to coordinate other lands of the empire in joining their union. With the previous rebellion greatly subdued by Thorton's intervention, its support was still strong among the Venotrist peasantry and local subdued populations. It was these groups Tosha meant the council to reach out to, bringing their strength to their cause and stabilizing their lines of resupply as they advanced inland.

Brokov's reconnaissance revealed the advance of their allies moving north from the Veneba River, making excellent time. The news was too good, for they needed to join with them before they advanced upon Nisin. It was decided that a telnic of apes and a telnic of Casians would remain at Pagan, while two telnics of the port's garrison would join the main host preparing to march. In a gesture furthering their mutual goodwill, the Earthers gifted the city a tissue regenerator, the second that Brokov managed to produce since departing Tro. Ular instructed the city matrons on its operation, which they quickly put to good use with throngs of people gathered in the city amphitheater to be treated. Three more regenerators were given the armies for the march to Nisin.

It was the march to Nisin that stirred the greatest debate among the crew of the *Stenox* as Tosha removed herself from her newly assumed duties with the city forum to join the others aboard the ship where it was conveniently anchored near the city palace.

"We can't all go, obviously. Brokov should stay with the ship and keep us updated on the enemy's movements. Zem should stay with him to safeguard the ship, and Kendra will want to stay with him, if I were to guess," Raven began as they gathered in the dining cabin, most of them seated at the table while Argos and Zem stood at the door, their imposing frames taking up far too much space.

"You are not going," Tosha insisted, poking Raven in the chest as she sat beside him.

"Of course I'm going. I'm the only one faster than Ben on the draw, and that's the primary duty we have to assume on this expedition," he pushed back.

"What of Cronus' warning?" she asked.

"What warning? All Lorken said is that I shouldn't go, but what's he basing that on? I'm guessing it must be another of these dreams everyone is having except me. I haven't slept better in my life lately," Raven said, though the looks he received from most of them indicated he was among the minority in that regard. One look around the cabin gave Raven pause.

"What? You have all been having strange dreams too?" he asked.

"I dreamt of a final battle, with gargoyles swarming over our armies in numbers too great to oppose." Kendra sighed, looking to Brokov who sat beside her, placing her hand in his.

"I dreamt of the same, though the faces change with every vision. The end result is always the same, the gargoyles swarming the land in untold numbers," Tosha said with a faraway voice.

Darpak and Gorbad, their new crewmates, spoke of their dreams, standing beside President Matuzak facing a horde of gargoyles, each waking before enemy spears fell upon them.

"Brokov?" Raven asked, his friend's look indicating he had dreamt something odd as well.

"I… I dream I am back aboard the *Stalingrad*, briefing Admiral Kruger on what happened here. It is so real that… well, I can't explain it." He sighed.

That was new.

"I dream of a great feast with strange foods I have never seen, but I can taste in my vision," Argos gruffly stated with pure sincerity.

"I always find myself in a great battle, fighting beside Lucas when the world turns dark," Ular said with his watery voice.

"I see Grigg smiling at me, asking me to follow him," Orlom sighed, taking Raven aback with his somber tone.

That was everyone except Zem, who stood there, staring back at Raven as if wanting to say something but holding back.

"You too, Zem?" he asked, wondering how an android could dream. Then again, what should he expect on a world with gargoyles, talking apes and winged men and lizard people? This entire place was crazy. It was like what his father used to say, *everyone around here is nuts but you and me, and you're a little bit off.*

"I have experienced lately what you humans describe as a dream or vision if you are so inclined. I was home again, but only for a moment, when Raven's mother drew me into her embrace, kissed my cheek and said they missed me, and that their home would always be waiting for me to return." Zem's metallic voice lowered, sounding almost human.

Raven didn't know what to say to that, for it was all so surreal.

"She also asked that I watch over her sons, who she loved so much," Zem added, sending goosebumps down Raven's arms.

They all sat there for a time, not knowing what to say, their original question of who would go and stay now seeming the furthest thing from their minds.

"Her sons." Raven shook his head, knowing she meant him and Ben, but that was impossible now. He had to kill Ben, and there was nothing that could prevent that now. It was then the Fates intervened to resolve the matter once and for all when Kaly's voice echoed over the comm, as they had given the devices to several of the commanders, including Kaly, Matuzak and the Casian and Ape generals.

"*Raven, I have an old friend of yours here,*" Kaly said.

"Who?" Brokov asked, lifting the comm from the table.

"Alen."

Chapter 29

They found Alen seated on a wagon, escorted by a flax of Troan cavalry, with another man seated beside him wearing the uniform of a Benotrist warrior. Save for Brokov, the entire crew came to meet him, finding Kaly leading the small procession toward the *Stenox* along the adjoining causeway, with a growing crowd gathering behind the wagon.

They were taken aback by Alen's appearance, the young man's youthful disposition replaced with the aged eyes of a million labors. Many battles, privations and his current wound conspired to bring about his transformation. He looked reasonably well fed, his limbs exposed by the brevity of his brown tunic, revealing a heavily bandaged right knee. His hair had grown past his shoulders, and he looked unusually dour for one finding his friends after so long. The last they heard he was leading the revolt in the north, but his appearance in a Benotrist warrior's company cast that in doubt, as said warrior wore mail and helm and was armed while Alen was not.

"Our patrols came upon them southwest of here, heading for Pagan along the road from Nisin. The warrior is a commander of flax from Nisin Garrison," Kaly said, looking back at Alen from his saddle, his ocran's hooves shifting along the fitted stone of the avenue.

"Why is the Benotrist still armed?" Raven asked.

"He came under a flag of truce, bearing a message for you," Kaly said, presenting a folded parchment from his satchel, handing it to Raven.

"It is penned by Thorton." Alen finally spoke, his voice breaking with emotion. He had thought to never see his friend again, and here he stood, looking the same as he remembered. He looked briefly to Kendra, recalling their time together, and then Zem and Argos, and finally Tosha, his former mistress, noticing her changed demeanor as she looked at him with empathy, disarming his angst in seeing her once again.

"What does it say?" Tosha asked warily, leaning over to look as Raven finished reading.

"Where is this village he mentioned?" Raven asked the Benotrist warrior as Tosha took the parchment from his hand, trying to make sense of it as it bore their native Earther text.

"Near Point. It lies thirty leagues southwest along the road to Nisin," the man answered.

"What does this say?" Tosha growled, waving the parchment in Raven's face.

"Stay with the ship until I return." He took the parchment back, stuffing it in his jacket pocket, causing an uproar among the others.

"Do not go, Raven. He killed most of my comrades, and his gargoyle friend carries Kato's pistol as well. They will kill you!" Alen pleaded.

"What?" Tosha was nearly apoplectic, fully realizing what the missive meant.

"You can't go alone, Raven," Zem warned.

"I'll go with Boss," Orlom insisted.

"No! I will go," Argos bellowed, stepping forth, brokering no compromise on the matter.

"And I also," Tosha insisted.

"You're not going, Tosh. You need to be safe," Raven said.

"I have a sword of light to protect me, in case you've forgotten. I AM going with you." Tosha would not relent.

Raven just shook his head, knowing when it was pointless to argue with her.

"How good is this gargoyle with his pistol?" Raven asked Alen.

"Very good, as much as I could determine. Thorton instructs him most zealously. But, please, do not challenge him, Raven," Alen pleaded, but Raven ignored him.

"Hope all three of us can fit on one air ski," Raven said, before telling the others to have Alen's leg seen to. Whatever ailed him would soon be fixed. With that, he turned back to the ship to prepare their departure.

* * *

Near Point. 32 leagues southwest of Pagan.

Ben Thorton sat in the back corner of the tavern, nursing a tankard of Bedoan ale, while a beleaguered barkeep nervously tended his duties. The tavern rested at the center of the village, which served as a stopover point for merchants and travelers traversing the main causeway connecting Nisin and Pagan. There were several municipal centers far larger along the route of travel, but Ben chose the smaller Near Point for his purposes, preferring fewer eyes to witness what was to come. Most of the villagers already fled once news of the Ape and Casian armies setting ashore reached them. Many more departed once Ben arrived, sensing trouble. The poor barkeep remained at Ben's insistence, serving him and his companions food along with Ben's daily tankard of ale, which he partook every afternoon. The tavern was fairly good sized considering its location, with the bar running the length of the wall off Ben's right and several tables spread out across the floor. Said floor was covered with large stones, joined by a mortar of some sort, which Ben took note of as he sat there the last few days with only Ella and Zelo as company. Zelo spent most of his time on the lookout for strangers, standing at the southeast edge of the village. He returned periodically, informing Ben of what he saw, which was nothing.

Ben took another sip, his eyes adjusted to the dim light, with only two lanterns hung from its high ceiling illuminating the structure. By now he must have counted every plank in the roof and the stones on the floor a thousand times whenever his mind wasn't consumed with what he must do. He wondered how it all came to this, calling out his old friend to meet him in this forsaken backwater of Arax, and for what? To kill each other. There was no going back at this point, not after Kato, not after the attack on the *Stenox*, and certainly not after Jennifer. No matter what course they desired, the Fates brought them to this juncture, like some sick joke of the cosmos.

He wondered if the boy had found Raven by now. Zelo had questioned his gentle treatment of him, sparing him torture and death, but such things were childish. Alen had no information that was useful, at least not to him. His own part in this war had gone for naught, for no realm would rule Arax, leaving the divisions in place that plagued this world for thousands of years, no matter what happened after this day. The Benotrist Empire was falling apart, beset with invasions without and rebellion within, as well as the populace tormented by dreams if what they told him was true. The Benotrists dreamed of an apocalyptic final battle, while the gargoyles had visions of their nesting grounds, calling them home, wherever that was. Only Zelo seemed resistant to its urgings, remaining with him out of some sense of loyalty. When he thought about it, the gargoyle was the only friend he had left, the two making an odd pair. Such thoughts brought him back to his *other* friend, former friend now, who was probably making his way to him.

Promise me you will protect him and see him home safely, Jennifer pleaded, extracting that promise from him. How easily he said yes, despite the impossibility of keeping the most reckless man he ever knew alive, but he did it for her. He would do anything for her, losing himself in her soulful brown eyes whenever she looked at him. There were times he thought he could almost touch her as she appeared in his thoughts, her visage as real as anything this mortal realm offered.

I miss you, Texas, he could hear her call to him, begging him to leave this place and join her wherever she now dwelt. He loved her more than anything or anyone, rendering life meaningless without her. What was life without love? What purpose was there for an individual without the one they were meant to be with to share it? Only serving a greater good gave you purpose in the absence of love, and even that purpose was gone now. All that was left was that promise he made to her, a promise that was beyond him now.

> *"From this valley they say you are leaving*
> *I will miss your bright eyes and sweet smile*
> *For they say you are taking the sunshine*
> *That has brightened my pathway a while*
> *Come and sit by my side if you love me*
> *Do not hasten to bid me adieu*
> *Just remember the Red River Valley*
> *And the one who has loved you so true..."*
>
> *The Red River Valley*

Ella's voice drew him from his melancholy as she stood off to the corner, signing the mournful refrain that he taught her, one of the special songs Jennifer would sing for him. Her voice was so like Jennifer's it made him ache. He hated it and loved it all the same, for it took him back in time, to a time when his life was whole and pure. He regarded the girl, wondering why she remained with him when he ordered her to depart with Alen, knowing Raven would give her shelter, but she insisted on staying. He wondered if she harbored feelings for him. He wished her to be safe and had protected her since the day they met, but he could never love another. His heart was forever bound to Jennifer, in this life and whatever life that followed.

Ella took him aback with her next refrain, again choosing one of those he had taught her, selecting this moment to sing it, as if the Fates couldn't conspire more against him.

> *"...So Bang the drum slowly*
> *And rattle your spurs lowly*
> *And play the death march*
> *As you bear me along*
> *Take me to the valley*
> *There lay the sod o'er me*
> *For I'm a poor cowboy*

BENJAMIN SANFORD

And know I've done wrong."

The Streets of Laredo.

She looked at him as she finished, now standing in the middle of the floor, the barkeep looking on, beguiled with her lovely voice and the mournful ballad she sang. Other than the two of them, he was the only other soul in the tavern, a simple bystander witnessing their strange interaction. Of all the songs he had taught her, she chose the very one that Raven loved, the mournful ode to a dying cowboy who succumbed to his poor choices.

The Streets of Laredo. He shook his head, realizing the song reflected his own sorry life instead of Raven's. Though he preferred *The Yellow Rose of Texas*, it was *Laredo* that most reflected his miserable state. And as if his life was but a page on a cosmic script, Zelo burst through the door.

"They are here!" he hissed.

With that, Ben lifted his Stetson from the table and put it on his head.

* * *

They stopped short of the village, dismounting the air ski atop the small rise overlooking Near Point. The village was modestly sized with the main road passing between rows of dwellings, each made of strong timber to weather the northern winds that blew off the sea. Open fields surrounded the village with a few copses of trees interspersed in each direction, giving the land a distinct character. The village looked empty from their vantage point, giving them pause before advancing. Raven walked straight down the road with Tosha on his right and Argos his left. He wanted her to remain on the ship where she would be safe, but as he came to know, she wasn't good at taking his orders. She was stubborn to a fault, a trait she shared with his sister. That thought gave him pause, for it was Jen's stubbornness that killed her. If that didn't happen, he wouldn't be here facing her husband at the end of a gun.

"What if this is a trap?" Tosha asked, keeping a tight grip on her sheathed sword with her left hand and her right on her pistol grip, with a satchel strapped over her left shoulder. Before departing the *Stenox* she changed out her attire for her Earth garb, clad in black from head to boot, a fitting choice as they entered the village.

"Ben doesn't want that," he said, though she doubted if that was true. Raven had a determined look in his eye, a look that would frighten her if she was on its receiving end. His confidence in Ben's intentions soon proved correct as Thorton stepped into the street from the structure up ahead on their left with the gargoyle Zelo holding at the edge of said structure, looking on with his right hand resting on his holstered pistol. Argos stepped farther left, his eyes fixed to Zelo as Raven stopped twenty paces from Ben, ordering Tosha to step away to the right. She paused, uncertain if she would obey before relenting.

They stood there for an eternal moment, neither saying a word, the village matching their silence with nary a sound in the air. The late day sun hung low in the west, symbolic of their setting friendship. There were no questions asked or answers given. There were no excuses for what had transpired to bring them to this point. What more was there to say but goodbye? With that, Ben went for the draw, and Raven followed, flashes of blue laser streaming through the air as Tosha screamed.

Epilogue

Beyond the North Sea, in a far-off land.

> *The time of our reckoning has drawn near*
> *The time of our ascension has drawn nigh*
> *Vengeance, mutilation, death chants cry*
> *Flesh of man, flesh of Jenaii*
> *Devour the favored sons of Yah*
> *Slay them child, lass and all*

Gargoyle war chants rose into the air in a deafening crescendo, echoing across the bay in a morbid symphony. They gathered upon those distant shores where sat their fell armada, forged through the centuries for this momentous time. Their ships were built by their human slaves, descendants of lost mariners that came upon their isle through the ages, being taken captive and set to the task of constructing the grand armada now prepared to launch. They gathered upon the wharves of the inlet bay, serried throngs of black and white leathery flesh, males and maidens of their foul kind, slather dripping from their pointed fangs. Their eyes shone crimson red or dull white accordant to their nature. They stood before the full moon, its image reflecting off the bay, chanting their death song since dusk, their blood rising with a savage lust.

Silence.

Their chants ceased with sudden aplomb, as if on cue, their minds linked to a single purpose as their great war chief attained the harbor tower, looking out to the masses gathered below, offering his words of war and slaughter.

"Our time drawsss near, my kindred. The Nordhenz has ascended and shall soon pass into shadow, heralding our ascension. We sail with the new moon, to fulfill our prophecy. To kill Jenaii. To kill mankind. Let themsss die by our swords, fangs and weaponsss of war. We chase them unto the ends of the world. Slaughter! Kill! Maim! Destroy!" he shouted into the night sky, his words relayed through the ranks, repeated in a haunting chorus. They would soon sail upon six thousand ships, to their destiny beyond the sea.

Post Epilogue

Somewhere in space.

Admiral Helmut Von Kruger stood upon the bridge of the Battle Carrier *Stalingrad* with his hands tucked behind him, staring through the viewport at the surrounding star systems, contemplating the decision before him. Of the eight vessels assigned to his task force, only the *Stalingrad* and the fleet destroyer *Javier Solis* remained, the others' whereabouts as much a mystery to him as their own location… unknown. The hull of their only companion rested off their starboard bow, its trundusium skin shifting in hues of silver and black, the standard of all Earth-based starships. The *Solis* was named after a 20th century Ranchero singer whose true name was Gabriel Levario, as musicians and thespians of that day took stage names as they were. He reflected on the many names of the ships he commanded throughout his storied career as a fleet officer, taking it upon himself to know the story behind each name, and why it was chosen. Such attention to detail served him well through the years, often preventing the mistakes that tripped others with expected regularity. The more obtuse among his contemporaries ascribed to luck what he considered sound preparation and planning. Opportunities would always present themselves, but the unprepared and dull-witted would either be unable to seize them or overlook them. That was the case throughout his career, until now.

Admiral Kruger considered his current position, lost in some unknown corner of space, his ships in desperate need of repair, with no means of communicating with Earth nor any sign of the *Magellan*, whose fate they likely now shared.

The *Magellan*, he mused, wondering where that ship was. The official designation for that ship was *Magellan XXI*, the twenty-first to bear that designation for space exploration. It disappeared shortly departing the Varan system, likely encountering the very deep space anomaly his task force passed through searching for them. It was one year ago now when he offered up half his fleet to seek out the fate of their missing vessel, which carried many esteemed members of Earth's Department of Exploration and Settlement, designated DES for those not wishing to say such a mouthful when referencing it. It was the importance of the missing high-ranking and renowned members of the DES that motivated the Space Fleet Directorate to prioritize the search, sending Admiral Kruger to lead the rescue expedition, though it was his own men that were missing he wanted to find. Colonel Chang, Raven, Thorton, Lorken, Brokov, Kato and Zem. To the politicians and bureaucrats, they were only soldiers whose deaths never warranted more than superficial reverence, sending their loved ones faux sympathies for their loss. To him, they were family, his brothers in arms, and he would be damned if he did not at least try to find them, and in that he failed.

His task force, centered upon the *Stalingrad*, included numerous vessels including the vital life support, engineering repair and quartermaster ships a long-term deployment might require if they lost contact with Space Fleet. Unfortunately, they came upon the anomaly, a mysterious cloud with a cacophony of colors spiraling in a dizzying array, that overtook them, spitting them out where they now sat, in unknown space. Once they emerged, only the *Stalingrad* and the *Solis* remained, the fate of their remaining ships as much a mystery as their current location. They were not even certain they were in the Milky Way as many of their long-range sensors were impaired along with many other vital parts of both ships, the most important being life support. Both ships were down to mere months before hard choices needed to be made.

THE CHRONICLES OF ARAX

Hard choices. He shook his head, the simple phrase drastically understating their dilemma. Hard choices meant he would have to decide who died first, but eventually they would all succumb unless they found what they needed in one of the hundred-star systems that fell within their range. Besides life support, the most critical impairment afflicting both vessels was the damage to their long-range drives, hindering their ability to jump between star systems. The engineering department were currently effecting repairs but required time to do so. That in itself was dire enough, but the latest report from the engineering chief, Commander Pham, was not promising even if they proved successful. They would likely only get to make one leap, and one only, but which star system should he choose? Their long-range sensors were drastically impaired, giving them no feedback on any of the neighboring solar systems' material makeup. Choose the wrong system, and they would find themselves stranded in a solar system lacking the raw materials they needed to refurbish their life support and permanently repair their engineering.

"I have the latest report from Lieutenant Lopez." Lieutenant Commander Bao Chang interrupted his thoughts, transmitting the comms officer's report to the readout affixed to his wrist while she stood at attention at his side, now wearing the gold form-fitting uniform of a bridge officer.

"What do you make of this?" he asked Bao, whom he had recently promoted to bridge officer before they undertook this mission. He found her performance to date to be exceptional, considering the dire situation they found themselves. She was further motivated to find her uncle, who commanded the *Magellan*, but that seemed unlikely now considering they too were now lost.

"Commander Pham had enough material to launch the probes you requested, but that will delay the repairs to the main drive. Considering the state of our situation, it was the only logical choice, Admiral," she stated honestly.

"Aye, but not without its own risk. That material is essential for our leap, and without enough, we are stranded here." Admiraal Kruger snorted, pointing out the drawback to his decision. Though he would repeat the decision if he had to do it over again, for he needed the information from the probes to help him sort out the promising star systems from the weaker ones. As it now stood, everything they could see was in the past, for the light of those stars were mere echoes of history. They needed the probes to draw closer to send them real-time information.

"Lieutenant Lopez should be receiving the initial reports from the first probe in thirteen solar minutes, Admiral," Bao said.

"Tell her I will be there shortly," Helmut said, dismissing Bao, who saluted and stepped away, leaving the admiral to his thoughts.

He again gazed out the viewport, examining the surrounding stars, wishing he could determine their promise by simple observation. He had no such luxury, and only one chance to choose, all their hopes for survival resting on that one leap to whatever system he chose. Choose poorly and they would all perish. Though they would retain power to move within that system, they could never leave it, and without the materials they required, they would quickly die there.

Helmut Von Kruger kept one thing from his subordinates, lest they think him mad. He had had dreams of late, dreams that repeated themselves every time he closed his eyes and with such clarity he thought he was going mad. They all showed one thing that was burned into his conscience… a SIGN.

A sign shall be given, a voice whispered in his mind.

    Thus ends Book Six of The Chronicles of Arax:
    The Fall of Empires.
    The saga concludes with Book Seven: Restoration

THE CHRONICLES OF ARAX

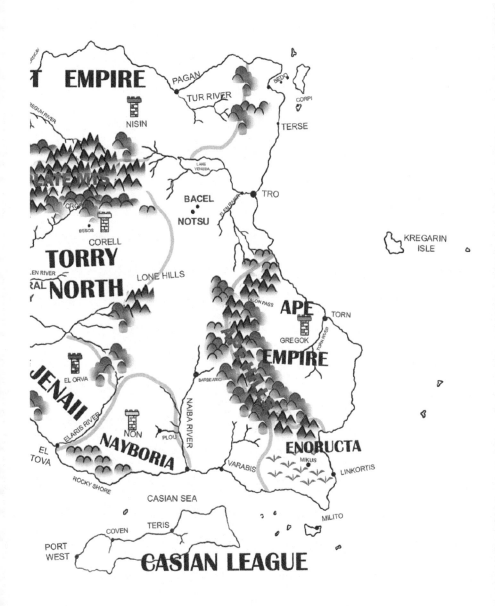

Appendix A

Armies of Arax

Torry Armies

Army	Location	Commander	Size
1st	East of Corell	Lewins	12-15 Telnics
2nd	West of Besos	Fonis	20 Telnics
3rd	Corell	Mastorn	10 Telnics
4th	Cagan	Farro	12 Telnics
5th	(Destroyed at Kregmarin)		
Torry/Macon army	Besos	Ciyon	15 Telnics

LARGE GARRISONS

	Location	Commander	Size
	Cropus	Torgus Vantel	3 Telnics
	Corell	Balka	3 Telnics
	Central City	Torvin	5 Telnics
	Cagan	Telanus	2 Telnics

(Currently split between Fleace and Cesa)

Cavalry

Army	Location	Commander	Size
1st	Corell	Unknown	100 mounts
2nd	Corell	Connly	524 mounts

Cavalry (continued)

Army	Location	Commander	Size
3rd	Corell	Meborn	305 mounts
4th	Corell	Avliam	200 mounts

Torry Navy

Fleet	Location	Admiral	Size
1st	Cagan (Includes 3 captured Benotrist warships)	Kilan (Grand Admiral)	31 galleys
2nd	Cagan	Horikor	50 galleys
3rd	Cagan	Liman	21 galleys
4th	Cagan	Nylo	22 galleys
5th	Cagan	Morita	17 galleys

THE CHRONICLES OF ARAX

BENOTRIST/GARGOYLE ARMIES

Legion	Location	Commander	Size
1st (gargoyle)	Telfer	N/A	10 Telnics
	(Survivors of Mosar reassigned to 2nd Legion)		
2nd (gargoyle)	Tinsay	Torab	24 Telnics
3rd (gargoyle)	Destroyed at Mosar (survivors reassigned to 2nd Legion)		
4th (gargoyle)	Surviving telnics absorbed by 5th Legion		
5th (gargoyle)	East of Corell	Unknown	15-18 Telnics
	(Includes all telnics of 4th and 7th Legions)		
6th (gargoyle)	Destroyed at Corell		
7th (gargoyle)	Surviving telnics absorbed by 5th Legion		
8th (Benotrist)	East of Corell	Unknown	13 Telnics
9th (Benotrist)	East of Corell	Unknown	13 Telnics
10th (Benotrist)	East of Corell	Gavis	18 Telnics
11th (Benotrist)	Notsu/Besos	Felinaius	20 T at Besos/ 15 at Notsu
12th (gargoyle)	Gotto	Unknown	15-18 Telnics
13th (Benotrist)	Laycrom	Trinapolis	50 Telnics
14th (gargoyle)	East of Corell	Unknown	15-18 (Est.) Telnics
15th (gargoyle)	Tuss River	Unknown	10-15 (Est.) Telnics
16th (gargoyle)	Destroyed at Tuft's Mountain		
17th (gargoyle)	Destroyed at Tuft's Mountain		
18th (gargoyle)	Destroyed at Tuft's Mountain		

Benotrist/Gargoyle Armies (continued)

Legion	Location	Commander	Size
GARRISON FORCES			
	Fera		29 T (Benotrist)
	Nisin		10 T (Benotrist)
	Pagan		5 T (Benotrist)
	Mordicay		10 T (Benotrist)
	Tinsay		20 T (Benotrist)
	Laycrom		20 T (Benotrist)
	Border posts		10 T Benotrist), 10 T (gargoyle)

Benotrist Navy

Fleet	Location	Admiral	Size
1st	Mordicay	Plesnivolk	48 galleys
2nd	Tenin	Kruson	7 galleys
3rd	South of Terse	Elto (Grand Admiral)	80 galleys
4th	Pagan	Pinota	50 galleys
5th	Tenin	Unknown	32 galleys
6th	Pagan	Silniw	50 galleys
7th	Tenin	Onab	24 galleys
8th	Tinsay	Zelitov	50 galleys

THE CHRONICLES OF ARAX

Yatin Armies

Army	Location	Commander	Size
1st	Mosar (Only 16 of 25 mustered at Mosar)	Yoria	8 Telnics
2nd	Faust (21 of 25 answered muster)	Yitia	20 Telnics
3rd	Destroyed at Mosar (3 surviving telnics joined with 1st Army)		
4th	Tenin	Surrendered to Torab	

GARRISON FORCES

	Mosar	Yakue	3 Telnics
	Telfer	Destroyed in Siege of Telfer	
	Tenin	Surrendered to Torab	

Yatin Cavalry

Army	Location	Commander	Size
1st	Telfer	Destroyed in Battle of Salamin Valley	
2nd	Mosar	Cornyana	475 mounts

Yatin Navy

Fleet	Location	Admiral	Size
1st	Tenin	Sunk in Battle of Cull's Arc	
2nd	Tenin	Sunk in Battle of Cull's Arc	
3rd	Faust	Horician	18 galleys

Jenaii Armies

Battle Group	Location	Commander	Size
1st	Besos	El Tuvo	7 Telnics
2nd	Corell	Ev Evorn	16-18 Telnics
	(Casualties suffered at Corell replaced with soldiers of the 1st Battle Group)		
3rd	West Bank of Elaris En Elon		24 Telnics

GARRISON FORCES

	El Orva	El Orta	5 Telnics
	(8 telnics attached to 3rd Battlegroup)		
	El Tova	En Vor	5 Telnics

Jenaii Navy

Fleet	Location	Admiral	Size
1st	El Tova	En Atar	20 galleys
2nd	El Tova	En Ovir	20 galleys
3rd	El Tova	En Toshin	20 galleys

THE CHRONICLES OF ARAX

Naybin Armies

Army	Location	Commander	Size
1st	Northern Border (7 detached to expeditionary force, destroyed at siege of Corell)	Duloc	3 Telnics
2nd	Plou	Rorin	10 Telnics
3rd	Non	Corivan	5 Telnics
4th	Destroyed along the Elaris (Survivors joined with the 3rd Army)	NA	1 Telnic

GARRISON FORCES

	Location	Commander	Size
	Plou	Cestes	5 Telnics
	Non	Rasin	7 Telnics
	Naiba	Tesra	3 Telnics
	Border Posts		5 Telnics

Naybin Navy

Fleet	Location	Admiral	Size
1st	Naiba	Gustub	10 galleys
2nd	Naiba	Galton	10 galleys

Macon Empire Armies

Army	Location	Commander	Size
1st	Fleace	Noivi	10 Telnics
	(5 telnics sent to siege of Sawyer, 5 remaining with General Noivi)		
2nd	Corell	Vecious	13 Telnics
3rd	Corell	Ciyon	8 Telnics
	(reconstituting into joint Macon-Torry Army)		
4th	Null	Farin	8 Telnics

GARRISON FORCES

	Fleace	Novin	3 Telnics
	Cesa	Clyvo	3 Telnics
	(Repositioning after truce of Fleace)		

Macon Navy

Fleet	Location	Admiral	Size
1st	Cagan	Goren	20 galleys
2nd	Cagan	Vulet	20 galleys
3rd	Cesa	Talmet	20 galleys
4th	Destroyed at the straits of Cesa		

THE CHRONICLES OF ARAX

Ape Empire Armies

Army	Location	Commander	Size
1st	Gregok	Cragok	20 Telnics
2nd	Torn	Mocvoran	20 Telnics
3rd	Talon Pass	Vorklit	10 Telnics
4th	Northern Coast	Matuzon	10 Telnics
5th	Southern Coast	Vonzin	10 Telnics

GARRISON FORCES

	Location		Size
	Gregok		10 Telnics
	Torn		10 Telnics
	Talon Pass		10 Telnics

Ape Navy

Fleet	Location	Admiral	Size
1st	Tro	Zorgon	9 galleys
2nd	Torn	Vornam	40 galleys

Casian Federation Armies

Army	Location	Commander	Size
1st	Coven	Gidvia	12 Telnics
2nd	Milito	Motchi	12 Telnics
3rd	Teris	Elke	7 Telnics

GARRISON FORCES

	Location		Size
	Milito		3 Telnics
	Coven		4 Telnics
	Port West		3 Telnics
	Teris		3 Telnics

Casian Navy

Fleet	Location	Admiral	Size
1st	Coven	Voelin	100 galleys
2nd	Milito	Gylan	80 galleys
3rd	Port West	Gydar	60 galleys
4th	Teris	Eltar	60 galleys

THE CHRONICLES OF ARAX

FEDERATION OF THE SISTERHOOD ARMIES

Army	Location	Commander	Size
1st	Bansoch	Na	20 Telnics
2nd	Fela	Vola	20 Telnics
3rd	Southern Border	Mial	20 Telnics

GARRISON FORCES

	Bansoch		10 Telnics
	Fela		10 Telnics

Sisterhood Navy

Fleet	Location	Admiral	Size
1st	Bansoch	Nyla	120 galleys
2nd	Bansoch	Carel	80 galleys
3rd	Southern Coast	Daila	50 galleys

Teso Armies

1st Army	Southeastern border	Hovel	4 Telnics
2nd Army	Corell	Velen	1 Telnic

Zulon Armies

1st Army	Northern Border	Zarento	2 Telnics
2nd Army	Corell	Zubarro	1-2 Telnics

BENJAMIN SANFORD

CITY STATE ARMIES

Sawyer	5 Telnics	100 Cavalry	
Rego	3 Telnics	100 Cavalry	

(Rego garrison size fluctuates with new conscription)

Notsu	1-2 Telnics	200 Cavalry	

(Notsu's surviving units are joined with Torry forces)

Bacel	Destroyed at Kregmarin and siege of Bacel		
Barbeario	8 Telnics		
Bedo	10 Telnics	100 Cavalry	40 galleys
Tro Harbor	6 Telnics	50 Cavalry	14 galleys
Varabis	5 Telnics		30 galleys

Other Books by the Author

Free Born saga
    Free Born
    Elysia
    Dragon Wars (coming soon)

Chronicles of Arax
    Book One: Of War and Heroes
    Book Two: The Siege of Corell
    Book Three: The Battle of Yatin
    Book Four: The Making of a King
    Book Five: The Battle of Torry North
    Book Six: Fall of Empires
    Book Seven: Restoration (coming 2024)

About the Author

Ben Sanford grew up in Western New York. He spent almost twenty years as an air marshal, traveling across the United States and many parts of the world, meeting people from a broad range of cultures and backgrounds. It was from these thousands of interactions that he drew inspiration for the characters in his books. He currently resides in Maryland with his family.

Made in the USA
Middletown, DE
14 April 2024